PENGUIN BOOKS

HOME GROUND

Lynn Freed was born and grew up in Durban, South Africa. She went to the United States to read for an M.A. and a Ph.D. in English Literature at Columbia University. She has lectured in English at several universities in America. She lives with her daughter in San Francisco.

Home Ground

LYNN FREED

PENGUIN BOOKS

PENGUIN BOOKS

Published by the Penguin Group
27 Wrights Lane, London W8 5TZ, England
Viking Penguin Inc., 40 West 23rd Street, New York, New York 10010, U.S.A.
Penguin Books Australia Ltd, Ringwood, Victoria, Australia
Penguin Books Canada Ltd, 2801 John Street, Markham, Ontario, Canada L3R 1B4
Penguin Books (N.Z.) Ltd, 182–190 Wairau Road, Auckland 19, New Zealand

Penguin Books Ltd, Registered Offices: Harmondsworth, Middlesex, England

First published by William Heinemann Ltd 1986
Published in Penguin Books 1988

Made and printed in Great Britain by
Richard Clay Ltd, Bungay, Suffolk

With my thanks to Yaddo, where
much of this book was written

To Mary and Vicky

Now that my ladder's gone,
I must lie down where all the ladders start,
In the foul rag-and-bone shop of the heart.

W.B. Yeats

1

To a child, nothing that is familiar in her world – not earth-quakes or revolutions, slavery or sodomy, poverty or riches – seems either exotic or wicked. So to me, Ruth Frank, white girl on a black continent, it felt only slightly odd to be diverting myself and my friend on an otherwise dull Sunday afternoon by pulling on the penis of the gardenboy.

It was 1953. I was eight, robust and presumed rich. The nextdoor girl Lucy, my friend when it suited me, was seven, skinny and poor. We had been placed side by side on a hill above the Indian Ocean by my grandfather's small ways with money. Forty years earlier, as an enlightened Englishman in a savage land, he had decided to build a new compound for his servants, featuring electricity and plumbing and a yard for them to sit in. The Irishman who built the compound took as his payment the derelict old servants' quarters in the hollow behind the house and a few feet of land on either side of it. Within a month he had painted the building pink inside and out, divided it into four flats and moved into one of them. The others he rented out cheaply in return for no complaints. My grandfather's objections were too late, and my grandmother never forgave him or the Irishman or the servants, whose good fortune had been bought at such expense. Lucy was born to uncomplaining parents in the smallest of the Irishman's flats –

three rooms, still pink, still cheap, and to me, when I made their acquaintance, a heaven of intimate containment.

'Lucy! Come for lunch!' I had yelled that Sunday across the lawn and tennis court that divided my bedroom from hers. In our house the telephone was not to be used lightly, certainly never to reach a friend within shouting distance. Besides, everyone except my father bellowed simply to be heard, upstairs to downstairs, across the great halls, the noise muffled by stone walls and heavy wooden doors. We had been taught how to raise our voices by my mother, who shouted magnificently. She would stand in the middle of the house and boom directly from her diaphragm in a low sustained bass, enunciating each syllable with pride. 'Ruth! You are wanted on the tel-e-phone!'

My parents were theatre people and to theatre people sounds matter. Voices, tone, diction, intonation, enunciation, articulation – all were considered more telling by them than handshakes. There was the assumption that a high squeak, a dead monotone, swallowed vowels, adenoidal wheezes were, if not intentional, careless. Anyone, they said, could have good delivery and decent speech. One just had to care enough. It was really a matter of consideration for others. There was the moral question of what right one had to subject one's listener to an awful noise, like radios turned up high, or dogs barking at night. 'Lower that voice,' my father would grumble. 'And modulate your tone, please,' my mother would add. As a team, they had the effect on one's speech of sheepdogs on the movement of a flock.

Audience mattered too. We needed one to witness the drama of our lives. To stylize the discord. To stand, like the theatre itself, between us and the world beyond. Even Lucy would do.

And so no one objected to my shouting the invitation across the quiet of a Sunday morning in a voice trained to carry. On our side of the fence it was Lucy's high-pitched whine in response, her undisguised indigenous accent – 'I'll ahhsk ma maa-aa!' – that was pitiable. More indicative than her father's alcoholism or her mother's ignorance, of the hopelessness of her prospects in life.

2

I knew that she preferred our Sundays and the noise and fighting at our table to the deadly piety of her own. I, on the other hand, loved to close my eyes and bow my head while Mr Knowles slurred his way through the Christian grace, and then to be allowed, as she was, to mash all my meat and vegetables into a heap and to pour bottled sauces over the top. I loved the festoons of wishbones that Lucy had collected for years and wrapped in silver cigarette paper and strung from corner to corner all around the room. I also loved the importance I had at their table, the way they watched how I ate and asked me leading questions. It was worth asking her over, even when I didn't particularly want her, just for the privilege of being invited back.

Lucy appeared quickly, taking the shortcut through the fence and across the tennis court. This saved her from ringing the bell on the front gate and agitating the dogs, which terrified her. A lot of things on our side of the fence terrified Lucy. Pillay the gardener, for instance, untouchable to his own Hindu race, delighted in threatening this low-caste white girl as she trampled through his bed of seedlings. 'Ay! Ay! You!' he screeched, and she, running two-at-a-time up the backstairs, landed panting in my room, barricading the door with her back.

'Will he tell your Ma?'

'Na.' Her terrors, so different from my own, seemed insignificant to me.

'But Sampson said *he'd* tell!'

'Tell what?'

'That I ran across the court.'

'He won't. My Ma's rehearsing and Nora'll never.'

'Hey, you! Naughtiness!' It was indeed Nora, the cook, down on the path below. She stood there wiping her hands on her apron and then looking up as she planted a fist on each huge hip.

'Ja!' I pivoted over the sill on my stomach.

'You going to fall, you watch out!'

'What?'

'You tell Miss Knowles she not allowed to run across the

3

court, please. Sampson he got to roll it now all over again, and this his Sunday off.'

'See!' Lucy shrank back against the door.

'Sorry, Nors.' I knew if Nora said 'Miss Knowles' and 'Naughtiness' that she was in a good mood. It was her Sunday off too and she didn't have time to waste on other servants' causes.

'There's the bell for lunch!' she shouted. 'You come down right now, please.'

Lunch on Sunday was a huge affair. Giblet soup and marrow on brown bread, duck, and at least four overcooked vegetables, cheese and pudding. My mother served at the sideboard from large silver salvers on to pink and gold china, handing each plate to Reuben the houseboy – 'For the Master,' 'For Catherine.' He stood at her side in his solemn Sunday face and bare feet, starched white cotton suit and white cotton gloves (to put something between his blackness and the food we ate).

The dining-room ran along half the length of the house, shaded from the heat of summer by a verandah upstairs and down, and by the mango and avocado trees in the garden beyond. It had been furnished by my grandmother before my father was born, something that numbered high in my mother's abundance of irritations. 'I really must redo this room one of these days,' she would sigh, looking around at the maroons and dark greens of a former era. The other woman's choices. Her voice would pause before it shrank into another sigh – 'Ah, well!' – and then it would die slowly into a whisper for the cadence – 'C'est la vie!'

This was said to the audience of her daughters. We were meant to be moved by the unfairness of her fate. To me, however, her complaints were simply lullabies. I welcomed them as a child embraces meaningless rhymes or the repetition of old, toothless rebukes. Gramma was, for the moment, the Queen of the Night. Circe. Medusa. And I loved to pretend that my mother was her victim.

Valerie, however, would never play along. 'I like this room,' she said, turning to my father. 'It feels like home.'

Valerie understood better than any of us the burden that enforced gratitude had placed upon my mother. My parents could never have afforded to buy our house. When Catherine was born, Abba, my grandfather, had given it to them, together with a small monthly stipend for its upkeep, so that we children could grow up, as he said, 'happy and normal'. He and my grandmother moved into a smaller house not far away. Then, a year later, after Valerie was born, and the theatre needed repairs, a new roof, more studios for the theatre school, he loaned my parents the money they needed. At my grandmother's wish the loan was drawn up in her name and considered as a purchase of shares. She wanted to be a partner, she said, to share in her son's career.

My mother, however, knew better. From the beginning my grandmother had let it be known that she considered her son bewitched by my mother, seduced three weeks after his return from England by her performance of Hedda Gabler. This my mother never denied. In fact she loved the idea. She considered my father spared by her talents from a life of buying and selling Persian carpets. What she dreaded now was the thought of her mother-in-law treating the theatre as she treated our house. Gramma had always behaved as if our house were still hers, sending over her chauffeur to pick mangoes and lemons from our trees without even asking, feeling free to criticize an arrangement of flowers or the neglect of the trellises on the summerhouse.

But my mother needn't have worried. Gramma only appeared at the theatre as she always had – to deliver my father's favourite biscuits in a special tin. She had what she wanted. It was the right to ask my mother at the Friday-night dinner table, her voice arched into a challenge, just how things were going at the theatre these days. To this my mother would answer by arching her eyebrows back, raising her wine glass, and smiling with particular graciousness into her mother-in-law's smile. 'To Ibsen,' she would say, 'my favourite playwright.'

My father smiled at each of us in turn. 'I hope,' he said, 'that you girls will always remember your home with nostalgia.'

It was something he said often, particularly after a morning of golf and a drink with other men. He loved to sit where his father had sat, separated from my mother by twelve feet of carved mahogany table and the three of us anchored between them. She had hinted to us that this hope of his sprang from his own unnatural childhood – ten years in an English boarding school and a vain, dominating selfish mother. Whatever the cause, his hope held no power over me. I couldn't squash it in with my hopes for myself. And even though I linked nostalgia with nostrils, his own perfect nostrils flaring with emotion, I suspected the word – as I suspected him – of wishing me pain.

Catherine rolled her eyes with exaggerated ennui. I rolled mine too, something that usually won me a laugh. This time, however, he didn't even smile at me. My mother, watching him, didn't either. Carefully, he laid his soup spoon down beside his bowl and turned to Catherine with dark, moist eyes.

'Is that such a terrible thing to hope for?' he asked. His voice was deep and smooth and pleading.

At sixteen Catherine had found the man she wanted. She had swept him off his feet, my mother kept saying – taken him with her on her broomstick, as I saw it, sweeping him into the air, swept away herself. We had all been at the wedding where it happened, but my father was first to understand its real significance. He could see that she had removed herself into the future with no trace of nostalgia, far from the house and the constant family dramas she seemed to loathe.

Catherine stared into the fruit bowl ahead of her and shrugged.

'Everyone take a dee-eeep breath!' Valerie shouted, raising one buttock slightly from her chair.

'Oh, nooo!' I leapt up from the table and ran behind the drapes.

'Valerie!' my mother barked. 'That is quite revolting! Ruth, open the door, please.'

6

Valerie laughed. She used her farts as she used her talent for making trouble, to create and control a scene.

I covered my nose ostentatiously with the hem of the drape and flung open the French doors.

My father flapped his napkin around his face. 'Please, my girl,' he said, 'leave the room if you have to make a smell.'

'You've missed the point,' my mother snapped. 'Ruth, come back and sit down.'

'Sis!' I said. 'I can still smell it.'

'Don't say "sis". And come back immediately or go to the kitchen.'

'Ruth should talk!' Valerie snapped. 'She never ever pulls the chain. She's repulsive.'

' "Never", not "never ever",' my father said.

It was true. They had tried everything to get me to flush, but no punishment could force me to endure the terror of that deluge with its chorus of cranks and gushes and wheezes. 'So what?' I spat back. 'You ran naked past Reuben in the passage.'

'When was this?' my father asked. His tan lost a little of its richness.

Valerie shrugged. 'Don't remember.'

'Yesterday!' I said. 'Last night.'

'How many times do you have to be told, Valerie?' my mother demanded.

'I thought he was in the kitchen, and I was late.'

My father drummed the table impatiently with the tips of his fingers. 'There is a rule in this house about dressing-gowns, young woman. At fifteen you are not a baby anymore. It is unfair to the servants to ignore that.'

'Reuben is *hardly* one's vision of lust and passion,' Catherine threw in.

Valerie laughed. She was always trying to engage Catherine as an accomplice, but Catherine would not be engaged by anyone. This was her power over us, the way she picked and chose.

'I'm surprised at you, Catherine,' my father said sternly.

7

'Reuben may be a native, but he is a human being and a grown man.'

My father's special knowledge of grown men and their passions silenced us. No one, not even my mother, wanted to carry the discussion any further.

But Valerie had not forgiven me. She stretched under the table and kicked me on the shin.

'Ow!' I shouted. 'She kicked me!'

'Baby! Tell-tale!'

'Valerie!' my mother boomed. 'If you can't behave like a civilized human being, leave the table.'

'Ugly, ugly, ugly.' I sing-songed. 'Catherine's got a boyfriend and you-hoo-hoo do-hon't.'

'Brat!' Valerie screamed. 'Can't anyone control that *brat*?' She lunged under the table and kicked me again. Then she pushed her chair back and ran crying from the room.

'Ow!' I shrieked. 'You bloody swine! Ugly! Ugly! You'll *never* have a boyfriend!'

'Ruth!' My father stared me into silence and then nodded to my mother to indicate that I was hers to scold. Valerie, the difficult one, had always belonged to him. He stood up solemnly and followed her out.

'Shall I have your lunch kept warm?' my mother called after him. But it wasn't really a question. It was an indication to him that by catering to Valerie's hysterics he was keeping the servants in on a Sunday. Without waiting for an answer she stepped on the kitchen bell, cunningly concealed under the carpet next to her chair. 'Ask Nora to keep the Master's plate warm, please,' she said to Reuben. And then, smiling suddenly, she turned to my silent guest. 'Well, Lucy, tell us how you're getting on at school.'

It was a replay of all the old auditions Lucy had been put through in our house. 'Tell us about your holiday, Lucy,' 'Sing something for us, Lucy,' 'Well, Lucy, what have you got to say for yourself, hey? Ha ha.' We all recognized the fun to be had.

'Fine, thank you, Mrs Frank.'

'Fine, thenk you, Mussus Frenk,' I mimicked.

8

Catherine snickered, acknowledging me, delivering my reward.

'That's enough, Ruth,' my mother purred. I was her favourite, child of her approaching menopause. 'Would you like a little more duck, Lucy?'

'No, thank you, Mrs Frank.' By now Lucy's freckles showed up pale in her purple face. Even her scalp was more visible than usual, glistening out like the skin of a caterpillar between the roots of her thin fair hair. Under the table, she twisted the fabric of her Sunday skirt into her hands.

'Na-w, thenk you, Mussus Frenk,' I tried again.

'Shut up, Ruth,' Catherine snapped. 'Once is funny.'

'Cheese, anyone?'

'Please may I leave the table?' Catherine asked quickly.

'In the middle of lunch?' My mother arched one eyebrow.

'I don't want cheese or pudding.'

'Well, don't you think that the decent thing to do is to wait until others have finished?' The other eyebrow shot up too.

'But I'm going for a drive.'

'With that Jeffrey, I suppose?' My mother's use of 'this' and 'that' as adjectives to delineate the world outside and suspect, always disturbed me. Catherine didn't answer.

'Have you asked your father?' my mother persisted.

'But it's an afternoon –'

'Afternoon? So what?' She pointed her long nose at Catherine, up and down, up and down, like an accusation. 'Who knows what this Jeffrey has got planned to fill your afternoon?'

We had all seen that nose wagging, accusing us of things we couldn't imagine, things missing from her own life. But only Catherine had learned to respond with silence. She pressed her lips together and stared down at the empty cheese plate.

'At least you could take Valerie with you. Can't this Jeffrey of yours bring a friend for her?'

Catherine didn't look up. She kept her voice low, appropriate to her resolve. 'I won't take her. I won't be responsible for her. I'd rather stay home.'

'I'll go,' I offered.

My mother laughed. The suggestion cheered her up enormously. 'What an *excellent* idea!' She laughed again. 'You can all go! How can any young man object to taking out the *three* Frank beauties?'

To be classed with Catherine and Valerie as a beauty, even by my mother, was something close to sensual pleasure for me – I, who was judged by the world to be plain, damned to make my way by my wits or by the love-blindness of some man. I laughed along to hide the extent of my pleasure, and Lucy, taking her cue from me, expelled a strangled little squeal.

'Hello? Is lunch over?' My father stood smiling in the doorway. Valerie's hysterics always seemed to cheer him up. 'Well,' he said, slipping into his chair and shaking out his napkin. 'Who's for a game of tennis this afternoon?'

'Me!' I shouted. 'Me and Lucy!'

' "Lucy and I",' my mother corrected.

I looked at him longingly, hoping to take Catherine's place on the court. They usually had a few sets together before I was allowed to come on after tea.

'Please may I go for a drive this afternoon?' Catherine asked casually, as if she wanted the mustard.

My father was not a man to do two things at once. His plate had been placed before him and, for the moment, he was manipulating his knife and fork with care and precision to remove the skin and fat from the flesh of his duck. Catherine waited and I watched her. Lucy watched me. My mother sighed and tossed her head to look out over the sunlit lawn. 'I think we'll have a good crop of avocados this year,' she said.

'Please may Catherine go?' I asked.

Catherine looked at me quickly and smiled. Her smiles, so rare in the company of the family, transformed her into a stranger, someone who could take pleasure in normal ways. It showed her lovely teeth, filled out her cheeks and lit up the green of her eyes. It was easy then to see how she could have swept off some Jeffrey. She swept me into a frenzy of delight, made me a partner in her cause without my even understanding what it was that I had done to deserve such a reward.

When my father had chewed and swallowed, he looked up slowly at my mother, and then, staging a careful arc, around to Catherine. He cleared his throat. 'With whom are you proposing to go for a drive?' he asked.

Her cheeks shone scarlet. 'With Jeffrey Goldman,' she mumbled.

'And where does he propose to take you?'

But the doorbell rang just then and Catherine sprang up. My father leaned back and wiped each corner of his mouth carefully with his napkin. 'Sit down, please, Catherine,' he said. 'We haven't finished lunch.'

'But *please*!' She stood still, hanging on to the table.

Reuben hovered at the door. 'Yes, Reuben?'

'A Master for Miss Catherine, Madam.'

'Show him in here, please,' my mother said.

We listened in silence to rubber-soled shoes squeaking across the boards and rugs of the hall and then thudding down the passage towards us. We heard Reuben lead him – 'Thees way, Seh,' 'Right in theh' – and then suddenly he was there, standing in the doorway like a thief, startled by the sight of all of us.

'Hi, folks!' Jeffrey Goldman waved an arm loosely in the direction of the table.

I had not really remembered him from the wedding. All I had noticed then was Catherine's smile as he swirled her into loops and dips on the dance floor. I had concentrated on the extraordinary sight of her happy in the arms of a man. She had smiled and laughed up into his face without once twisting her own into a look of forbearance. By comparison, he hadn't been worth watching.

Now, however, I scrutinized him with interest. He was large and pink and freckled. Tufts of coarse chest hair sprang out above the V of his T-shirt and a few curled through the weave of the fabric itself. There was nothing in his presence – or in his voice or in the words he had chosen to greet us – of the magic I had imagined would lend itself to Catherine's sweeping. No dark, searching eyes or delicate mouth or smooth, muscled body like my father's cast him in the role of lover. I turned to

11

look at my mother, fixed into her stage smile, and wondered whether she'd noticed all this. 'I loathe hairy men,' she often said, looking on with satisfaction at her own hairless one. She also loathed men whose aim missed the toilet and those who jangled their genitals with the change in their pockets. Somehow I had come to associate all these shortcomings into one syndrome – a man without style. I waited impatiently to see Jeffrey plunge his hands into his shorts.

But he just stood there under our scrutiny, blushing as he caught sight of Catherine, and then raising his arm to wave at her as if she were on the other side of the street. 'Hi, Cath!' he said. 'Ready?'

My father stood up, gripping a claw at the end of each arm on his chair. 'Pardon me, young man,' he said. 'Unless I'm mistaken, I don't think we've actually met.'

'Oh!' Jeffrey hopped from foot to foot and turned deep red. 'Sorry!' He thrust out an arm and swung himself in my father's direction. 'Hi! I'm Jeff Goldman. Pleased to meet you, Mr Frank, Mrs Frank.' He lurched down the length of the table to my mother.

My mother held out a hand. 'How do you do?' she said.

'Oh, fine thanks!' Jeffrey grinned, showing lots of teeth.

'Will you let them go?' I asked. I knew it was going badly for them. I could see and hear that this Jeffrey was all wrong for the part.

'Do sit down,' my father said. 'Catherine –' He turned to her graciously. 'Are you going to finish your meal?'

But Catherine stood fixed and still, gripping the table. Her soft brown hair had sprung into a halo of short curls from the heat of her head. And her fright seemed to have enriched the blush in her cheeks, camouflaging her acne. In contrast, the rest of her face had blanched so that its shading, its roundness and symmetry, cast her perfectly for the bust of an angel in the Italian Renaissance.

'Catherine?' My mother coaxed her with the voice she used to handle stage fright. 'We're all going to have pudding now. Please sit down.'

Quickly Catherine dropped on to her chair and stared at her hands. The bell rang in the kitchen. Reuben came and went in silence.

Until that day only Valerie had brought boys to the house. Usually they were boys from the beach, muscled and tanned, whose families were unknown to us. She seemed to enjoy watching them stare into the mysteries of finger bowls or hold their fish knives upside down. She got them to use 'sis' and 'ag' and 'shiksa' in front of my parents. And then she dropped them, one by one. But Catherine dreaded scenes. She preferred to bring her friends home when we were out, when there was just Nora, with the dispassion of a servant, to make their acquaintance.

'Thanks for keeping my lunch hot!' Valerie stood in the doorway now, flashing eyes and teeth. She had changed into a yellow sundress to reveal her lovely breasts and neck to Catherine's man.

'Jeffrey,' my mother said. 'I don't think you've met our second daughter, Valerie.'

He turned and grinned at Valerie as she took her place next to him. 'We met at the wedding. Howzit?'

Valerie lowered her lids and smiled mysteriously. She breathed in deeply to expand her breasts above the neckline

'Valerie,' my mother said loudly. 'If you want lunch, suggest you go and arrange it in the kitchen.'

'I'm not really that hungry.' She pulled a litchi off the bunch and peeled it delicately.

My father turned to Jeffrey. 'Sunday afternoons we generally play family tennis,' he said. 'Would you care to join us?'

But Jeffrey needed help with this. He looked at Catherine, who pulled her mouth into a thin smile in response. 'I'd rather go for a drive,' she said softly.

'Well,' he said, shifting from one side of his bottom to the other. 'Why don't we play tennis with your dad for an hour and go out afterwards?' He smiled happily at his solution.

'Go where, may I ask?' my mother boomed, sitting up straight and raising her eyebrows. Only one man in this family was allowed the liberty of staging the show.

13

Jeffrey blinked under the unexpected fire. 'Up the north coast, maybe?'

I raised my hand and flapped it wildly. 'They're worried Catherine will be chopped up by natives,' I explained. 'That's what happens off the beaten track.'

My mother laughed, and Jeffrey laughed too, not at all understanding the joke.

'We'd like you to stay in town,' my father announced quietly. 'And I would like my daughter home by six-thirty.'

Jeffrey looked quickly at Catherine. He had hoped to have her to himself after dark. But she lowered her eyes to the table, more helpless here than he. 'I'll have her home on time,' he said. 'I promise.'

'Shall we have coffee?' my mother asked no one in particular.

We all rose on her cue and followed her into the lounge. At her approach the four Ridgebacks spilled off the furniture and wagged around our feet. She tolerated them for the sake of the rest of us, and for the look of four large dogs in a large house, but nothing in her past had prepared her to love an animal. If anything, she seemed a little afraid that they would find her out. She called them by their names and made a show of patting their heads. But they knew. They heard the falseness in her voice. They saw her rush off to the cloakroom to wash them off her fingertips. There was no gesture she could make, no tone of voice that would bring them to her as they came to the rest of us. They stood back now, smiling in their guilt, waiting to be scolded for jumping on to the furniture. But she ignored them and rang the bell for the coffee.

The heat of a summer afternoon, full of the smell of the sea, had filled the house and was settling everyone into a daze. A flock of hadedahs wailed off into the distance. Catherine and Jeffrey removed themselves to the window seat at the other end of the room and stared in silence out over the city. My parents dozed behind the Sunday paper. Valerie draped herself across the rocking chair, setting it in motion. Anyone looking in on us there, the meal over, the dogs at our feet, could have mistaken the quiet for peace, or for happiness. Probably Lucy did. In her private hopes for what she'd have and what she'd be, she must have imagined such a scene for herself – the faded elegance of a huge room in a huge house, and all the people spread out in it, even the dogs – just as I imagined myself in her three rooms, contained and safe, never out of earshot.

'Let's play something,' I suggested to everyone to end the silence. Between lunch and tennis this quiet in the house was always severe, the way I imagined boarding school would be, or prison. It carried for me, even then, some of the oppression of Sundays to come, with homework still to do and no sure future of my own to look forward to. On that day it seemed particularly unrelenting, so full of other people's miseries that I felt at odds myself, as if I were separated by oceans and continents from anyone to whom I really mattered.

My mother sighed. 'Just listen to them,' she said, waving one hand towards the street.

The blacks outside were celebrating a Sunday afternoon with noise. It was their time of the week, when the sounds they made, like the roar of the first bus in the morning, filled the white man's silence with the incontestable legitimacy of their existence. They hailed each other with shouts and halloos from opposite sides of the street. Or swaggered down the middle laughing. Or sat along the edge of the pavement in groups, under the Jacarandas, smoking homemade cigarettes. One of them strummed on a slack-stringed guitar, repeating the same three or four notes again and again in simple syncopation. Another blew a similar tune out of a mouth-organ.

Out of uniform, in their Sunday shoes and white shirts and long pants, they could pretend they were free of us. And if we did see them there on the pavement, if I hung over the fence and claimed them back – 'Reuben! Sampson! Look!' – they turned away to talk to their friends in Zulu, or they all got up as a group and moved to another street.

'Can we play something?' I repeated. 'Can we all do something together?'

'Not now, darling,' my mother said. 'Daddy and I would like to have our coffee in peace.'

' "All do something together"!' Valerie mimicked, clasping her hands before her. 'What a little drip you are!'

'Come, Luce,' I said. 'Let's go outside.'

I plunged out of my chair, across the red verandah and down into the garden. Lucy followed. The dogs, brought alive by our exit, almost tumbled both of us in their wildness to get to the fence and bark at the black men on the other side.

'What should we do?' I asked her, rolling over and over, down the slope to the lower lawn.

She followed me on foot. 'I don't know,' she said, breathless. 'Anything.'

I sat up, and she sat down beside me. 'I'm sick of making all the suggestions,' I said spitefully. 'Why don't *you* think of something for a change?'

'I don't care,' she said. 'Anything's OK with me.' She opened her pale eyes in fear of what I'd say next.

Suddenly there was a commotion at the back gate. The dogs had bolted up there and were jumping up against the wrought iron, snarling and snapping. Outside two black men stood brandishing sticks at a safe distance, waiting for an escort to remove the dogs and lead them to the servants' quarters. One caught sight of me and smiled sheepishly. 'Awu! Nkosazana!' he said, hiding his stick behind his back. White men's dogs were not to be threatened lightly.

'Simba! Chaka! Temba!' I shouted, mainly to show him that I was on his side. I recognized him now. He was Temple, the Millers' gardenboy, who made some extra money in his time off by cutting other servants' hair.

'Temple! Can we watch?' I ran up to the gate, pushing my way through the dogs. I had seen his satchel under his arm, the one in which he kept his tools – strange silver clippers and trimmers and long-toothed combs. I loved the ritual that his trade involved: the client on a crate in the middle of the yard with a sack around his shoulders, the piece of mirror held up to a serious face. And I loved to see the dense mass shaped and pruned, to strain the fuzz through the spread of my fingers as it fell to the ground, to pick up one tight curl and squeeze it

16

between a thumb and fingertip, more like a millipede shell sucked dry than hair as I knew it to the touch, to feel it spring back against my skin, and then to drop it quickly, as if it were alive, to jump up and stand back against the wall, wiping my hand on my dress. They would laugh at me then in their generosity, and I would laugh too, a little ashamed.

'Let's not watch,' Lucy said quietly. Ida, her servant, lived ten feet from her back door in the communal shack that housed all the servants from the flats. There was no mystery for Lucy in the cutting of a black man's hair.

But to me the servants' compound was forbidden. To be caught in there meant not only punishment for me, but a scolding for the servants who had let me in. And yet I often got in anyway, and sometimes they would let me stay, making jokes in Zulu I couldn't understand, sizing me up, I suppose, as to the adult I would become.

'Can we watch?' I asked again.

'Nkosazane must ask Sampson,' Temple replied diplomatically.

Just then Sampson ran down from the tennis court, waving a stick and filling our nostrils with the raw-onion smell of his young man's sweat. At his approach the dogs turned their attack on him, prancing around his legs with their lips curled back above their gums. But Sampson was used to this contest. He poked first Chaka and then Simba, the two males, on the chest, whacked them each on the nose. Then he shouted at Temba and Nomsa, the females, who sprang around on the outside of the circle, darting in when they found a space to snap at his ankles. It was a display that they staged daily whenever they caught sight of him. Walking, pushing a wheelbarrow, squatting down to dig or to weed, he was never safe. And if one of us was there to watch they were much worse, as if they expected encouragement for their efforts. They would run up to us, like now, with their tails wagging, only to dash back again to their victim to renew the attack.

There were other victims too. When Pillay arrived each morning from his Indian house in his Indian part of town with

17

his Indian smells about him, the dogs would dive at him from all parts of the garden. But he would screech back, standing quite still as he guarded his old felt hat between his hands. For some reason, Pillay's screeching scared the dogs. They were only fierce until he bared his betel-red teeth and emitted his shrill warning – a meandering scale of menace ending in a stream of pink spit. And so, although the uproar they created together never lasted long, it was as timely as afternoon tea. 'There's Pillay already,' Nora would say. 'Time to go to school.' The dogs and their victims meant nothing to her, or to Reuben, or to Beauty the laundry girl. As household servants, with the magic of their access to the white man's house about them, they were immune from attack. Or perhaps it was the white man's smell, like the manure in which the dogs themselves loved to roll, that protected them, shielded them from being detected for what they really were.

'Stop it, dogs!' I screamed, waving my arms in circles. 'Temba! Nomsa!' But my voice held as little authority for them as it did for the rest of the family. All three black men looked at me for another solution.

'Come!' I shouted, running back towards the house with Lucy clambering behind me. Like magic, the dogs turned away and raced behind me to the sewing-room door. I opened it quickly and slammed them all inside.

'Quick!' I called to Sampson. He opened the gate and his friends rushed in, holding their sticks ready. They ran like bush warriors, quiet and swift, in single file, along the path, behind the kitchen, up the stairs to the laundry garden, under the washing lines and through the wooden gate of the compound just as the dogs emerged from the other side of the house in a pack, wild with the game, ready to tear at a calf or a foot in the chase.

'Just *what* is going on here?' my mother boomed from the kitchen. Dogs running riot in the house terrified her into a fury.

'Sampson's friends,' I explained through the kitchen window. 'The dogs were biting them.'

She sighed and clicked her tongue. 'I don't know why he has

18

to have these hordes traipsing through here continually. What on earth does he *do* back there that brings them in in such droves?'

There was no point in taking the blame myself for her jangled nerves and Sunday discontent. I beckoned Lucy to follow me out of sight behind the mulberry tree until she went away.

'We'll get into trouble,' Lucy whispered as I led her, after a few minutes, to the compound gate.

'Shut up!' I said. 'Scaredy cat.'

We slipped through the gate, taking care not to let the dogs in with us. They whined and scratched on the other side. Only the presence of a white person in the servants' compound induced them to think of entering themselves. Usually they hung back outside, even if the gate was open, and played and rolled on the laundry lawn until Sampson emerged.

'Shh!' I whispered to them through the slats.

In the yard beyond, voices stopped. 'Ubani lowo?' Sampson called out.

'It's only me,' I said. 'Miss Ruth.' I plunged along the dark pathway, with Lucy behind me, as if I were entering a cage in the zoo.

'Look!' I whispered to her as we passed the open door of the toilet.

'I *know*,' she sniffed. Nothing about this place was going to impress her. For a moment I found myself considering her with respect.

I could never pass that room without stopping to look into it with a shudder. Inside, dark-green mould dotted the rough concrete of the walls, turning to black slime at the corners, in the cracks, and around the edges of the floor. The floor itself sloped quite steeply to a porcelain-rimmed hole at its centre, and a chipped porcelain handle swung from a chain above it, like a noose. I had never approached closely enough to see to the bottom of that hole, whether it had water in it like ours, or whether, as I preferred to imagine, it was open to the sulphurous centre of the earth and would suck you down bottom first, if you lost your footing. Nora had told me that it was often

19

blocked up because the servants used newspaper to wipe themselves, that squares of it were skewered on to a nail behind the door for this purpose. She meant to horrify me into pressuring my mother for real toilet paper, which I did. But nothing came of it. My mother considered my concern quaint but silly, an indication already of what she came to refer to as my 'championing of the underdog'. Like Catherine's sweeping, this role, I knew, would type me in the family until I could perfect another to take its place.

Lucy pulled at my shirt. 'Ugh, it stinks,' she said. 'Let's go.'

This time I followed her away from the fetor of the toilet to the tobacco and paraffin smells of the yard itself. We stood together at the end of the path, looking in on the square concrete enclosure and the haircutting scene at its centre. It was just as I had expected it to be, with Sampson on the crate, and the sack, and the mirror, and Temple bending his knees to reach Sampson's neck with his clippers. Temple's friend squatted up against the building, watching, pulling on a cigarette, talking and laughing with the others as he waited his turn.

In the far corner of the yard the incinerator had been stoked and lit. Smoke curled out of its stovepipe and trailed in wisps across the yard. My father had installed the contraption there a few years before to dispose of the burgeoning number of sanitary pads used by a house full of women. And my mother had hoped that it would encourage Nora and Beauty into civilizing themselves out of the reusable rags and shreds they seemed so attached to. She could smell them in their periods from the other end of a room or a passage, and would sigh and call them aside for a lesson in hygiene. 'Yes, Madam,' they would say softly, and 'Thank you, Madam,' as she gave them a packet of Kotex for their own use. But then one day she found a row of soggy pads pegged by their loops to the servants' washing line. Beauty had been laundering them each month and saving the monthly packets for her future. What could one *do* with these people, my mother wanted to know? And then she would shake her head in the manner of a disenchanted colonial administrator. They were all hopeless, she assured us, even the best of them.

At first Sampson and his friends pretended we weren't there. They looked at us but they refused to see us. And when we giggled, they didn't stop their conversation to find out what was funny. I crept in closer and beckoned Lucy to follow. I wanted to know how close I had to get to come alive for them.

We squatted beyond the edge of the circle Temple was tracing around Sampson. Some of the fuzz had fallen within our reach. I stretched in and swept up a handful.

'Yuch!' Lucy curled up her nose. 'Kaffir hair.'

'Shh!' I whispered urgently. 'We're not allowed to use that word.'

'It's dirty,' she said, backing away from my hand.

The trio of black men still seemed blind to us. They smiled and nodded to each other. But they had stopped laughing and their voices were lower. I felt them listening, over their own words, to what we were saying about them.

'Rubbish!' I retorted loudly, peering nevertheless into the airy black mound I held for signs of life. Blacks were always picking nits and bugs from each other's hair during their time off, sitting along the edge of the pavement and taking turns. Suddenly I wanted to dump the hair and run my hand under a tap, to douse it in disinfectant. But I felt them watching, waiting for my next move. I glanced up into Sampson's face and smiled. He turned away. In a desperate show of bravado, I threw the whole handful up into the air and let it fall around me, some on my head, some on my blouse and shorts.

Lucy jumped back and stood against the wall. 'Ag, sis!' she spat out. 'That's revolting, man!'

The trio began to laugh again. The friend at the wall hung the cigarette between his lips and clapped his hands together rhythmically. I felt rewarded. I stood up and began to dance behind Temple, exaggerating his movements. They laughed more loudly. Lucy laughed too, and I became intoxicated with the power of my performance. Darting and dipping around Temple, I scooped up more handfuls of hair and strewed them

21

over Sampson's head, over Temple, over myself. I shrieked and whooped, bared my teeth at them, copying the way they laughed.

'Awu, Miss –' Temple stood back smiling, waiting to be allowed to continue cutting the hair.

'Awu, Mees,' I mimicked. 'Mees, Mees, Mees!'

Sampson smiled politely. The joke was over, I knew, but I was wild to have it back. I began to skate my sandals over the hair on the ground. 'Look!' I shouted. 'Look!'

They looked in silence. I pulled at my own hair, making it fall over my face. I contorted my mouth into a baboon's smile and loped around them. Nothing. Only Lucy laughed uncontrollably, doubled over herself at the wall. I squatted in front of Sampson as if he were in a cage and I outside it, contorting for his attention. 'Uh! Uh! Uh!' I grunted.

I picked up some hair and threw it on to Sampson's feet. Lucy exploded. I put some more on his knees, but it fell off. Again I scooped it up, again it fell off.

'I'm a baboon!' I shouted up to him. I pulled my cheeks away to reveal the skeleton of my teeth and jaws. He stared down at me soberly. 'You're a baboon!' I shouted, desperate. But he just looked. And Temple stood waiting. The friend rolled up another cigarette.

Above Sampson's knees, his thighs were flattened over the edge of the crate, smooth, muscled, and hairless. Usually he wore the long khaki shorts and shirt of his uniform. But this was his day off. He could wear anything he pleased.

'What are you wearing?' I demanded, pulling away the sack.

'Boxing shorts, Miss,' he mumbled.

'Boxing, boxing!' I sang. 'Will you box for us?'

'Awu, Miss –'

I peered under the sack at the shorts. They were broad and roomy and fell away from his thighs. I took a hem in each hand. 'Look, Lucy! He's got no underpants on!'

'Awu no, Miss,' Sampson said softly. He pressed his thighs together and crossed his feet at the ankles. Neither of the others moved or spoke.

'Come, let's look at his big wee!' I shouted to Lucy. I unhooked his feet and pressed open his knees, lifting up his shorts
again. 'Look!'

This time Sampson didn't close his legs. He stared out soberly
over our heads in silence. Lucy crept up, giggling, and stood
behind me. Between his shorts and his left thigh I had reached
in and caught hold of a man's penis for the first time. It was
exquisitely new to the touch, sensuous, erotic, even then. I
shrieked in delight and jumped back. 'Try!' I suggested to Lucy.

But she fell back. 'Na,' she said. 'We'll get into trouble.'

I flew around Sampson in a circle. 'Scaredy cat! Scaredy cat!' I
sang.

Again I reached in, up his shorts, and pulled and yanked. The
flesh in my hand seemed to grow. Temple and his friend
exchanged a glance and grinned.

'Awu, Miss!' Sampson rasped. 'My manhood, Miss!'

'Men-hoood! Men-hoood!' I shouted. 'Come on, Luce! It's
fun!'

This time she crept up, the colour high in her cheeks, and
darted one bony hand up his shorts. 'Uh!' she cried, jumping
back. 'Sis!'

'Go on!' I urged. 'We'll take turns.'

And so we did, growing bolder in our attempts, even fighting
over turns. As the penis hardened Sampson's eyes grew wild. He
pulled the sack off from around his neck to reveal a smooth,
black, sweat-gleaming chest. Round and round we flew, as if in
a game of musical chairs, bending to reach into the shorts as we
passed in front of him.

'I'm getting dizzy,' I gasped.

'Me too.' Lucy ran back into the shade of the wall and wiped
her face on her dress.

By now Sampson had set his mouth into a ghastly grin,
showing all his teeth. He muttered something and threw his
head back so that we could see the black stipple under his chin.
His chest heaved, he thrust his hips forward to the edge of the
crate. The two men at the wall had crept in closer to watch.

But the thrill was fading already. It wasn't me the men were watching anymore, it was Sampson. 'I'm bored with this,' I said, panting with exhaustion.

'Let's go,' said Lucy.

Just then I heard my mother's voice raised to carry over the entire block. 'Ruth! Ruth! Where are you?'

'See, I told you,' Lucy whispered. 'Now we'll get into trouble.'

Sampson sputtered out a phrase or a curse. He sat up and spat on to the ground. Without a word, Temple and his friend glided into Sampson's room and closed the door. Sampson stood up, his penis still bulging out of his shorts, and strode past us to the toilet, slammed the door there.

'Ruth!' My mother's voice was nearer, somewhere outside the kitchen.

Lucy hung back. She even grasped the back of my blouse in her terror.

'Come on, it's OK,' I said, unworried myself. 'Coming!' I shouted.

We trotted up the path and through the gate, out into the sun and greenness of the laundry lawn. The dogs were still there, gathered now in the shade of the laundry itself. They rushed up to greet us as if we'd been away for weeks, wagged and jumped and licked our feet.

'Down!' I shouted. Lucy clasped me from behind, in terror now of the dogs.

'Ruth! *Where* have you been?' My mother stood on the path outside the dining-room, shading her eyes. 'I've been calling and calling.'

I smiled at her, screwing up my nose and eyes, which I knew she found charming. 'In the compound,' I said.

'For God's sake!' She clicked her tongue in irritation and started walking back towards the house. 'Come with me,' she barked back over her shoulder. 'And Lucy should go home now.'

Lucy vanished silently, taking the legitimate route, and I followed my mother down the path. She was leading me back for something serious, that I knew, but I was almost sure it had nothing to do with the compound. There was, in the slight bow of her head and shoulders, in the deliberate moderation of her stride, in the clasp of her hands before her, an attention to detail that she usually exercised only in preparing for a new role. She was someone else for the moment, not a mother who would punish me for playing with the servants. She stopped, turned, and inclined her head towards me.

'Ruth,' she said slowly. 'Something serious has happened.'

'What?'

Slowly she stretched out her arms and held me by each shoulder. 'No one knows why these things happen,' she said in a deep rich voice. 'I wish we did.'

I waited. The compound wasn't completely ruled out.

'Darling –' her voice dipped. She pulled me close to her. 'Gramma died this afternoon.'

'Died?' I said, struggling free. 'Dead?' This was new. Until then only animals had died in my world.

My mother always warmed to the subject of death. Bereavement was her favourite role. She folded her arms and nodded solemnly to emphasize the eternal finality.

Thoughts of the north coast suddenly occurred to me. 'Who killed her?' I asked.

'No one "killed her", Ruth, for God's sake!' My question had shaken her out of the role.

'How then?'

She breathed in deeply and closed her eyes, on stage once more. 'She slipped on a poker chip this morning,' she whispered. 'It was just a terrible accident. Terrible,' she repeated, rolling the r's.

I had all sorts of questions to ask about poker chips, but I could see from the difficulty she was having finding the face and voice for this information that I should stick to 'how' and 'why'.

'How did she slip?' I asked.

'Come,' she said, ignoring my question. 'We all need to be together now.'

But I stopped where I was. The thought of spending the rest of the afternoon together with the others, inside, depressed me.

'Where's Jeffrey?' I asked, stalling.

'He went home.'

'And Daddy?'

'He's at the hospital.'

'But she's dead.'

'Ruth! Come inside, please, and stop this nonsense.' She began to walk off down the path, herself again, taking large strides and flicking her wrists in irritation.

'Can Lucy come back?' I called after her.

'No.'

'Well, can I go back to the compound? I don't *want* to go inside.'

She swung around on me at the corner of the path, gave up completely in the face of such inappropriate audience response. 'What do I have to say, my girl, to get you to understand that your father's mother died a few hours ago?'

Hours or years, I still couldn't see why I had to be indoors. 'I do understand,' I said.

My indifference seemed only to inflame her, to offer her, in its innocence, a mirror of her own.

She took a few steps towards me and stopped. 'And just *why* can't you leave the servants in peace?' she bellowed. Her voice must have carried at least into Sampson's room, where I guessed him to be sitting with his friends, waiting in silence. 'Have you ever considered that it's unfair to them to invade their privacy in the compound? Huh?'

I bowed my head and waited. I knew that the servants' privacy hadn't made her bellow. There was something else, something I couldn't name, that had taken the place of death as the real passion between us.

'Madam —' Beauty had come up behind me.

'Yes?'

'Does Madam need sandwiches for rehearsal tonight, Madam?'

'Can I come to rehearsal tonight?' I asked quickly.

'*Rehearsal!*' she boomed. 'God knows if there's even going to be a show!'

It was out, then. My heart leapt against my ribs. The theatre. My grandmother's half gone, our world opened to the sky like my dolls' house without a roof. 'Will they take Gramma's half away?' I asked.

'Who on earth knows what that old cow's done?' she shouted. jerking her head up to the sky in the direction I presumed she thought my grandmother had taken.

I looked up too, half expecting to see the theatre winging away into the clouds.

'No sandwiches tonight!' she snapped. 'Ruth, come along, please.' She swivelled around and stalked off.

I followed her down the path wondering which half of the theatre they would take. And what would become of us when they did. About tennis after tea. Whether my father would come back from the hospital to play now that his mother was dead. I thought of Gramma dead, the thin elegant lady who had always made a joke of calling me by boys' names. And I couldn't imagine the difference her death would make to me. It was parents dying that was the worry, the terror that visited me in the night. I ran up and clasped my mother around her corseted bottom, sniffing in the heavy sweetness of her Black Narcissus. I buried my face in the flesh of her waist and hugged her tight. 'I don't want you to die,' I pleaded into the silky fabric of her dress. 'I don't ever want you to die.'

2

My grandmother didn't manage to take half the theatre with her as my mother had predicted she would. Nor did she leave it to my father's sisters, another dread. She left it to Abba, who gave it back directly to my parents. The relief in the family was like a holiday.

'I think we should consider bringing out Gwendolyn Stit for *The Women* one of these years,' my mother said merrily.

'Gwen won't do for Sylvia, if that's that you're thinking,' my father said.

'I was thinking of Mary.'

'I think we'd do better to bring out Jocelyn Hopswith for Sylvia, don't you?'

'Jocelyn!' my mother snorted. 'Her price is sky-high these days.' She stared up at the ceiling, running her eyes along the intricate mouldings. 'We'd have to use an amateur then for Mary, you know.'

'No, we must have a pro.'

She sat forward. 'What if we asked Lorraine and Noel whether they'd like them for a stint in Jo'burg? Share the cost of bringing them out, sort of thing. They're always asking us.'

'I think we should ask everyone, Cecil too. July's their off-season, remember. They might be quite glad to come out if we make it worth their while.'

'Oh, why not cast the whole show with overseas actresses?' Valerie put in. 'We can always borrow the money, you know.'

But the excitement of the purchase floated my mother far out of Valerie's reach. She took my hand in hers and kissed it. 'Darling, what kind of a story would you like me to record for this run?'

Before they went into rehearsal for a stage or radio production she always recorded a serial of bedtime stories on to a huge tape in a giant tape-recorder. The episodes were carefully arranged so that there would be one for every night that she was gone. She never read the stories out of books. She made them up. They were full of magic animals and witches and lost children. And in the end people got what they wanted. Fantastic rewards. Jewels. Castles. Holidays without end. Nora had been taught to switch the machine on and off and to resist any begging from me to play just one more episode.

'Why don't you just read a proper story for a change?' Valerie asked. 'You really can't compete with Enid Blyton, you know.'

'Enid Blyton!' my mother laughed. 'Who on earth would want to compete with Enid Blyton?'

'Your stories are boring.'

My mother smiled the poised public smile that always infuriated Valerie. 'Then don't listen, my dear,' she said. 'You're too old for stories anyway.'

Valerie leapt to her feet. 'Listen! Who wants to listen to your stupid stories? I never did, even when I was Ruth's age.'

'Oh, really? That's not what Nora used to say!'

'I want a story about the theatre,' I said quickly.

'*What*?' Valerie demanded spitefully.

'The theatre,' I repeated. Since Gramma's death I had been thinking a lot about the theatre. How it made us different from other people. Not just the way we were, but how we thought of ourselves. How other people thought of us. I had begun to understand that losing the theatre, or even half of it, would have cast us all out like orphans. Without it we would have been exposed to the small concerns of ordinary lives. My father to a job like other fathers. My mother to the lives of other women. Sewing circles. School fêtes. And the causes of the unfortunate. It was unimaginable. To have to lose our audience. To measure our happiness in normal ways. To look with clear eyes into the face of Catherine's withdrawal. Or the pathology of Valerie's viciousness. Or even the first signs of my own aversion, like some rudimentary allergy, to the discrepancy I was beginning to find everywhere between the naming of things and the nature of the things themselves.

'Shloop!' Valerie spat out at me. 'The the-a-tre,' she sing-songed. 'What a little drip you are!'

'Take no notice of her, darling,' my mother crooned. 'I think it's a *marvellous* idea for a story! Let's see, let's see –' She swirled her Scotch in a glass, this way, that way, with the concentration she generally devoted to solving a staging problem.

'Don't make it about me or us,' I said. I wanted to see the story from the outside, invisible in the audience. A real story that I could believe, without the lie of myself in it.

'Shloop! Drip! Dweet!' Valerie sneered.

'Let's see – I think I have it. Yes! I'll record it after supper tonight.'

I

'Once upon a time in a country called Lithuania, there lived a poor Jewish family – a man and his wife and their three children. They lived in a tiny house with cracks in the walls and not much else.

'One day the father heard that there was a country at the bottom of Africa where people, even Jews, could go and find diamonds and gold and riches. He sold everything he owned and bought five tickets on an old leaky boat to take his family to that magical country.

'On the boat they met other Jewish families. "Where are you going?" they asked them.

' "To the gold mines."

' "To the big hole in the ground where they dig up diamonds."

' "To a place where there are natives."

' "Natives?" they asked.

'The others laughed. "There are natives everywhere," they said. "Black and wild. They steal your babies and eat them. They run naked in the streets."

'But when the family arrived at the bottom of Africa they found out that the others on the boat knew as little as they did about the place. Indeed, the native girls walked about with bare breasts and beads and huge mud cones on their heads. But they didn't steal children. And the native boys wore clothes and would do anything you told them to do for just a few pennies.

'The husband opened a trading store to sell blankets and tobacco to the natives. Soon he had enough money to buy a whole house just for his family. Five rooms, with a bathroom outside. He promised to teach his wife to read English so that she could help him with the books.

'But every year there was another baby. At night she was so tired that her eyes wouldn't allow her to concentrate. The older children went to school and learned to make fun of her ignorance and her funny accent. With the birth of her seventh child she seemed to become an old woman. The child was wild and angry and refused to be pleased. Somehow the mother found it difficult to love this baby as much as she had loved the others. "I think," she said to her husband, "that God is telling us to have no more children. Why else would He have sent us such a child?"

'Her husband agreed. "We should call this baby Leah," he suggested, "because she has made you so weary of life." '

II

'One day, when Leah was about eight or nine, she peeped into the convent chapel on her way back from school. She loved to hear the Christians singing and often stopped to listen. But that day there was a show too. In front of the altar sat a girl dressed in old-fashioned clothes with a doll wrapped up on her lap.

31

Three girls dressed up in beards and robes were presenting gifts and making speeches. The choir sang. Convent girls watched reverently from the pews. Leah stood at the door transfixed by the magic of it. To be someone else whenever one wished, a whole audience silenced – this she understood quite suddenly was what she wanted for herself.

'She felt a hand on her shoulder and turned, startled. A nun stared down at her out of a pale face.

' "Is there something you want, child?" the nun asked.

' "Yes. Please. Excuse me, but how much does it cost for acting lessons?"

' "Acting?"

'Leah gestured towards the show.

'The nun looked into Leah's serious face. "Of what faith are you, child?" she asked.

'Leah blushed. "I'm Jewish," she said.

' "Ah," said the nun. She patted Leah's serious face with her papery white palm. "Elocution is only one of the subjects we offer the young ladies in our school."

'On her first day at the convent Leah found that elocution class was not included in the school curriculum. It took place after school and cost ten shillings a year.

' "Ten *shillings*!" her mother said. "Lele, we don't have money to waste."

' "It won't be wasted," Leah promised. "I don't care about anything else."

'Leah had never asked for anything before. Not even clothes. Her mother cocked her head to one side and frowned. "All the fuss to change schools was for this one thing?" she asked.

'Tears began to spill down Leah's cheeks. She had to catch her breath so that she wouldn't choke.

'Her mother stretched out her arms and pulled Leah to her, wrapped her up and rocked her gently. "All right," she crooned in Yiddish. "Don't cry, don't cry. I will find you the money." She loosened her arms and lifted Leah's face to hers. "Not a word to anyone, hey? Who will understand ten shillings a year for this whatever-it-is?" '

III

'At six o'clock the next morning and every morning after that Leah woke up the household with her A-E-I-O-Us and meaningless rhymes and huffs and puffs. Her mother would hear no complaints. "She's happy now," she said. "Leave well alone."

'Within six months Leah was winning prizes at the local eisteddfods. One year the nuns even chose her, the only Jewish girl in the school, to play Mary in the Christmas play. Her parents didn't dare to object. They had even become a little proud. When she recited for the whole family on a Friday night, they were very proud indeed.

' "Perhaps we're lucky after all to have such a daughter?" her mother said one night.

'Her father nodded. "Who can tell where talent like hers can lead?"

'Leah's elocution teacher told her about a famous acting academy in London and its representatives who came out to the colonies each year to find local talent. "London is the goal of all serious actors," her elocution teacher said, And so, right then and there, Leah decided that she herself should go. Every day of the week, every week of the year, she worked and hoped and prayed to go to London. By the time she reached her last year of school she was ready for the audition.

' "Number fifteen!"

'Leah stepped on to the city hall stage. The heat was stifling. The audience of mothers and teachers and other students shuffled and coughed. The adjudicators didn't even look up. They were tired after their long journey. And cross that they hadn't found any talent so far. One of them tapped the bell for Leah to begin.

'But Leah did not begin. She stood quite still, her eyes closed, waiting for silence. Then, when the coughing and shuffling had absolutely stopped, she raised her head and took a deep breath. She began to recite from a poem by Robert Browning called *Andrea del Sarto*.

'The adjudicators sat up. They looked first at Leah and then at each other in astonishment. There on the stage was a pale slip of a girl with a big bust and big nose. But her voice! It was deep and rich and subtle. It shaped Browning's phrases with passion. Her face too, her whole body, gave expression to what she was saying.

'When she had finished they whispered together and nodded and slapped their pencils down on the table. One of them stood up behind the table to make an announcement. Number fifteen, he said – he glanced down at the sheet in front of him – a girl called Leah Moskovitz – would she please come back on to the stage, they had something to announce?'

IV

'When Leah's parents realized that she would have to leave her home and country for the great honour she had been given they refused to let her go. It wasn't the money, they kept saying. They could find the money now. It was the thought of Europe again and she a girl alone. Her threats and temper tantrums were useless. They were quite used to them. Things had gone too far this time, they said. They blamed themselves. They blamed the nuns. They blamed the Englishmen who had sailed out all that way to choose her.

'Finally the Mother Superior herself came to plead for Leah. Leah's mother and father and brothers listened politely. But they remained unmoved.

' "Gifted or whatever," Leah's father said, "Leah is too ambitious for a girl." '

' "Too serious," Leah's sister explained.

' "Serious?" the Mother Superior asked.

'Leah's brother Moses cleared his throat. "She's eighteen already," he said. "Time for a girl to get married. Like the others."

'Then Leah's mother cocked her head to one side and smiled kindly at the Mother Superior. "Leave to me," she whispered. "I do."

34

'And so Leah went to London. Everyone came to see her on to the boat, even the nuns, and a newspaper reporter. 'Local Girl for London Stage' was the headline spread across a photograph of a pale thin girl on the steps of the gangway. The family framed the cutting and hung it above the mantelpiece.

' "See our girl," they said to anyone who would look. "There's our famous actress, our Leah, our little one." '

'Who the hell does she think she is?' Valerie demanded. 'A bloody heroine?' The spite in her voice and face stilled the echo of my mother's words.

'It was a *story*,' I said. 'And anyway, you weren't supposed to be listening.'

'I can listen to what I damn well want to listen to!'

Nora heaved herself up and pressed the stop button. 'Awu!' she said. 'Madam other stories much better.'

'I liked it,' I said. I wanted it back, my mother's world. Herself as herself as she really had been.

'Twerp! A *theatre*! It wasn't about a *theatre*! It was about *her*!'

'You couldn't even tell the story of Cinderella!' I shouted. 'Jealous! Jealous! Jealous!'

'*What?*' she screamed.

'Bedtime,' Nora said. 'School tomorrow.'

'*Jealous*! Of *her*? You ugly little drip!'

'Jealous, jealous,' I sang.

Nora heaved her bulk between us and shook her head. Valerie had to shout around her shoulder.

'Don't you realize, you hideous little creature, that I am the real talent in this household? I could act her under the table! That's why she never puts me in her shows! They'd laugh her out of town!'

'Ha! Ha!' I mocked.

She narrowed her eyes as if to sight me for the kill. 'Just wait and see,' she sneered. 'One day she's going to get the shock of her life.'

3

My mother never encouraged any of us to think of a career on the stage. None of us, she said, had either the passion or the talent for it. Neither did most of her students. Neither did most of the actors she could find in this Godforsaken place we lived in. It was one of her laments, like the dining-room decor. Only Valerie and Abba ever dared to protest.

'But Sarah, my dear, you're producing a fine *Doctor's Dilemma*, with a very tolerable local cast,' Abba insisted.

'Tolerable? It's intolerable!' She sighed at my father down the length of the breakfast-room table. 'I have to replace that Blenkinsop before it's too late. But whom am I going to find at this point? Just whom?'

'I thought he was rather amusing,' Abba offered. He loved to be allowed in on rehearsals, knew every word and every move by opening night.

My mother laid her hands in her lap and closed her eyes. She loathed this sort of layman chit-chat. Everyone in the family knew that. But Abba still had to be taught. 'Dad,' she said, opening her eyes and nodding briskly to cap the issue, 'Blenkinsop is not supposed to be amusing.'

A few weeks after my grandmother died, Abba had come to live with us. He brought back the furniture Gramma had taken with her when they moved out, and suddenly the house was filled with coffee tables, couches, armchairs, oil paintings, rugs, even a second grand piano. It felt at first as if we didn't belong there anymore, as if the house had been reclaimed by my grandmother from the grave to compensate her for her half of the theatre left behind. I found myself taking care to avoid using the new things too freely lest familiar treatment encourage them to usurp the legitimacy of our own things in the house, challenge our right, in fact, to be living there at all.

Not so my mother. Reclaiming my grandmother's half of the theatre seemed to have liberated her from her distaste for her mother-in-law's possessions. And to have softened her resistance to Abba's invasion. She busied herself for weeks finding a place for each piece, standing in the middle of a room and pointing out where she wanted a chair or a table or a picture to go.

She decided to lodge Abba in my grandmother's old boudoir – a cavernous room smelling of moth-balls and camphor. All around the room in enormous wardrobes were old costumes and props – ball gowns with bustles, ostrich-feather capes, boas and crinolines. Under the dresses, satin slippers and ladies' boots rested on racks. And in boxes on top were all sorts of hats. Otherwise the boudoir was hollow and unwelcoming, with only an old couch and a threadbare carpet waiting out the time until their shabbiness destined them for the servants' compound.

Abba flattened himself against the boudoir door as the movers carried in his bedroom furniture. He laughed in embarrassment when my mother asked him what he'd like where. 'Only the necessaries, my dear,' he assured her. 'A bed and a tallboy and my personal effects. My needs are simple, you know.'

My mother ignored him. She had my grandmother's velvet chaise longue put in there, her best antique side tables and Queen Anne desk, a small loveseat and Abba's favourite armchair. As each new piece of furniture was hauled into the room, Abba lifted up his hands in defeat. Finally, he tapped my mother's shoulder and stood to attention. 'Now, Sarah, that is sufficient, my dear,' he said. 'More than sufficient for my needs.'

But she simply suggested that he call for his chauffeur and take himself off for a drive. She was about to go into rehearsal and didn't have time for arguments. While he was gone she laid the fine Persian rug from the front hall in the middle of the room and hung my grandmother's velvet drapes over the two window walls. In the window corner, she placed a small white wicker table and two chairs for Abba's breakfast and tea The room was transformed into a beautiful apartment – a bedroom, lounge and breakfast-room all in one. Early in the morning the sun rose full into it from over the sea, gold and brilliant. The tops of the flame tree waved scarlet and green against the windows of the other wall. It was an elegant room, cosy, rich and contained, smelling of seasoned wood and fresh linen.

From his first day with us, Abba welcomed me into the boudoir with unusual enthusiasm. He bought a jar and filled it with cheap, coloured sour balls for my visits. I complained once to my mother that the sweets cut my tongue and asked her for a suggestion on how to refuse them. But she just stared at me in disbelief. '*Tell* him!' she snorted. 'What on earth's the matter with you?'

At dinner that night, she herself exploded into a diatribe about people who bought the cheapest of everything. She crushed her shoulders together and drew in her lips to give a few lines as Scrooge. She even mentioned sweets. I stared across at Abba in an agony of betrayal, but miraculously he seemed to find her performance funny. He nodded and laughed quietly. Then, in the manner of a teacher to the very young, he offered us his own views on household economics and the wisdom of thrift. 'Yes, yes,' he chuckled, looking around the table at our silent faces. 'Moderation in all things, hey? Remember the ant and the grasshopper, Ruth?'

Abba didn't seem to care about *things* the way we did, the way my grandmother had. Unlike my father, he didn't require French underwear or Italian silk scarves or specially fitted suede covers for his golf clubs. He even bought normal brushes from local shops and kept them until the bristles curled and fell out. My father's brushes had to be ordered from Kent in London. He could not be happy without two military-style hair-brushes, several oddly shaped real bristle toothbrushes and a tortoise-shell clothes brush that no one but him was allowed to use. Abba, however, didn't understand the magic of things acquired at great cost from places far away. What he loved best was to show me his bargains – a bone shoehorn he had bought for twopence fifty years before, or four identical pairs of black woollen socks found that morning in a sale at the Bon Marché.

Between Abba and me there developed a closeness of extremes. No one in the family really listened to what we had to say. Nor were we valuable as an audience at the dinner table. But Abba loved to have my opinion on this and that. And I in return pretended to be interested in the stories he told me of his past. I was used to sagas. I had often been grabbed by Uncle Leon, my mother's oldest brother, to hear his tale of the old world and its horrors, Cossacks and anti-Semitism, long journeys and hard-won success. I distrusted Uncle Leon and his suffering. I couldn't quite believe the tears in his fat, pink eyes or be grateful on his command for what had not happened to me.

With Abba the saga was different. He shrank himself small amongst the events he described, vanished entirely at times so that I had to ask him to put himself back into the story. For the most part, however, the story itself exerted no grasp over me. What held me there as he talked was the anticipation I had at first that he would really cry. When he didn't, it was the sight of his plump brown hands folded and still, the undulations of his voice, his soft consonants and perfect, rounded vowels, the words he chose – strange and neutral in our house – to describe his first small business in South Africa, the Boer War, his trip back to England to marry my grandmother.

One day he pulled out an old leather photograph album and held it in his hands like the sour ball jar. 'Would you like to see what your grandmother looked like as a young girl?' he asked.

I knew already what she had looked like. Our own albums were full of her – a plump and sneering young woman with pale skin and dull, lashless eyes. I nodded anyway, and he sat down beside me with his treasure on his lap.

Abba smiled at me kindly as he pointed out her great beauty and high spirits. He shook his head and chuckled when he told me of the life she had left behind in London to live with him at the bottom of the world. He seemed to feel rewarded, honoured, quite unaware that the poverty from which she had come could have coloured her choice and daring.

I watched him close the album and caress the leather with the palm of his hand. 'Quite a woman,' he said. He turned to me and nodded. 'Your grandmother was quite a woman.'

It was then – as I heard him flatten his voice into that familiar eulogy, as I watched him pull out his handkerchief and wipe under his glasses – that I understood the main point of his story. I realized how homesick he felt for his life with her, how lonely it was for him to be living in that room, in that house, inhabited as it was by so many ghosts, and by all of us intimate strangers.

'What were you two talking about up there?' my mother asked me.

'Gramma,' I said.

'Gramma?' She looked up from her script. 'What about her?'

'Their wedding and things.'

She sniffed, returned to the script.

'Do you think she was beautiful?' I asked.

'Oh, yes,' she said. 'Beautiful she certainly was.'

'I don't think so.'

She smiled down at her pencil.

'Is Catherine beautiful?' I asked.

'Yes.'

'As beautiful as Gramma?'

She shook her head.

'Is Valerie?'

She looked up at last, right into my eyes. 'You're all beautiful,' she enunciated slowly and carefully, 'in your different ways.' She reached out and cupped my chin in the palm of her left hand. 'One day, my girl, you will grow up to be a *very* beautiful woman. Mark my words.'

But I could find no comfort in marking her words. They were nothing like 'the three Frank beauties' I remembered so well from Jeffrey's first visit to our house. The kindness in her voice. the regal smile, the mist in her eyes as she said '*very* beautiful woman' were standard stage tricks. She was really thinking of her new Blenkinsop.

I eased my head away and somersaulted on to the floor. rolled there on my back amongst the dogs. Being pulled into one of her performances always settled a great loneliness around me. It made me want to prick her back.

'I want to be rich one day,' I said. This, I thought, might do it. She was always deriding the rich. There were only two forces that she seemed to respect without reservation. One was the power of female beauty. The other was the passionate ambition of a genuine talent. Just to be rich was like just to be happy, she said. It meant nothing.

'Don't kiss the dogs, darling,' she said. 'They're full of germs and God knows what.'

I grabbed Temba's head and kissed her loudly on her whiskers.

She didn't look up. 'Rich?' she said vaguely. 'Well, you'd better start thinking of how.'

'Will Catherine be rich when she marries Jeffrey?' I asked.

She looked up at last. '*What!?*'

'When she marries Jeffrey,' I repeated. I smiled up at her. The *fait accompli* of the question always infuriated her. Everyone knew that. And so everyone, especially the family – aunts and uncles and cousins – loved to torment her by asking it. I had heard her telling Catherine that the weight of all those questions was giving my father migraines for the first time in his life.

'Catherine is seventeen,' she snapped. 'Who gave you the idea that she's marrying anyone?' She swished her foot from side to side.

'But if she did marry him, she'd be rich as anything, wouldn t she?'

That was enough for her. 'Ruth! *For God's sake!* Go and do

your homework! Do you realize that I start the new Blenkinsop tonight?'

'I've done my homework. I'm going to play with the rabbits.'

I was quite aware that mention of the rabbits would make things worse. They had become a symbol in our household of the trouble Jeffrey was causing. Two months before, he had arrived with them as a gift on my ninth birthday, causing pandemonium amongst my parents, the servants and the dogs.

'What kind of damned unimaginative fool would give a child such a gift?' my father had demanded that night at the dinner table.

'Jeffrey,' Valerie said.

'They're my present,' I reminded everyone. 'They're my rabbits.'

My mother sighed and rubbed her eyes. 'I suppose,' she said, 'they'll have to stay in the flower pantry until we can find a more suitable place for them. We'll just have to do without flowers in the house for a while.'

Within hours the rabbits had jumped out of their crate in the flower pantry and were found gnawing on the handles of the cupboard doors. The next day my father had a hutch built close to the compound. He bought me a book on rabbits so that I could tell the servants how to look after them. But it was Sampson I was going to have to tell and I didn't know how. Since that day in the compound he would snicker to himself as I passed him in the garden. Or cluck and laugh about me to other gardenboys out in the street. I felt he must have told them all about it, and now it didn't seem so funny anymore. When I thought of his penis in my hand my stomach rose and twisted in shame. The thrill was gone, the drunkenness of that mad performance.

Before I could even read the book through, the rabbits had burrowed out of the hutch and my mother ordered Sampson to find them. The dogs, locked into the sewing-room, gouged the inside of the door in their madness to get at Sampson. The next day my father summoned the cement man to lay a solid floor in the hutch. But as soon as that was done, Nora and Beauty began to complain about the smell of rotting cabbage leaves and rabbit urine that wafted into the laundry and the compound yard. And then my mother pointed out several times that the sewing-room door was ruined beyond repair and that Sampson was spending his weeding and compost time catching rabbits and cleaning out the hutch. Everyone except Catherine and Abba had something to say about my rabbits.

'Why don't we eat them?' Valerie suggested at dinner one evening. 'We can invite the Goldmans on Friday night and tell them it's chicken.'

'Shut up!' Catherine snapped.

'Don't you dare go anywhere near them!' I shouted. 'And don't you dare ever feed them anything.'

'Why not?' she demanded. 'I'll feed them anything I like!'

I looked at my mother for help. 'Don't let her feed them!' I pleaded. 'She'll give them dahlia leaves and they'll die.'

'No she won't,' my mother said. 'Who on earth would think of giving a rabbit dahlia leaves?'

But I knew that Valerie was like no one on earth. 'The book says that they're poison,' I insisted.

' "Poisonous",' she corrected.

'No one will poison your rabbits, my dear,' Abba offered softly. 'Just look after them and feed them regularly, and they'll grow to a ripe old age like me.' He patted my hand.

'Well, anyway,' my mother grumbled, 'I am getting a little sick of having to beg Moosah for discarded cabbage leaves and carrot fronds and things for them. It pushes the price of everything else up.'

'But how is that, my dear?' Abba asked. Any discussion of the marketplace intrigued him.

My mother sighed. She couldn't bear the time he took to ask a question, the softness of his voice, the way he spaced his words out evenly without colour or emphasis. 'It's a question of bargaining, Dad,' she boomed. 'They feel that if they give me their rubbish, they shouldn't have to come down on the price of mealies or beetroots.'

Abba laughed softly. 'That is nonsense. You are doing them a

43

favour to carry away their discards.'

'Oh, well!' She threw up her hands to indicate how bored she was with petty economies. 'What's the difference anyway? It's only pennies!'

'Pennies add up,' he chuckled softly.

'Has anyone here seen the way this child kisses those disgusting animals, and squeezes them?' Valerie demanded. She tossed back her hair. 'It's quite revolting to watch.'

'Then don't watch,' my mother snapped. 'Just leave her alone.'

'Yes,' I joined in, 'mind your own beeswax! You're just jealous.'

'Jealous!' Valerie screeched. 'Of a hideous little creature like you? What a joke! Ha! Ha!'

Catherine turned languidly in her chair and we all waited in silence. Her special connection with the donor of the rabbits gave her first place in this conversation. 'That Martin of yours looks not unlike a rabbit,' she said to Valerie. 'All he needs is a pair of ears and a lettuce leaf. Shall we serve him instead on Friday night?'

I roared with laughter, pushed my chair back and clasped both arms across my stomach in ecstasy.

Valarie flared immediately. 'And Jeffrey? He's got the face of a tortured camel!'

All of you stop this immediately!' my father growled. 'Or you can all go to the kitchen!' He stared at Catherine for a moment and shook his head. 'Those wretched rabbits are causing nothing but trouble in this house.'

'Did anyone see the rainbow over the bay this evening?' Abba asked. 'I had such a lovely view of it from the boudoir window.'

By the time I got to the hutch after leaving my mother, the rabbits were dead. A few half-eaten dahlia leaves and some browning flowers were stuck through the wire of the cage. On the other side, the rabbits lay stretched out as if they were running across a canvas, their mouths wide open and their teeth bared and menacing.

I dropped to my knees and hooked my fingers through the mesh. With everything around me just as it was – the washing machine rumbling, Beauty singing as she ironed, Indian mynahs in the trees and the dogs at the fence – I wanted it to be a joke. I poked my finger through the wire and touched the black rabbit's paw. The wind picked up the edge of a lettuce leaf, ruffled the fur of the white rabbit's tail. Dead. Deader to me than Gramma. And no way back from dead to alive. I rested my forehead against the wire and began to sob.

'Wê, Ruth!' Nora shouted from the kitchen window. 'Tea time!'

After a few more calls she came out grumbling, stopped on the laundry lawn and called again. Then she gave up and shuffled down to the hutch to see what the matter was.

'Awu!' She came to a sudden halt behind me. 'Kwenzenjani?'

The dogs, who had followed her out, sniffed and pranced around the wire.

She tiptoed closer and peered over my head into the hutch. 'Who done that thing?' she whispered. 'Who done that bad thing?'

When we reached the lounge Nora handed me over, still sobbing, to Abba. Then she planted herself behind the tea tray to face my startled mother.

'What's happened now?' my mother demanded.

Nora straightened her cap and composed her face, folded her hands before her as if waiting for some cue.

'For heaven's sake, Nora!' my mother barked. 'What is it?'

At this Nora began to speak, punctuating her tale with a dumb show of gestures: two hands flopped lifeless to one side of her head for the rabbits' ears, and then held rigidly before her to indicate the contortion of their paws. As a finale she bared her own enormous teeth in a startling imitation of their death grimace. 'All dead, Madam,' she said, shaking her head from side to side as she turned it to me. 'Awu, shame for Miss Ruth.'

All through Nora's speech Abba patted my back, clucked his tongue and rocked me gently in the chair as if I were an infant. But suddenly his gesture of mourning inflamed me out of my misery and I sat up on his lap. 'I told you she'd kill them!' I shouted at my mother. 'I told you and you wouldn't believe me!'

My mother pushed the tea tray away and stood up. 'Nora, were there dahlia leaves in the cage?'

'Yes!' I shouted. 'Go and see!'

'Yes, Madam. In the wire.' Nora hung back now in the doorway, pulling her lips self-righteously over her huge teeth as she waited to see justice done.

'Nobody knows yet exactly what killed the rabbits,' Abba offered, holding me firmly by the arms. 'It may have had nothing at all to do with dahlias.'

But my mother was already out in the hall. '*Valerie!*' she roared. 'You come down here *immediately!*'

As soon as Valerie sauntered into the lounge, I disentangled myself from Abba's grasp and leapt on to centre stage to confront her. But she ignored me, turned her back on me and smiled into my mother's wild eyes. 'Something wrong?' she asked.

My mother glared at Valerie in silence as she deliberately folded her arms. Ten scarlet nails dug into the soft white flesh of her upper arms. The heat of the day and her rising anger had traced two damp semi-circles around the armpits of her dress. Finally she breathed in deeply, opened her mouth as if she were about to sing, and then boomed out at full force. 'JUST WHAT DO YOU HAVE TO SAY ABOUT RUTH'S RABBITS?'

Valerie raised her eyebrows and tried to stifle a smile. 'Nothing,' she said.

'You poisoned them!' I shouted.

My mother lowered her head and pointed her nose into Valerie's smile. 'Did you or did you not feed those rabbits dahlia leaves?'

Valerie never took advantage of a lie under duress. It was as if she were so in love with trouble that a lie would have served more as a deprivation than as a rescue. 'I did not,' she said.

'Liar!' I shrieked. 'Bloody swine liar!'

'I fed them flowers and leaves,' she said. 'Not just leaves.' She

46

turned to me and twitched her mouth into an unconvincing sneer. 'I wanted to see if Ruth knew what she was talking about.'

In one leap I grabbed her upper arms in both hands and dragged my nails right down through her smooth, tanned skin to her wrists. At first, for the few seconds before she felt the pain, we were all shocked into silence. But then, holding out her arms as the blood welled up into the welts, she opened her mouth wide and screamed at full force. She turned on me with her own hands clawed, but my mother grabbed her wrist in a vice and Nora rushed in from behind to pull me away to the verandah door.

'I'm *glad* I killed them!' Valerie screamed at me through her tears. She tried to pull away but my mother held her fast. 'I'm *thrilled!*' she shrieked. 'I hope they died in *agony!*'

Even Abba was up now, turning and turning in one place. 'Please!' he said loudly. 'Please, Sarah, Valerie, Ruth –'

'I hate you *all!*' Valerie sobbed. 'I hate this family! I hate everyone in it!'

From my prison in Nora's strong arms I could only thrust my head forward. 'And everyone hates *you!*' I screamed. 'Not one person in this house loves you, not even Daddy!'

'Nora,' my mother boomed, 'release that child and go and tell Sampson to bury the rabbits behind the paw-paw trees.' She flung Valerie's wrist away from her as if it were the neck of a snake. 'As for *you!* You just go right now and cancel that party on Saturday night! I'll teach you to cause trouble on the day I start a new member of the cast.'

Valerie flew screaming from the lounge and Abba padded out behind her. My mother sighed and flapped a perfumed handkerchief at me. 'Here, darling, take this.' She lifted my face and kissed me lightly on each cheek as she squinted over my head at the clock on the wall. 'We'll get some more rabbits,' she promised. 'Just wait a few days until Daddy's used to the new Blenkinsop before you start nagging.' She winked at me conspiratorially and made off for her study.

I knew the scene was officially over. Any upset at the theatre always shortened the span of our domestic dramas. My mother's heart just wasn't in the role of mother. Apart from anything else, she believed in saving her voice so that she could shout at the cast. But official or not, I couldn't feel satisfied that no party and five scratches down each of Valerie's arms compensated for my rabbits dead and buried behind the paw-paw trees.

I blew my nose and waited for the study door to close. Then I crept out of the lounge and up the stairs to the second landing. As usual, Valerie had locked herself into the toilet. I could hear her syncopated gasping, and Abba in the passage coaxing her to come out. Quickly, I slipped out of my school shoes and climbed over the balustrade that divided the children's wing from the central hallway. Valerie's door had been left wide open. I hesitated for a moment as I stared into her room. No one crossed that border without Valerie's permission, not even my mother.

But I knew that Valerie would soon tire of crying to the audience of Abba's concern. She would have to come out at five anyway to practise. I tiptoed across the passage and poked my head through the doorway. Her room was north-facing and hot, choked with the alien smells of her perfumes and powders. She herself stared out in fixed smiles and glances from snap-shots stuck all over the walls and around the edges of her mirror. I shivered. The grandfather clock in the hall began to roll through its five o'clock prelude. Somewhere outside the dogs were barking furiously. I thought of Sampson burying my rabbits and dashed into the middle of the room. As the chimes began, I pulled open the top drawer of her tallboy, scooped out its contents into the skirt of my uniform, pushed it closed, and bolted out again, around to the top of the stairs.

There I stopped to listen. From the study came the faint dull thud of my mother's voice timing her script. 'God is a Spirit' – Nora's requiem for all dead things – floated up the backstairs in her high-pitched vibrato. Abba and Valerie were still on either side of the toilet door. Holding my skirt together with one hand and the banister with the other, I flew down the stairs and then raced into the sewing-room, closing the door behind me. I spilled the treasures from my skirt on to the sewing table and stared down at them in wonder.

What I had bagged was most of Valerie's collection of dolls' clothes – tiny dresses with bloomers to match, booties, matinee jackets, bonnets and nighties, even her special pram set of leggings, jacket and bonnet, all handknitted in fine pink wool. Valerie collected everything – miniature bottles, autographs, porcelain animals, Coronation paraphernalia, china dolls, and dolls themselves that she had played with as a child. When the Zionist ladies from the United Jewish Appeal came around collecting for orphans in Israel, Valerie loudly refused to give them any of her things. She maintained that she was saving them all for her own children, and even snatched back some of the articles Catherine and I had donated. If we had given dolls, Valerie would pull them out of the cast-off box and peel off the clothes she wanted for her collection. Then she would throw the naked bodies back on to the pile and leave them there contorted and dead-looking, like the pictures we had seen of concentration-camp victims in my parents' Holocaust books.

Of all Valerie's collections, her dolls' clothes were the most prized. I was never allowed to touch them and seldom even to look at them. But I soon discovered how easy it was to infuriate her simply by claiming some of them back for myself. Or by laughing at the ones she had sewn. Or by reminding her that my mother had made the best ones with her own two hands. Valerie could never allow my mother a skill that she lacked herself.

Staring down now at all the familiar garments laid out on the sewing-room table, I felt very powerful. Valerie's murder of my rabbits had lifted the terror of retribution from me. I picked up a tiny sweater and poked my fingers through the sleeves, tore the tissue off her most precious voile-and-lace christening gown, dancing it up against the light to test its varying trans-parencies.

The front gate slammed shut. I ducked behind the sewing machine and peeped out of the window. Cathering was stalking across the front lawn, home from her hockey match, flushed and cross. I was safe. She would go to the kitchen for tea and hear the rabbit news from Nora. Then she would slip up the backstairs, trying to avoid my mother so that she could phone Jeffrey in peace.

Still squatting, I opened the scissors drawer and pulled out the pinking shears. I snapped them open and shut in the air like a crocodile's jaws and smiled. The christening gown was still in my left hand. I shook it out by the throat just above the tips of the shears. I fluttered it up and down, swanned it coquettishly around and around the upright steel blades. The voile floated and dipped and billowed like a bird. Slowly I opened the jaws of the scissors and then squeezed them shut in a convulsive snap. A huge zig-zag gash slit the skirt up to the yoke. It was easy. Holding the victim steady, I lunged with the shears from every angle, snicked and snacked in a steady percussion all the way around. A few horizontal crunches severed the remains into a heap of feathery tatters around me.

For a while I was satisfied just to stare at the mess and to think of my rabbits. But then I pulled myself up and shook out my legs. One christening gown was not nearly enough revenge.

It took me about fifteen minutes to demolish everything on the table. I was haphazard about it, cutting here into a sleeve, there into a skirt, causing just enough damage to make sure the garment was irreparable. The knitted garments I annihilated with an embroidery scissors, poking a hole somewhere first and then pulling at the wool until the sweater or bonnet disappeared before my eyes into a pile of spaghetti. It was fun. By the time I had finished, I had completely forgotten about Valerie.

The debris, however, did worry me. My mother hated a mess. And it was accepted as a truism in our family that only servants knew how to clean things up properly. Staring down now at the chaos around me, I accepted without question that I would have to ask for Nora's help.

'Hello, my darling!' Nora said as I came into the kitchen. 'Here –' She held out a piece of raw liver, 'I keep this for you.'

Catherine and I loved raw liver and used to eat it quite openly until Catherine got worms and my mother forbade it. Nora, however, assured me secretly that the worms had nothing to do with the liver. She seemed to take the doctor's pronouncement personally, as if she were the one accused of making Catherine sick. My mother's opinions on food and its dangers she discounted completely. And so, proving her point, we shared this disobedience without my ever getting worms. I gobbled the piece she offered me and wiped my mouth on her apron.

'Nors,' I sing-songed. 'Please would you help me clean up?'

She frowned, put her hands on her hips. 'Can't you see I'm making the supper? What have you done?'

'I made a mess in the sewing-room.'

She clicked her tongue, but I knew the liver had put her on my side. 'What kind of mess?' she asked.

'Material I was cutting up,' I said. '*Please*, Nors!' I threw my arms around her enormous hips and then ran out of the kitchen before her mood could change.

My mother was in the lounge when I trotted in. She was always there at this hour, even on a rehearsal night, with the evening paper and the dogs and a glass of Scotch. It seemed to be the time of day she liked best – the half hour before my father returned from his class at the theatre. She smiled up at me. 'Feeling better, darling?' she asked.

I nodded and jumped on to the couch next to her.

'Now, please,' she said, 'I don't want you girls fighting while we're gone.'

'Tell Valerie,' I suggested without much hope.

Suddenly she sat up and peered through the doorway out into the hall. 'Where's Nora going with that broom?' she asked. But without waiting for an answer, she walked to the door. 'Nora!' she boomed. 'What are you doing?'

'Cleaning, Madam,' came the reply.

My heart began to gallop in my throat.

'Cleaning *what*?'

'Sewing-room, Madam. There is a mess.'

I heard my mother draw breath. She took a few steps out into the hall. 'Just *who* has made a mess in the sewing-room?' she resonated loudly enough so that anyone anywhere in the house could own up.

Nora made no answer.

I leapt up and ran into the hall. 'It's Valerie's dolls' clothes,' I mumbled.

'Valerie's *what?*' My mother began to stalk towards the sewing-room.

'*My what?*' Valerie shouted from the doorway of the music-room.

'Mind your own beeswax!' I replied, running off behind Nora and my mother for protection. But then I heard my mother's '*Good God!*' and hesitated. I turned and bolted back out across the hall and up the stairs. As I made the top, Valerie launched into her wild animal shrieking. It was already spiralling into its frenzied crescendo when I burst without knocking into the boudoir.

Abba looked up startled from his armchair. He held a tomato juice cocktail in his hand. On his lap lay a copy of the *Jewish Chronicle*.

'Abba!' I whispered loudly, closing the door behind me. 'Please save me!'

He placed the glass carefully on a coaster, laid the paper over the arm of the chair, and stood up to consider me and my request formally. 'From what, my dear?' he asked softly, 'or from whom?'

'From Valerie. I cut up her dolls' clothes.' I stood panting with my back up against the door. 'Please may I lock the door?' I asked.

He nodded ponderously. 'Yes,' he said, 'go ahead if it makes you feel safe.' Then he shook his head, lifted the fabric of his trousers at the knees and sat down again carefully.

I slid the bolt of the door across the frame but didn't jump as usual on to the chaise longue.

Abba peered at me across the room. He took off his glasses to see me better. Although the boudoir was in shadow at this time of day, he wouldn't switch on a light until he had to. In the gloom his eyes and the folds and folds of dark-grey skin around them seemed very black. 'Are these dolls' clothes beyond repair?' he asked.

I nodded.

'And you are sorry now?'

I stared at him and nodded again. I had to lie, knowing the simple way he saw sin and redemption, punishment and remorse. But I longed to tell him the truth. That it was myself I felt sorry for. That I hated Valerie and wished her dead instead of my rabbits. Hated them all for refusing to listen or see. I wished with all my heart I could replace them, even him, like my mother replaced Blenkinsop, or a servant who had been caught stealing.

There was shouting now downstairs – Valerie's and my mother's – footsteps running across the hall. Catherine's door opened next to us. 'Shut up!' she yelled out.

'Well, come on, sit down,' Abba whispered to me. He patted the arm of his chair. 'Come over here and sit right down next to me.'

I rushed over and flung myself across his lap, knotting my hands behind his neck.

'Shall I go on with the story of Napoleon?' he asked gently. 'Or Shakespeare? What about him?' I could hear his voice breaking.

'Shakespeare,' I whispered.

He cleared his throat. 'Fine, fine. Now where did we get up to in *Julius Caesar*?'

'The murder,' I muttered. 'The temple.'

'The Capitol,' he said. 'Yes. Well, that will do. I'll tell you about Mark Antony and his speeches. That will take our minds off things while we wait for the storm to break, won't it?'

4

As soon as Catherine was eighteen Jeffrey started trying to ask my father whether he could marry her. But my mother saw to it that the two men were never alone. When Jeffrey asked for an hour with my father my mother would explain that he could never be disturbed while he was learning his lines. Or before opening night. Or during the run of the show. When there wasn't a stage production to use there were radio theatre rehearsals. Jeffrey was simply not equal to the battle.

'Ha!' my mother would say. 'That'll stall him for another week.'

What neither of my parents seemed to take account of was that Catherine herself was bent on marrying only Jeffrey. She didn't seem to mind his tight vowels and fidgeting and banging into things like a large puppy. When he came into the room, she was like a prisoner given an unexpected reprieve. She burst into a smile. She couldn't keep her hands from touching his sleeve or stroking his arm. 'Let's go,' she'd say, and she'd lead him quickly out of the door.

I came to see her happiness with Jeffrey as a sort of revenge on my parents for all the roles they had tried to cast her in. Sleeping Beauty. The Princess and the Pea. Tamina. What they had wanted for her, for all of us, was a man of style and breeding. Someone in command of the English language. With backbone, quiet good humour. A Mr Knightley, perhaps. Or a Mr Darcy. And Jewish of course.

My father would have done. But he was already our father. My mother, for all her complaints about him, felt herself the luckiest of women. His beauty counted for a great deal. So too did his manners. In breeding she considered him her superior by far. In intellect too. She loved to have him praised as a gentleman. It gave her a chance to point out that he was no fool either. She pulled books off the study shelves. Look, she said, he had won every prize going at school. Then she gestured around at all his silver cups and trophies. Rowing. Boxing. Golf. He was more than a gentleman, she boasted. He was perfect. And he was hers.

My father himself never boasted. He seemed to understand that he had left real triumph behind him when he'd left England. His natural love of style and ease, nurtured there amongst the boys with whom he'd grown up, had robbed him of the sort of ambition that men in our world needed to succeed. We were his triumphs now, his women. The stage he'd set, the style in which we lived. There was a sense of abdication about him, as if he'd withdrawn to a high place and had taken us with him. As if we owed him something from our lives and from our futures for what he'd left behind. My mother seemed to understand this. And that he was jealous of us, as she was of him.

So when I thought of all the boys I knew – on the beach, at synagogue, cousins and cousin's friends – I understood that there was really no man, no real man, my father would ever welcome in to carry one of us away. Such a man didn't exist in our world.

Compared with the real choices Jeffrey didn't seem so bad. At least he had lots of money and spent it freely. He loved Catherine. And she made a point of loving him just as he was. She never tried to coach him in the day-to-day drama of our lives.

'Coming to opening night, Jeffrey?' my mother asked casually. She knew that he always came, sat right there in the front row even though she'd pointed out again and again that those were *not* the best seats in the house.

'Certainly!' he said.

My mother tossed her head. She had often imitated the intonation of his 'certainly' for us, giving it all the sing-song import that he thought it carried.

'My parents are coming too,' he added.

'Hmm.'

'They saw it in London last year.'

I held my breath. People with money and no taste who went to London at the drop of a hat and saw plays that my mother could only read about in *Theatre Arts* both enraged and depressed her. I glanced at Catherine. Colour had risen to her cheeks. I saw her take Jeffrey's hand under the table-cloth.

'Well, then,' my mother boomed, 'I wonder why on *earth* they're bothering to come and see *my* show?'

Jeffrey turned pink and shook his head. 'No!' he blurted. 'They think you're better – they didn't even know you were going to put it on!'

'Ah!' She dropped her voice to a whisper. 'How grateful I am to have *their* good opinion.'

I had noticed that she would glance at my father at the start of one of these scenes and that he would close his eyes and nod, as if he were her coach. He never stepped in to save Jeffrey. Nor did he take part. But I saw something between them every time, a sort of agreement that she would deliver the blows with his blessing. And I began to wonder whether they were just playing at cruel parents. Or whether they really hated Jeffrey. Appropriate or not, why did he deserve such punishment just for wanting Catherine? And how would I bear it if I were she? I couldn't bear it as it was. I wanted to shout at my mother to leave him alone. More than that, I wanted to be free myself from the power of her performance.

We always went backstage after a show. The theatre school student posted at the stage door was given instructions to let in only the immediate family and friends. But this was merely for the effect of exclusivity. In fact everyone who wished to go through was let in. The chaos of exaggerated whoops and hugs was what my parents adored.

Catherine led Jeffrey and his parents through the door. Valerie hunched her shoulders and hobbled behind them in an exact imitation of Mrs Goldman. I snickered into my hand and copied Valerie.

'Daahling!' my mother cried when she saw Catherine. She took both Catherine's hands in hers and held her at arm's length, beaming. 'Well, how was it? How did you like Daddy's Goring?'

Catherine pulled her hands free and shrank back against Jeffrey. She didn't look my mother in the eye. 'Yes,' she said.

'He's too damn old for Goring,' Valerie announced.

A few people turned to stare. My mother laughed. 'Too *old*! Don't you see, my dear, Lord Goring is *supposed* to be older than he acts?'

'In his thirties, not his late forties!'

My mother turned from Valerie and surveyed the crowd. She let her glance fly past the Goldmans, standing in a trio behind Catherine, and land on Adrianne Prescott, a radio actress.

'Adrianne!' she boomed. 'Daahling!'

'Sarah! It was a triumph!' The two women hugged. 'Roger was – Roger was –'

My mother patted Adrianne gently on the back as if to comfort her. She rested the side of her forehead against Adrianne's cheek and closed her eyes. Adrianne, she had told us many times, was *hopelessly* in love with my father. But because Adrianne was old and ugly my mother didn't blame him for this as she blamed him for the students who stared at him with ga-ga eyes or for the unknown women who posted fan letters to him under the theatre door.

Someone elbowed past me. It was Mr Goldman. I held my breath.

'Sarah Frank!' he bellowed. 'Con-gra-tu-*la*-tions!' He grasped my mother's shoulders. 'Better! *Much* better than London, I can tell you!'

I glanced at Catherine. She stood dead still in fright. In her strapless yellow taffeta dress and the choker of pearls Jeffrey had given her for her eighteenth birthday she did indeed look like Cinderella at midnight.

'And where is your famous husband?' Mr Goldman demanded in his Old Country accent. He smiled broadly as he waited for an answer, still hanging on to her shoulders.

Like his son, Solomon Goldman was hairy and pink. But his hair was grey and the skin on his face taut and veiny, pulled thin over the prominent bones of his cheeks and nose. Nothing about him matched. His teeth were too long for his lips to cover, his eyes too wide and too small for the size of his face. His hips were too narrow to hold up his trousers. But his chest was massive and pushed the closure of his shirt into scallops, with his hairy white flesh bulging out between the buttons. Even his thin, straight hair fell unnaturally around the strange outcroppings of his skull, leaving slashes of pink and red baldness shining through like scars above his ears.

My mother wrenched her shoulders free. He grabbed her hands. To my amazement she didn't seem to terrify him as she did his son. I wondered how it was possible that someone so ugly dared to touch her or to make such a demand on her so loudly, in such an accent, and with such laughing condescension. He seemed nice all of a sudden.

'Hello? Anyone at home?' My father, still in costume, peeped out from the wings.

The crowd swarmed towards him and he, beaming, stepped out to greet them as Lord Goring. It was a part he loved. We had been treated to its speeches and gestures for years.

'Ah!' Mr Goldman cried. He abandoned my mother and parted the crowd with his pigeon-breast, cutting a straight line to my father.

My father paled and stepped back, but it was too late. Mr Goldman threw an arm around his shoulders. 'And what is the famous actor up to Monday?'

'I beg your pardon?' Despite the calm in his voice his chest heaved. His eyes darted around the crowd for my mother.

'Lunch?' Mr Goldman asked. 'I come to town on Mondays. I

would like the privilege to take the greatest actor in the world to lunch.'

And so it was done. Soon after the engagement had been announced, Mr Goldman began pleading for a grand wedding, a thousand guests, smoked salmon flown in from Scotland, crates of Dom Perignon from France. He would arrive at our house with gifts of brandy and cigars, French perfume for my mother, expensive silk scarves for Valerie and me. He coaxed and wheedled my parents, waving his arms in wide arcs, arguing feelingly against their preference for a garden wedding, a tent in case it rained, homemade food and the household servants serving.

'Sarah! Rô-ger!' he implored them. 'Not for a wedding! The engagement, OK; but the wedding, no!' And then, quickly, he would flatter them, defer to their choices of colours and flowers and music, respectfully ask their permission to be allowed to pay for it all. 'Who cares about the money?' he kept asking anyone who would catch his eye, even me if I happened to be hanging around.

It was not a question I had ever considered before, and I wasn't at all sure how one was meant to answer it. Beyond the most elementary observations on the rising prices of food and servants, the subject of money and its power was as seldom aired in our house as the words 'sis' and 'shiksa'. And yet my mother always rose to Mr Goldman's question with, 'Oh, come along, Sol, you know *perfectly* well that that isn't the point!'

What then was the point, I wondered? I watched every choice she made with interest. On Saturdays I trailed behind her as she went from shop to shop looking for the wedding fabric, watched her plead with the sales ladies to bring out what they kept 'behind' – imported silks, taffetas, tulle and special laces for special customers. I noticed that she turned away brocades and bright colours, things I would have chosen. And then, when she would say, 'Ah, that's more like it,' I reached out quickly to touch the sanctified offering, to stare into its particular magic of threads and dyes, hoping to learn from it the secret of good taste.

Clothes mattered enormously to my mother, almost as much as voices. Her own wardrobe was chosen with the same care and passion that she devoted to directing plays. Each detail was scrutinized – the application of the sequins, the way a pocket had been set in, the cut and the finish and the trim.

With our clothes it was the same. Until we were eleven or twelve she had made all our best dresses; drafted the patterns. ordered dotted Swiss, fine lawns, laces and organdies from England. No dress would be released until the 'effect' was right. By this I imagined she meant the effect of the dress on my aunts, my father's two sisters – who, she said, for all their pretensions to taste and finishing schools, had no dress sense at all and couldn't do more for their own daughters than sew 'a simple smock.

Money evidently mattered too. I could see this in the look on her face when she asked for a price. And then, if the price seemed too low, in her scrutiny of the fabric in hand for hidden flaws. It mattered to have money when one needed it. It mattered to know how to spend it. I came to understand that the Goldmans had more than they needed but spent too much on the wrong things. That Abba lacked the talent to spend his at all. And that we, the deserving, had somehow been deprived of our birthright by a world insensitive to taste and discretion.

The wedding was set for December. My mother postponed her annual Christmas production until Easter so that she could sew tiny pearls on to Catherine's wedding dress, and rank and seat a thousand guests. Everyone agreed that the reception should be held in the theatre. But four hundred of the guests would have to sit outside in two marquees. Which guests to choose was the problem. She also worried about the bridesmaids' dresses. Mrs Samuels, our dressmaker, could only commit herself to Catherine's dress and three others. So Tillie – 'Hannah's little coloured woman' – had to be hired to make the rest. But the creature's work was slapdash. She couldn't even *cut* properly. And if the bolts of pink tulle didn't arrive soon there would be no time to make the dresses *anyway*! Catherine would just have to put up with a retinue swathed in makeshift material, like a procession of *Indians* in *saris*! My mother sighed and closed her eyes. This wedding was turning out to be more work than a production. At least on the stage she didn't have to *answer* to anyone! It was *bound* to rain, had anyone thought of *that*? The heat would be *fierce*! And what if the *fish* went off? Wasn't it just *typical* of the Goldmans to insist on kosher food?

Eleven bridesmaids and flower girls had been chosen from almost forty eligible cousins. Most of them were picked for size and beauty. Giants and midgets were eliminated. So were huge busts and hunched shoulders. We were measured for height and then matched as evenly as possible to make pairs. My mother even made a scaled drawing of the synagogue so that she could plan the entrances and exits. Valerie, the maid of honour, was cautioned on her demeanour. She was not, at all costs, to upstage Catherine.

The prospect of being a bridesmaid did not thrill me at all. It would, I knew, take more than tulle and high heels to transform me for the job. My mother knew that too. She began to pounce on me every time I walked through a door. 'No, no, no! *Not* like that! Now look. *This* is how you enter a room.' She marched out of the lounge, waited a few seconds, and then flung the door open. Catherine rolled her eyes. Valerie, who never needed to be taught how to make an entrance, refused to look. My mother smiled graciously. '*Hello*, everybody!' she said. She stalked to the couch, executed an elegant turn, and then sat down swishing stockings and skirt. 'See, darling? Now go out and do it yourself.'

I stalled, hoping for an escape. 'It's ridiculous,' I muttered. 'Normal people don't walk like that.' I was still in my school uniform – a navy serge gym tunic, shirt and tie, and black lisle stockings with meandering seams. My feet were weighted down by heavy, black, rubber-soled, laced-up shoes.

'Go on, ugly,' Valerie taunted. 'Give us a laugh.'

But just then Reuben arrived at the door in his whites and sash. 'Dinner is ready, Madam.'

My mother sighed. 'Does anyone realize that we have barely six weeks until this wedding?' One of my knees caught her eye as she passed. She tapped at it to remind me that it was spread too far from the other one. 'Darling, *please*! Try to be a little more graceful. A little more *feminine*. Practise your walk and your smile.' She smiled herself to show me she had faith in me. 'Remember what I told you? Come along then!'

After my bath I closeted myself in my room and examined my nude body carefully in the mirror. It was pasty and full of lumps, like unkneaded dough. I turned to catch my profile. My nose was already hooked high like my mother's, dominating my face. When I smiled my lower jaw receded and the lip curled back over my bottom teeth. My top teeth were spaced out in an assortment of sizes and shapes. My hair hung in strands. My stomach protruded and my legs were too short for my body. There was no hope.

I sat on my bed and attempted to weep at the unfairness of it all. Our study was full of Edwardian novels in which half-starved orphan girls wept themselves to sleep every night in attic rooms. But it was easier for them. Somewhere at the end of the novel a rich father or uncle would emerge out of nowhere to punish the oppressors and to buy fantastic clothes and jewels. My situation wasn't so easy to solve. And playing parts had never given me comfort. I couldn't even blame anyone. If I complained about my nose or my teeth my mother simply pointed out that they were just like hers. And that *she* had always managed perfectly well.

I shrugged and pulled on my pyjamas, galloped down to the kitchen to find Nora.

She was setting dough to rise for the next day's bread. 'You coming to give me work?' she demanded.

I shook my head.

Satisfied, she returned to the bowls and dough and damp dishcloths. She began on 'Silent Night' with exaggerated vibrato, inviting me to harmonize.

'Do you think I'll ever get married?' I asked.

'Awu!' She stopped singing and turned to look at me. 'What the matter with you?'

'Nothing. I'm only joking.' I lifted my feet on to the chair to avoid a huge cockroach gliding towards them.

'You too young to be thinking those thoughts,' she muttered.

'I'm not thinking. I was just wondering.'

'You!' she said accusingly. 'You the best of the lot! You wait and see.'

This was what I had come for. Although her servant's eyes and strange African standards of beauty counted for nothing in our world, I loved to have her praise and assurances.

'Husbands?' she went on. 'You going to have a better one than Master Jeffrey.' She lifted her apron over her head and hung it on the hook behind the back door. 'Humph!' she said.

Then suddenly she thrust her hand into her uniform and unravelled one huge breast. 'See?' She let the breast drop down to her waist. It hung there massive and still, with its strange black nipple staring ahead like a doorbell.

I looked at it politely. Nora often did this. Perhaps it was her way of avowing the kinship of all women. Or perhaps she was proud of the size of her breasts. She was certainly assured that the sight would cheer me up. And that the demonstration would somehow clinch the subject of my chances in life as a woman. She smiled triumphantly as she stuffed it back into her bodice. 'Tomorrow I put two fairy cake in your little break,' she promised. 'One vanil, one chocolate.' And then she left the kitchen to join Reuben for the night.

Nora and Reuben were lovers. A few years before, soon after Reuben had come to work for us, I had seen them both hefting first the mattress and then the iron bedstead from his room into hers. I ran off immediately to tell my mother. She stared up at me from her script, keeping her finger on the place. 'What?' she roared.

'They're moving Reuben's bed into Nora's room.'

'Nonsense,' she snapped. 'Go and play.'

But I saw her mark her place in the script, and sigh, and walk out to the compound quickly so that she could arrive there without warning. I climbed into the mango tree and waited.

'Do you know what you're *doing*, Nora?' she asked.

'Yes, Madam,' Nora murmured.

'This won't upset the other servants?'

Reuben had vanished back into the compound, leaving the women to themselves.

I could see the vast bulk of Nora's buttocks quivering as she defended her right to love as she pleased.

'What about your church?' my mother demanded. 'What about Constance?'

Nora clasped her hands in front of her and stared at the grass. Constance, her daughter, was a year older than I was and lived with her grandmother in Zululand. She visited her mother twice a year. Nothing had ever been said about the child's father. Nora had no answer to these questions.

'Well, then,' my mother said, turning to leave. 'Just be careful, please. I don't want any trouble.'

'Yes, Madam.'

After that, Nora and Reuben became a family joke. But it was mostly Nora that they laughed at – the thought of any man wanting her.

'There's something about all that flesh, you know, that seems to appeal to them,' my mother would say, waving her cigarette in the air. 'I think they consider her *quite* a beauty!'

To me, however, Reuben was the lucky one. I found him very ugly. He had come from the Belgian Congo and was thin and bony and very black. His eyes and teeth were a bilious yellow and his gums a dark grey. I was also afraid of him. He never smiled. Unlike the other servants, he wouldn't allow me to joke with him or to tease him. There was menace in his unintelligible mutterings and in the sneer he wore when I delivered a command from my mother. We often heard him yelling at Nora in the compound, heard things banging about there, and heard her crying. But my parents refused to interfere. Sometimes my mother would warn Nora that the noise had to *stop*. And Nora would promise that it would. No one but me ever seemed to blame Reuben.

Reuben was, in fact, my parents' favourite servant. His aping of my father's personal habits delighted them, convinced them of his superior intelligence and discerning judgement. 'Damned shame, isn't it?' they would say. 'In another country he'd really go far.'

Everything about my father's style seemed to appeal to Reuben. He wound a low, rich purr into the timbre of his speech, eliminating the deferential whisper that characterized the English of other servants. And he was personally vain. He had Nora launder and starch his uniforms daily, and loved to swathe the scarlet sash across his chest on Sundays and other formal occasions. After he moved in with her, he converted the houseboy's room into a dressing-room for himself, like my father's, with an old full-length mirror, a tallboy of Nora's, and three crates draped with a tablecloth to form a chaise longue.

When Reuben copied my father's hair ritual, however, he became famous all over town. Every morning, after his bath and cold shower, my father rubbed Brylcreme into his curly hair, made a careful side parting, and then combed and brushed his hair as straight and as flat as he could. After this, with a large triangle of beige silk, he would tie the hair into place and leave it like that until he had completed his toilet.

A week after Reuben arrived he appeared behind the vacuum cleaner with a beige cotton scarf tied around his head in just the same manner as my father's. He didn't seem to notice or to care that we laughed at him. But when I reached up one day to pull the scarf off, he turned on me and bared his teeth and hissed.

'Don't play with Reuben special scarf,' Nora warned. '*Every* day, *every* day he make the hair straight, same like Master.'

All the servants were to come to the wedding, even Sampson, and Johannes, Abba's chauffeur. They were to be seated at tables like everyone else and served the same food. I was delighted. Even though I was about to emerge from the gap inhabited by white children – between servants and parents – I still owed allegiance to both sides.

'What are you going to wear?' I asked Nora.

She laughed and held her hands in the air as she wiggled her fat hips. 'Ai, ai, ai!' she cried. 'I am going to look *smart!*'

'Will you show me?' I asked.

She looked at the kitchen clock. 'Come,' she said. 'Quickle.'

I ran ahead of her to the compound, wound myself into the sheets on the line as I waited for her to come up the path.

'You dirty the sheets, I tell the Madam,' she said happily.

I stood behind her as she unlocked her door, pinching lightly at her bottom in my delight. Since Reuben had moved into her room, I was welcome there only when Constance came to visit and he had to move out.

'Mafuta! Mafuta!' I chanted.

She turned the key and pushed the door open. Beyond that threshold I couldn't tease and she couldn't scold. We had to play at host and guest.

'You sit there,' she said. She flicked at the seat of an old globe chair with a feather duster.

As cook and housekeeper Nora had the best room in the compound. It was larger than the others, had its own basin in one corner, and looked out over the laundry garden, not the yard. Even so, with the two beds squashed together into a corner, there was barely enough room for a small wardrobe, chest of drawers, and the chair I was sitting on. Above the wardrobe and under the beds cardboard suitcases and boxes had been crammed. The walls were covered with old chocolate-box covers – puppies and kittens and bowls of red roses. A bouquet of dusty florists' bows in a chipped pink glass vase almost obscured the cracked mirror of the chest. And next to it, framed and unsmiling, Nora and Constance stared out of a photograph taken against a fake backdrop of mountains and waterfalls. Like Lucy's flat or the shell of a snail, Nora's room seemed to me to contain a whole world in one place.

'Here it is,' she said shyly. She hung the dress on the wardrobe door.

I jumped up off the chair and stood before it in amazement. It was a real dress, the sort that Aunt Hannah and Beatrice and Ruby had. Not at all the homemade sacks in cheap floral cotton that Nora wore on her day off. On the bed she was laying out a hat, gloves, a handbag and a huge pair of high-heeled shoes, all in matching grey satin and pink lace trimmings. One pink rose had been pinned on to the bodice of the dress and another on to the crown of the hat.

'Can I touch?' I asked. My mother never allowed me to touch her clothes.

Nora laughed as I put the dress to my cheek. 'You like my outfit?' she asked.

'It's better than Ma's,' I said.

'Awu!' she said, turning to hide her smile as she put the dress away. 'Don't say that!'

'But it *is*!' I insisted. 'Everything matches.'

She wrapped the shoes carefully in their tissue and placed them back in a box. The bag and hat and gloves were wrapped too. Then she folded her arms and considered me seriously. 'Big surprise,' she announced.

'What?'

She laughed again. 'Old Nora going to have her hair straightened!'

'What! How?'

'I know a person knows how,' she said mysteriously. 'Make-up too,' she said to me through the mirror. 'You not going to recog-nize your old Nora!'

'What kind of make-up?' I couldn't imagine what make-up would be visible on Nora's black skin.

'Same like yours,' she said quickly. 'Lipstick. Roodge. Moos-cara.' She pulled off her cap, patted her hand over her braided head and then pulled it on again at a different angle. 'Jewish people,' she announced emphatically, 'are *very* smart.'

I had asked my mother several times where the servants would be seated. I couldn't bear the thought that Nora, in her pink and grey lace and hair and make-up, would be hidden from view.

'But where're you seating Nora?' I stared down at the seating chart on the card table before her.

She threw her eyes up to the ceiling. 'Aren't you a little too old to be championing the underdog?' she boomed.

'Don't put her outside,' I pleaded.

'For God's sake, Ruth! Do you suggest I put her at the top table?'

She was in no mood for persuasion, I could see that. Nevertheless, I persisted. 'She's bought a special dress and everything.'

My mother tapped her pencil lightly on the edge of the table. 'Nora would feel very uncomfortable inside.'

'Why?'

'Because they like to be amongst their own.'

'But she's having her hair straightened –'

'*What?*'

'At a special hairdresser.'

'Good Lord!' She stared at me in alarm. 'I hope to *heaven* she doesn't get herself up like one of those awful American negroes!'

All the women were crammed into the office of the synagogue, waiting for a signal from the rabbi. It was ninety-five degrees and so humid that the walls ran in little rivulets. Lizards darted in and out of the shade.

'Sis!' Valerie shrieked. 'Get those lizards away from me!'

'Shut up!' Catherine snapped.

'Valerie!' my mother boomed. 'Control yourself. And watch your language!' She had made a fan out of some papers on the desk and was fanning Catherine. With her other hand she dabbed at Catherine's cheeks and nose with a lace handkerchief. 'Now remember, darling,' she purred in her low and steady backstage voice, 'move slowly, walk on the balls, chin up, a slight smile on your face.'

Catherine tossed her head but said nothing.

'Can I do anything, Cathy?' It was Ettie Goldman, Jeffrey's mother, in her high-pitched, girlish whine.

The colour suddenly rose in Catherine's cheeks. 'No, thank you,' she said in the cold precise tones she reserved for those she loathed.

'Oh, Ettie! Yes!' My mother turned to her. 'Why don't you go out there and find out what on *earth's* holding them up? It's already half past.'

Mrs Goldman shrank her short neck even further into her hunched shoulders. She cupped her jewelled hands before her like a mendicant. My mother had often mimicked her for us – the voice, the hands held just like that. 'But they told us to stay in here –' she sing-songed.

'Mrs Goldman!' I shouted, suddenly very excited. 'You've got on almost the same outfit as Nora!'

Valerie let out a whoop and a shriek and then led everyone but Mrs Goldman and me into crippling laughter. Even Catherine smiled at the funniness of it.

'Ruth! Don't be absurd!' my mother boomed. I could see she was as delighted as the rest.

'But she has!' I insisted. 'They are both in grey and pink!'

Mrs Goldman pursed her thin lips into a straight line and said nothing.

Just then Rabbi Levy's face popped around the door. 'Ready?' he asked.

'Valerie! Elizabeth!' my mother boomed, suddenly serious again. 'Catherine! Girls! *All* of you! We're on!'

As we lined up along the corridor, the choir began to sing and the crowd became still. Mrs Levy's quavering voice rose into 'Baruch habah' as Catherine, on my father's arm, entered the synagogue. The rest of us, three feet apart and stepping lightly on the balls of our feet, followed behind her.

When we had come to a stop, the rabbi began the wedding service. He was sweating profusely in his black beard and robes. The cantor too glistened in the heat. Women opened Japanese fans and fluttered them about their necks. Soon the whole place hung heavy with the perfume of women and the woolly sweat of men.

I searched out my mother under the hupa. She was staring upward, over the rabbi's head, her chin at an angle, her face fixed into a familiar expression of forbearance. The sight made me feel less strange. Since Catherine's engagement she had repeatedly offered the rabbi voice and speech lessons at no

69

expense. But he was a complacent man and couldn't see the need or find the time. And so here he was as usual, talking through his nose. And such *rubbish*! She glanced up at my father to record her disapproval. But he had turned his head away, close to tears at the loss of Catherine to another man.

I looked up at the balcony. The servants sat there, where women usually sat. They hung over the balustrade to watch the strange show below.

Then suddenly Jeffrey had smashed the glass, and people were saying 'ah' and 'mazeltov'. And Jeffrey kissed Catherine, and my parents embraced her too. And Catherine and Jeffrey turned, smiling, and we all turned behind them, smiling as we had been told to, and trooped out like the winning team at a rugby match.

'That one's going to be a killer,' a male voice said deep and clear as I passed. I stopped. The crowd milled and swarmed, waiting for us to clear the aisle. But I stood where I was. I turned deliberately to see if the words were meant for me. A man smiled into my eyes and bowed from the waist. He was about Jeffrey's age, bearded and dark, blue-eyed, manly.

'Go on! Move!' hissed Barbara, my partner, behind me.

But I was fixed to the spot, shocked out of self-consciousness by the happiness he had given me.

'Ruth! For God's sake!' Barbara gave me a shove. 'Silly fool!'

I pitched forward under the shove and galloped along the aisle towards the door. Ungraceful. Unfeminine. But I didn't care. I laughed as I ran. I had a future as a woman. One day I was going to be a killer of men.

We could hear the band playing as we emerged into the heavy dusk and crossed the road to the theatre. I spotted Lucy in the crowd of onlookers gathered along the pavement, and behind her Mr and Mrs Knowles. I waved regally. They waved back, enjoying the stares they got from the crowd around them. For some years Lucy and I had been waving to each other as we passed in the street. We had moved beyond the shared territory of childhood now and into our different worlds. We never spoke at all anymore.

In the theatre it was as hot as my mother had feared. And the smell of fish overwhelmed the perfume of hundreds of pink roses that festooned the hall and the marquees. Everywhere was pink. Pink and white lights had been strung and looped into a false ceiling. Their glow shimmered into an iridescent haze with the moisture hanging in the air. Even the swarms of flying ants that flew in with the guests fluttered in thick pink clouds under the lights. Their wings floated down in a light-pink blizzard to the tables and the floor. A few of the younger boys, holding flying ants by their wings, chased each other between the tables. And wingless ants were crunched underfoot as the guests marched to their places.

At the theatre entrance an Indian major-domo in a turban announced table numbers and locations in a strained officious voice. I glanced at the door just as Nora arrived. She looked magnificent, black and round as a plum. Dozens of sausage curls glistened around her face. Her cheeks gleamed pink and moist. Her lips shone red. Pink pearls dangled from her ears. With the net of her veil hooked under her broad nose and her head held high for everyone to see she did indeed look like an American negro. A hundred times better than Mrs Goldman.

The major-domo took a few steps towards her, forcing her to retreat to the top of the stairs. I knew she was explaining to him that she had a right to come in, that she and the others behind her had been invited as guests like everyone else.

I jumped up and waved to catch my mother's eye. It wasn't difficult. She sat at the top table scanning the hall like a searchlight. Furiously I nodded my head towards the entrance until she noticed Nora. She climbed down off the platform and stalked across the dance floor to the major-domo, snatched the list from his hand and pointed imperiously to Nora's name. She stood, arms folded, as he explained to Nora with elaborate politeness which marquee to go to and how to find her table. And then she walked back to her place looking as harried as if the lights had failed on opening night.

The band trumpeted everyone to attention and Catherine and Jeffrey walked down the centre of the theatre arm in arm.

We clapped and champagne corks popped.

'The lucky beggar!' my cousin Sharon said. She was twenty-one, fat, and still unmarried.

I looked around. Eleven bridesmaids, all dressed the same, were waiting to be lucky like Catherine. But the boys seemed oblivious. The younger ones threw things at each other – nuts and ants and name cards made into missiles. The older ones crossed their legs and pretended to listen to the speeches.

Food was brought. And then the dancing began. This was the moment I had been dreading. In all the fuss about my walking and sitting, dancing had somehow been forgotten. I hoped that by looking into my lap I wouldn't have to waltz with Richard, the appointed cousin, for the bridesmaids' dance. But there he was behind me, tipping me off my chair to demonstrate that he too was unwilling.

People clapped as we danced. Richard held me far from him, pushing me backwards with two bony arms as if I were on wheels. Round and round we went in silence.

At last the tempo changed to a foxtrot. 'OK,' the bandmaster said. 'Everyone on the dance floor.'

Richard pushed me away. 'That's that,' he said, looking around for someone nearer his age.

As I turned to go, warm fingers touched the nape of my neck. 'May I have this dance, Madame Defarge?'

It was my redeemer. He held out his arms. 'Come,' he said. lifting me up so that I could feel the softness of his beard against my cheek, 'let me sweep you off your feet.' He whirled me into the middle of the dance floor and then put me down without losing a beat. We swept backwards, forwards, my head swirling in dizzy happiness. 'The littlest Frank,' he crooned in a deep baritone. 'Who would have thought it?'

'Thought what?' I managed to ask.

The music changed again into a samba. 'I can't do this,' I said. My cheeks were on fire.

'I'll show you.' He held me more tightly.

But I planted my feet where they were and stared soberly into his face. 'Thought what?' I asked again.

He took his hand from around my waist and lifted my chin with his fingers. 'I'll tell you something –' he said.

'Hello, Bernard.' My father arrived at my side and smiled his stiff social smile at my partner. 'I see you're teaching my youngest daughter to dance.'

Bernard bowed.

My father placed a careful hand around my shoulders and drew me away. 'May I claim her from you for this dance?' he asked.

Again Bernard bowed, but this time he backed away, smiling at me as he went.

'I don't want to dance anymore,' I said to my father. I wanted to cry. I felt punished and wanted to punish him back.

'Come on, Chopsticks,' he coaxed in a burlesque of disappointment. 'I saw you hitting the high spots with that young man. Won't you give your old dad a chance?'

'Who is he?' I managed to ask.

'Bernard Rubenstein? Oh, he's a funny sort of chap, isn't he?' He looked soberly at me.

'What does he do?' I asked.

'Follow, don't lead.'

'What?' I insisted.

'Some sort of a painter or artist or something, I believe.'

'Is he rich?' I asked.

He frowned down at me in surprise. 'Is that very important?'

'I dunno. I'm just asking.'

'Do you wish we were wealthy?' he asked.

'Yes.'

The muscles in his jaw tightened. 'It saddens me that you should feel that way.'

The music stopped and the drums rolled. 'The bride will now throw her garter,' said the bandleader. 'Will all the young ladies please gather around.'

'That means you too,' my father said. 'Go on.'

'No.' I stood where I was, balking at the indignity of wanting a husband so publicly. Valerie too had refused to join in and smiled sardonically as the other girls gathered in front of the stage. Catherine, with her garter held high in the air, looked like the Statue of Liberty.

Suddenly I saw Bernard Rubenstein lean over Valerie and bite her shoulder lightly. I saw her throw her head back and laugh with all her teeth. He sat down in the chair next to hers and leaned forward to look into her face. He seemed to be telling her jokes. I could hear the swoop of her laughter over the shrieks and cries of someone catching the garter.

The band struck up again.

'One more dance,' my father said, 'and then it's Valerie's turn.'

I could barely feel his hand around my waist as he led me into the foxtrot. I concentrated on taking quick, shallow breaths.

'That's it! he said triumphantly. '*One*-two-side-together, *one*-two-side-together. Don't pump with this hand. Let it rest on mine as light as a feather. And *smile*! Don't be so serious! Lift up your chin! You've a lot to be proud of, you know. Follow, don't lead. *There*. *Now* you've got it.'

5

'But it was only a propeller pencil!' I shouted.

Abba shook his head. 'It's the principle, my dear. Theft is theft regardless of the object.'

My mother sighed. 'Oh, Dad, don't bother arguing with *that* child! She's the great champion of the underdog, you know.'

'But you don't even absolutely know that he took it!' I howled. 'Nora just found it in his *room*! You shouldn't even have sent her in there anyway! You have no right to invade his privacy like that!'

'Ha! Listen to who's talking!' She laughed. 'Until *very* recently you were in and out of the compound all the time.'

I blushed. I was thirteen. I knew now what I had done to Sampson. Worse than knowing myself was knowing that he knew too. For years I had almost managed to forget that it had happened. But now he was packing his things to leave. I felt responsible.

'Last time it was the torch from Dad's car. Today it's a propeller pencil. Next time it could be a watch. Or worse. We should have thrown him out long ago. Once they start stealing, that's it.'

'We're just fortunate that Nora's the faithful servant she is,' my father said, sipping his coffee.

'She's a spy!' I shouted. '*You* made her into a spy!'

75

He reached over for a piece of glacé ginger and posted it carefully between his teeth, licked the syrup off the tips of his fingers.

'Can't you give him a chance?' I wailed.

'We've given him too many chances already.'

'But he'll never get another job!' I shouted at them in misery for his wanting the pencil so badly. And in disgust that I had touched his penis. And in shame at the thrill I still remembered.

My mother smiled at me. 'Darling,' she said. 'Don't you see? It's not just the pencil –'

'It *is* just the pencil! It *is* just the pencil!'

'It's the principle, my dear,' Abba repeated.

'When you grow up and have to run a household of your own –'

'I'll *never* have servants! I'll *never* live like this!'

'Oh, *really*?' My mother arched her eyebrows and smiled. She loved this kind of statement from me; all the adults did. It seemed, in its madness, to reaffirm for them the transitory nature of my adolescent revolt. And to give them a foil for comic scenes. 'Who's for guavas and cream?' she asked.

It was quiet in the compound when I got there. Nora and Reuben were still in the kitchen, and Beauty was out. I pushed open the gate and felt my way along the path, past the toilet, to Sampson's door. There was no sound from within, no guitar strumming or noisy laughter. But I knew he was there. A shadow moved back and forth across the ribbon of weak yellow light that wavered under his door. I knocked.

'Ubani lowo?'

'Miss Ruth.'

I waited in the dark, smelling again the strangeness of that other world – rubbish and paraffin and disinfectant. Half Madam myself, I felt uncomfortable there now.

The door opened a few inches and Sampson looked out. With the light behind him he was very black. I couldn't even see his face.

'I brought you a present,' I said.

He pushed the door wider. I could see now that his eyes were red from crying or drinking. He wore his Sunday clothes.

'Here –' I held out my red propeller pencil.

He hid his hands behind his back. 'No, Miss Ruth. You make more trouble.'

'It's a present. It's mine. Take it with you.'

But still he shook his head, wouldn't even look up. Behind him, on his bed, I could see a cardboard grocery box tied up with string. My father's old felt hat sat on top.

A lump rose to my throat. I closed my fist around the pencil and stared at the floor myself. This man a thief? And Abba with all his principles eating guavas and cream. Where did I belong in all this, I asked myself? Sampson wanted me to go away, I could see that. But I felt that I had nowhere to go. I wanted him to know that.

'Where will you go, Sampson?'

He said nothing.

I knew he didn't want my pity, the tears spilling down my cheeks. Perhaps he already understood what was only just beginning to make itself clear to me. That my presence there, the offering, the tears, were for myself, not him. Pleasure in misery. Useless for anything else.

'Awu, Miss Ruth –'

I turned and fled, ashamed.

'Where you been?' Nora demanded.

'None of your business.'

She shuffled up to me in her yawning pom-pom slippers. 'Don't say none of your business. *My* business you make trouble with Sampson.'

'I didn't make trouble.'

Suddenly she frowned down at my hand, bent close to see, as if I held something in it alive and dangerous. 'Where you get that pencil?' she demanded. 'I tell the Madam –'

'Tell-tale! Spy! Traitor!'

'Awu!' She turned on me. 'Why you call me bad names? Hey?'

I hung my head. 'You told Ma about Sampson.'

'Sampson no-good rubbish. He steal the Madam special pencil for her scrip.'

'Why did you have to tell on him? Couldn't you just have put the pencil back?'

She pulled her lips closed self-righteously as if to stop herself swallowing the teachings of the devil.

'Where will he go now?'

She shrugged.

'Reuben will have to garden, you know, until Ma finds someone else –'

Her eyes darted at me over the mounds of her cheeks. 'Reuben he *never* be gardenboy!'

'Well who will garden then?'

She turned away and hovered over one of the servants' pots on the stove. Nora was a poor actress. When she was unsure of a part she had to hide her face to say her lines. 'Reuben he know a boy for the garden.'

I stared at her back, the familiar expanse of bottom, the bow of her apron, monkey ropes of varicose veins under her stockings. And I thought of Sampson's head shaking side to side. 'No, Madam, I no take. No, Madam.' I felt the pencil in my hand and felt a fool.

'What boy?'

'From the Congo, same like him.'

'I'm going to tell Ma,' I said, walking to the door.

'The Madam she like Reuben,' Nora said quickly. 'She want another boy same like him. Not lazy like Sampson.'

'I'm going to tell her *you* put the pencil there.'

Nora turned to me at last. Her chest heaved, small beads of sweat glistened on her nose. 'You don't tell lies!' she whispered. 'You mind your business!'

The door flew open and Reuben came in with the coffee tray. He brushed behind me, stopping a second so that I felt squeezed between them, breathing too close the starch of their uniforms, their Mum and Lifebuoy soap.

'The Madam she want you,' Reuben muttered to me. He carried the tray on to the sink.

'No, I didn't want you,' my mother said. 'He must have wanted to get rid of you. You know, you're getting a little too old to be hanging around the servants all the time. They don't like it.'

'Sampson didn't take the pencil.'

'Oh, don't start *that* again, for God's sake! Look, haven't you got any homework?'

'It's done.'

'Well, how about listening to Lux Radio Theatre with us? It's *A Tale of Two Cities*; Dad plays Sydney Carton. You've read the novel, haven't you?'

I nodded.

'Go and have a quick bath. But *hurry*! Dad says it's quite a good production.'

I lay across the couch with my head in my mother's lap. It was a cool August night, the sort that gave us the illusion of life in the north. I wore flannel pyjamas and a winter dressing-gown. My father had plugged in the heater. The wind, blowing fierce and strong from a storm at sea, tipped over one of the verandah chairs. My mother turned her hands in front of the heater and then ran the tips of her fingers lightly over my face.

We listened together in silence. It had always seemed strange to me that we heard the same thing differently, were moved in different ways. For them it was not the story as much as the performances that counted. They would smile at each other when they recognized a voice, shake their heads at an awful accent or someone hopelessly miscast. They never seemed to mourn, as I did, the ending of a play. Or to wonder about the story itself, what had happened before, what would happen after. The play was a device. And they measured its success in the details of its effect.

Although I could identify the voices of the radio actors almost as well as they did, I had never before let that knowledge spoil the story itself. I could forget them in their real lives, who they were and how they looked. That night, however, I failed to make the leap from player to play. I heard my father playing Sydney Carton, saw him sitting in a chair opposite me, listening too, his legs crossed, smoking a cigar. I knew the ending of the story. But that night, somehow, his voice was more real than he was. He had become Sydney Carton – reckless, romantic, clever, heroic. And he was going to die. I heard it coming, the crowds shouting for his death, the Marseillaise' playing as they marched him to the scaffold. I turned my face into my mother's lap and wept, trying to draw breath quietly so that she wouldn't know.

She patted my head. 'Darling,' she said, 'it's only a story!'

'Hey, hey!' my father laughed. 'Chopsticks? Here I am! Look! Alive as a spring chicken!'

My tears had delighted them both. But I resented that delight. And I didn't want their reassurances. I wanted him beheaded truly, that joyful misery back again.

'Why on earth did Cecil have you gabble that last speech?' she asked him, her hand still on my head. 'Was the timing off?'

'I wasn't aware that I was gabbling.'

'You threw the whole damn thing away. Pity.'

'I could have slowed it down a bit, I suppose.'

'*Cecil* should have seen to that. That's what he s *there* for. after all. Seems to me he must have miscalculated, and then had to fill in with all that unnecessary music and that *endless* crowd scene.'

'What did you think of Ian?'

'Oh, Ian is Ian whatever he does. Cecil should have used Julian.'

'Julian was in Jo'burg.'

'Hmm.'

I turned my face upwards to listen.

'Cecil hasn't a *clue* when it comes to cutting, you know. He could have left out that whole spiel with the girl at the beginning. It made no *sense*. Even Mrs Average Listener would know *that*! Maybe he's just lazy.'

'No, it's more to do with ear. I don't think he's got an ear, do you?'

'You're *quite* right! Even his pauses are haywire!'

'Well, you said it yourself. You've either got it or you haven't. So where's the solution?'

They eyed each other in silence, and frowned, thinking of ears and pauses. And I, listening, after all the years of just such conversations, suddenly heard them differently. This was their real world. The truth mattered to them here. Good was good, bad bad, and they knew the reason why. For the rest – the roles they played at home, ourselves as they saw us, our lives, Sampson's stealing, Nora and Reuben – we took the parts and shape of a loose performance, unpredictable, uncontrollable and messy. The truth in real life had no rules, no standards. And so they could only try to impose on us the forms and shapes they understood. Like trying to build a fence around a frightened flock of geese. They took no comfort in facing the chaos that surrounded them.

The new gardenboy was even darker and uglier than Reuben, smaller and much younger – about sixteen or seventeen – and with yellower eyes and teeth. He smiled a lot to make up for not speaking English.

'What is your name?' my mother asked.

'Call him John, Madam,' Reuben answered.

'But, Reuben, does he speak no English at all?'

'He will learn, Madam. I will teach him.'

'I certainly hope so, Reuben. I can't have a gardenboy who doesn't even know what a wheelbarrow is. What standard did he reach in school?'

'Standard five, Madam. But they learn French there, Madam.'

'Hmm.'

'Does he want to go to that night school the university students run?'

'I ask him, Madam.'

John learned quickly. Soon he was saying 'Good morning, Madam,' and 'wheelbarrow', and 'Need soap, Madam.' And he was funny. His clowning at the sink made Nora scream with laughter. Even Reuben would smile occasionally, baring his teeth like a horse.

One day, as I stood with a plate of cake in the kitchen after school, John approached me, smiling. 'Please, Miss –' He held out a dirty exercise book on which someone's name had been scratched out. He stepped back. 'My school work, Miss.'

Inside, in a closed, pencilled scrawl, were simple sentences. 'The farmr feed the pigs.' 'Fech the buket.' 'The shopp opin nino clok.'

'Is this dictation?' I sat down at the table, thrilled with this new role.

He nodded.

'I mean from night school. Someone read this and you wrote it down?'

He smiled. He had no idea what I was asking.

I looked down again at the sentences. They were uneven and smudged. I longed to take a red pen and circle the smudges as our teachers did at school. Or to draw a line through the whole page and write 'one hour detention'. I had never taught anyone anything.

'Good?' he asked, still smiling.

'There are some mistakes,' I said.

He frowned and stared down at the page in a burlesque of close attention.

'Here, see, it should be "farmer", and here, "fetch". "Feeds", "shop", "open" and "nine o'clock".'

He hung his head.

'But it's *good!*' I said. 'You've only been learning for three months! You're *very* clever!'

He stared at me with his yellow eyes and smiled politely.

'Look, I'll just write the right words here and you can copy them.'

He hung above me as I wrote, then ran one finger under my words, leaving a meandering trail of soil across the page.

'You can bring your work to me whenever you like,' I said magnificently. 'And I can help you with your reading too.'

John came to me quite often, a few times a week. But after a while teaching him lost its novelty. And I didn't like the way he stood too close, and pretended to understand what I said, and then came back the next time with the same mistake. If I passed him in the garden he would smile and wave at me like an old friend. 'I bring my book tomorrow,' he would promise, as if I were the one wanting the lessons.

'I don't know why you're bothering with him,' my mother said. 'That's the job of the night school bods, you know.'

'It's not their *job!* I shouted. 'They're *volunteers! They* really care about what happens to people like John.'

She sighed. 'I don't know why I even bother with you! If you want to spend your time teaching the servants to read, go right ahead. Just make sure he doesn't neglect the garden, please.'

'Oh, no! Neglect the garden! Perish the thought!'

It was easy to play champion of the underdog with my mother. With her face cast in bored disdain, the disregard in her voice, she fed me my lines. But my responsibility to John weighed me down. I didn't like it. I didn't like him, or his smiling familiarity. I wished I could cancel his access to me, but I could think of no excuse that wouldn't expose me for the fraud I was. I found myself avoiding the kitchen, slipping upstairs with my cake and tea before he could catch my eye.

'It is a very good thing for the African to strive for an education,' Abba said. He approved of John and was always stopping on the path to the front gate to ask him about his studies.

'How can a person strive if he's got to spend his days digging in the garden or hoovering carpets?' I demanded.

'Nothing worth having is easy, my dear. Consider the history of our Jewish people.'

'But this is *their* country!' I said. 'How dare the government just come in and tell them where they can go and what they can do?'

'It is no more their country than it is ours, my dear.'

'Well, they were here first.'

'To whom, then, would you say England belonged? The Angles and the Saxons? Or the Celts?'

'The Celts.'

'Dad,' my mother sighed. 'I don't know why you're bothering with this child.'

Abba held up his hand to my mother and smiled. 'Patience, my dear. I've had a little practice, you know.'

'Well, maybe *they* won't be patient!' I shouted. This, I knew, would scare them. The papers were full of protests and pass burnings in the African townships.

'Yes.' He nodded his head up and down. 'If only our African would understand that violence will get him nowhere.'

'I think they're right to be violent,' I said. 'Why shouldn't Africans be treated just the same as us?'

'As *we*,' my father said.

'Not quite just the same.' Abba smiled. 'They have centuries to develop, you know, before they catch up to us.'

'They're barely out of the trees!' Valerie sneered. 'That's why Ruth's so mad about them. She's always had a thing about baboons.'

'Valerie!' my father said. 'There's absolutely no need to be rude.'

'Who cares?' I shouted. 'I'd rather spend my time with them than with you!'

My father closed his eyes for silence. 'Your mother has rung the bell,' he said. 'Would you kindly change the subject while Reuben is in the room?'

I stared down at my plate, at Reuben's white-gloved hand taking it away, and tried to think of him in another world, wearing normal clothes like my father, reading the paper, sitting with his family at a table. All I could imagine was Reuben just as he was – servant, solitary, disengaged from real life, with all the dignity he had a shadow of our own.

'For pudding, Madam?' He wouldn't look at her. He hated women, I knew. He hit Nora. And yet, still, I couldn't see him as a man. I tried. I squinted my eyes to blur his outline.

'Bring the rest of the baked quinces, please. And whatever's left of the gooseberries. And the ice cream. That'll do.'

'Exit baboon,' Valerie said.

'You a nice girl to teach John,' Nora said. It was six months now since he had come to us. She had taken a motherly interest in him and liked the fact that he was clever. But to me she confided that he was too dark-skinned. Ugly, she said. No Zulu girl would have him.

I sat at the kitchen table and he stood at my side. 'Sit down,' I suggested.

'He can stand,' Nora said.

He stared down in silence at the grammar book I'd opened. I was glad she was there. Her presence in the kitchen seemed to impose a formality on him that he dropped when we were alone.

'I *take* the book. I *took* the book. I *have taken* the book. The book *is taken*. See?'

He nodded.

'All you have to know is three words – take, took, taken.'

'Yes, Nkosazana.'

'Do you have these exercises for homework?'

'Yes, Nkosazana.'

'Nkosazana' was getting on my nerves. I knew he didn't mean it. Out in the garden he called me nothing. Like Catherine, who wouldn't call Mrs Goldman 'mom'.

'You can call me Ruth.'

'He call you *Miss* Ruth!' Nora carried the tea tray out to the lounge.

As soon as she was gone, John moved closer. He rested one hand on the table and leaned casually over my shoulder. I shifted to the edge of the chair to avoid the stream of his warm breath. I zig-zagged my finger down the page of his notebook. 'This looks all right,' I said.

'Thanks.' He had even picked up the currency of casual conversation amongst whites. He knew how to use it and when.

I closed the book and handed it to him. 'I don't think you really need so much help anymore,' I said.

He slapped the book rhythmically against the palm of one hand. It was just an exercise book now, no longer some found object of forbidden treasure. 'Maybe I need help with arithmetic,' he said.

'Maybe I *will* need help.'

'Tea time,' Nora announced. 'And John he must go back to the garden now.'

'You know,' my mother said, 'you shouldn't get too friendly with that John. It's not a good idea.'

'I'm not.'

'Nora says you've helped him a lot. It's enough now.'

I drank my tea in silence. I hated to hear my misgivings given shape by her.

'It's not really fair to him, you know,' she said. 'These poor devils are only human.'

John was in the front flower bed when I came through the gate the next day. He thrust the trowel into the soil and jumped up with a smile. 'Today I need help with arithmetic,' he said.

My chest tightened. 'Oh, John, I've got a lot of homework –'

His smile dropped.

'OK,' I said. 'But after supper.'

'John he still washing up,' Nora said when I came into the kitchen.

'Suka!' Reuben spat out. My visits to the kitchen for John seemed to irritate him. He walked out on to the kitchen porch and slammed the door.

John smiled at me over his shoulder from the sink. He hummed a tune to himself. The dogs sat around his feet staring up at their bowls on the counter. They seldom attacked the servants indoors and never when they were about to be fed. For this reason, John only fed them as he was about to leave for the compound.

I pinched up Temba's ears on to the top of her head, and then Nomsa's with the other hand. 'Look!' I said. John laughed. I lifted Simba and Chaka's tails together and made a farting sound with my mouth. We both laughed. The kitchen was hot and steamy after the afternoon rain. Flying ants fluttered around the light bulb over the sink. John reach up and caught one in his hand.

'Ugh!' I said.

He tilted his head back and opened his mouth, held the

wriggling flying ant above it. Then, snap, he bit the brown body off the wings and chewed, crunch-crunch.

'*Ugh!*' I cried. 'That's revolting!'

He laughed, very pleased with his power to revolt me. Dancing from foot to foot he plunged his hands back into the soapy water in the sink. Then suddenly he peered down into the sink. I stepped forward and looked too. But there was only water there, and a rag. He lifted his hands a little. I looked closer. The forefinger of his right hand was pushing through a circle made by the thumb and forefinger of his left, in and out, in and out. He laughed as I watched, and nodded his head. The gesture made no sense to me. I pretended to laugh, but he could see that I hadn't caught the joke. He lifted his soapy hands out of the sink and held them in the air. In and out, in and out. And then I saw his hips moving rhythmically with the movement of his hands, his grin, the way his eyes rolled. I understood. I tried to smile again, but I could only think that I'd be blamed. He began to sing a song. His hips swivelled now, all his teeth showed. He didn't seem human; he'd never seemed human to me. I stepped back so that he couldn't touch me, even by mistake. But I bumped into Nora. She stood quite still, with her jaw dropped and her chest heaving. 'Go back to the lounge,' she said. 'The Madam she want you.'

'Probably some sort of faction fight,' Abba said at supper the next night.

'No,' my father said. 'It had something to do with that uproar in the compound last night. Couldn't get a thing out of any of them.'

I felt like the real murderer watching the execution. They knew nothing, they didn't really even want to know the truth. And all I had got out of Nora was, 'He too cheeky, Reuben he teach him a lesson.' But when I had come through the gate, home from school, I had seen John move off quickly to the tennis court, ducking his bandaged jaw in front of one shoulder. I ran upstairs to look at him through the venetian blinds of my bedroom window. I remembered the farting noises of the night before, our laughing. I was to blame, I knew. And now I couldn't even think of why his presence had disconcerted me. I tried to remember the shrinking, the affront of his familiarity. But it all seemed innocent now. And his punishment some horrible joke.

'When he came in for an aspirin this morning his eyes were swollen into slits and oozing, the whole jaw bandaged up.' My mother shook her head. 'If you ask me he must have tried to venture into Reuben's terrain.'

My stomach turned for Nora now. Reuben's terrain. I tried to think of how it would feel to be so fenced in. Like Temba or Nomsa closed into a pen when they came into heat, and the male dogs fighting over them outside. And even so, I wished my mother were right. That it was Nora who was the cause of the trouble, not me. I felt like a spy myself, a traitor to both sides, cast out of the magic circle of guiltless guilt.

'Well, there's certainly enough of her for two,' my father said.

'How would you divide her up?' Valerie asked. 'Horizontally or vertically? Maybe by days of the week. Not so messy.' She loved to engage my father in risqué banter.

'Valerie, don't be vulgar,' my mother said.

Valerie leapt to her feet, her black eyes flashing. 'Vulgar! *You* should talk! Who brought the whole thing up in the first place?'

I was up now, shouting too, and tears had sprung to my eyes. 'You're all vulgar! You're revolting! You talk about Nora as if she's not a person! I *hate* the way you laugh –' My eye caught the diagonal of Reuben's red sash. He was standing in the doorway waiting for a pause.

'Yes, Reuben, what is it?' my mother asked.

'Telephone, Madam. Miss Catherine for Madam, Madam.'

6

Catherine seemed to have gone much further than around the corner where she lived. Her house had been a wedding gift from the Goldmans. It stood even higher on the ridge than ours, and looked more widely over the city and the sea. Symmetrical huge white columns, sash windows, french doors and verandahs upstairs and down imposed a formal majesty on two acres of manicured lawns, flower beds and rockeries that descended from the house to the street below. In one corner was a swimming pool with its own waterfall. Two tennis courts took up some of the land behind. Gula-gula and mango trees lined the driveway. Flamboyants camouflaged the servants' quarters – a double-storey building far from the main house, with a real toilet, a dining-room and a lounge. It was the grandest house I had ever seen.

Inside I had imagined there would be magnificent paintings, draperies, antiques, receiving-rooms trimmed in gold-leaf and damask. But what I found on my first visit were twenty-one huge empty rooms, carpeted by the Goldmans in pale green, and an enormous gilded bed with cherubs climbing up the bedposts.

My mother bent forward to scrutinize the cherubs. 'Good God!'

Mrs Goldman, who had brought us to see the house, stood back beaming.

'Who chose this bed?' my mother demanded.

'Me,' tittered Mrs Goldman. 'We had to have it brought all the way from Jo'burg in a lorry.'

'But didn't it *occur* to you that Catherine might have her own preferences in beds?'

Mrs Goldman only tucked her head deeper into her shoulders and blinked at my mother. She had the money. No amount of shouting was going to unseat her now.

When we were in the car my mother exploded. 'Ugh!' she spat out. 'Argh!'

'Didn't you like the bed?' I asked.

'It's a *travesty*!' she boomed. 'Catherine will have to start by throwing that out! And those carpets! Those lovely parquet floors hidden under that ghastly green!' She sighed. 'I'll just have to set aside some time to go shopping with that girl when she gets back.'

But when Catherine returned from her honeymoon she didn't ask my mother to shop with her. For months my mother would ask, 'What are you going to do with that *lovely* sun-room, darling?' or 'Don't you think the patio simply *cries* out for white wicker?' Catherine would just shrug and turn away, as if her own house were as unimportant to her as ours. Perhaps it was. To my mother's exasperation most of the rooms remained empty. And Catherine didn't even seem to care about the cherubs on Mrs Goldman's bed. She seemed, in her own silent way, determined to deny my mother the chance of turning her house into a set for the staging of her married life.

'She's pregnant,' my mother announced at lunch.

'Ah,' said Abba.

'How do you know?' Valerie demanded.

My mother dropped her eyelids and waved her nose at Valerie. 'A woman knows these things,' she said.

'A woman!' Valerie snorted. I could see that she wished herself pregnant, the object of my mother's mysterious woman's knowledge.

'Did she tell?' I asked.

'No, of course not!' My mother laughed. 'And you're not to

90

say a word. To anyone!'

Family secrets. My mother specialized in them. The mysterious visits of Dr Slatkin when my father had a migraine. The injection he gave and then the long sleep afterwards. This was never mentioned. Nor was Aunt Hannah's mental breakdown. Nor money problems of any kind. Unless they were someone else's. Problems with productions and members of the cast were for our ears only. This one hating that one, threats and hysterics – these were sacred trusts, not to be divulged. I found myself filtering every statement I made, hesitating before I answered anyone's questions about my family or the theatre.

'And that Jeffrey's got very big for his boots lately, hasn't he?' she said. But she wasn't asking. She was simply letting us know that she knew things had changed between Catherine and Jeffrey.

It was true. I had noticed that Jeffrey took pleasure in ordering Catherine about now. Now that she was his wife. To fetch the honeymoon photographs. Or to put another cube of sugar in his coffee. And I saw Catherine quiver when he addressed her, jump, run, scuttle to his command. Soon he took to smacking her on the bottom in pretended jest. Or to pulling her hair for her attention.

'Darling!' she would protest, but smiling, never cross.

One Sunday evening at their house he pushed his plate away with both hands. 'I can't eat this!' he announced.

Quickly Catherine was at his side, removing the plate.

'Mine's perfectly all right,' my mother said. 'What's wrong with yours?'

But Catherine threw her a nervous glance. And then Jeffrey grinned, clamped a hand over Catherine's upper arm so that her flesh turned white around his fingers. 'Full of fat,' he said. 'I don't eat fat.'

'Darling!' Catherine tried to writhe free. But he held on tight.

'Don't you think it's about time she learned to cook?' he asked us all.

Valerie snickered.

'Look at her,' he went on. 'The perfectly brought-up young

lady. And she can't cook an egg!'

'What about Philemon?' my mother demanded, pointing her nose at the food on his plate that had not been cooked by Catherine.

'I'll cut you some without fat,' Catherine said quickly.

'Not hungry anymore!' Jeffrey smiled at my mother. It was his house, his wife. My parents couldn't have Catherine back. They couldn't even defend her, not unless she asked them to.

My mother raised her eyebrows and pursed her mouth into an expression of incipient triumph. '*None* of my girls has been terribly interested in *cooking*!' she said. 'There really are more interesting things in life, you know.'

'Rubbish!' Valerie said. 'I love cooking. But that bloody Nora won't let me anywhere near the kitchen.'

Jeffrey frowned as if deep in thought, tossed himself about in his chair. 'Catherine!' he commanded down the table. 'Ring the bell for Philemon.'

Shadrak, the houseboy, summoned by Catherine's hidden bell, appeared at the door.

'Tell Philemon to come here, please,' Catherine said.

We sat in silence. In our own house servants were never scolded by the master of the house, and never, never in public.

Philemon, the cook, came in, wiping his hands on his apron. He was a grisled old man, Mrs Goldman's cook for twenty years. She had given him to Jeffrey along with the house and the bed and the carpets. To perpetuate, as my mother said, the dreadful Jewish food on which Jeffrey had been brought up.

'Philemon,' Jeffrey said. 'I want you to teach the Madam to cook.'

Philemon stared down at his bare feet and then glanced sideways at Catherine.

'Understand?' Jeffrey asked.

'Yes, Baas.'

'OK. You can go.'

I looked across at my father and saw his lip quiver. My mother was clearing her throat, ready to make a stand.

But Catherine looked quickly at them both. 'We've got ice

cream for pudding,' she said. 'Walls.'

My mother smiled suddenly. She clasped her hands together in ecstasy. 'How lovely, darling!' she boomed. '*Walls* ice cream! That's just what I'm in the mood for.'

'And hot chocolate sauce,' Catherine added. 'And nuts.'

Sometimes, after school, I walked to Catherine's house for tea. I was proud of her, of her house, and of her baby. My pride was so great, in fact, that it overwhelmed the assurance I always had on walking up her driveway that she wouldn't welcome me.

'Hello.' I stood at the edge of the patio flagstones. 'I haven't got Hebrew today,' I explained.

She sat alone on the canopied swing seat, knitting in the shade of the giant wild fig, with her dogs curled up around her feet. Her second pregnancy had swollen her arms and legs, brought her face out in livid spots. She looked up without a smile. 'Tell Philemon there's an extra person for tea,' she said. 'And don't shout. The baby's sleeping.'

We drank our tea in silence.

'What are you knitting?' I asked at last.

'Booties.'

'Can I see?'

She tossed her head in the direction of her knitting basket. 'Look but don't touch.'

There were three and a half pairs in blue and white, each carefully laid out on a piece of white gauze. Everyone wanted a boy this time – the Franks because we were all girls and the Goldmans to carry on their name.

'They're super,' I said. 'And the cake's lovely. Did you make it?'

She said nothing. Her needles clicked lightly. Somewhere out of sight the lawnmower whirred, the traffic hummed, a ship hooted in the bay. I longed to know what to say to her, something that would make her my friend. But she seemed to hate everyone except Jeffrey. She seemed more irritated by our access to her than I had been by John's to me. She frightened

93

me. I couldn't even imagine how she loved her daughter.

'Remember your wedding?' I asked.

'What kind of a stupid question is that?'

I blushed. 'I mean people who were there.'

'So?'

'Do you remember Bernard Rubenstein?'

She nodded slightly, but didn't look up.

'What's he like?'

'Rubbish.'

'Rubbish?' My ears caught fire. I'd seen her mouth turn down as she said it. My mother's sneer. The only man who'd ever wanted me. 'He seemed nice at your wedding,' I said.

'He's rubbish.'

I felt the tightness start in my stomach, the heat in my head, the way her damnation worked on me just as my mother's did. I knew I should have gone on keeping Bernard to myself. And yet, even as I regretted telling, the rudeness of her response was beginning to cure me of my pride in her. I was fourteen now. I wanted to tell her she had no right to treat me that way. All those silences she used to close herself off, the chill in her voice – they had the same effect on me as Valerie's viciousness. It was like war amongst us, of which I didn't yet know the cause. But there it was, war, and I saw it for the loneliness it left me with. Watching her knit now as if I weren't there made me stand up and reach for my hat.

'Master on the telephone for you, Madam,' Shadrak announced.

In one leap, Catherine was off the swing seat and across the patio. The four dogs rushed after her. They had been chosen by Jeffrey as soon as he returned from honeymoon, to make his household more like ours.

When Catherine returned her cheeks were flushed. 'Oh, you!' she said. She picked up her knitting and sat down again on the swing seat. 'Please tell Ma we can't come tonight.'

I stared at her as I buttoned up my blazer. On Friday nights we were always together. My parents made a thing of it. I didn't want to be the bearer of such news to them. 'Ma thinks you're coming to us,' I said.

'Well, we're not now.' She turned one shoulder towards me, as if to ward off germs. Her needles clicked furiously. 'And make sure the back gate's locked behind you. Last time you left it open and the dogs got out and bit the boy next door.'

'Vay'hi erev, vay'hi boker, yom hashishi –' My father's lovely baritone rose into the ancient melody of kiddush. Twenty members of my mother's family stood behind their chairs waiting for the final 'amein'.

When it was our turn for a Friday night, my mother came home early from the theatre. She took care to maintain her reputation amongst her sisters and sisters-in-law for lavish food and an exotic table.

Down the centre of the long table she had arranged anthuriums and flame-tree pods, elephant ears, banana leaves, hibiscus, frangipani and bottle brush. Amongst the jungle of fronds were bowls of brandied prunes, bunches of litchis and ladyfinger bananas, mounds of honeyloaf buns on silver filigree platters and dishes of rolled butter. At each place a blown-glass figurine held a name card. And my grandmother's silver was laid out on the cloth in careful order – soup spoons, butter knives, fish knives, fish forks, with pudding spoons and forks at the top. The napkins, Reuben's specialty, sprang out of the wine glasses like swans in flight.

'You always do things so nicely, Sarah,' Hannah said. 'Who would ever think of Kaffirboom pods?'

My mother sighed. She no longer needed to remind the family that she led two lives. That by Friday night she was exhausted from her week at the theatre.

Hannah blinked at her through thick lenses and giggled as she snatched a roll. 'I don't know how you do it!' she exclaimed.

'Where's Catherine?' Beatrice asked. Her envy of my mother prevented her from ever wondering how anything was accomplished at our house.

'At Ettie's,' my mother said. 'Tomato or sweet corn soup?'

Beatrice winked at Cissie. 'Got to share her now, eh?'

'Share and share alike,' sing-songed Cissie.

'Don't be absurd, Cissie!' my mother snapped. 'Tomato or sweet corn soup?'

The men on my mother's side seldom joined in with the women's conversation. They discussed synagogue politics, the rabbi's sermons, the Jewish club, matters of common ground amongst them. In deference to my father, my uncles never mentioned affairs of business. They were far more aware than he of his indebtedness to trade for the survival of the theatre.

That night, however, my father was distracted into silence by Catherine's absence. He listened politely to my uncles, but I could see the effort he made to compose himself as host. His eyes often wandered to my mother. She had to remind him to pour the wine. And then to offer the men cigars. After everyone had left he slumped down at his end of the couch and stared ahead of him blankly.

'This is the first Friday night since I can remember that we've been divided,' he said.

'We've always been divided,' I said.

'Keep your clever comments to yourself!' my mother snapped. She too slumped on to the couch.

'What exactly did Ettie *say*?' he asked.

'I told you. She insisted that "we have the children to ourselves for once." ' She imitated Mrs Goldman's squeak and hunchbacked delivery. 'I asked them all to come here, but she wouldn't hear of it.'

'That's all?'

'That's all.'

'And Catherine?'

My mother sighed. 'Ruth, go to bed.'

'No, I want to hear.'

She shrugged. 'Catherine is under some sort of spell,' she sighed. 'I can't imagine Ettie Goldman's is any pleasanter for her than it is for us. That Jeffrey must have forced the issue.'

'Nevertheless,' my father insisted, 'she chose to go there.'

'I'm telling you! *She* didn't choose. *He* chose.'

My father was silenced. He closed his eyes and squeezed his forehead on either side with both hands.

'Roger! You haven't got another head coming on, have you?'

He looked up at her through liquid eyes and nodded.

'My God!' she boomed. 'That's two in one week! Damn! Ruth, run upstairs quickly and fetch Daddy's pills. And a glass of water. *Quick!*'

I was upstairs and back in a minute.

'Here,' she said. 'Take these. Damn that Ettie Goldman! Damn her son! I'm just going to have to speak to that Catherine!' She sighed and rubbed both eyes vigorously. 'Dear God! Eight days till Jocelyn and Gwen arrive!'

'Just who are we going to cast as Crystal?' my mother demanded a few nights later. She had been asking the question for months, after each hopeless audition. And now the English actresses were coming, and rehearsals for *The Women* were to begin, and still there was no Crystal. No one but my father dared to answer her.

'I thought we'd agreed on Valerie,' he said.

'*We* didn't agree. *You* suggested her.' She closed her eyes and stretched her neck back to suggest the noose around it. 'It's a huge risk,' she sighed. 'She's not right, you know as well as I do! She just hasn't *got* it!'

'I think she could do it.'

'*Think!*' She sat up and glared at him. 'It's our big production! We can't risk another flop.'

'Well, don't rule her out,' he pleaded. 'I think we should give her a chance.'

My parents never seemed to consider the carrying power of their own voices. I slipped past the door of the study and up to Valerie's room.

'What do you want?' she snapped.

'I've got something to tell you,' I whispered.

She unlocked the door and opened it a few inches. 'What?'

'They're talking about casting you as Crystal –'

She opened the door wide and pulled me into the room. 'How

do you know?' she asked, jumping on to the bed.

'I just heard them.'

'What did they say?' Her eyes looked sharp and black into my own.

'I'll tell you if you promise to get me out of Hebrew.' Valerie's promises were worthless, but so was giving her something for nothing.

'What?'

'When I ask them to let me off Hebrew you've got to promise to back me up.'

'Yes, yes.' She flicked at her hair as if my request were stuck there, like a dead fly. 'What did they say?'

'Ma said you'd be good.'

'And Dad?'

'I forget what he said.'

'Liar!' She reached out to grab me, but withdrew her hands quickly. 'What did Dad say?'

I knew that she would use my words any way she wished. 'He said he needed more time to think. It was a big risk or something. That's all.'

In her last year of school, just before Catherine's wedding, Valerie had announced that she intended to become an actress. Both my parents tried to persuade her to do something else, anything, to go to university perhaps. But Valerie was adamant. The theatre was her passion, she said. If my mother wouldn't train her, she would simply apply to Janet McGuire's studio. Her threat only saddened my mother, who thought nothing of Janet McGuire. But she thought nothing of Valerie's talent either, or her 'so-called passion for an acting career'.

'Darling,' she said. 'It's a lousy life, you know. You can see what Dad and I have to go through. Is that what you really want? Work, work, work, and worry, worry, worry?'

Valerie saw only the audience in her grip, her name in the papers. Our name. Grace Kelly and the Prince of Monaco. 'It's what I want with all my heart,' she said.

After Valerie's first few weeks at the theatre school my mother became strangely diplomatic. 'Perhaps you're trying too hard with the *Merchant*, darling,' she would say. 'Why not give it a break for a while? Who're you going out with on Saturday night?'

Men came all the time for Valerie. And then they went again. They were grown men now. Some madly in love, sending flowers, giving her things. But sooner or later she always found things wrong with them. Dark, moist, secret, horrible things, she hinted. Sometimes I heard her weeping in crescendos after a night out. Then my father would knock lightly on her door in his silk dressing-gown.

'It's me, my darling,' he crooned, using the voice of his stage lover. Never for anyone else. Not for my mother. Not for me.

My mother didn't understand. She'd given up on princes now and seemed content to settle for Valerie safely married. 'Don't encourage her, Roger,' she said. 'There's something odd about that girl. All this hysterical nonsense. She's not a baby anymore. And we both know perfectly well she's never going to make it on the stage.'

My father, however, seemed to enjoy Valerie's refusal to fall in love. They laughed a lot together now. He told her jokes he had heard on the golf course, jokes about men and women and the complications of sex. We could hear Valerie's shrieking laugh as they walked up the path together. And then her stifled giggles as they came through the front door.

My mother seldom caught a joke. And she seemed particularly unable to understand sexual jokes. But when she heard them laughing, she insisted on being included. 'Come along now, you two,' she would say. 'Let's *all* share the fun.'

Carefully, my father tried to explain. 'You see, when he opens the wardrobe door, there is Abie, naked, and Rachel's on the bed, naked too –'

My mother stared back, waiting. 'So?'

'Don't you see?'

'See what? Is that all?'

'That's it.'

Valerie exploded.

'Well!' my mother said, picking up her Scotch. 'Frankly, I

99

don't see what's so funny about a naked man in the cupboard and a naked wife on the bed. It's all just a *little* bit silly, if you ask me.'

The day the actresses were to arrive, my mother was in a fine mood. 'I've told Beauty to start moving your things into Catherine's room, Val, so that Beauty can get your room ready for Gwen,' she said. 'Jocelyn should have the spare room, don't you think? Ha!' She laughed. 'Five years of talking and writing letters and drawing up contracts – I can't *believe* they're actually coming at last, can you?'

'I want Nora to move my things,' Valerie insisted. 'Not Beauty. And *not* the pictures, or the things in the top drawer.' She glanced at me with hate. 'What's left of them anyway.'

'Oh, let's not start on that again, please!' My mother nodded regally from Valerie to me. 'Girls, *please*! I implore you! No fighting while our guests are here. These are very famous actresses –'

'Just tell that child to keep out of my way then,' Valerie sniffed. 'The mere sight of her offends me.' She was playing prima donna already, playing herself playing a part in my mother's play. And already my mother was treading carefully around her for the sake of the show. She always did this with the raw ones and the difficult ones, the ones who couldn't take criticism. I knew that if Valerie wanted me out of the way I'd be kept away from her. 'Don't be difficult, darling,' my mother would say to me. To be difficult during a production was to be a terrorist. But with Valerie taking part I'd have no choice. She'd find me in her way even if I were at the other end of the house. And I could think of no way to protect myself.

'Can I miss Hebrew today?' I asked.

My mother smiled absent-mindedly, counting out the silver for lunch.

'Why should she?' Valerie snapped. 'Catherine and I had to go on till matric!'

'It's stupid. I never learn anything.'

Knives into piles, forks into piles. 'Well, I can't imagine why not, a clever girl like you.'

'Lots of people are allowed to stop at fourteen,' I wailed.

'Ruth! Stop this at once!' My mother slammed down the pudding spoons and began to count again. It was useless. Having famous actresses in the house was going to be like a full-scale production. Two productions. One at home, one at the theatre. And Valerie taking part in both. I was invisible already, my mother in her other world. I pulled on my hat and left the house for school.

7

My mother never went on with the story of Leah. For her that story ended on the boat. And her own story began when she came back. What happened in London, for the years in the middle, became one of our secrets, a secret within secrets. Even Valerie usually left those years alone.

London swallowed up my mother's girlish success and left her mad to have it back. She worked harder than ever, every morning before classes, every night, every weekend. Some of the other students at the academy laughed at her. She didn't care. She had no time for friends. And anyway, she was too serious to attract them. But the teachers too found her strange. Not just because of her seriousness, but because of the way she concentrated on every word and every phrase they spoke. They felt uncomfortable with her. She certainly wasn't the most talented student there, they said to each other, but by Jove she was driven!

Her letters home were full of plays and concerts and famous people she had met. London was everything she'd dreamed it would be, she said. She'd even seen the King!

Her father read her letters formally to the whole family at the dinner table. They were collected in a silver bowl and handed around like sweets on a Friday night. Their replies were filled with the formalities of life – celebrations and funerals. And with questions. When would she come home? Had she met any nice Jewish men lately?

In the four years that she was gone, my mother never answered these questions. She couldn't explain to them that she never wanted to return. That she prayed, like a Catholic, for a miracle. That the life and the man she imagined for herself had nothing to do with the marriages they so carefully listed at the ends of all their letters.

As soon as her training at the academy was over, she set out full of hope to find work. First she tried every theatrical company in London. Then she tried Nottingham, then Birmingham, then Brighton, then the smaller provincial theatres, right down to the bottom of her list. Sorry, they said, there was nothing for her. Yes, they were quite sure. Why not try again next year?

Meanwhile, she wrote home of triumphs with Ophelia and Hedda Gabler. They needn't send money anymore, she said. Didn't they realize that she was not a professional?

After nine months of looking she went back to visit the academy and asked her old coaches for more introductions. They simply patted her on the back, told her to buck up and promised to think of something. For the first time she saw condescension in their smiles. She felt small and misshapen and odd in their eyes. Not English enough. Not talented enough. She began to despair. Her money was running out. The only friend she had was Mrs Cohen, her landlady. The miracle she had prayed for all these years simply hadn't happened.

Meanwhile, the questions from her family became more insistent. Was there a man in her life yet, they wanted to know? When would she give up this acting craziness and come back home? Why didn't she come back now, while she was still young and so famous?

Even though she still refused to answer, my mother at last began to consider going home. Perhaps there, after all, she could do something, be someone. She could start a rep company, maybe, with whatever sort of talent she could find. She could even train the actors herself if necessary. Open a theatre school. Build something up from scratch. Anything would be better than the waste and humiliation that her life had become in London.

In her letters now she wrote of the cold and the prices of everything. She mentioned a cough and then a spot of blood on her handkerchief. Then she wrote nothing for a month. But she prayed every day for a letter commanding her to go back. Leaving her no choice but to return unwilling. They sent Leon instead.

'Someone who says he's your brother,' said Mrs Cohen. She threw her head back in the direction of the parlour and her eyes rolled with it.

'Leon!'

'Sarala! How thin you look!' He stood up, still wearing his hat and coat, and held out his arms to her.

'Never eats, that's why,' said Mrs Cohen.

My mother stepped into the room but stopped short of his open arms. 'Why didn't you tell me you were coming?' she demanded.

He shrugged his fists into the pockets of his coat and sat down again.

She stared down at the wet, baggy cuffs of Leon's trousers. 'Mrs Cohen,' she said, 'do you think we could have some tea?'

'With pleasure, my dear. I'll leave you to it, then, shall I?'

My mother nodded. 'You should take off your hat indoors, Leon.'

He took it off and held it on his lap. 'What a lady you are now,' he said.

She blushed.

'No boyfriend?'

She shook her head.

'Tea, Miss Moskovitz.'

'Thank you, Mrs Cohen.'

They left London together three weeks later. Leon had been instructed to be firm. But she gave him no cause. Whatever she was weeping for, it wasn't a man. No one had even come to see her off. They hung over the railing of the ship and watched Southampton recede into the haze.

'Things have changed at home, you know, Sarala,' he said at last.

She nodded.

'More people, more money.'

She watched the gulls swoop and dive. Leon's small red eyes and large purple nose reminded her of a Shylock she had seen somewhere. She shivered.

'There's money for you too. A dowry, if you like.'

'Money? My own?'

He laughed. 'Your own, yes. But it's in the business, of course.'

'Can I take it out?'

He looked alarmed. 'Sarala, you have to think of your future.'

'I *am* thinking of my future!' she insisted.

The family were gathered into a sombre clump on the quay. For them reunions or farewells always occasioned solemn clothes and faces. My mother, however, had dressed herself in bright-red silk, with her finger- and toenails varnished to match. She wore lipstick and short crimped hair and a feather in her hat. She paused at the top of the second-class gangway, nodded to the group below, and then descended slowly with her head held high and Leon behind her carrying her coats and bags.

A newspaper photographer greeted her as she stepped on to the quay. She looked down her nose and over one shoulder, right into the eye of his camera. 'Sarah Returns Triumphant!' appeared above her photograph the next day. By the following week it had joined 'Local Girl for London Stage' in a matching black frame above the mantelpiece.

Within the first month my mother had been introduced to every eligible man in the town. Most of them were businessmen like the men in her family. One was a dentist. One a rabbi. They came into the parlour with greased hair and polished shoes, only to be treated with the same cool haughtiness with which she had looked into the camera. Otherwise she spent a lot of time weeping. Her eyes were often red, but she would say nothing about what troubled her, not even to her mother.

'Sarah needs a man,' her mother whispered to the rest of the family with a sigh and a shake of the head. 'But what can we do? She only wants the King of England.'

One day my mother arrived at the family warehouse in a taxi. None of the women in the family had ever come to the business before. Her father and brothers shuffled her quickly into the little glass office and closed the door. Well, they asked? What now, Sarala?

'I want my own theatre,' she demanded.

They coughed and recrossed their legs. This was something new.

'You know already,' she said, 'that without the theatre my life is nothing. But consider this –' She lowered her voice to strike a humming resonance in the small bare room. 'I never intend to marry.'

They stared at her. Ben opened his mouth to speak, but she interrupted him. 'If you are intent on keeping me here at the bottom of the earth to rot without a vocation, my misery will be on your heads.'

Intrigued, they waited for more. Eternal damnation was not something that was emphasized in the Talmud.

'All I ask,' she said, 'is for the right to use my own money for my own purposes.' Suddenly she raised her voice so that it rolled and rumbled around their heads. 'What on earth is the point of a dowry when I'm never going to marry? Can you tell me that? CAN YOU?'

She glared at them for a few seconds and then left the office and the warehouse without another word.

The men conferred. Ben was adamant: it was a waste of money. She would be sorry one day and then it would be too late.

'Why not take a chance?' Leon suggested. 'It's not so much she's asking. Just a couple of thousand.'

Her father chuckled. 'That girl always gets what she wants, you know,' he said to his sons. 'Just like my mother. She's the

106

only one of my children that's turned out like my dear late mother.'

It was done. For the year it took to build the theatre, my mother paced and worried and fretted. Her father and brothers had bought a lot on the edge of town, opposite the new synagogue. But before the work could begin, thick bush had to be cleared away. Every morning she caught a bus and then walked a mile to the building site to check up on things. She argued with the builder about the plans, threatened him in front of his natives, raised her voice like a man for everyone to hear. She stood with the foreman and watched the native boys swing their axes at the tangle of bush and monkey ropes. One day a green mamba fell out of a tree and bit one of the workers. Within five minutes he was dead. The others ran away in fright. As soon as another gang had been hired, monkeys, angry at being dislodged from the bush, pranced and sprang and screeched around the natives as they worked. After a few days the monkeys became bolder and stole the workers' lunches. One man was bitten on the hand. By the time the third gang had been hired, six months had passed and the foundation had only just been laid.

At home my mother frowned and stood apart. Sometimes she refused to eat. Often she was heard muttering and sighing in her room. The family whispered and wondered.

'Don't worry,' her mother told them. 'She's enjoying herself a whole lot.'

When the theatre was finally built my mother was twenty-four. Everyone in town knew that she had sacrificed a dowry on its account and they decided it hadn't been worth it. All that fuss and there it was – a hall full of globe chairs with a stage at one end. Plain wooden floors. Tin roof. No gilt or plush.

My mother too refused to be pleased. The place was a barn, she said. The acoustics were all wrong, and it was like a Turkish bath in the hot weather. If she opened the doors to get some air, dogs roamed in off the street. One day a troop of monkeys loped in. When she tried to shoo them out they bared their teeth at her and screeched. The chanting from the

107

synagogue across the road was beginning to unnerve her. And so were the native boys who gathered outside the doors on their way to or from work. They stood there shouting and laughing and clapping, like monkeys themselves. How was it possible to teach or rehearse under these conditions? Could they tell her that?

Her mother shrugged. 'Sarala,' she said, 'nothing will ever satisfy you.'

But my mother would have been satisfied with perfection. She had imagined a grand theatre, like the ones in London. A balustrade around a gallery, painted in cream, the same colour as the walls. Dark-brown velvet on the seats, and a cream and brown geometrically patterned carpet. Five dressing-rooms charmingly done in peach and gold. And next to the theatre, the theatre school. A voice-production room, a movement room, a room for props and costumes. Auditions to get in, lots and lots of raw talent to choose from. And the whole complex – theatre and school – standing back from the street, with a portico and columns, and a large circular driveway lined with trees.

The school opened with six pupils. Their parents sent them to learn how to speak like ladies and gentlemen. But first my mother boomed and badgered them out of the wide-mouthed prating that passed in the colonies for polite speech.

'Not *awsk*,' she mimicked. 'Take your chin off your chest. It's *ahsk*. See? Say *ahsk*.'

'Awsk.'

'Now look. Listen to me.' She held her chin high and breathed in. '*Ahsk*. Smile when you say it. *Ahsk*.'

'Ahsk.'

'There! Now say *Ahnold ahsked his ahnt for ice cream*.'

'Ahnold ahsked his ahnt for aws cream.'

'NO! No, no no! Not *aws cream* but *ais cream*. Try that.'

'Ahno –'

'NO!! Just *ais cream*.'

'Aws cream.'

'*Ais* cream! *Ais* cream!'

108

'Ai-scream.'

'That's it.' She let out a deep sigh and ran the back of her hand across her forehead. 'All right. Now for breathing.'

Producing *Hedda Gabler* had been my mother's dream ever since her third year at the academy. She still knew every line of the play. And more than that, she knew every gesture, every move. She had played Berte, the servant girl, in the second string student performance. One of the coaches had actually praised her performance. He had tapped her on the shoulder in the corridor and said, 'Nicely done, Sarah.' Now that she had her own theatre she would produce it herself. And play Hedda herself. Never mind the audience. Never mind the snakes and the monkeys and the barn of a theatre. She wanted to surprise the whole town. The whole country in fact!

The actors she found had no idea how to take direction. Most of them had only been on a stage as children, to recite or to sing. She had to walk each step for them, speak each phrase.

'Fools! Dolts! Philistines!' she raged to herself.

With them she was more polite. Men in this place were not used to being shouted at by a woman. There was no guarantee that they wouldn't just walk out. She couldn't give them a contract. So far she could only pay her cast with free tickets.

At half-past seven on opening night, cars began to draw up along the dirt road. Fairy-lights lit up the contours of the theatre. Their glow obscured the grey corrugated iron of the roof and the plain brick walls and the grass shoots pushing up weakly here and there through the raw red soil around the building. Over the doorway the lights spelled out 'HEDDA GABLER' and 'SARAH MOSKOVITZ'. It was like the grandest of weddings.

Women in taffetas and ostrich feathers, furs and velvet evening hats gathered in the foyer. Their men wore silk hats and tails, and carnations in their buttonholes. Leon's children sold programmes at the door. Beatrice's sold boxes of chocolates from a card table in the middle of the foyer. It was July, the height of the season. Even a few of the Johannesburg critics had come down to see the show.

109

Backstage the actors, under my mother's firm eye, sat quiet and calm, waiting for eight o'clock to come. The house bell rang.

'All right, everyone,' she whispered. 'Five minutes to curtain time.'

Few of the actors had voices to speak of, but my mother had taught them to shout if necessary above the din in the audience. She knew what to expect. In her search for a cast she had attended every church hall musical and two-night melodrama in town. The audiences whispered and waved and crinkled chocolate papers and creaked and scraped their chairs.

She watched and waited in the wings. Her Tesman and his aunt were trying valiantly to roar out their lines, but she could hear that they were having trouble. Someone in the audience hissed 'Shh!' Others joined in. She closed her eyes and prayed. She stood up, watching, waiting for her cue. Then she made her entrance, stood centre stage and paused.

Two seconds, three seconds.

The prompt mistress panicked. 'Good morning!' she called out.

But my mother simply raised her chin. The rumble in the audience dropped to a murmur. The chairs stopped scraping.

'Good morning, my dear Miss Tesman,' her voice rang out at last. She lowered her lids slightly in scorn, just as the academy Hedda had done. 'What an *early* visit! How *kind* of you!'

Everyone listened now. They watched my mother take the play by the throat. Every move of hers, the turn of a wrist, the toss of her head, stole their attention from the rest of the cast. It was as if a deadly snake danced before them. They felt themselves in peril, like Tesman and Thea and Lövberg.

At interval they swarmed out into the foyer and wondered aloud what would happen next. As soon as the bell rang they swarmed back in and sat as still as mice. Although the theatre was hot, no one fanned or blew. They watched in horror as Hedda carried Lövberg's manuscript towards the fire. A few of them gasped. Someone shouted 'Oh, no!'

'Shh!'

'Shut up!'

And then they relaxed and laughed when they heard the piano. They jumped when they heard the shot ring out. The whole audience gasped. It was all over. The curtain closed and the lights came up. They leapt to their feet and roared and clapped. 'Hooray!' they shouted when my mother came out to take a bow and accept bouquets of flowers. 'Bravo!'

Then they all swarmed out into the cool night air and shook their heads at the strangeness of the play. Such passion, such a crime. It was shocking, they said. Fantastic. They spoke of my mother as if she were indeed Hedda Gabler. Not the youngest of the Moskovitzes, who had gone to London for years and years and then come back again to build a theatre at the bottom of the world.

'Hey! Shakespeare! Next line, please!' Mr Shapiro, the Hebrew teacher, remembered us by the names of our fathers' businesses. Catherine and Valerie had both been Shakespeare. Now I was Shakespeare, three afternoons a week for two hours each, in the bleak classrooms behind the synagogue.

'Umm – And the Lord God said unto Moses – Umm – Tell the children of Israel to bring unto me   ' They would be there when I got home. Five weeks of them. Even Nora had asked my mother for new uniforms and a cap in their honour.

'Press on! Press on!' Bubbles of spit flew out over our heads. Several people ducked. Girls giggled. I kept my finger on the word I didn't know and looked up at him.

'Your uncle tells me you're winning prizes at your school.' Elastic strings of white saliva stretched between his dry lips. He loved to claim acquaintance with Uncle Leon and all his money. 'Your school' meant Rangston, two Jews per class, the Franks and all their airs and graces that got us in there.

'Rangston snob!' Avril Polovsky whispered into the back of my head.

Mr Shapiro hitched up his trousers and scratched one hip. He shook his head so vigorously that he displaced the long piece of hair combed from one ear to the other over his bald crown. Several people turned to stare at me. 'One day you'll see how important it is to know the language of your forefathers.' He looked around the class. 'Who knows the word?'

'Offerings!'

'Gifts!'

'Sacrifices!'

He nodded. These were his people. They understood the language of their forefathers. 'There, you see? "To bring unto me offerings." Now you, Liebowitz and Sons P-T-Y, you try. See if you can do better than Shakespeare.'

The classroom smelled of boys' sweat and Jik cleaning fluid. Of all the places I didn't belong, this felt the strangest. The place itself, the people in it. Mr Shapiro's whine, his bulging glare. 'Poor devil,' my mother said, because he still had a tattoo from Auschwitz. The government school girls wore skirts high above their knees and were at ease with boys – loud, fat boys who called me 'yok' and 'goy', words I never used. They belonged to Jewish youth movements and wanted to live in Israel. Ghastly speech, my parents said, ghastly manners. The Jewishness I'd been sent there for was of little value at home.

When I came home they were all on the verandah.

'Ah!' my mother cried. 'Here's our little one now!'

'Little one' was not the role I wanted. I walked on towards the front door as if I hadn't heard them.

'Darling! Ruth! We're on the verandah! Come round and say hello to our guests!'

English guests were always brought out to the verandah. They loved to sit there in the faded wicker chairs sipping Scotch and looking out towards India. It gave them a sense of Empire. So too did Reuben in his starched whites and sash, the sun on everything, the fragrance of the frangipanis just under the verandah wall. I trudged down the path and up the steps.

'Ruth, darling, I'd like you to meet Miss Jocelyn Hopswith –' She gestured grandly towards a huge, beaming horse of a woman whose face I recognized from *Theatre Arts*.

'And this is Miss Gwendolyn Stit.'

Miss Stit nodded to me and smiled tolerantly, as if she belonged there more than I did. She looked like some of the mothers of girls in my class. Bright-pink make-up covered her thin white skin and ended abruptly at her jaw line. Her hair had been permed into tiny curls flat to her head – not teased and sprayed into a winged helmet like Valerie's. She was pretty in an English sort of way, as if she'd be cold to the touch, and dry.

'Ruth has just been at Hebrew school,' my mother explained. The fact never embarrassed her as it did me. She didn't seem to see the curiosity that washed lightly across the faces of both actresses. Or to care at all if she did see it.

'I want to stop going,' I heard myself saying. 'I hate it.'

My father laughed, a deep paternal chortle. 'This is our little revolutionary,' he said. 'Wants to reform the world.'

'I'm not a revolutionary. I don't want to reform the world. I just don't want to go to Hebrew school anymore.' If 'little one' was going to involve me in humiliation for five weeks I was determined to stop it at the start.

'Would you rather learn another language instead?' Jocelyn asked. Her voice was as deep as my mother's, smooth and thick. It fitted her enormous face and teeth and hands and feet.

'Ah, you see it's not just the language,' my mother explained. 'It's part of our tradition.'

'I see, of course.'

'But –' She threw a maternal arm around my shoulders. 'I think this little one has had a jolly good innings, don't you, Roger?' She smiled at him graciously, benign mother to master of the house. 'I don't see why we shouldn't consider letting her off now, do you?'

My heart leapt in hopefulness for what I could achieve before the run was over.

Valerie sighed. 'She's so much younger than my sister and I, you see, that she gets away with murder. *We* had to go on with all that until we left school.' She hit each syllable with precision and projected her voice over the verandah wall to the dahlias and marigolds beyond.

'My sister and *me*!' I said. I smiled into her astonished face, then turned to Jocelyn. 'I'd rather take French. But we have to choose between French and Latin at school and I take Latin.'

'Didn't you win the Latin prize one year, Chopsticks?' my father asked.

I looked away. I couldn't bear playing my part in Happy Families.

'*Junior* Latin prize,' Valerie said.

Jocelyn reached one paw over for some nuts. 'Have you done Virgil yet?' she asked. She tipped her head back and poured them into her mouth.

'We've just started Ovid. I think we get Virgil next year.'

'Ovid!' She sprayed some chewed nuts around. 'How splendid! Which one?'

'*The Metamorphoses*. Do you want to see?'

'Why should Miss Hopswith want to see?' Valerie sneered. 'She knows Ovid already. Don't be absurd, child!'

I looked quickly at Jocelyn. She nodded furiously at me, pointing at my suitcase.

'Ah!' She snatched the book greedily and flapped through the pages. 'Ha! – Aha!' She looked up, her nostrils flared into round, black caves. 'Do you know the Dryden translation?'

It was a real question, without the usual adult need to triumph over a teenager's ignorance.

I shook my head. Draidin? Drydin? I wished desperately that I even knew who or what it was.

'You should! He's *wonderfully* elegant. So much better than the Humphries!'

Humphries? 'We're not supposed to read any translations yet,' I said.

'Well!' my mother boomed. 'That's just silly, isn't it?' She looked from Jocelyn to Gwen, a woman of letters now. 'Why don't I phone Putmans tomorrow and have them send up a copy?'

'Certainly you should,' Jocelyn muttered, paging on. 'One mustn't ever bother with small minds.'

I loved 'small minds'. I'd never heard such a dismissal so naturally uttered. Small-minded Miss Grindrod and her passion for Mary Renault. It felt right. So did loving Ovid, especially after you'd already left school.

'Why don't you lend Miss Hopswith the book?' my mother suggested grandly. 'I'm sure that if you explain to Miss Grindrod that the famous Jocelyn Hopswith is reading it she'll let you off your homework!' She really seemed sure herself, so sure that she didn't notice Gwen's thin little English sneer of a smile, or the glance that Jocelyn gave her to see if she was joking.

I blushed. 'Oh, Ma!' I said.

'Here –' Jocelyn handed me the book with a wink. 'Sell it on the hockeyfield as a relic.'

'Ha! Ha!' My mother picked up the cue and laughed back. My father too. It wasn't even funny, but Jocelyn had outacted them both. She'd fronted for them, taken over already. Gwen and Valerie watched in silence, lost somewhere upstage.

'I think I'll get the Dryden tomorrow,' I said.

'Oh, *jolly* good! Let's read it together, shall we?'

I felt her liking me, this stranger. And I liked myself with her. How easy it was to say things to her. How I felt under her observation. Myself. Ruth Frank. At home in the strangest way.

115

8

I fingered the small square of folded paper, scotch-taped shut against the curiosity of Nora and Valerie, and tried to repeat in my head what I had written inside.

'Dear God, please let me marry Bernard Rubenstein one day. And may I be first in the class this year, please? I shall thank you for ever and ever, every day of my life. Ruth.'

Unlike the fierce God of the Jews or the confusing tripartite God of the Christians, my God was relatively simple. He hovered somewhere beneath whatever ceiling I happened to be under. His function was to give me hope. And to increase my chances of success in life. Bargaining with him was the beginning of informal religion for me. Like any gambler, I began to establish complicated rituals for invoking his favour. The small wad of paper that I now pressed deep into the hinge of my Bible had only recently come into use.

Miss Robinson, the new headmistress, glared down at us from the teacher's elevated platform. We stared back at her in silence, rows and rows of girls in navy-blue serge, feet crossed at the ankles, hands in laps, waiting.

'It has come to my attention,' she said, 'that some of your mothers are unaware of our rule regarding the giving or selling of Rangston uniforms to our African servants.'

I flushed in panic. Constance had all my outgrown uniforms.

116

She wore them every time she came to visit Nora, even the Panama hat. My mother was no help. She ignored school rules. Anyway, she said, the uniforms were like sacks. Not even Israel would accept them.

Miss Robinson slapped the desk hard. 'As I have reminded you on many previous occasions,' she said, 'the Rangston uniform is a symbol of the traditions and standards of our school. To have African children going about in our dresses and gyms – *even* if your mothers cut off the collars and cuffs – is to make a mockery of everything we stand for!'

It was the tradition at Rangston for the headmistress to teach scripture to the seniors. Miss Robinson, however, liked to turn part of every scripture lesson into a forum for her wacky opinions on race and sex.

She frowned down at her notes. '*Ah!*' she cried. '*Parties!*'

Edwina Sloane poked me between the shoulders from behind.

'Low lights, soft music, I know *perfectly* well what goes on at these parties of yours!' Miss Robinson closed her eyes and clutched the sides of the desk with her smooth English banana hands. 'Boys want one thing only, whatever they say. It's *quite* biological, you know!'

I stared at her familiar frown of emphasis and wondered what it was that she actually *did* with Miss Powers. Hugged? Kissed? How could it be?

Miss Robinson was a lesbian. Within two weeks of her arrival as headmistress, Francina, her maid, had whispered this to some seniors passing the gatepost.

'Ag, sis!' she whistled through toothless gums and flaccid lips. 'Isn't it?' she asked.

By the following week Francina had a daily audience at the gatepost. ' "Make up the other bed in *my* room for Miss Powers." ' she mimicked in an African parody of Miss Robinson's throaty English voice. ' "You just leave early tonight, Francina! We make our own supper." ' She pulled a hairpin out from under her cap, cocked her head to one side, and delicately scratched inside one ear.

We stood around and waited for more.

'Suka!' Francina plunged the hairpin back into her hair and shook her head to signify that the entertainment was over. 'Things is no good since Battie isn't here no more.'

My parents had lesbian friends, but they were theatre people. They wore men's clothes and hats, and sat with their legs apart and blew smoke all over the room. It was almost as if they were playing at being men. But here was Miss Robinson in a faded cotton dress, stockings and shoes, a brooch at her neck. A real lesbian.

'One pinch on the bottom and the next thing you know you're in an unmarried mothers' home,' she barked. 'One day you will be out in the world, making a future for yourselves. What chance do you think you will have with an illegitimate child behind you? I'll tell you. None. None at – MYFANWY JONES! Bring that note here at once!'

We stared in silence as Myfanwy shuffled up red-faced with her note. Miss Robinson tore it up without reading it. She loved to be above things.

'Well, where were we?' she asked us. 'Edwina?'

'Careers,' Edwina said. 'The future.'

'Ah, yes. Careers. There are only *two* careers, so-called, that I recommend for women. Teaching and nursing. Most of you, of course, will be wives and mothers. And this is all very fine, I suppose. But don't, for heaven's sake, come and tell me you want to be *psychologists*! Or *so*-ciologists! Or any of those "ologists" we read about in the newspapers these days! Fads and fancies all of them!'

She smoothed one hand over the cover of her Bible. This meant she was dangerously near diverting us into scripture. I raised my hand.

'Yes, Ruth.'

I stood up. 'I think psychology sounds quite interesting, Miss Robinson.'

'A lot of stuff and nonsense!' she exploded. 'Read Dickens! Read Jane Austen! Read Shakespeare! That's *all* the psychology you'll ever need!' She beamed at me pushing both lips up flat under her nose. 'I think, Ruth Frank, that you're simply being perverse. Psychology indeed! Poppycock! You were *born* to be a teacher.'

She'd won. I sat down completely depressed. Of all the things I did not want to be, a teacher was first. Year after year, class after class, where was the glory in it?

'Teaching is the noblest of professions,' she went on. 'It exercises power over the *mind*. Remember that, gels. Teachers are the mothers of the mind.'

I tried hard to imagine myself as Bernard's wife. Children and servants, a house, a garden. For years I had been falling asleep at night imagining Bernard watching me fall asleep. But now all I could conjure were the words themselves. H-ouse, as in m-ouse. Serv-ants. Serve. Ants.

Girls in my class stuck photographs of boys to the lids of their suitcases, next to pictures of horses. The boys had names like Nigel and Hugh. Pale eyes stared out of pale faces. The faces themselves seemed half-made, still missing their masculine effects.

I stared down at my inkwell and focused my eyes on the stains around it, squinting to expand the blotches into a map, a face, the future I couldn't imagine for myself. I reached into my Bible and touched the paper prayer. Nothing.

'The great religions of the world –'

I gazed out of the window at the ships on the sea. Miss Robinson's voice, a question from someone, the clicking of hockey sticks on the field below – all blended and faded into a hum against the silence of the other worlds and their possibilities beyond those ships. I knew that it was there that I really wanted to go, carried away from this fertile underbelly of the earth, this boring place. I wanted to be a stranger somewhere. To complicate my life. But how? Alone? With Bernard? I thought of Jocelyn and Gwen, the way they could come and go because they were famous. Really famous. Not like my parents in their small bowl. Our small bowl. An ache began to make itself felt right under my ribs.

'Ruth Frank! You may learn by heart Samuel one, verses

seventeen to twenty-seven for inattention, and recite them to me in my office tomorrow after school.'

'I'm sorry, Miss Robinson.' The ache transformed itself into a huge lump the size of a granadilla and rose immediately into my throat. It almost stopped my breathing. I had never been punished by Miss Robinson before.

But when I arrived outside her office the next day, she welcomed me with a smile.

'Come in, Ruth,' she said. 'Are you ready with Samuel?'

'Yes, Miss Robinson.'

'Well, come along then. Begin.'

I stood on the small Persian rug, on the worn spot famous in the history of transgression at Rangston. I had repeated the passage so many times in a day and a half that it had lost all meaning for me.

'And David lamented with this lamentation –' I began.

'Don't gabble, gel!' she barked.

'I'm sorry, Miss Robinson.'

'Don't be sorry. Begin again. Speak the *poitry* of the piece.'

I blinked in panic. 'And David lamented with this lamentation over Saul and over Jonathan his son: Also he bade them teach the children –'

'Stop!' She stood up in her agitation. 'Ruth Frank! Surely *you* can do better than that! Good heavens, gel, buck up!'

By now I could hardly push any voice through my throat at all. And the words of the passage had jumbled into a heap in my head. Saul and Jonathan, daughters of Israel, battles and lions and mountains of Gilboa.

'I'm so –'

'And for both of our sakes, stop pretending to be sorry!'

I stared at her through watery eyes.

'Come on, Ruth Frank! You are a Jewess. And the daughter of two fine actors. Surely you can do credit to one of the finest pieces of poitry in the English language?'

The thought of the English laying claim to what wasn't theirs cheered me up. 'May I try again tonight and come back tomorrow?' I asked.

'I should think so!' she said.

'May I be excused, please?'

'Just a minute,' she said, lifting some papers on her desk. 'I have received a letter from the headmistress of the Brighton School for Girls.'

'The Indian school?'

She put on her glasses and scrutinized the letter. 'Mrs Naidoo asks whether our middle school debating team would like to debate against their middle school debating team.'

This was new. Indians. 'Middle school?' I asked.

She looked up. 'I would like you and Edwina Sloane and Pamela Smuts to form a middle school debating team. Go to Miss Harding. She will drill you in the formalities and procedures. Attend all senior school debates as of tomorrow. I told Mrs Naidoo that we will be ready to meet her team after Michaelmas.'

Once, when I was walking to my grandparents' maisonette, an Indian stepped out of the shade of a flame tree and into my path.

'Want to buy some earrings, Miss?' he asked.

Such an approach, on such a street, miles from the Indian part of town, was unorthodox.

'No, thank you,' I said. And then, to prevent him from begging, I added, 'I haven't got any money.'

'Look here, Miss. Something nice.'

I turned to him. But he just grinned at me, glanced down towards his trousers several times.

So I looked too. There, in one black hand, he held a wrinkled black penis, pulled through the slit of his ragged trousers. I saw the penis and then his bare feet below, cracked and grey.

'Nice, hey?' He was still grinning, holding out his offering as if it didn't belong to him.

I stood still and stared. No more than thirty seconds could have passed since he had first spoken, and yet the silence and politeness had stretched the meeting into a minuet.

Suddenly I turned and fled, raced so hard to my grandmother's front door that I was almost crippled by a stitch in my side.

'Who invited you, Algernon?' she asked, the usual joke when I came to visit. 'Come in, come in. You didn't bring the dogs, did you?'

'No.' I could barely talk.

'My goodness, you've been in a hurry to get here. Go to the kitchen and ask Regina for a mineral, whatever you want.'

I never told my mother about that Indian. And now, bringing home the news of the debate, I thanked my private God for the caution that had held me back.

'Darling!' she exclaimed. 'How lovely!'

Everyone was home early for tea. The silver tray was out, silver teapot, best crockery, everything.

'Where are Jocelyn and Gwen?' I asked.

'I sent Nora to call them down,' she said. 'Real pros, I must say. Got stuck into their lines first thing this morning.'

'*I've* been word perfect for a week!' Valerie said.

My mother beamed her duchess smile at me. 'Tell me, darling,' she said. 'What made them decide on Brighton?'

'Brighton!' Valerie shouted. 'Curry-munchers! Urgh! *Sis!*'

'Why not?' I snapped. 'Just because they're Indians doesn't mean they're as stupid as you are!' It was still fairly safe to be difficult with Valerie. Rehearsals didn't begin until Saturday.

'No wonder they chose you! You look just like an Indian yourself!'

'So do you! So do you!'

'Indians,' my father pronounced, 'can be fine people.'

'Quite so,' said Abba. 'As a matter of fact, they are not unlike Jews.'

My mother stretched her neck, and pointed her nose up towards the ceiling so that she could bring it down in emphasis on all the definitive syllables. 'Some of the most cul-tivated people I know are In-dians,' she said. 'Just look at Devi Chow-dree.'

'Yes,' said my father. 'Quite so. And like us Jews they look after their old people and their poor.'

'Ha!' Valerie sneered. 'Then why're there so many bloody Indian beggars? You can't tell *me* Indians don't cheat and lie!'

'So do you!' I shouted. 'You cheat and lie!'

'Valerie! Ruth!' My mother glared at each of us in turn. 'What on earth do you think Gwen and Jocelyn would think of this?'

The door opened and Jocelyn's face peered round. 'Tea?' she asked.

'Come in! Come in! We're all here, you see, discussing politics as usual! Ha! Ha!' My mother lifted the tea cosy and patted the pot. 'Ruth, darling, nip off to the kitchen with this and ask Nora to send in a fresh pot. *Piping* hot, please! And some honey for the crumpets.'

'Every race and nation has its poor,' my father was saying as I returned with the teapot and honey. 'Even Israel. One can't help them all, you know. One can only do what one can.'

Something about the way he delivered his platitudes, the reverence he always put into 'Israel', the nod of his head as he said 'race and nation', 'do what one can', made me tip up the honey pot over the carpet.

'Ruth! Argh!' he spluttered, leaping to his feet to inspect the beads of honey glistening on the surface of the rug.

Abba leaned forward and adjusted his glasses. Removing stains from Persian rugs was his special pride. 'Nooo damage done!' he pronounced. 'A little water will clear it up in a minute.'

'It's all our fault for coming down late, I'm afraid,' Jocelyn chortled. 'Do let's go on with the discussion!'

'Ma,' I asked quickly, 'will you help me with a piece of Samuel?'

'A piece of whom?'

'Samuel, from the Bible. I have to read it as "poitry",' I said, imitating Miss Robinson's high, looping, throaty English voice.

'What?' Jocelyn laughed. '*Do* that again!'

' "Come along, gel!" ' I whooped, ' "where's the *poitry* of the piece?" '

Jocelyn scrunched her whole face into an ecstasy of silent laughter.

'What happened to "men and their urges"?' Valerie demanded, wanting a laugh for herself.

'We left that ages ago! Now we're on illegitimate children.'

'You're on *what*?' my mother boomed.

' "One-pinch-on-the-bottom-and-the-next-thing-you-know-
you're-in-an-unmarried-mothers'-home!" '

With this Jocelyn exploded so loudly that two of the dogs
jumped up and ran in terror to the door. My parents laughed
too, and Gwen, even Valerie.

'She's much madder than Battie!' I shouted, mad myself with
the stir I'd caused. 'She's a *lesbian*!'

But suddenly the laughing collapsed into coughs and throat
clearing. My mother leapt at the pot and held it up. 'Gwen?'
Jocelyn? Anyone?'

'She *is*!' I insisted. 'Francina told us –'

'Isn't it time you helped this child with the Bible?' Valerie
suggested. 'It's not going to be easy, you know, squeezing
"poitry" out of such a lump.'

'Darling,' my mother said as soon as the study door was
closed. 'I'd lay off lesbians if I were you.'

'Why?'

'I hear Jocelyn's a lesbian.'

'Jocelyn!'

'Shh!'

'With Gwen?' I whispered. I thought of Miss Robinson's
brooch, and the way Jocelyn sloshed on bright-green eye
shadow. There was clearly no knowing.

She smiled and shook her head. 'Nooo! Not Gwen!'

'With who then?'

'*Whom.*'

'Whom? How does it happen?'

'There doesn't have to *be* someone. People are just born
queer.'

Years before, in the summerhouse at the bottom of the garden,
Lucy and I had ordered Indra, Pillay's daughter, to take off her
pants and lift up her skirt. We asked her to urinate. She tried but

couldn't. So we commanded her to open her legs above us while we lay face up on the floor and peered into the smooth folds of brown and black and pink satin skin between her thighs.

'Shall we touch?' I asked, trembling as if I were chilled.

Lucy giggled.

And Indra stood there, still, obedient, scared and mute.

But when I reached my hand up and touched her thigh, she jumped. 'Nooo!' she whispered. 'Naughty!'

'Well, you know that the man inserts his penis into the woman's vagina?' my mother was saying. She had composed herself in the vast leather armchair as Mary Livingston, MD. 'And that he plants his seed there?' she added.

I turned away quickly and ran my hand along the book spines on the top shelf for the Bible. Why had I asked? I might have known that the words she would choose, the way her lips would curl with clinical precision around them, even her favourite gardening metaphor, would make me shrink once again in disgust. Nothing she could tell me could explain what I really wanted to understand. The vast spectrum of desire. When it happened. Why it happened. And how it accomplished the great miracle of falling in love.

'I know all that!' I said. 'That's not what I asked.'

'Well, I'm getting on to lesbians if you'll hold your horses.'

But I couldn't stand to hear her explanation of what lesbians did. It would be full of perfectly articulated vaginas and clitorises and God knows what else – far worse than men planting their seeds. 'I haven't got time,' I said, placing the Bible on her lap. 'I'd rather get the Samuel over with.'

'Eendians! Oooh! Smelly a lot!' Sandra Peters shrieked.

The classroom was in an uproar at my news of the debate. Everyone had an opinion on Indians.

'They stink because they put that revolting oil on their hair,' someone said.

'And they chew raw garlic.'

'Ja! Our gardener chews it all the time! My mother won't

even let him come on to the verandah.'

'I *hate* them,' Cheryl McCormack said.

We stared at her. Her hatred had the validity of experience. We all knew that when she was seven an Indian man had pushed her into an alley and made her undress there. The incident had been printed in both the newspapers.

'I hate them too,' said Lynda Jones cosily.

'That's rubbish,' Edwina said. 'They're just like everyone else.'

Cheryl turned her flat pink face to Edwina. 'You're so stupid!' she spat out. 'If you love them so much, why don't you go and live in Indiantown?'

'You've missed the point as usual,' Edwina said. She turned to me and rolled her eyes. 'Talk about stupid!'

I blushed from my ears to my shoulders. I hated these classroom fights, but there was no avoiding the showdown now. 'You can't condemn a whole race of people just because you don't like some of them,' I said to Cheryl.

'Oh, yes I can!' Cheryl shouted. She jutted her chin towards me accusingly, her whole head – face and scalp – livid red. 'You think you're the bee's knees, don't you, Ruth Frank? Just because you were chosen for the debating team!'

'Just as well she wasn't chosen for the hockey team!' Fiona Brunton shouted.

Behind me I heard smothered laughing. Someone whispered 'Jew' and another 'Indian'. Someone else hissed 'Shhh!'

Suddenly the lump was back in my throat. I lifted the lid of my desk and pretended to look for a book. My father had told me that he'd learned to box at school so that he could fight the boys who called him 'Jew'. But I didn't want to fight. I had no one to accuse, nothing I wished to defend. They could have made me just as miserable by laughing at my nose or at my teeth.

I found the paper prayer and slipped it into the palm of my hand. 'Please, Lord,' I prayed, 'don't let me cry. Let me have a boyfriend. Let them like me.'

'Ruth!' Edwina leaned over my shoulder. 'Can you come to my house for tea after netball?'

I nodded but didn't look round. Edwina had never invited me over before. My mother said that they would have nothing to do with Jews since her father had married a Gentile and changed his name from Slomovitz to Sloane. My mother loved to expose this sort of treachery. 'Oh?' she would say when I mentioned Edwina, 'That Slomovitz girl?'

'They're so stupid they make me sick!' Edwina said as we walked together to her house.

'Me too,' I said. I was exhilarated to have so sudden a friend, someone with whom I could look down on others.

'That Indian didn't even rape Cheryl,' she said. 'My mother told me someone saw them and called the police before he could even do anything.'

'I know.' I didn't know. It was hard to imagine rape anyway. How *did* they do it when you didn't want them to?

I laughed. 'Once I was walking right here and an Indian exposed himself.'

'Here? Right here?'

'Ja.'

She laughed too. 'What did you do?'

'I ran.'

'Ugh!' She screwed up her face. 'Men are revolting.'

Edwina had four brothers. Apparently she had more reason to be revolted than I. When I thought of my Indian saying 'nice, hey?' or of Cheryl's Indian undressing her, my thighs felt weak, as if I'd drunk some wine.

'I'm never going to get married,' she said. 'I don't care what happens.'

'Why not?' I asked.

'Can you imagine having to wear high heels and make-up and join a sewing circle? Ugh!' she said again.

I had only seen Edwina in school uniform or jodhpurs. It was, in fact, difficult to imagine her heavy body balanced on high heels. She belonged on a horse. She wore down the outsides of her school shoes by walking with her legs too far apart and rolling outwards with every step. And her skin was thick and ruddy like orange rind. Make-up would only make her ridiculous.

'What about children?' I asked.

She shook her head. 'Not for me.'

I touched my pocket and the piece of paper in it. 'I think I'd like to get married if I met the right person.'

'Good luck!' she said.

But Edwina and I vied for first place in class. I wished her to consider me a worthy foe. 'I mean an Italian count. Or even a Swedish prince,' I flourished. 'A lord, an earl, the king of kings.'

She laughed. 'Still,' she said. 'They're still men.'

'What did you have for tea, darling?' my mother asked at dinner.

'Orange squash and biscuits.'

'What kind?' She always asked this. It was her measure of what divided a house from a home.

'Tennis biscuits. And lemon creams.'

'Bought biscuits!' she snorted. 'Serves Arthur Slomovitz right!'

'Nothing wrong with bought biscuits, Sarah my dear,' Abba said. 'Why, I often used to request Baker's Assorted with my tea.'

'*That*,' she snorted, 'I find hard to believe of Mother.'

Abba chortled to himself.

'I love lemon creams,' I said, in case Gwen and Jocelyn, behind their dinner table faces, loved them too. 'I wish we could have them all the time.'

'Oh, Ruth, Ruth, Ruth!' My mother beamed a gracious smile at her guests. 'If I advocated bought biscuits you'd be asking for Nora's flower pots, now wouldn't you?'

I said nothing. There was no winning with her on the subject of taste. But I was ashamed of her in front of Jocelyn and Gwen, the flimsy things in which she placed her pride, the smallness of our world compared with theirs. I longed for Saturday so that she could concentrate on the play and its own particular crises. Stop playing duchess and woman of the world at home.

'Why don't you ask that Slomovitz girl over here one day?' she suggested.

'Her name is Sloane. Edwina Sloane.'

'Edwina!' Valerie said. 'It sounds as if they wanted an Edward and got her instead.'

'Oh, no,' said Gwen, 'it's a very old Anglo-Saxon name, you know.'

'See? See?' I said. 'How can I ask her if everyone's going to laugh at her name?' I wanted Gwen and Jocelyn to know the trouble I had here. And that I took people for what they were. Even lesbians. Even Indians.

'I find it very odd that people use names they don't even understand,' Gwen went on. Small blue veins showed up in her neck as she raised her chin to lecture us further. 'And the combinations! The Seamus Shapiros and Christopher Cohens! It's too absurd!' She wiped the edges of her mouth delicately with my grandmother's linen and lace napkin.

Abba slowly brought his knife and fork to land. He stared at the table ahead and seemed to be breathing lightly. 'I think,' he said at last, 'that even if Arthur Slomovitz had kept his name, he would have had every right in the world to name his child Edwina.'

'I disagree!' my mother snapped. 'If that Arthur Slomovitz wants to go about pretending to be someone he's not, his children will just have to suffer the consequences.'

'But, my dear,' Abba said softly, 'that's not at all the poi–'

'Why?' I shouted, fighting off the infection of her words. 'Why do you have the right to teach everyone a bloody lesson?'

My mother slapped her hand on the table. 'How dare you swear like a fishwife? Leave this table at once and finish your supper in the kitchen.'

I leapt to my feet, tears already streaming down my cheeks, and rushed to the door.

'Gwen, Jocelyn,' my father said with a breathy little stage laugh. 'Do excuse our little revolutionary. Now who's for pud? Sarah, ring the bell, darling.'

'Awu!' Nora flung her fists on to her hips as I appeared at the kitchen door. 'What you done now?'

'I hate them,' I mumbled.

'Awu! You hate Mrs Joc-e-leen? You hate Mrs Gwin? You naughty with Madam special actress?'

'Not them. I just hate the others.'

'Don't say bad thing!' She marched over to the stove and lifted a few lids. 'You want some marrow, Naughtiness? You want some chicken feet?'

'I've just got to finish pudding. Reuben'll bring it.'

'Phuthu? Look!' She held up a spoonful of the white spongy porridge. It was servants' food. Usually I loved it.

'No thanks,' I said. 'I'm full.'

'You got the doings?' she looked into my face.

I shook my head. 'The doings' was a period. Nora loved the idea of our sharing this biological nuisance.

'Constance she still got no doings.'

'She'll get them,' I said. 'Don't worry.'

Nora laughed. 'I only worry when the mens come around for her.'

Like dogs, I thought, like hyenas.

'Every night I pray to the Lord to keep my child pure and good.' She began to hum 'Gentle Jesus Meek and Mild'.

Reuben crashed my pudding dish down in front of me.

'I don't want it,' I said.

In one swipe he snatched it up again and handed it to John at the sink. John never looked at me anymore. When I came into the kitchen he stopped singing and clowning.

'Nors,' I said, 'could you cut the collars and cuffs off my uniforms when you take them for Constance?'

She stopped humming and turned to look at me.

'The headmistress said it's against the rules – I can get into trouble –'

'Why the Madam she didn't tell me?' Nora demanded.

I blushed. 'Because she doesn't care about those rules.'

'Why they make those rules?' she demanded. 'Black children they can't go to white school.'

'I know.'

Her massive chest heaved. 'What I must cut off the hat?'

Reuben and John stopped their talk at the sink and turned to listen.

I stared down at the wooden table in front of me, miserable and ashamed. 'Forget it,' I said. 'I don't care. It's just a stupid rule.'

She turned away, pulled out the tea trolley and began to set out the cups for coffee. 'God made the bees,' she sang loudly, the old familiar song she had taught me long ago. 'The bees made honey.' She clattered the spoons on to each saucer. 'The honey made the white man –' Poured out the hot milk, holding back the skin with the lid of the pot. 'And the white man made some money.'

9

The first day of rehearsals was like the prelude to war. Disaster was everywhere, even though it seemed, in its separate occurrences, to add up to nothing as a whole.

I sat at the back of the theatre next to Abba. I was there because Jocelyn, sorry for me after the dinner table fight, had asked my mother if I was allowed at rehearsals. And my mother had said of course she's allowed, but she never comes, she never wants to. And so I had to say of course I'd love to come, even though the boredom of rehearsals, and particularly of first rehearsals, was like physical pain to me.

My mother stood at the edge of the stage, staring down at her script and then up over the tops of her reading glasses to give the cast directions.

Valerie had planted herself next to Jocelyn. For the last few days she had often been planting herself next to Jocelyn, and talking softly to her, just out of earshot, as if they were intimates. I wondered whether Valerie were perhaps a lesbian too. Lesbians seemed to be all over the place lately, and in all sorts of disguises. The thought unsettled me. If Valerie were a lesbian she'd never get married. And I was counting on marriage to carry her out of the house before much longer.

'Sylvia – act two, scene one –'

'Ready!' Jocelyn stared down at the script on her lap with her pencil poised. She seemed to be taking special care to behave as if she weren't famous. Gwen, however, was playing prima donna. While my mother talked to Jocelyn she sighed and closed her eyes and rubbed her temples. Although it was a cool July day she flapped her script around her head noisily.

Somehow, even though I didn't like her, it was to Gwen I felt responsible for the shabbiness of the theatre, the globe chairs, the chipped enamel kettle that Jim, the theatre boy, was carrying in with tea. Jocelyn was different. Nothing needed to be excused to her. Perhaps, I thought, it was because she was a lesbian, and looked like a horse, and was more famous than Gwen, and more expensive.

Gwen crossed and recrossed her legs with a swish of stockings. She tapped her foot on the floor. She fluttered her fingers in a wave to my father sitting in the third row.

I stared down into my lap. The fingers of my right hand were lashed together by the thread I'd pulled from the hem of my skirt. Shame had shot blood into my cheeks and ears. But my heart ached for my mother. She seemed so unashamed herself, innocent almost. I hated to think of Gwen laughing about her and about our theatre, about all of us. It was as if I were being forced to watch some blood sport and couldn't look away in case my favourite contestant fell down dead.

'We're going to have trouble with that Gwen,' my mother said to my father as they dressed for dinner that night.

I hung over the balustrade of the upstairs verandah, just outside their room, staring out to sea.

'If you anticipate trouble, that's what you'll get.'

'Ghugh! I don't know why I ever expect help from you! You're too busy flirting with her to notice!'

I stared out at the darkening sky as they fought about his flirting. The wind blew sharp and cold through my jersey. Lights were coming on. Blacks were out on the street already with their music and chatter. Rowena Tittlestad was having a party, with boys. I hadn't counted enough with the girls who had been invited to stop them talking about it in front of me.

A door slammed. My mother crashed drawers open and shut, pulled the curtains closed, turned on the heater. She reached through the curtains to close the verandah door.

'Ruth! What are you doing out there?'

I trudged into the room and plumped down in her special armchair – soft and cosy like a padded green cave.

Someone knocked.

'Come in!' she shouted.

'Madam', Reuben mumbled, 'The Master he want to know when the Madam she want the supper?'

'Tell him seven o'clock as usual.'

It was going to be a siege. 'Ask your father to pass the salt, please,' and 'Please inform your mother that she's wanted on the telephone.' Valerie would run from one to the other and make things worse. She loved a siege. For me, though, it was always awful. The more my mother suffered, the more she would dig in. There was nothing anyone could do, not even my father. If he apologized she exulted and he suffered. If he didn't, the siege continued. And now there was an audience of guests. It was going to be awful.

My mother sat in grim silence at the foot of the dining-room table, making a point of placing an empty dinner plate in front of her and drinking only water. Gwen had ordered supper in her room. My mother stared furiously at Gwen's empty place, as if she were about to cast a spell on it. She was Hera now, her favourite role for a siege.

My father, on the other hand, tried to cheer things up for the sake of appearances. 'Well, Chopsticks! How's our little Bolshevik today, huh?'

'Not funny,' I said.

'Agreed!' my mother pronounced.

He set his mouth and flared his nostrils and breathed out with a rush. This meant he had been driven to the fringes of his endurance by the impossible woman with whom, for some reason, he had chosen to spend his life.

'Aiiiee – eeeaah – aaaagh!'

We all jumped. The unmistakable shrieking of African

134

women in a fight filled the room. Swooping screeches, soprano yells, and then ululating loops of fury reached the dining-room in waves. My mother stepped on the bell.

'Reuben! What on earth is going on?'

He bowed his head. 'Trouble in the compound, Madam.'

'What trouble?' she barked.

'Beauty and Nora, Madam.'

'Oh, for God's sake!' She grabbed the edge of the table. 'Roger! Will you go and sort this out, please?'

My father wiped his mouth and laid his knife and fork together. Despite the triumph of her being forced to address him during a siege, he was not pleased. He hated sorting out the servants.

'If it's Beauty and her teeth and bones again, she can take her things and go!' my mother boomed. 'She's had her last chance.'

'Am I handling this or are you?' my father asked.

'Gugh!' she exploded. 'He'll probably utter a few meaningless phrases in dulcet tones. And then *I'm* left without a cook again. That's all I'm short of now! This house to run, a production coming off, and no cook!'

'Oh, don't worry, Sarah,' Jocelyn boomed cheerfully. 'We can all muck in, you know. Can't we, Val?'

I held my breath. This wasn't the way to handle my mother during a siege. She hated being jollied along, especially when she was in a fury.

'She came back after two days last time,' I said quickly.

'You keep your oar out of this!' my mother snapped.

'But just consider, my dear,' Abba said, 'that Nora would have to go a long way to find a situation as satisfactory as this one.'

Tik-tik-tik, she tapped the tips of her scarlet nails on the table.

'May I be excused?' Valerie asked. 'I'm being fetched in half an hour.'

My mother turned on her. '*Fetched!* Don't think you're on holiday just because you only come in in scene four!'

I jumped up. 'Me too. I've got to do my history essay. Please may I be excused?'

Without waiting for an answer I ran out past the pantries to the kitchen. It was empty. Only the servants' pots bubbled and hissed on the stove. Outside, the screeching had subsided into 'yes, Baas,' 'no, Baas.' I crept across the laundry lawn to the mulberry tree.

They were standing on the path – my father, Nora and Beauty. Reuben and John hung back against the compound wall. The dogs, locked away from the fracas into the laundry, scratched and whined and jumped to be let out.

'You admit, then, Beauty, that you set this curse on Nora?' my father was asking.

Beauty hung her head. It was her weekend off and she wore the costume of her trade as a witchdoctor. Around her head, her arms, her breasts, her waist and knees she wore dozens of furs and skins of different colours and lengths. Bones and teeth hung from her neck and wrists. And around her ankles bracelets of shells shivered and shook as she moved.

'Well?' he demanded.

'Hhawu, isanusi!' John muttered.

Beauty nodded.

'Is that yes?'

'Yes, Baas.'

'And what is this curse all about?'

'Master!' Nora flapped one hand out, palm down in deference, for his attention.

'Yes, Nora?'

'She curse me so that the mens won't want me no more.'

Beauty stamped one foot and set the shells into a frenzy.

'But, Nora! That's simply not possible, my good woman!' My father gave her one of his public school chortles. 'Now you're a sensible woman. Surely you don't believe all this nonsense?'

'Hawu, Master, it is the truth.'

I shrank into the shade of the mulberry tree. Perhaps something amazing would happen. Nora's breasts would explode or Reuben would spit on her and move his bed out.

'Well, what does Reuben have to say about all this? Reuben?'

But Reuben just spat on the ground and walked away, past me, back to the kitchen without a word. John followed.

'Reuben, he from the Belgian Congo, Master,' Nora explained.

'Well, there you are then! There's nothing more to worry about, is there?'

Nora shook her head but didn't move.

'Well, now look,' my father said, losing some of his valuable patience. 'What is to be done?'

'Beauty she must take away that curse,' Nora insisted.

'Hhayi!' Beauty shook her head and stamped her foot again.

'Beauty!' he barked. 'I must insist that you take this curse away. All this nonsense has to stop! The Madam and I are very busy with our play at the moment. We simply don't have time for all these high jinks.'

'Master,' Nora said, 'she want me to pay to take away the curse.'

'What!' he exploded. 'That is downright blackmail! Why didn't you tell me this at first?'

Nora said nothing.

'Beauty,' my father said, 'I order you to take away this curse or I shall call the police.'

Beauty let out a shriek, threw back her head, and shook all her bones and shells.

'Enough!' my father shouted. 'That's quite enough of that! Have you been drinking?'

Beauty shook her head.

'Well, I'm off for the police –'

'No, Baas!' she gasped. 'I do it.' Tears had started in her eyes. 'Nora she give me bad food.'

'What?!'

'Awu, unamanga!' Nora shouted.

'What is this, Nora?' my father demanded.

But Beauty stepped forward now. 'She give Reuben my meat,' she said. 'She give me rubbish.'

'Well, now –' My father slipped his hands into his trouser pockets. 'This casts a different light on things, doesn't it?' He looked from Nora to Beauty. 'I shall give you two my last word on the subject. And then I don't want to hear any more about it. Ever. Or you'll both be out on your ear. Ears,' he corrected. 'And no references. Do you understand?'

'Yes, Baas.'

'Yes, Master.'

'Beauty, you will remove this absurd curse from Nora, right away, by whatever means you customarily employ. And Nora, you will divide your food equally amongst the four of you. If there is any more trouble, the Madam herself will handle the rationing of your meat. Do I make myself perfectly clear?'

'No, Baas.'

'No, Master.'

'What do you mean "no"?'

'Yes, Baas.'

Nora nodded. 'Thank you, Master.'

He turned and walked past me, back into the house. Nora followed Beauty into the compound in silence.

When they had all gone, I trotted back into the house, through the sewing-room door and into the lounge. Only Jocelyn and my father sat there drinking coffee and discussing the fight.

'Finished your essay?' Jocelyn asked.

I blushed. No one usually listened when I made that sort of excuse. 'Uh, no, not really.'

'What's it on?' she asked.

' "The More Things Change the More They Remain the Same",' I chanted.

'Ahhh! Plus ça change, plus c'est la même chose! *Les Guêpes!*' She seemed to have been cast into unintelligible ecstasy by my history essay.

'I don't really understand French,' I reminded her.

'Famous, famous!' she cried. 'When's it for?'

'Monday. We've got to choose an episode from before Cromwell and apply it to something that happened after.'

'Why?' she demanded.

My heart dropped. If she didn't understand, how would I?

'I mean how very unimaginative of your history mistress to apply such a subject to English history when you have such perfectly wonderful subject-matter right here under your very nose.'

Oh. 'Miss Harding won't teach us anything after 1914 because she says it's still undecided. We only learn up to the Boer War.'

'*What?*' She sat forward. The flesh on her face seemed to come away from the bone and rearrange itself into a deep frown.

'Still undecided,' I explained. History wasn't my favourite subject. Everything seemed undecided.

'*Undecided!* When is anything of or from or about the human condition ever decided?' she demanded. She collapsed her chest and shoulders into a heap of despair. Her eyes, under the hood of her enormous brows, scanned my face. 'Just look at what happened tonight –' She turned to my father, who was glancing as discreetly as he could at the newspaper folded on the arm of the couch. 'Just think of what's-her-name – that washerwoman – practising as a *witchdoctor*! Now! In this day and age!'

I couldn't imagine how Beauty's hobby had any bearing on history, and could only think of Miss Harding's face if I brought up such an idea.

But I didn't need to comment. Jocelyn was spinning webs for the essay I wasn't allowed to write. 'You've got the history of the Zulus right here. Chaka and Dingaan for one. Now look –' She sat forward confidentially. 'We could take the attitudes of the European colonists towards the African people, some incident to illustrate this, let's see – what about that business with Dingaan killing off those Boers and then that awful revenge –'

'Blood River?'

'Yes! Blood River! All to do with land, of course, and the superior claim of the European to it. And then, you see, you jump to what's going on now, pass books and separate areas for Africans and so forth – which really amounts to the same thing, doesn't it?'

My father looked up nervously and smiled. 'Hey, hey, Jocelyn! Steady on, old girl! Our little revolutionary doesn't need any encouragement, you know.'

She didn't seem to understand how little I knew or cared. I prayed, in those seconds as she turned, frowning to him, that she wouldn't find out. I even wished I could find the subject as thrilling as she did. But South African history seemed third rate to me. There were no kings and queens, or walled cities, or wars lasting a hundred years. So what about the Zulus spearing seventy Boers? Or even the Great Trek? How could that compare to the ten causes of the French Revolution? Or the six wives of Henry VIII?

'All right then,' she declared, winking at me. 'We could simply deal with the washerwoman. Surely we could find some witchdoctor episode from the early days, and then, you see, this contretemps between her and the cook tonight?' She looked eagerly into my face.

'The trouble is Miss Harding won't allow that.'

'Ah, yes!' She thumped the toe of one heavy brogue on the carpet. 'The rule of small minds over large.'

I started to rise from my chair, to flee while she still thought me large-minded.

'Which university were you thinking of going to?' she asked suddenly.

I sank back down. 'I don't know. I'd like to go to England, maybe.'

'Well,' she said. 'What about Oxford? Wasn't papa there?'

I nodded, glancing to see if he would now join in. But his eyes were closed. His head hung towards the newspaper. And he snored lightly.

'I was at Somerville, you know, back in the Dark Ages. Before I went off the rails to become an actress!'

'Oh!' What was Somerville? I had no idea.

She leaned towards me suddenly and whispered. 'You *must* get out of here, you know,' she said. 'This is a country with no future.'

'I know,' I whispered back. But no future for the country had no teeth for me. We were always hearing that. It was like the Jews and the Messiah.

'It would be a waste to stay,' she insisted.

My heart leapt. She'd found the right word. Waste terrified me. Wasting invisible chances. The real world spinning out of reach while I wasted time waiting for my chance to get there. And even if I got there, where were the guarantees? What about all those years in England my mother had wasted by coming back again? My father too?

'When I decided for the stage, my family almost disowned me, you know. Everyone said I'd gone mad.'

'What did they want?' I asked. What did my family want, I wondered? They didn't seem to notice my future. It lacked the potential for tragedy that Valerie's had.

Jocelyn grinned. 'They wanted me to marry the curate and settle into a house and have some children.'

I thought of my mother in her boarding house in London. Mrs Cohen the landlady. All that hard work, and no men, no adventure. She had the husband now and the house and the children and the theatre as well. And yet it seemed that there too something had been wasted. Even though she seemed to have everything. Even so.

Suddenly the doorbell rang, both doorbells. One shrieked continuously in the kitchen, the other bing-bonged loudly in the hall. I ran off after the dogs to see what the matter was. But when I reached the hall I stopped in fright. A face was squashed up against the bubbled glass of the front door. When it saw me a tongue came out and squashed there too, pink and white. Teeth. A beard.

'Who's there?' I asked.

'The big bad wolf.'

I knew the voice. The vision cupped its hands around its eyes.

'Ah ha! The littlest Frank! Let me in, let me in or I'll blow your house down!'

But I could only think of the ragged skirt I still wore. And my hair that needed a wash.

'I'll huff and I'll puff!' it growled.

141

The lounge door opened behind me. 'What is all this racket?' my father demanded.

I gestured to the door.

'Who is it?'

'Bernard Rubenstein.'

'It's for me!' Valerie shouted.

'Excuse me for a minute –' My father unlocked the door and held it open. 'Come in, please.'

Bernard bounced in in a pair of thick rubber sandals made out of car tyres and inner tubes, the sort that Africans wore. He leapt over to the kist and clanged the brass mortar and pestle. 'Val-e-ree!' he boomed.

'Would you like to come in and sit down while you wait?' my father asked, staring in amazement at the sandals.

Into the lounge he hopped and jumped, right across to Jocelyn. 'Madam,' he said, doubling into a bow, 'your humble servant.'

She waved a huge hand at him in a regal dismissal. 'Sit, sir, and let us talk this matter out.'

With a roar he threw himself across one of the armchairs and then beamed his attention on me. He curled back his lips against the bush of his beard, bared his white teeth like the jaws of a trap. 'Stand up!' he ordered.

I stood. But I had to hold the back of my chair for support. I felt as if I'd been struck by the plague. My head, my chest, my skin were all on fire. Even my bones ached.

'Turn!'

My father cleared his throat and opened his mouth to object. But he wasn't quick enough. Bernard wasn't Jeffrey. He didn't care about approval or consent. And he didn't seem to notice people like my father, or to understand the rule of manners in other people's houses. In fact his presence there seemed to have made the room and the house his own. Me too. Valerie too. Anyone he wanted.

'Champion!' Bernard shouted. 'She'll turn into a bloody prize in another few years!'

I heard what he meant me to hear – the hope he thought he

was giving me again. But suddenly I felt like a slave rejected in the marketplace. And then the shame of having stood up for him at all. Despair that she had him now, had pulled him like a thread out of my dreams, all the fine paths he'd been filing between me and my future quite empty suddenly. So quickly, without warning.

Valerie trippled down the stairs and arrived breathless in a cloud of Shocking Schiaparelli. Bernard leaned far back across his chair and squinted, as if he were trying to look up her legs.

'Hmm!' he grunted. 'Turn!'

She turned just as I had done and then curtseyed. 'Sir,' she said.

'Sir, she said, sir, she said,' Jocelyn sang. 'I'm going a-milking, sir, she said.'

'Not bad, hey?' he asked my father.

But my father was too stunned to respond.

'Come on then, my beauty,' Bernard growled, leaping to his feet. 'Let's hit the road.'

'What an astonishing young man!' Jocelyn said after they'd gone.

My father shook his head and blinked like an old man, like Abba. 'Such a creature,' he mumbled. 'What on earth can she see in such a creature?'

I shivered. The fever had gone now and I was cold. 'I'm just going to get another jersey,' I said.

Gwen met me at the first turning of the stairs. She wore an ivory wool dressing-gown and satin slippers to match. But her face had been washed of its pinks and greens. Her skin seemed thin and finely wrinkled like old tissue paper.

'Do you know where the servants are?' she asked me, as if I were the servant in charge of servants. 'I've been ringing that bell for over ten minutes.'

I looked at my watch. 'It's half-past eight,' I said. 'They must have gone already.'

She stamped one slipper. 'Well, how shall I get my glass of warm milk?'

I stared up at her, wondering how to handle this without my

mother knowing. I could ring for Nora from the compound, but then she'd complain to my mother the next day. 'I don't know,' I said.

'Well, surely there's *someone* who can heat up milk in this establishment? Can't you?'

'I?' It seemed like a mad idea. 'Do you want me to bring it to your room?'

She nodded and turned up the stairs again.

I ran to the kitchen, flipped on the light, and stood back so that the cockroaches could skitter back into drawers and cupboards. It was probably a good idea that Gwen hadn't come down herself. English people were terrified of our cockroaches. The room smelled damply of washing-up soap and dogs and dough rising. Moisture had condensed on all the windows. I marched in and stared at the panel of buttons and knobs on the stove, trying to remember how Nora switched on a plate. I had seen her there hundreds or thousands of times, turning and switching and stirring, but I had never noticed which and how. Just to be sure, I turned them all right up to number 10, and then looked around for a pot. I had no idea where the pots were kept. All I could find were the servants' pots under the sink, and two huge frying pans hanging on the wall. I took one down and put it on the stove.

By now the plates were turning from black to red and warming the kitchen beautifully. The frying pan hissed and spat as I poured the milk into it. I grabbed a wooden spoon from the jar and stirred. This was fun. I flew off to the cake pantry for a tray and then to the dining-room for a tray cloth and a good glass. Perhaps she would want sugar too, I thought. Back to the cake pantry for the silver sugar bowl and then to the dining-room again for a silver spoon. I set the tray down on the sideboard and spread my mother's best-drawn linen cloth over it. The glass, the bowl, the spoon, it all looked lovely. Warm milk seemed cosy, the sort of thing people in England would drink.

As I carried the tray back down the corridor to the kitchen I heard the hissing and spitting there with a satisfaction I'd only read about in school books and novels. It was the pleasure that the farmer's wife took in turning out food for her family. Wives in other times, in other countries, doing it all themselves, start to finish. Cosy, like the Knowles' flat was cosy. But even they had Ida.

Milk frothed and foamed over the edge of the pan and down underneath it. It smelled like custard. I sang as I picked up the pan and held it over the glass. Cursed as most of it spilled on to the stove itself and was sucked up by the dishcloths over the bread. So. I'd have to warm some more. I whistled back to the fridge for the milk.

'WHAT ON EARTH IS GOING ON HERE?'

I swung around to the door, but my mother had swooped in behind me and was already at the stove, twisting madly at the knobs.

'Good God! There's burned milk everywhere! And everything's on high! The edge of this dishcloth is scorched! *My God!* You've cracked one of my best glasses! Do you realize that the house could have burned down? *What on earth are you doing?*'

I backed up against the shelves of the fridge.

'What?'

'I was heating up some milk.'

'But why?'

'For Gwen.'

'For Gwen!'

'She –'

'She asked *you* to heat up milk for her?' She turned to the stove, touched the glass, the cloth, as if choosing which one to throw. 'Where is that woman?' she demanded.

'Upstairs.'

She flew back out and up the backstairs, lifting her skirt as she climbed. I kicked off my shoes and followed. Up the dark stairs, along the dark corridor to the children's wing. I stopped at the end of the tunnel. I heard her knock. 'Yes?' came Gwen's voice.

'It's Sarah here, Gwen. I'd like a word with you, please.'

The door opened. 'Yes, Sarah,' a weary voice said.

'Did you ask my youngest daughter to warm some milk for you?'

'I did.'

'Well, I think we had better get a few things straight right now!' She never lost control of her voice when she lost her temper. It only deepened and boomed more loudly. 'First, I would like you to understand that this house is *not* an hotel. My servants are household servants. They have tasks and duties that pertain to the *household*. They are not here expressly for your comfort. Second, my family, my daughters in particular, are *never* to be given orders by you or anyone else! How dare you ask my youngest daughter to warm up your milk?'

Gwen took a deep breath. 'I'm sorry, Sarah. I had no idea I had committed a *faux pas*.'

'A *faux pas*! Trays carried up to your room, my daughter nearly burning the house down warming milk up for you! Oh, no, my dear, we've gone far beyond any *faux pas*. Just consider your performance during rehearsal this afternoon – all that flittering and jibbeting like a silly little schoolgirl! And then the reading itself! Like the most crass of amateurs! I tell you –'

'What?' Gwen's voice rose to a shrill high F. 'Amateur!? Have you gone mad, Sarah Frank, or are you just ignorant?'

'Oh, no, I'm not ignorant. I've seen the best of them, I can tell you. And let me tell you, the great ones don't behave the way you do. Just take a look at Jocelyn! *That's* what we're paying for! Not only the name, the *performance*! Let me tell you right now, Miss Stit, unless your whole attitude improves you can just pack your bags and leave.'

'Ha! You make me laugh! Ever signed a contract before, Sarah Frank?'

'Perhaps you didn't read the contract, Miss Stit. Read again. Look especially at clause nine. Yes, oh yes, you may smile. But believe me, I know what I want and I get it! If you can't give it to me you can just get out! You have until tomorrow morning to make up your mind.'

I flew back down the tunnel and hid at the top of the

backstairs. The door slammed. It was over. She'd stay or she'd leave. Either way my mother had won. My heart leaped and danced. I pounced out as my mother emerged from the tunnel and hugged her tight. She kissed my hair and held me cheek to cheek. There was shuffling and murmuring in the hall, Jocelyn starting up the stairs. We waited. She came down the passage towards us, held out her hands to my mother.

'I was going to warn you,' she whispered. 'She tries it on, you know, every damned show. By Jove I wish we had more producers like you in London!'

10

The following morning Gwen came down to breakfast for the first time.

'Awu, Miss Gwin, I lay you a place.'

'Has everyone had breakfast already?'

Nora shook her head. 'The Madam and the Master they have the tray in their room. Miss Jocelyn she still asleep.'

Gwen avoided looking at me. 'Is there a newspaper one can read?'

'The Madam and the Master they got it.'

'I can go and ask them if you like,' I suggested.

'Oh, no, thank you very much. I'll fetch myself a book.'

As soon as she was gone Nora came to stand at my side. 'What the matter?' she asked.

'Gwen and Ma had a fight.'

'I know that.' She bent down to peer into my face and then pointed at my empty plate. 'What the matter with *you*? You sick?'

I shook my head, but I was sick. I had woken in my dark room to a great loneliness. Valerie and Bernard. Valerie and Bernard. Valerie and Bernard.

'Why you give your breakfast to the dogs?'

'I didn't.'

She clicked her tongue. 'God he punish you if you lie.'

'I'm not hungry.'

But she wouldn't move. She had folded her arms now, and peered down at me sitting there slumped and pasty, wishing for a man of my own.

'You got trouble with the boys?' she demanded. She always asked me that. Boys were the only sort of trouble she could think of having. 'What boy?' she asked.

'Nora! Leave me alone! You're a pest! You're a gossip!' For some reason Nora hated to be called a gossip. It was the sound of the word itself that seemed to offend her, all that hissing in the middle. She would never say it herself.

'You call me bad words because of my black skin!' she stormed.

'Rubbish! It's got nothing to do with the colour of your skin!' Black skin was Nora's new weapon, since all the upheavals and the pass burnings.

'You don't call Valerie no bad word like that! You don't call Miss Gwin no bad word like that!'

'Valerie *is* a gossip! I *do* call her a gossip!' The argument, stupid as it was, had brought me to tears.

'Awu! Why you cry? Old Nora make her baby cry?'

I snorted and hiccoughed into her stiff starched apron, clasped her around her huge hips, sniffing the morning fragrance of her Lifebuoy soap, her Mum and Pond's cold cream.

'Awu!' She stood back a moment and stared into my pale, streaked, miserable face. 'You jealous of Val?'

I shook my head vigorously.

'Awu!' she said again. 'You want that tsotsi come for Miss Val last night?'

I hid my face in my hands.

'What you want that tsotsi for? Cheap Zulu-boy shoe, jump and shout like meshuganagob while the Master he there? What you want with that meshuganagob?' She stood back and bared all her teeth in one of her mighty laughs. She found madmen hilarious and had several names for different sorts of derangements. 'Meshuganagob' she applied only to Jews.

'When did you see him?' I asked.

'*I* see! Nora she see *every*-thing! That tsotsi never makes no girl happy! That tsotsi going to running-running with girls, girls, girls. You listen! You too clever for that kinds of meshuganagob. Val she bad-luck sister here. What you want her bad luck for? You meshuganagob too?'

My father was dressed for golf when I arrived at their bedroom door. 'Hello there, Chopsticks! he said.

'Heard the news?' my mother chortled. 'Her majesty remains! Slipped a note under my door, if you please! Ha! Don't think we'll have any more trouble with that one!' She was more than recovered. She was jubilant.

My father did a neat kneebend in front of the dressing table mirror. He stroked down a few invisible stray hairs.

'How about bringing home one of your cups for a change?' my mother boomed. She stood back to admire him. 'The seam there's a bit skew,' she said, winking at me.

The siege was over. He patted her lightly on the bottom. 'Cheers queers!' he said.

I settled into the green cave chair to watch her dress.

'He loves to think we're counting on those cups of his,' she explained cosily. 'It's important, you know, to encourage a man in his sport.'

'Ma,' I sing-songed, 'tell me how you met Dad and all that.'

She stopped unravelling her stocking at the knee. 'What?'

'I mean that first night at *Hedda Gabler* –'

I meant had he flirted with her then the way he had flirted with Gwen? The way he flirted with everything? With us, with himself in the mirror? Even with the parts he played? And why did she encourage him in this? 'What a Lear you make!' she'd say. 'I wish you could just *see* yourself from the floor!'

'Ha!' she exclaimed, and went on rolling up her stocking. 'Still love stories, hey, after all these years? Ring down, darling, and ask Nora to bring us up another pot of tea.' She looked at her watch. 'It won't hurt to give Gwen a little more time to save face.'

We sat across from each other with our cups of tea, I in the cave chair, she on the chaise longue. The room still smelled of unmade beds and breakfast eggs. Sunday morning, the great loneliness still with me.

'*Everyone* was there on opening night,' she began, 'the mayor, the city councillors, everyone who was anyone in the town (which wasn't saying much, mind you). *That* was a performance! You haven't seen me as Hedda, but I tell you, *that* was a performance! I remember standing on stage after the final curtain, just standing and listening. I *knew* I'd done it – before the crits, before the box office, before everything. You can always hear success, you know, in the sound of an audience leaving.'

I stared across at her. I hadn't meant my request to put a platform under her feet. But she was on it now, and I could only sit watching.

'I remember wishing that just *one* of my coaches could have been there to see me, just *one*. No one could have outacted me that night.' She sighed. 'Ah, well. Sometimes one's chances come along at all the wrong times.'

'Tell me about Dad,' I said.

'Dad?' She sat forward suddenly and lowered her voice. 'It was my performance he fell in love with, you know. He adored me in that role, always has. Made me do it again and again over the years until I was simply too old for the part.'

'Before I was born.'

She looked up, interrupted. 'Not just the performance, mind you. The voice too. He told me that hearing my voice nearly broke his heart. He was terribly homesick for England. Only been out for three weeks. Mark my words, my girl; voices matter a great deal. One might even say that I fell for that lovely baritone of *his*!'

'Why did he come back from England?' I asked.

'No one forced him to return!' she boomed. 'He could have joined the family firm in London. But he wanted to *be* someone. On his own home ground.'

I hated the idea of both of them settling for less. 'I don't see the point in being someone where it doesn't even count,' I said.

She raised her chin and lowered her lids, the look she used on Hannah or Mrs Goldman. 'Your father would be someone wherever he was. Even selling carpets in a shop.'

I tried to believe her, but still I couldn't imagine him without us, without her, without every hair in place. And I didn't understand. How had he fallen in love with her performance? In spite of the play? If it was Hedda Gabler he'd fallen in love with, he loved a mad woman who burned other people's books and then shot herself. If he'd fallen in love with the performance, where was my mother in it? It was the old secret between them, like a conundrum only they could understand.

'What did you think when you met him?' I asked. What did you feel, I wanted to know? How does it feel?

'Well! He was simply the most beautiful creature I'd ever laid eyes on! That dark skin with the pale, almost luminous cheeks and forehead. The mouth wonderfully red and full, the black moustache, those wide, dark eyes, and that aquiline curve sweeping down from the eyebrows to those wonderfully inflected nostrils!'

My whole body twitched into an involuntary shiver of disgust.

She laughed happily. 'Heigh ho! Did I ever tell you about the dress I wore for that final scene?'

'The blue taffeta.' I knew the story. It was one of her favourites.

But she wasn't taking any cues from me. She stretched her legs out along the chaise longue. 'It was in the most exquisite sort of midnight blue French silk taffeta, cut on the bias, down to the ground, with a bustle of course, and a bit of a train behind. High frilled neck, perfectly fitted to my figure.' She closed her eyes for a few seconds to accent one of her pauses. 'I opened the dressing-room door and there he was, about to knock. "My God!" he said. Just that. Ha!' She held out her cup and saucer. 'Pour me another cup, please, darling.'

She was good at triumphs. But it wasn't a triumph I had wanted. I had wanted to know the truth. To understand the flop we had at home – the furies and the sieges and the war amongst us.

'Was he happy?' I asked.

'Happy?' She stared at me. 'We fell madly in love!'

Madly in love. Only the King and Mrs Simpson had been allowed to fall madly in love. And characters in books, or on the stage. And she and my father. Not Catherine and Jeffrey or Nora and Reuben or anyone else I knew.

'Until he met me he'd been escorting Gramma around the town to soirees and dances. Abba was always an old stodge, you know. Refused to dance, didn't like to go out every night. And then, of course, Gramma was so much younger and so *very* beautiful.'

'I don't think she was.'

She smiled at me as she always did when I was on her side for the wrong reason. 'She was, you know, whatever else one might have thought of her.'

'But was Dad happy? Before he met you, I mean?'

She narrowed her eyes on to me and pointed her nose. 'All I know is that he told *me* how out of place he felt. He didn't feel as if he belonged anywhere. British here, South African there, uncomfortable with Jews, a Jew amongst Gentiles. You can just imagine! Poor Dad! I was the first person he'd been able to talk to since he'd come back. And, of course, I could be very sympathetic.'

'Were you sympathetic?'

'I just said I was.'

'You said you could have been.'

'Oh, come along, Ruth, stop quibbling. In a manner of speaking I was *exactly* what he'd been hoping for.'

I believed her now. But I felt, somehow, that he hadn't stopped hoping. 'Was he exactly what you'd been hoping for?' I asked.

'Ha!' She threw her head back and barked. 'He was the very spirit and image!'

'But him himself. Was it him?'

' "*He* himself", darling. "Was it *he*?" '

It was the difference between us, between her truth and mine. I couldn't have a vision out of nothing. First I had to see Bernard. Then I could make him into something for my future.

'When did he ask you to marry him?' I asked.

The question sobered her back into the present. 'Oh, all along he kept asking. But what's the good of asking? He wouldn't do anything without their OK. Which, in effect, was *her* OK. He couldn't really. Didn't have the wherewithal, nor did I.' She waved her nose around the room as if my grandmother still hung in the air. 'If I hadn't pushed things he'd probably still be asking . I went to see her, you know.'

This was new. My heart leapt in hope.

'One day I simply phoned Abba at the shop and asked whether I could come to see them both after dinner. Dad was in one of the student shows that night. I told Abba I wanted the meeting kept confidential.

'He must have forced her to stay home that night, God knows how. He never had much control over her. But she was there, all right, pale and grim. She didn't even get up when I came in, didn't offer me a thing, not a drink, nothing. He had to order tea. Always been a decent chap, you have to give him that. A bit lacking in imagination, but *decent*.

' "I came to tell you that I'm prepared to give Roger up," I said. "I know you think me unsuitable. I'm older than he. You don't want your son to marry an actress or to make a career for himself in the theatre. All you have to do is to tell me to end it and I shall tell him that I'll never see him again."

'They stared at me in absolute silence. Couldn't believe their ears. Gramma even offered me more tea.

'I took the tea and sipped and kept them waiting a bit. Then I delivered the blow. "If I do end my relationship with your son, however, I want you to know that I shall have to tell him the reason why. Roger is madly in love with me, as I am with him. I'm not at all sure how he'll take the news. But I will not marry your son without your blessing and that is that." ' She raised her chin and held me in one of her pauses.

Then suddenly she collapsed into a triumphant laugh. 'Ha!

Ho! Ha! It was *Traviata* of course, only in reverse! I *knew* it would work and it did! Hand me my cigarettes, darling.'

She smiled up at the ceiling with her hand stretched out to receive the cigarettes. Perhaps she was still listening to her success, all this time away, still playing Hedda Gabler. She certainly wasn't hearing the dogs barking or smelling the Sunday duck, as I was.

I stared at her, the curtain down, and wondered whether she was as lonely on her platform as I was watching. The truth seemed to be somewhere between us, shifting and changing. Last night. Dad and Gwen. Perhaps *Traviata* had worked for her back then. Or perhaps it worked only now, in the telling. There was no knowing. Things only seemed to happen for her if they worked. Other things, ordinary things that just happened – messy, unformed things – needed time so that she could shift the ground beneath them. The ground seemed to be shifting underneath us all the time, sets switching, scenes changing. We had no real history. I was going to have to find the truth another way.

One Saturday night, many years before, my parents had gone to a party in Silverpark, on the other side of town. Nora sat with her knitting on the front stairs while I leapt and shrieked from room to room with Lucy, who had come to spend the night.

Suddenly we heard Nora's voice. 'Ubani lowa?' she called out.

We flew to the top of the stairs and stood in silence behind her. A key was turning in the front door, someone struggling with the lock.

Nora's buttocks began to quiver. 'Ubani lowa?' she whispered.

And then suddenly my mother burst in through the door. She held her satin evening shoes in one hand. Her hair stood out wildly from her head. Her stockings were torn and laddered.

Nora moved slowly down the stairs and we moved behind her. 'Madam?' she said.

My mother just stared at her. Her mascara had smudged all around her eyes. 'You can go now,' she said in a sort of croak.

'Hhawu! How did Madam come home?' Nora asked.

'Walked.'

'Awu, Madam she pass the Umgeni Bush?'

I followed my mother up to her room and Lucy followed me. She didn't seem to notice us behind her. She was breathing loudly, as if she'd been running. I stood back as she closed her bedroom door and heard the key turn in the lock. Then the door to my father's dressing-room. Then the verandah door. The door from their bathroom to the passage. She'd locked us all out.

After a while there were loud sobs, with gasps between, as if she couldn't take in enough air. They went on for a while and then stopped. And then we heard the garage close and the front gate slam, my father's measured tread up the front steps, his key in the lock, and the bunch dropped as usual into the brass bowl on the kist. Lucy and I hid in the dark tunnel to the children's wing. We heard him climb the stairs and try the bedroom door, then the dressing-room, the verandah, the bathroom.

'Sarah!' he said. 'Open this door at once!'

We waited, holding our hands over our mouths to muffle our breathing.

'Sarah! I don't want to have to raise my voice!'

Nothing.

He went downstairs into the flower pantry where he kept his tools. Then up he came with a screwdriver and some spare keys. He fiddled with the dressing-room lock, tried different keys, screwed and unscrewed things, until he had the door open.

'Get out!' she boomed.

'You *walked*! Are you quite mad? Do you realize you could have got yourself killed?'

There were murders in Umgeni Bush, and troops of monkeys that bit you if you got out of your car. Not even street lights. A huge dark tangle of trees and monkey ropes and monkeys and murderers. The thought of my mother marching past there all the way home almost stopped my breath with pride.

'What kind of blithering fool are you anyway?'

'*Me?*' she bellowed. '*Me* the fool! *Me* the fool? ME?' She went on shouting 'me', 'me', at him until her voice began to crack.

'You and your damned fool temper! What kind of a scene do you think you left behind you when everyone discovered you were gone?'

'Me! Yes! I suppose I am the fool! Fool to have married you! Twopenny-halfpenny cheap flirt! Kissing that tart, that bit of fluff, where you *thought* you couldn't be seen! How dare you?'

He moved into his dressing-room and she followed him, shouting the names of women, some people I knew.

'Sarah, calm down. You'll wake the children.'

'*Playboy!* Leon always called you a playboy!'

His shoetrees clicked shut and he placed his shoes outside the door. 'Perhaps you can explain to me how walking home past Umgeni Bush is meant to punish me?'

Even I knew she must have wanted to worry him to death. But she couldn't tell him. She slammed some cupboard doors and blew her nose. I wanted to leap out of the tunnel and tell him for her.

'Where do you think you'd be without me?' she asked, crying now. 'Nowhere! A *bit part* schoolboy amateur! In your father's shop selling carpets!'

'Perhaps,' he said. 'And perhaps I'd be better off. Now shall we spend the night hurling acrimony at each other or should we continue the discussion in the morning when we've both had a decent night's sleep?'

In the morning there was only silence. She didn't speak to him for a month. She hardly spoke to any of us. It was the first siege that I could remember.

11

Two weeks into rehearsals I knew the show would be a failure. I could hear it all around me, like my mother heard success. All day Nora sang hymns, as if someone had died. She dried out the chicken and undercooked the fish. Even Reuben had to be told his uniform needed washing and that there was a hole in one glove. Night after night Bernard picked Valerie up from the theatre and delivered her home at two or three in the morning. There was nothing my father could do about this. She made a point of being grown up and she didn't seem to need his special comfort anymore. He took to visiting Catherine's baby every evening on the way home from the theatre. But Catherine didn't want him either. He complained to my mother that she was barely civil. My mother didn't hear. She sighed a lot and took sleeping pills to sleep. Gwen was making trouble all round, she kept saying. She'd gathered a whole coterie around her, whispering and muttering. And her performance was lousy. They'd made a terrible mistake bringing her out. And to top it all the theatre roof had leaks. The pest control department said the place was riddled with white ants. Hundreds of pounds to fix things and where would we find it? I began to worry too. About us and about me. I couldn't bear to be dragged into their failure. But I saw no way out.

Only Jocelyn cheered me up. Somehow, talking to her gave

me hope. She read the paper every day and asked me what I thought of separate universities for blacks and the Treason Trial and boycotts. No one in the family had any time for what was going on in the country. And I didn't have much interest. But it was like Abba and his stories. I talked about politics to Jocelyn and she talked about leaving a sinking ship. There was my hope. It was all I had to think of when I saw no way out.

A week before opening night Gwen announced that her throat was sore and she'd lost her voice. She went to bed.

My mother sat on the couch staring into her cup of cold coffee. The rehearsal had gone badly that day. I'd heard her say that she'd had to give Gwen what for. 'That's all we're short of now!' she kept saying. 'What are we going to do if she's ill?'

No one dared to answer her. Jocelyn frowned ahead as if she were considering the question seriously. We both knew that Gwen was putting it on. It was the best way she could find of getting back at my mother.

'Her performance may be lousy, but her name's a draw,' my mother wailed. 'It's in all the ads.'

The doorbells rang and shrieked.

'Run, darling,' my mother said to me. 'See if that's Dr Slatkin.'

'It's Bernard,' I said. 'He rings both bells.'

'Go anyway. Run!'

I hated answering the door to Bernard. He and Valerie tried to outdo each other with lateness. And she always won. She would wait in her room for at least ten minutes after he arrived. Lately he'd taken to stroking my bottom or holding me tight by my arms to stare into my eyes. He could still force blood into my cheeks and ears and deprive me of my voice. I began to dread the effect of our encounters.

'Little one!' he crooned as he came in.

I backed up against the kist.

'Who is it?' my mother called out.

'The big bad wolf,' he growled.

I heard her snort. With things the way they were she didn't even have thought or voice for him.

He came to stand right up against me. 'Let's have a look at you,' he said. One half of his mouth curled up into his beard exposing a flash of teeth.

I heard Valerie's door slam. 'Here she is,' I said.

He'd heard it too. But he just stood there with his hips at my waist, with my chest heaving and my eyes trying to find somewhere else to look. As she started down the stairs he leaned over me and bent his head to the nape of my neck. His lips and his beard moved so lightly over my skin that all my senses strained to follow their touch. Not even Valerie's shadow coming down towards us, her gasp, her Shocking Schiaparelli, warned me of danger. I heard her scream at a great distance, felt the clasp of her bag slamming against my temple. But I only wanted him back, his lips on my skin again. My mother flung open the door. My father came out into the hall. Jocelyn loomed somewhere behind them.

'My God!' My mother ran to me and held my chin in her hands. 'Roger! There's a gash right down her face!'

'Bitch!' Valerie screamed. 'Cheap tart! Bitch!'

Bernard held her arm, but she hit out with the other, and kicked at him. He laughed. 'The fighting Franks!' he said. 'Come on, my beauty! Christ, you're gorgeous when you're worked up!' He pulled her out of the door, still laughing.

'Got a little Gentian Violet?' Jocelyn asked.

'Perhaps it needs a stitch!' my mother boomed. 'Roger! Stop standing there gaping and give me your hankie before the child bleeds to death!'

Nora arrived to say goodnight. 'Hhawu!' she whispered. She tiptoed up and peered at the side of my face. 'Who done that thing?'

And then I saw Nora's face and felt the sting, and my temple ached, and I burst into tears.

The doorbell rang.

'Slatkin at last!' my mother boomed. 'Don't worry, darling, here comes the doctor. Someone let him in!'

My parents didn't approve of physical violence. They never spanked us, and seldom hit, except occasionally when my mother lost control of her temper and an arm at the same time. She, I think, would have made a natural hitter, but my father's horror of corporal punishment, nurtured by all the canings and cruelties of his boarding school days, prevailed. Oddly enough, his horror of formal violence, and of the violent actions of others, didn't extend to his own schoolboy delight in practical jokes. Or prevent him from giving surprise half-Nelsons to bring one begging to one's knees. Or from flicking a napkin at an arm or a leg like a whip. Or whipping the back of his hand across one of our bottoms as he passed. Our yells and protests only made him laugh more heartily at his success. Not even my mother could convince him that that sort of pain wasn't at all funny.

Dr Slatkin pronounced my wound superficial and could see nothing wrong with Gwen's throat. He didn't ask how I had been hit and my parents didn't say. Except for my father's jokes, the violence that happened amongst us was another family secret. It was turned, over time, into passion. Or lack of inhibition. We were a family of fighters, my mother would say with a laugh! Passions ran high!

Only Nora acknowledged the value of corporal punishment. Although she had been forbidden to lay a hand on us, she had often slapped us while she was nanny. And she still liked to pinch and pull hair. She knew we'd never report her. There was a delicate balance to be maintained between servants and parents. Betraying one to the other only made things worse for us.

'Hee! Hee! She grabbed a handful of my hair and pulled. 'Remember how I make you eat?'

She'd been ordered to sit with me while I bathed in case I fainted from the pain of Valerie's blow.

I laughed politely. Nora seemed quite sure that the slapping and hairpulling had been hilarious for us both.

'How's Constance?' I asked.

'Still struggle to pass standard four.'

'She'll pass, don't worry, Nors.'

'She *got* to pass. You already in standard six. She fail, fail, fail, every year. Every year she want money, money, money.

She got to hurry up, I say. I'm getting old. She must hurry up to take care of her old mother.'

'You're not old!'

'Too old! Too much worry! Too much work!' She pulled off her cap and bent her head to me, pointing here and there at her little plaits. 'Look the grey!'

'You shouldn't give her money till she's passed,' I said. Constance irritated me with her demands on Nora. She was massive and solid and sullen. Stupid too.

Nora replaced the cap and closed her lips. I never knew how she considered my advice to her on Constance. She never responded.

'I mean why should you keep sending money when you don't even know whether she'll pass?'

'She pass this time. I hit her if she fail. She know.'

'Hitting won't help.'

She looked down at me in the bath. 'We got our own ways,' she said.

My eye kept catching the pink of the Elastoplast as I sat drinking tea with the others. The skin stung now. I felt heroic under their glances. No one had asked about Bernard. They knew he was to blame and why. But he stood far beyond the compass of their disapproval. It was as if Valerie had chosen an Eskimo or an Inca, as if both of us were under the spell of his dangerous heathen powers.

I touched my neck, where his beard and lips had been. I was glad that Valerie had seen us, thrilled with my power to take him back. Even though I knew he was still hers. I didn't even care why he had done it.

'That Gwen is putting it on,' my mother said. 'She's been trouble from the start. Her performance is lousy and she knows it. What I simply don't understand is how she's got where she has.'

'Sarah –' Jocelyn sat forward and lowered her voice. 'If worst came to worst couldn't you take the part yourself?'

I knew then that Gwen would not go on. Jocelyn didn't play

games with words and cheap comfort.

'Me? I'm far too old for Mary! I'd never get away with it.'

'Rot! I'm far too old for Sylvia in that case, aren't I?'

My mother shook her head. But I could see she was thinking about herself in the part, about the money, how much they'd still have to pay Gwen if she didn't go on. 'I'll bet she doesn't pull this sort of thing on the Jo'burg crowd,' she said.

'We're not absolutely sure she's "pulling" anything,' my father said.

'Well!' Jocelyn clapped her hands on to her thighs and stood up. 'I'm off to bed. Nine to six tomorrow, hey Sarah?'

My mother bit her lip and nodded. She'd dropped all her roles now – Duchess of Windsor, world-famous director. She didn't even notice Jocelyn leave.

I jumped on to the couch between my parents, laid my hand lightly on my mother's shoulder as if she were a lost child who might scream at the touch of a stranger. 'Don't worry,' I said.

She looked up at me and her eyes filled with tears. 'I'm the only one who does worry!' she cried. 'I'm sick and tired of being the only one who worries!'

'I worry too. I worry all the time.'

Her eyes narrowed on me even through the tears. 'You! What've you got to worry about? Don't be stupid!' She shook her shoulder free of my hand and turned away.

My father reached over and patted my knee. 'Better leave your mother alone, Chops,' he murmured.

I stood up to hide my own tears. I had wasted the truth on her and I felt stupid. And cheap for the cheap comfort I'd tried to give her. Who was I to tell her not to worry? We weren't even playing at Happy Families anymore.

'Valerie's ghastly!' she wept. 'I told you she wouldn't do. But no, you had to have her! She still can't use her hands. She can't even walk across the stage! And now this creature's letting us down! What are we going to do?'

She'd forgotten me already. Without a role, just herself as she was – worried and angry and lonely – she seemed to notice only my father.

'Good night,' I said.

'Watch out for that wound,' she called after me. 'Don't sleep on that side. You don't want a scar.'

By Wednesday Gwen had taken her money and left for a rest cure in Rob Roy. My mother settled into the part of Mary. All the tricks of timing and technique, the way she used her head and her hands, her voice, her walk – everything she did evoked the grief and pride of a woman betrayed.

Valerie was put out. 'It's stupid to be acting against you,' she said. 'It's beyond belief. You're too old for the part.'

'Nonsense!' Jocelyn guffawed. Valerie's flirtation with Jocelyn had ended the first night Bernard came to the house. 'One doesn't act *against*, one acts *with*. And from what I've seen your mother could play Ophelia if she cared to.'

Valerie tossed the hair off her face. 'Well, I don't want *my* career affected,' she said.

'Your what?' my mother boomed, herself again suddenly.

'My career.'

'Ha! Roger! Did you hear that? That's a laugh!'

'Sarah, don't rise to the bait. Think of what lies ahead, please.'

My mother cocked her head like one of the dogs. Then something seemed to come to her, the survival of the theatre, perhaps. Or even of the family. She smiled at Valerie. 'I think I'll ask Devson to give you and me a splash in *The Times* Friday, shall I? Mother and daughter sort of thing. We could certainly use the publicity. What do you think?'

Valerie looked up quickly. She suspected all acts of kindness. 'What are you wearing for your final bow?' she asked.

'Why, I'll wear what I wear in the last scene. What choice do I have now that I'm in the show?'

'That should do admirably!' Jocelyn said. 'You look absolutely gorgeous in that scarlet chiffon!'

'So you'll get a white orchid as usual,' Valerie sneered. She smiled triumphantly. My father's orchids were always given and received as a great surprise.

He stared down at his place mat. When Valerie's viciousness wrapped itself around him he was bewildered by the pain. 'There will be orchids for the three of you,' he said. 'All white. I always send white.'

I watched Valerie smile, the way she glanced sideways at my mother, her black eyes darting from her to him.

'Jealous swine!' I shouted. I had to swallow. I was crying for them, for my mother and father. 'You want everything she's got! You're like a thief! Well, ha! No orchid's going to stop you being a flop! You're only getting one because Dad feels sorry for you! Everyone says you can't act to save your life!'

'Get her out of my sight!' Valerie screamed. She leapt up in her place and grabbed the salt cellar and threw it hard at me. But it missed and banged against the drinks cabinet.

'Darling,' my mother said, calm again in her new role. 'Don't provoke Valerie now. Please. For my sake.'

I grabbed my own salt cellar and held it back to throw. 'You'll never, never be a quarter as good as Ma is! An eighth! A hundredth! You're a hopeless flop! You can't even find your own husband!'

It worked. The truth sent her screaming from the room, gasping and raging and knocking over chairs. I didn't need to throw anything.

'God!' My mother rested her elbows on the table and her forehead in her hands. 'Did you have to start something *now*?'

Abba stood up in his place to face me. Towards opening night we tended to forget about him. He got quieter and quieter so that no one could blame him for what went wrong. 'Perhaps you should apologize to your sister,' he suggested.

'I never will!' I shouted. 'I never will because it's the truth!'

'Apologies won't help!' my mother snapped. 'At this rate we're going to need a bloody miracle!'

I had never been able to read a play properly. I missed the dialogue for all the stage directions and I could never remember who was saying what. On stage things were only slightly better. Most of the actors I had seen couldn't give life to the words they spoke or to the parts they played. They exaggerated their smiles and 'Ohs' and 'Ahs' so much that I shuffled in my seat with embarrassment. And their words had the sort of elocuted magnification that no one but Janet McGuire's students ever used in normal speech.

Jocelyn was different. She wasn't Jocelyn anymore up there. She was Sylvia, the bitch. She waved her fingers so delicately around her mouth that one didn't notice the hugeness of her hands. She crossed her long legs carefully, as if she creamed and cared for them every day. Smiled in the way other women smile, with menace. I could even hate her as I sat forward in my seat.

When my mother made her entrance, a few people in the audience clapped – they'd seen *The Times* article on her and Valerie and Gwen's illness. She paused for silence. She raised her chin and voice. 'Sylvia, must you always send me woebegone creatures like that lingerie woman?'

My ears caught fire and my breathing almost stopped. I stared down into my lap.

My father patted my knee. 'All right, Chops?' he whispered. I nodded.

He was tense. His nostrils were flared as if he would weep. Perhaps it was for my mother up there again. Or for Valerie making her début. I couldn't bear to look at him. Or at Abba smiling up at scene after scene as if he were watching *Peter Pan*.

'Here comes Val,' my father whispered as the curtain rose on scene four.

I looked up, my heart clopping in my chest. I had lost track of the scenes and the story, thinking of my mother and of Jocelyn. Of England, of *being* someone. Valerie was nothing. I didn't even see her.

I saw only my mother. She smiled up there as Mary would have smiled, and glanced at herself in the mirror with the misgivings that Mary would have had. She was gone into her other self now, far away again. Her real self playing Mary.

But she wasn't Mary. Next to Jocelyn my mother was just an actress. I understood now why she had come back from England. I believed now what I knew already to be the truth. She never could have been a Jocelyn Hopswith. Never ever. And I didn't believe the myth about Hedda Gabler anymore.

The cast stood in a row on stage, with my mother in the middle. Jocelyn and Valerie pulled her forward for her bow as director. She smiled and nodded, she bowed her head and raised her hands. She mouthed 'Thank you! Thank you!' And she clasped her hands over her heart and closed her eyes. Someone brought on a bouquet of flowers. She gasped in mock surprise. I could barely breathe.

'Going backstage?' Abba asked. He always asked this. He loved his pride of place there.

People shook our hands and patted our shoulders as we squeezed towards the stage door. I looked into their faces as they spoke to my father. And listened to their voices. They hadn't liked the show. I could see, I could hear that for myself.

'Mr Frank! There you are!'

I spun around. Miss Robinson was mowing her way through the crowd towards my father.

'And Mr Frank senior, how do you do, sir? I'm Emily Robinson, headmistress of Rangston.'

I smiled and tried to shrink away. But she fixed her frown on me.

'And young Ruth up till all hours! Do you really think this play suitable for young gels, Mr Frank? Ha! Ha!'

The laugh meant nothing. I knew this was why she'd come to find us.

My father gave her the delicate John Barrymore gaze that he used to charm difficult old ladies. 'Oh, Miss Robinson, one can't protect them from everything, now can one? Would you care to come backstage with us?'

She whooped out another laugh. 'Oh, no, thank you very much! I can't imagine what I'd say! And there's Miss Powers now, waiting in the cold. I *do* hope you're coming to support your daughter in the Rangston–Brighton debate? *Jolly* good fun I should think it'll be! We're counting on Ruth, you know! Well, good night, Mr Franks two! Good night, Ruth!'

The debate now, my own performance to worry about. And my mother's failure infecting everything, even Rangston. I wanted to cry.

Backstage, I hid myself on the prompt's chair behind one of the wings. I was terrible at pretending enthusiasm. I couldn't even get the right smiles, or the arms spread wide in ecstasy. Anyway, all words of praise had vanished. I could think of none to lie with, not even for Jocelyn.

'Sarah! Congratulations! What a splendid job!'

'*Darling!*' she said. 'How *lovely* of you to have come!'

But I could see from the smile on her face that she knew they were lying. I could see from the way she breathed.

'Your mother was wonderful,' someone said.

I jumped. This is what I dreaded. Being lied to myself. Sucked into lying back.

'Want to go on the stage one day like Valerie?' It was one of my mother's students. He hunkered down next to me.

I shook my head.

'Why?' He grasped the chair and bounced up and down like Jeffrey.

'I hate acting,' I mumbled.

He laughed and pushed my arm playfully. 'Junk, man!'

I blushed now to have been touched by him and stared into my lap.

'Go to Rangston?' he asked.

I nodded.

Bounce, bounce, he seemed to want to stay. 'Who d'you mix with?'

I shrugged. Edwina? Who could I name? I had no one. 'People you wouldn't know.'

'Ever been to Habonim?'

I looked down at him and shook my head again. I knew of Habonim from the students at Hebrew school. It seemed to be a sort of military youth movement for the children of people who liked to pretend they would rather be living in Israel. The members wore uniforms and used Hebrew words whenever they could. They sang Israeli songs and the Israeli national

168

anthem and saluted the Israeli flag. The whole thing sounded horrible to me. But there would be boys. Suddenly I wanted desperately to be invited. I didn't even care if he only wanted me because I was my mother's daughter. 'I'd like to go one day,' I said.

He pounced on to the back of my chair and shook it. 'Saturday night? I'll give you a ring.'

'Well, darling!' My mother stood before my chair now. 'Well?'

'Well what?'

'How did you like it?' How was the show?'

A few of the actors and stagehands had gathered behind her and looked eagerly into my face, as if I were a critic or a connoisseur.

'I don't know,' I mumbled. I shrugged myself back into the chair as far from her as possible.

'My generally articulate youngest daughter!' she boomed. She laughed. They all laughed with her.

But when we got home and were picking our way behind my father and Jocelyn and Valerie to the front door, she threw an arm around my shoulders and asked again.

'Well, what did you think of me in that part, darling? You haven't seen me on stage for ages now.'

I shrugged off her arm. 'You were stupid!' I spat out. '*Stupid!*'

She stopped and stared at me. Her chest heaved, her nails dug into the flesh of her upper arms. 'You are turning into rather a nasty little piece of work, aren't you?'

I shrugged again. She had never branded me like this before, like she branded Valerie, or a servant proved to be disloyal.

'Would it have hurt you to give your mother a little encouragement? Even if you didn't mean it?' There was a sob in her voice and tears in her eyes. She swung away from me quickly and disappeared into the house.

I stood stunned under the glare of the front lawn spotlight. 'A little encouragement'? Encouraged by me? She, so full of courage, encouraged if I were to approve? Or even to pretend to approve? A whole audience had clapped her and she had closed her eyes, covered her heart with her hands. But she wanted *my* approval. She had asked me for it. Twice. 'Well, what did you think of me?' she had said. I knew that question. I knew the voice, the bluff. They were my own. Even the sob, the tears, the rage. We both knew the sound of failure.

The dogs were out now, prancing around me, lifting legs against trees, barking at shadows.

I ran up the front steps and through the hall, up the stairs two and three at a time. She was in her bedroom, struggling to unzip her dress.

'I'm sorry!' I sobbed. I clasped her tightly from behind. 'I'm sorry, I'm sorry!'

'Hey! Hey!' She unfastened my arms and turned to me. 'What's this now?'

I buried my face in her neck. 'I'm sorry!' I gasped.

'Oh, come on! Enough of this sorry! We all say things we don't mean –' She held up my chin in the palm of her hand. 'Look! I've got a present for you.'

She pulled up the skirt of her dress and knelt before the bottom drawer of her tallboy. It was the place where she kept her perfume, boxes of razor blades, her jewellery, small gifts of bath salts in porcelain jars, still unopened – things locked away like alcohol from the servants. I watched her kneeling there in her stockinged feet, her dress gaping open across the white skin of her back, the determined movements with which she searched the drawer for some treasure to end my misery. Our misery.

'Ah!' she said. 'How about this?' She held up a little white and gold box that I knew well.

'No,' I said. 'It's yours.'

'Take it! Here!'

I took the box and held it in my hand unopened.

'Darling, I *want* you to have it!' She looked up into my face wanting only to see me happy.

I knew what was in the box. The ring her mother had given her when she returned from England. A faceted amethyst – 'not a particularly good one' – with tiny pearls arranged in a circle around it. And underneath a filigree basket of gold to hold the stone off the finger.

'But it's yours,' I said. 'I can't have it.'

She pushed the drawer closed and turned the key. 'Not anymore,' she said. 'Don't look a gift horse in the mouth!'

I opened the box and stared at the ring. I couldn't give it back. I knew she wouldn't take it. But it felt like a theft. I began to weep again.

'Good God! Now come alone, darling! Get undressed and I'll come and say good night. And put the ring in your locked drawer, by the way. It's not a particularly good stone, but it's probably worth something.'

171

12

My mother sat in her bedroom chair letting her egg grow cold. It was eight o'clock. She had been up since five, waiting for the Sunday paper to arrive.

'How will we tell her?' she asked my father.

He sat in bed, grey and yellow in the morning light. 'Let me handle this,' he said.

'Handle what?' I asked.

'Here.' He handed me the paper. 'You may as well know. But not a word to Valerie, please. Either before or after I have spoken to her.'

'Frank women fail in *The Women*,' I read. 'Why, oh why, did Mrs Frank put her daughter on the stage? The wonderful team of Roger and Sarah Frank that has served us so well all these years has suffered attrition by the addition of Valerie Frank, their daughter. Not only can Miss Frank not act, but she was positively embarrassing to watch last night in the opening performance of Clare Boothe's *The Women* at the Frank Theatre.

'If there is any reason to see *The Women* it is for the performance of that marvellous English actress, Miss Jocelyn Hopswith. Miss Hopswith was indeed the saving grace of the evening. What timing! What care! And what a voice! But unfortunately not even Miss Hopswith could float this production. It was sunk from the start.'

I put the paper down and looked at my mother. 'Sunk?'

She didn't wring her hands or rub her eyes or march furiously between the window and the wardrobe as she usually did after a bad write-up. This was far beyond our usual dramas. She just ran her long nails lightly along both arms of the chair. 'How are we going to finish the run?' she asked.

'She wasn't that bad,' I said. I too was scared. And thrilled too. Nothing like this had ever happened to us.

'Just how will we finish the run?'

My father flared his nostrils. 'What, may I ask, is the point in repeating such a question *ad nauseam*?'

'And Devson!' she exploded. 'How could Devson of all people do this to us?'

'Do what?' he snapped. 'It's his job! He's paid for his opinions!'

'To be so ruthless –' Her voice was breaking. 'He's never been so ruthless befo –' She looked up suddenly. 'Has he ever taken the girl out?'

'Possibly. Yes, perhaps, once.'

'Ah!'

'Ah what!? He's a critic. Why should he bring his personal feelings to bear –'

'Oh, don't be stupider than you can help!'

'I'll choose to ignore that remark in view of the circumstances.'

'Gugh!' She folded her arms and turned away to look out over the bay. ' "Attrition-addition"! He can't even write!'

'It's one bad review, for heaven's sake. Try to see the thing in perspective.'

She twitched further away and folded up more tightly.

Valerie burst into the room. She snatched the paper out of my hands. 'Well?' she demanded. 'How did I do?'

The box office was the worst ever. They decided to cut the run from two weeks to one. Every house had to be papered. My father delivered rolls of tickets to Our Jewish Home for the Aged and to the School for the Deaf and the Blind. He even sent

173

some next door for the Knowles and the other people in the flats. Jocelyn told tale after tale of flops she'd been in in London. Publicly my mother continued to blame Charles Devson. She wouldn't even invite him to the cast party. But I heard her shouting at my father behind their bedroom door. 'You and your bright ideas! You're the one who wanted her for Crystal! And who's left holding the baby, hey? Can you tell me that?'

Only Valerie herself seemed unconcerned. Happy even. She seemed to enjoy her power to ruin the show and my mother along with it.

'Charles Devson!' She sneered. 'It's not Charles Devson! It's Ma! She's a has-been! She's a flop! If Charles Devson were less of a drip he'd have just come out and said it!'

We were waiting to light the candles on Friday night, the night before the final performance. My mother had gone off to find her matches.

Catherine yawned. 'How long is this going to take?' she asked.

'Here we are then,' my mother said. 'Jocelyn? Want to come in and watch?'

Catherine rolled her eyes. I rolled mine too. Jews on stage embarrassed us both.

Jocelyn bustled in. 'Oh, jolly good! I shall always remember the Frank women best around their Friday-night table! Wish *we* could get Friday nights off. Perhaps I should convert. Ha! Ha!'

I hadn't spoken to Jocelyn since opening night. She was always either at the theatre or asleep. I longed to be alone with her so that she could stop pretending nothing was wrong. Now more than ever I wanted that special way she had of making the truth matter-of-fact.

We waved our hands over the candles and covered our eyes. Jocelyn, her face composed in deadly horsey earnest, copied us.

'Hail, Mary, mother of God,' Valerie intoned.

Catherine laughed a little. I snorted into my hands.

My mother sighed loudly. 'Baruch atah adonai,' she started. We all joined in. I peeped through my fingers at Jocelyn, who

174

was peeping back at me. I smiled. Perhaps she saw through this too. I hoped so.

'Shel Shabat!' we chorused.

'All right, men!' my mother boomed. 'Come on. I'm ringing the bell.'

'So, what's next on the agenda?' Jeffrey crashed down his pudding spoon and grinned.

My mother raised an eyebrow at him. 'Agenda?'

'The next show. What's next?' He pushed himself back in his chair. He was getting fat like his father. His shirt pulled at the buttons and he wore a gold ring on his little finger.

Jocelyn's kind eyes swept around the table in her large still face.

'As soon as we decide,' my mother assured him with one of her public smiles, 'you'll be the very first to know!'

But she had lost most of her power to bring him down. 'P'raps this one's a bit much for the locals,' he suggested. He blushed. He guffawed and slapped at Catherine. 'Hey, Cath? All that wife-swopping, hey?'

She smiled at him. There was apparently nothing he could say that wouldn't bring out a smile.

'Oh, no, surely not?' Jocelyn said. 'In this day and age! I must say I haven't had so much fun for ages!' She held up her wine glass. 'Here's to wonderful shows in the future and the continued success of the Frank Theatre!'

We reached for our glasses and drank.

My mother just held up her glass and then put it down again. She was superstitious and hated to toast continued bad luck. 'What time is this affair of yours tomorrow night?' she asked me. 'And how do you propose to get there?'

'What affair?' Valerie demanded.

'Ruth's been invited to Habonim,' my mother said. 'I suppose there's no harm in it.'

'*Habonim!*' Valerie shouted.

'No harm at all,' Abba said. 'Quite the contrary, my dear.'

Valerie tied her napkin around her head like a scarf. She jumped up and leapt around the table. 'Hava nagila! Hava

175

nagila! Hava nagila! Ve nishmagha!'

'Valerie! Sit down!' my father barked. 'Do you realize this is Friday night?'

'From Indians to Zionists! Perhaps she'll take on the Matabele next! Who asked her?'

'Could someone explain to me what "Habonim" is?' Jocelyn asked quickly. 'I'm so hopelessly ignorant, you know!'

Abba cleared his throat. 'There's no question of ignorance, my dear,' he said. 'Habonim is one of several Zionist youth movements all over the world. It was founded for the encouragement and training of our Jewish boys and girls between the ages of about thirteen and seventeen who wish to contribute to the building of the state of Israel. The word itself means build —'

'Abba,' I shouted, 'can Johannes pick me up from Habonim tomorrow night?'

'Certainly, my dear,' he said.

'And just how are you getting there?' my father asked.

'Garth Finkelstein,' I mumbled.

'Garth Finkelstein! Valerie shouted. *Garth Finkelstein!*'

'Oh, come along, Valerie,' my mother snapped. 'What do you think you're achieving by shouting "Garth Finkelstein, Garth Finkelstein"?'

'*Edwina* Slomovitz and *Garth* Finkelstein! Ha! Ha!'

'Who is the family?' Abba asked.

It's what I had dreaded. The jokes, the questions, the 'this' and 'that' of my mother. The family's standard punishment for anyone who tried to leave, even for a night. I'd taken part in the fun myself, we all had. But now I was beginning to understand the fear behind the ridicule, the terror really of the real world and the people out there in it. As if their touching us would make us disappear. Catherine had disappeared. Perhaps they thought that I would too.

'The father's a salesman of some sort,' my mother said. 'Simple sort of mother. The boy's one of our poorer students.'

'One can only hope his Zionism is of a higher calibre than his acting,' my father said. He never had any difficulty finding objections to the males who laid claim to his daughters.

'He's half-witted,' Valerie said.

'So are you!' I spat back.

My mother sighed and rubbed her eyes. 'Valerie, don't be rude.'

'Me? What about *her*?'

'Rude, rude, rude,' I sang. Only one more show. Things couldn't be worse than they were already.

'Sorry, Madam –' Reuben stood at the door, staring at his toes.

'Yes, Reuben, what is it?'

But he just stood there, silent.

This meant that what he had to say was for her alone. She sighed and pushed back her chair. 'Carry on without me, please,' she said.

But being left to carry on with the rest of the family didn't appeal to me. I excused myself and followed her to the kitchen.

'What's going on?' she demanded.

'In the compound, Madam.' Servants were very good at answering the wrong question.

I followed them at a distance, hung back in the shadow of the mulberry tree. Low bleats and moans came from the compound yard. And a sort of rhythmical beat, like the flapping of sheets in the wind.

'Nora! Nora!' My mother's voice rose from the compound to carry over five blocks. 'Stop it this instant! I shall call the police! I shall call the Flying Squad!'

I ran to the compound gate and slid past it, down the path.

'Gha! Gha!' Nora rasped.

'Someone switch on the light out here!'

Two floodlights immediately exposed the yard and the people in it. Nora stood like a lion-tamer in the middle, waving a switch from the mulberry tree. John and Reuben hung one behind the other against the wall in front of me. In the far corner, up against the incinerator, Constance lay curled on the ground weeping. She held one arm up to protect her face.

'Good God!' my mother boomed.

A gash across Constance's short-cropped massive head oozed thick, dark blood. Smaller gashes criss-crossed her fat arms and legs.

'Gha! Gha!' Nora panted.

'What has happened here, Nora?' My mother demanded.

Nora dropped the switch and turned to the wall to hide her face from my mother. 'Constance, Madam. She trouble.' She bent her face into her hands and began to weep – awful, broken gasps, as if something were stuck in her throat. The sound was unlike anything I had ever heard from her. I had often seen her cry. But it was usually for things lost in her life or people dead. This new sound, the turn of her back, the bend of her head, the awful cries, seemed to have nothing in them for anyone else.

'Constance!' my mother shouted above the din. 'Are you all right, my girl?'

Constance tucked her head in even further, as if my mother too would hit her.

My mother lowered her voice, didn't step any closer. 'Can you stand up, Constance? I need to know this. Otherwise I must call an ambulance.'

'I can stand, Madam.'

'Well, shall someone help you? John! Reuben! Come along, please!'

Nora looked up quickly. She curled her lips back from her teeth and bent to pick up the switch.

John stumbled back into me. 'Awu! Miss Ruth!' he said.

'Ruth!' my mother boomed. 'What are you doing here?'

And then Nora saw me. And I saw, in that second, a stranger. Someone who would use the switch on me, perhaps. Or worse. I backed up the path a little further into the dark.

'I'm going to have to help her up myself, I suppose?' my mother barked.

But Constance had managed to heave herself to her feet without help. She stood alone to face my mother. She hung her head in silence.

'Well!' My mother folded her arms and pointed her nose up and down, up and down. 'So this is what all the fuss is about!'

Despite the extra panels sewn by Nora into one of my old gym tunics, Constance's huge bulk had split the seams at the waist and sides. The hem rose high above her knees. The sleeves of the shirt cut into the flesh of her upper arms. The bodice, reinforced by top sewing and a yoke, forced her breasts down to her waist, around the child she carried in her enormous stomach.

'Nora!' my mother boomed. 'I'm going to have to call in Dr Slatkin. This girl of yours may need stitches for that cut in her head. And I want him to make sure the baby is all right!'

'Madam,' Constance muttered, 'I all right.'

'We'll see about that!' My mother wheeled around to leave. 'Wait here, please, until the doctor arrives.'

But an hour later, when Dr Slatkin arrived, Constance had vanished into the night. John and Reuben were sent to find her. They made a show of searching the bushes at the back of the house. Then they came back into the kitchen and shrugged. 'Gone, Madam. Nora she say she don't know nothing.'

'Aren't they simply maddening?' my mother fumed. 'One thinks one is helping them, but then just look at what one is up against!'

Jocelyn frowned, trying to understand. 'What could have made the girl run off like that?'

'Oh! They have this completely absurd notion we send them off to hospitals to die!'

'Well –' Jeffrey snapped his fingers at Catherine as if she were one of his dogs. 'I'm taking my wife home.'

'But it's early!' my father pleaded. 'We haven't even had coffee.'

Jeffrey raised his eyebrows in mock surprise. 'Doesn't look as if there's going to be any coffee here tonight.'

'Of course there is!' my mother boomed. 'Ruth! Go and tell Nora to hurry up and make the coffee. Sit down, you two.'

The kitchen was empty, the lights still on. No dough had been set for tomorrow's bread. I rang the bell to Nora's room and waited. The dogs milled around the sink, still waiting to be fed. They even looked hopefully at me. But I didn't know how to feed them, or what. Nora had to come back. I pushed the bell again and held my finger on it.

A shape separated itself from the darkness and moved down the laundry path towards the house. I ran to the window and rubbed away the steam. The front door slammed. I heard the staccato clicking of my mother's heels down the kitchen passage.

'Sure to stay one minute more than they have to,' she said.

The dogs jumped up and whined and barked. Someone switched on the back porch light.

'No one's fed the dogs,' I said.

'Who's there? Nora?'

'John, Madam.' He stood still, just inside the wall dividing off the sink area. The dogs leaped and wagged around him for their supper. In his hands he folded and unfolded a ragged piece of exercise book paper.

'What is it?'

'I get a letter, Madam.'

'Oh, for God's sake!'

'My uncle, Madam.'

'The same one who died last year, I suppose? Come off it, John!'

'He sick, Madam.'

'When?'

'Tonight, Madam. Please, Madam. My wages for the doctor, Madam.'

'Tonight! What about the cast party tomorrow night?'

He stared down at his feet.

'You haven't even got the proper papers, John. What if you're stopped by the police?'

He didn't look up. She was always saying you couldn't stop them if they really wanted to go. I knew she couldn't stop John now.

'Oh, God!' She spun around. She pushed one palm against her forehead and then flung it down. 'All right! Go and ask the Master for your money. I'll just have to borrow Shadrak, I suppose, although he's next to useless! John! I want you back by six o'clock Sunday *without fail*! Do you understand?'

John nodded. He couldn't look at her or at me. I knew he'd never come back. A weight began to lift off my heart.

'You haven't fed the dogs,' I said.

Nora's slippers shuffled across the back porch and through the kitchen door. John flew past me and out of the kitchen.

'Nora!' my mother barked. 'Where on earth – GOOD GOD! What is the meaning of this?'

Nora headed slowly for the tea tray. A strip of white sheeting bandaged up her lower jaw. Blood, dried dark and black, ringed her swollen lips. Both eyes oozed and blinked.

My mother folded her arms and observed Nora shrewdly. 'Where's Reuben?' she asked.

Nora tilted her head towards the compound. She pulled out the tray and smoothed a tray cloth over it.

'Did he do this to you? Because if he did he's gone too far this time. I shall get the Master to talk to him!' My mother folded her arms and shook her head. 'I just don't understand you people.'

Nora smoothed and smoothed the cloth. Every now and then she snorted and shuddered.

'Nora! I'm speaking to you!'

'I kick him out my room, Madam.'

'Well, isn't that about time? I'm surprised you didn't throw him out the first time he ever laid a hand on you!'

'I forgive him, Madam. Like Jesus he says.'

My mother stared at Nora in wonder. For a few moments the wonder seemed to lift the brick on brick of disasters that hemmed her in all round.

'But now he double-cross me, Madam.'

'What? How?'

Nora stopped and looked over her shoulder towards the kitchen door. John hovered there, holding his money between both palms.

'Well, come along, John. What are you standing there for?'

'Madam,' he said. He edged his way along the fridge and the stove to the sink, grinning and dipping and holding his cupped hands before him.

'He hasn't fed the dogs yet,' I said.

'All *right*, Ruth! John! Those dogs must be fed before you leave, please.'

We all stood in silence while he dropped the meat and bones into bowls, carried them out to the porch in a rush of dogs.

'What's all this then about double-crossing, Nora?'

'John he get Constance, Madam. Reuben he know all the time, all the time. He double-cross me, Madam.'

'What? Do you mean to say that John is the father of that child?'

'Eh-hê!'

Coffee spoons and demitasse, sugar bowl, tiny gilded sugar spoon.

My mother sighed and shook her head. 'Oh, dear! Well now, Nora, these things happen, you know, my girl. Would you like the Master to talk to them both?'

'Congo rubbish, Madam.' She set the coffee pot on the stove, switched on the plate.

A dark head passed the window. The dogs left their bowls and flew off after it, barking and snarling.

'John he tsotsi, Madam. Much worse as Reuben. Always running, running after girl, girl, girl.'

'Be that as it may, John's a good servant. You said so yourself. They're both fine servants. I want you to find a way to live with all of this, Nora.'

But I could see from the set of Nora's head that she had no intention of living with all this. The garden gate slammed shut. The dogs roared along the fence, down to the bottom of the garden.

'We find another gardenboy, Madam.'

'What?'

Nora folded her hands one over the other as she did when she asked for a favour. She bowed her head. 'Madam. Please, Madam. Beauty she bad woman. Worse as John. She curse me, Madam.'

'Don't start on that again, for God's sake, Nora!'

'Please, Madam, let Beauty go, Madam.'

My mother poked her nose forward in disbelief. She followed it for a step or two towards Nora. 'Have you gone quite mad? Good God, where am I going to find the patience to deal with this?'

Nora never had any trouble finding patience. She twisted her head and peeped up at my mother through her slitted eyes. From my corner next to the fridge, with her cheeks swollen wide, she looked almost amused.

'I've got a bloody disaster at the theatre! Thousands of pounds to find from God knows where! No gardenboy all of a sudden! My cook bandaged up like a survivor of the wars! A bloody cast party tomorrow night. And you suggest that I dismiss the laundry girl? *For God's sake!*' She raised her voice to resonate around the kitchen and Nora's aching head. 'IS THERE TO BE NO END TO THIS? HOW AM I SUPPOSED TO GO ON? CAN YOU TELL ME THAT? HEY? CAN ANYONE TELL ME HOW I'M SUPPOSED TO GO ON??'

The cooking began early the next morning. Nora moved slowly around the kitchen and pretended she couldn't speak. Reuben, with a pink plaster across his forehead, sat on the back porch polishing the silver.

Jocelyn and I were the only ones down, sitting in the warm winter sun of the breakfast-room.

'Might we go for a walk in the garden?' she asked. 'Do you know, I've been here almost a month and I've never even been into the garden proper.' She smiled her kind smile at me, so different from the sneer she wore on stage.

'I could show you the summerhouse,' I suggested. 'Or whatever you like.'

'Oh, everything! I want to see and smell it all before I return to dreary old England.' She was still making public statements. Dreary old England. I knew she was longing to get back.

We walked out on to the side lawn, down the rockery path to the summerhouse. Jocelyn followed me through the camouflage of shadows to the bench.

'Oh, how very lovely this is!' She was herself again. She

plopped on to the bench and stretched her arms up towards the canopy of bougainvillaea leaves and flowers and twisted branches. She sat forward and smiled across the lawn. 'Oh, Ruth!' she whispered urgently. 'Look at those marvellous huge black birds!'

'Hadedahs,' I said. 'They come every morning.' The English seemed so satisfied with things like birds and the smell of flowers. 'I never come here anymore,' I said.

'Oh, you will, you will. After you come back.'

I looked at her. 'From where?'

'Ruth, my dear, I want to say something to you before I leave. I'm so glad we have this chance.'

Blood rushed to my cheeks and ears. I'd completely forgotten she was a lesbian. Perhaps she would tell me that she loved me. Or grab me and kiss me.

'Shakespeare, you know, seems to say everything we want to say so much better than we can ourselves.'

She was going to do it now. 'Shall I compare thee . . .' or 'When in disgrace . . .'

'Do you know Brutus' speech, "There is a tide in the affairs of men"?'

'Yes.'

'That tide is almost here for you, you know. This country is about to explode. One has to be deaf and blind not to know that.'

I was relieved it was only the same old story. But still I didn't want to hear her *say* that my parents were deaf and blind. I knew they were. I knew I was too. The strangest deafness and blindness that let me hear and see and yet not care.

She stared at me. 'But not just the political situation, Ruth. Actually, I think that's the easier nut to crack. May I be frank?'

She smiled. I smiled at the pun.

'There are some situations – households, families, if you will – that one must remove oneself from in order to save oneself. Oh, what an awful way of putting it! I sound like one of those ghastly evangelists!'

'I know what you mean.' I thought I did. I thought she meant save myself from landing up like Catherine. Or Valerie if she married Bernard. I thought she meant marriage.

'Well, let me explain anyway. I grew up in a terribly middle-class, terribly unimaginative family. Without even knowing that they were doing it, my parents and grandparents and aunts and uncles and so forth gave us a very clear picture of what we would grow up to be. My world was very simple, really. A small village, the village school, the curate I told you about. Ha! Ha! When I was about your age I began to know that I couldn't fit into the life they'd planned for me. I thought I wanted to go to the university and become a teacher. But that's not important. What is important is that I knew what they wanted and I rejected it.'

She spread her legs and crossed her arms over her knees, like my father watching cricket, chin forward, eyes forward out over the lawn. 'With you, my dear, it's going to be a little more difficult.'

My heart began to gallop. How did she know that? And how had I known, seconds before her words were out, just what she would say? Before I even understood what the words meant?

'I don't think things have been made so clear for you, you see. Every family hangs curtains. They make up myths about themselves, almost as if they were taking part in a play. The curtain hangs between themselves on stage and the audience out there – the real world, you see. My family hung such a curtain. But our myth was quite simple. The same one really that most other families I knew had. And as familiar as "Hansel and Gretel". Players and audience, we were all the same. I knew *exactly* what I was up against. I'm not sure yours is so simple.'

My head was spinning with her words – curtains and myths and 'Hansel and Gretel' I didn't try to understand as I would have done in class. I didn't need to take a test. And yet, not knowing exactly what the words meant, I understood her meaning in every way. She was giving me words for the madness by which I felt myself infected. She was calling mad mad.

185

'You see, if the curtain is opaque one day, diaphanous the next, rising and falling at odd times, and if, as the case may be, the myth itself is murky and obtuse – well then, how are you to know what part to play? And who's the audience? How are you to know?' She peered at me through the mottled gloom. 'It's so much easier, don't you see, when one knows what one is leaving behind.'

I felt it again, the point miles above us at which anticipation met utterance. It was the point of truth.

'And in this country, well, what do you find even if you know your part? You lift the curtain and find another. And another. Curtains upon curtains upon curtains. Ruth, my dear, you are not, I think, the revolutionary your father jokes about.'

'No.'

'If you were, things would be so much simpler, wouldn't they?'

I nodded.

'Yes. Revolution is someone else's show, not yours. What you have to find out first is what you don't want.'

'Catherine did.' I wanted to test the words every way, everything I felt to be the truth.

'Ah, I have a sister like Catherine. Don't run and hide, my dear. That's the easy path. At first. It's not for you.'

I wanted to tell her that I couldn't think of my future without a man. I wasn't like her. I could never be.

'If you were a revolutionary – not just politically, in every way – I'd say stay and battle it out. But you're not. You like to please too much. You love them all too much. You would, I think, give them your head on a platter for a mess of potage!' She laughed. Her laugh was lovely. I couldn't bear to have her leave, to be left alone again.

'I have to wait till I've finished school. And even then –'

'I know all about the money. You'll just have to work for a scholarship. You have to think beyond the curtain. Far beyond the stage itself. There are many, many ways to take one's leave.'

I was lonely already. And desperate to leave. And worried

186

about being an old maid. It was easy for her to say. She didn't need a man, she was a lesbian. She was famous. She could come and go.

'May I write you now and then, Ruth?'

It was the sort of question I usually hated to be asked. But with Jocelyn there was no fake in it. She truly wanted my permission.

'Yes. Please. I mean, I'd love to write.'

'I hate to lose new friends. One never loses the old ones, you know.'

'Look,' I said. 'See the way you can see the Rutledges' verandah through the jacarandas? And the morning glory up the pillar? And the palm tree like a sort of lamp post?' I pointed across the road. 'I always used to think that's how England would look.' I laughed. 'I don't know why, I always did.'

Jocelyn narrowed her eyes at the scene, framed by the shade of two jacarandas. I'd never thought of the Rutledges' verandah as England. I knew that morning glory and palm trees and verandahs belonged to us. But my eye had stopped there as I searched for something to give substance to what I wanted her to say.

She smiled at me. She threw her huge arm around my shoulders and gave me a hard squeeze. 'Oh, Ruth Frank, how lucky you are to have all this to leave behind. It's the *place*, you know. You'll come back for the morning glory and this summerhouse and that marvellous frangipani.'

The gate slammed and the dogs flew out and Pillay began his meandering screech. The hadedahs took off in a wailing rush.

'Will you take me now and show me the rest of the garden?' she asked. 'I'd particularly like to see the fruit trees.'

13

I had tried to approximate the Habonim uniform by wearing a blue blouse and a skirt. But the only skirt I possessed was red velvet and gathered at the waist so that my hips looked enormous.

'Hhawu!' Nora said, peering through her swollen eyelids. 'Umuhle!'

Nora's praise only panicked me further. She loved bright colours and large hips. But the Habonim girls I knew wore make-up and earrings and tight, tight skirts in khaki.

'You can go, Nors,' I said. 'I'll answer the door.'

But she lowered herself on to the stairs and sat staring towards the front door. 'Who this boy?' she demanded.

'A student at the theatre school.'

'Father?'

I shrugged.

'Awu!' She cocked her head to one side. 'Why the boys start coming so soon?'

I couldn't even mention Constance now. We would be separated for ever, Constance and me, woman from girl. 'It's not so soon,' I said. 'I'm fourteen.'

The doorbell rang. Nora heaved herself up, but I got to the door first.

'Hello, Garth.'

'Howzit?'

She folded her arms and squinted at Garth – his hair, his Habonim uniform, his veldskoen. 'You take a jersey?' she asked.

'No,' I said. 'It's hot.'

She vanished into the cloakroom and returned with my school raincoat.

'No!' I said.

A car hooted. Garth glanced nervously towards the street.

Nora held the raincoat out to me with her lips pulled closed. I grabbed it and plunged out of the door with Garth.

'Who gave her the hiding?' he asked as we picked our way to the front gate.

'One of the other servants.'

'What did your Ma say?'

It had started already. My Ma. What this, what that. 'Nothing really.'

He snorted. 'Whew! Things must be hellova different at home!'

Habonim meetings took place in an old, single-storey Victorian house, close to the race track, in the poor part of town.

'Ilana can tell you where to buy the uniform,' Garth said as he steered me up the path and across the verandah. He seemed very sure of me. 'She's the madricha.'

'I hate this skirt,' I said.

'Why?' He stared at the skirt, then at me, as if I had admitted that I hated my mother.

But people came up to us before I had to explain. 'Shalom! Shalom!' they said.

'Shalom, everybody! Ruth Frank – Mike, Dave, Elaine, Mel, Shoshanah, Josh –'

I tried to cover my skirt with the raincoat. 'Thanks a ton for having me,' I said.

A few of the girls sniggered. 'Don't thank us!' Elaine Berkowitz said. I knew her from synagogue and Hebrew school. Her father sold magazines with naked women in them in a little shop near the beach. She always kept a copy in her suitcase to show her friends. But she made a point of never showing me. If I walked past, she slammed her suitcase shut until I'd gone. 'Have a look around,' she said. 'There's not much to see.'

She was right. In every room the floors were bare and dusty. Torn posters of workers in Israel and of soldiers waving Israeli flags plastered the walls. A few old wooden tables and chairs, crudely painted in blue and white, stood here and there throughout the house. There seemed to be no central place, no division of function, nothing done to encourage nostalgia in the people who met there.

'It's nice,' I said.

'Did Garth tell you we're having Simon Mngoma tonight?' Mike asked. He spoke with reverence, like the girls at school when they mentioned the Queen or her children.

'No,' I said. I'd never heard of Simon Mngoma.

'The ANC chap,' Garth explained. 'You know. He was kicked out of Natal 'varsity.'

For what, I wondered? That kind of politics was never discussed in our house. 'I thought you had a social?'

'Afterwards. We always have a meeting or a speaker first.' He wandered off to help with the chairs.

'Let's put him here,' Elaine suggested. She glanced at my skirt. 'Some of us,' she said, 'will just have to sit on the floor.'

'He's here!' someone shouted. 'Come, everybody!'

People came in from everywhere, about forty in all. They filled the room, sprawling over the floor and spilling out of the doorways. Simon Mngoma, a young black man sweating in a tight wool suit, accepted a glass of Coke and waited, unsmiling, for silence.

He looked at his watch. 'We have not got much time,' he said in an educated African accent. 'As you all know, I must be off the streets and out of the white areas by eleven p.m.'

No one spoke. Several people shook their heads.

'And that means – if someone drives me to the bus – that I need one hour and one half to obey the laws of this country.'

I shook my head too although it was an old complaint, still without teeth for me.

'What people may not realize,' he went on, 'is that we Africans will not be obeying your laws much longer. We will not be "good boys" anymore. You do not hear what I hear in the townships. You do not see what I see on the buses and in the streets where black men live.'

I had never heard such threats from a black man or woman. The menace in his innuendo began to unsettle my boredom.

'Seventy-nine per cent of our children in the kraals are starving. "Education", the government says. Our women need to be "ed-u-cated" how to feed their own babies! But I tell you this: we were here long before any white man came to tell us how to feed our children! Where was kwashiokor then? You tell me!'

No one moved. A few people coughed.

'We were nomadic farmers. We knew how to feed ourselves and our children. What now? What now, I ask you?' He hung his head and shook it heavily from side to side.

Even though I knew a bad performance when I saw one, I wanted to be shocked with all the others. I tried to think of kwashiokor babies. The distended stomachs, sunken eyes, skinny arms and legs. But I had only seen photographs. And even they didn't hold the horror of the Holocaust chronicles. Starving black babies seemed far from me – white girl, Jew.

'Think of your own mothers and fathers,' he said, staring at us again through cold eyes. 'What can they do for you when there is a knife at your throat and a gun at their heads?'

My heart jumped. When? How? Who?

'It will happen,' he sing-songed. 'Oh, yes. If not this year, next year. Or years after that. Who is safe? No one. It can happen tonight. Those servants you think love you, they do not love you –'

Reuben – he was certainly right about Reuben. It wasn't hard to imagine him with the carving knife at my throat. But what about Nora? Nora turning on me with the mulberry switch when my mother called my name –

'And the ones you are so sure of. Those dee-voted servants who changed your own nappies –' He curled up his nose and lip

191

in disgust, and then paused while we waited, hearts beating in terror. 'They will go next door. To your neighbour. Oh, don't you worry. No one will be safe when the black man rises.'

My upper lip had beaded over and my armpits ran. He was becoming very effective.

He smiled at us, a bloodless, sarcastic smile. 'White men,' he said, 'think that we black men want their women. That is the reason, they say, we must be kept apart.' He pointed a pink-nailed finger at us. 'You tell them we prefer our black women. You tell them to keep an eye on their own women and what those women want!'

Once, years before, Lucy and I had made a stage on the top of the bookshelf in my mother's study. We cleared away the ashtrays and silver cigarette box and danced to each other's audience. Outside, black men sat along the pavement playing guitars and drinking tea out of tins. I turned to the window and banged on the glass. Two of them looked up. I threw my hands above my head and danced. But my dancing bored them and they returned to their playing and laughing.

'Come,' I said to Lucy. 'Let's take off our blouses.'

'Na,' she said.

I unbuttoned my blouse and pulled it off, banged even louder on the leaded glass.

They turned again and watched, this time with sober interest. I had no breasts yet, but I danced as I had seen Valerie dancing, squashing my elbows into my sides and swivelling my hips.

One of them laughed, said something in Zulu. They all turned now to look.

In ecstasy I threw off my sandals and then pulled down my shorts and pants, kicked them to the floor.

'We'll get into trouble,' Lucy whispered crouched out of sight.

But I was wild with my daring, with the audience of black men outside. I lifted each leg and stamped like a gum boot dancer. I turned my back on the window and bent over to look at them between my knees.

A few more came from further up the road. They stood soberly at the fence to watch the spectacle. 'Come on!' I urged Lucy. 'It's fun!'

'Na!' she said.

And then Mrs Knowles walked past, back from the bus stop. I didn't see her, but I heard the phone ring, and Nora answer. And then my mother's voice, wild with rage at the interruption of her afternoon sleep. She came in her dressing-gown to the door of the study and asked me questions I couldn't answer.

'What on earth do you think you are doing?'

'Why in God's name have you been prancing naked for all the world to see?'

'Wasn't he great?' Garth asked me.

We were dancing now, to Frank Sinatra. He held me close.

'Great,' I said.

'I'm getting out of this place as soon as I can,' he said.

'Where will you go?'

He looked at me in surprise. 'Israel, of course.'

'You'd be sooo nice to come home to,' Sinatra crooned.

Garth pulled me towards him so that my breasts squashed against his shirt. 'Want to go for a walk?' he asked.

My pulse tripped up my breathing and I coughed. I knew from the girls at school what walks meant. And I didn't feel quite ready. I didn't really know what to expect, how far to go. 'OK,' I said.

He led me by the hand through a messy kitchen and down some stairs to a small garden. It was rank and unkempt. Other couples were already kissing in the shadows. Silently. As if the darkness would lift if they spoke.

'Here,' Garth whispered. He had found a spot near the hedge. 'Want to sit down?'

I sat. Who would he tell, I wondered? Everyone said that boys told. Certainly the whole theatre school class would be waiting to hear. That, I was sure, was the point of the walk.

He drew me towards him and then clamped two thick, wet

lips over mine, sucked my own lips in between them. Torrents of warm breath flowed from his nostrils into mine. I couldn't move or even gasp. After a while his tongue pushed its way between my lips, snaked along until it reached the barrier of my teeth.

'Open your mouth,' he mumbled.

I opened my mouth slightly and took a few quick gulps of air.

This time his tongue shot right in and explored the entire interior of my mouth. All the assorted teeth, the gums, everything. Nothing I had ever imagined about kissing approached this humiliation. I closed my eyes and tried to pretend that he was Bernard. But my disgust made it impossible.

'Let's go,' I said. 'I have to go.'

He was breathing fast now. In the gloom his eyes looked crazed, unfocused. 'No!' he said. 'There's time.'

He pulled me down over him, leaned back, crushed my lips against his teeth. His chest heaved under me. His hips ground against mine. To my amazement something about all this was beginning to appeal to me. I seemed to like the smell of him. Or his thighs tight around my skirt. My heart clumping madly against his shirt. Or my own thighs weak and hot under all the velvet. He could have been Bernard after all. I could almost imagine myself in love.

'Ruth Frank!'

I jumped. 'Coming!' I shouted.

'Shh!'

I leapt to my feet and flapped the grass off my skirt.

'Is it your parents?' Garth whispered, following me up the stairs and back through the kitchen to the front of the house.

'Your chauffeur!' someone snickered.

'Coming to the beach tomorrow?' Garth asked.

I nodded, my heart lifting through the top of my blouse.

Outside the gate Johannes held the car door open for me. Garth hung back in the doorway and watched as I climbed in.

'Goodbye!' I waved. 'Thanks a ton!'

'Shalom!' he shouted. 'See you tomorrow!'

'Well, my dear?' Abba patted my skirt. 'Well?'

'It was OK,' I said. I smiled into the dark of the car. With exquisite secrecy the pulse still throbbed in my groin.

He patted my hand. 'The play was very amusing!' he said. 'Very amusing indeed! A triumph for your dear mother. And for your sister. You have got a lot to be proud of, you know.'

The cast party had already begun when we got home. Someone played the piano and Valerie stood next to it crooning 'I've got you under my skin.' In her hands she held her orchid, browning a little from its week in the fridge.

The crowd milled and laughed and drank champagne. People draped themselves over the piano to listen to Valerie. They threw their arms around my mother and praised everything – the play, the food, the house. I longed to tell someone that I had been kissed.

'*Hello*, darling!' my mother boomed in a voice full of cast party cheer. 'Come and join us!'

I shook my head.

Suddenly she lowered her voice. 'What an extraordinary outfit, darling! Why not nip upstairs and slip into something more appropriate?'

'I'm not staying.'

'And your hair! You look as if you've been pulled through a bush backwards!'

Suddenly Bernard was at my side. He crept around me sideways with bent knees and hands slicing the air, as if I were a wild horse and he looking for the safest way to mount. 'Hey, hey!' he growled. 'Been out on the town, I hear.'

I blushed.

'Hello, Ruth!' Jocelyn, munching several canapés at once, engulfed me in a hug.

'Ruth's just going upstairs to change,' my mother explained, turning away from Bernard as if he weren't there. 'She's been to that meeting at our Jewish youth club.'

I backed out of the lounge, ran up the front stairs and then down the back stairs to the kitchen. The servants were flying about with platters and trays, sauces, dishcloths.

195

'Awu, Ruth!' Nora shouted from the stove. 'We busy, can't you see?'

I sat on one of the chairs and picked an olive out of a platter of chicken.

'No!' Nora bustled over to fetch the platter. When Philemon was there she was always bossy. She knew what my mother thought of Philemon's cooking.

But as she reached for the platter she stopped and cocked her head to one side and squinted at me. She planted her hands on her hips. 'What happen to you?' she demanded.

'Why?' I smiled mysteriously.

'That boy, what he do?'

'Oh, nothing.'

'What he do?' She stepped closer and picked some grass off my skirt.

'He kissed me.'

'Aiii!' She threw her hands in the air and closed her eyes. She shook her swollen head wildly from side to side. 'Aiii!' she shrieked again.

'*What on earth is going on in here, Nora?*' My mother stood furious at the kitchen door.

Nora lifted the platter of chicken but said nothing.

'We're waiting for the chicken! We're waiting for the rice! I have to bring in extra servants because you're in no condition to serve. And you're standing there shouting like a maniac!' She turned her fury on me. 'Either go up and change into something civilized, or go to bed! How many times do I have to tell you to leave the servants alone?'

I skipped past her and up the back stairs. I sang as I washed my face. Pranced naked in front of the mirror, pushing out my breasts as Valerie had done at the piano. It was done. I had done it. 'You'd be sooo nice to come home to,' I sang.

'Hey!' Valerie burst into my room. She hopped on to my bed, her orchid still in her hand. 'Tell me,' she said confidentially. 'What happened?'

'What do you mean?'

'Nora told me –' She smiled at me as if she knew, as if she too were happy.

It was easy to tell Valerie what she wanted to know. Like the most grateful of beggars, she made you want to turn out your pockets to show her you had nothing more to give. 'Go on,' she urged. 'And then?'

'That's all,' I said, wishing there were more.

'All?'

I nodded.

Suddenly she winced. She shuddered. '*Sis!*' she spat out. 'How utterly repulsive!'

I grabbed my dressing-gown and pulled it on quickly.

'His tongue in your mouth!'

I could feel it again, rough and smooth, round and round each tooth.

'Germs and saliva! He might just as well have put his *thing* in your mouth!'

His thing! Where had his thing been in all this? I'd completely forgotten the planting of the seed.

'Did he ask you to do anything else?' she demanded.

I shook my head. All I could think of now were his eyes, half-closed, closing me out; his hands pulling me down on top of him As if I were anyone. Any cheap girl. And he someone I didn't even know or love. I remembered that he was stupid. That he couldn't act. I was ashamed.

She stood up. 'Well, at this rate, my girl, you're going *one* way!' She pushed past me, checked her face in the dressing table mirror and then looked at mine in disgust. 'Sis!' she said. And slammed the door behind her.

I rode to the beach the next morning on the bus, with my heart leaping as if I were about to go on stage. Most people my age went to the beach on a Sunday – Jews to north beach, Gentiles to south beach. I'd tried it a few times and hated it.

The bus swung around on to Shorefront Road. From upstairs I could see both beaches – two fifty-yard strips of sand covered with people and umbrellas and vendors and lifesavers. Crowds of young people milled around the wall dividing the road from the beach. At the edge of the surf nannies with their skirts tucked into their pants hung on to small children. The screams of the swimmers and the crashing of waves and the smell of salt and popcorn and hamburgers filled the air.

I plodded down the hill and over to the wall, hovered on the pavement. Boys shouted and wrestled each other or snatched the girl's bags. Girls screamed and chased after them. It was what I had dreaded, not knowing how to behave. I shaded my eyes with one hand and pretended to look for someone.

'Hello, Ruth!'

I jumped.

A hand tapped me on the shoulder. 'Long time no see!'

'Lucy?'

She smiled. One arm clutched the brown waist of a boy I knew from Hebrew. His hand nestled just under her left breast. She grinned at me in triumph, not just of having Clive Spilkin's hand under her breast, but because she saw my eye on her perfect nest of bleached hair and the chaotic palette of colours she'd painted on to her face.

'Want to put your things with ours?' she asked. 'Come –' She took me by the wrist as I used to take her and led me along the wall.

People noticed us as we walked by. They stared at her large breasts and tightly nipped-in waist and giggled and whispered. I wondered whether she knew what they were saying – Look at her! Cheap south beach shiksa! Poor Clive! And, ha! ha! look who's with them! Miss Stuck Up! Hey, Garth! Look who's come to the beach today!

I saw Elaine Berkowitz and smiled and waved. But she turned away. She whispered something to Sharon Gevitsky and they both shrieked loudly.

'Here,' Lucy said. 'Clivey, give me a jump.'

He held her waist in his hands and hoisted her easily on to the wall. Then he turned and offered the same service to me.

'No thanks. I can't stay long. I've got to go home for lunch.'

'Crumbs!' Lucy said. 'You just came, didn't you?' Her voice was still high and shrill, and her vowels tighter than ever.

I nodded.

'Shame! You could've come and watched me and Clive at the rink. You know I'm on the Natal junior team?'

'No, really? What team?'

'Ice-skating, man!' She grinned up at Clive.

'Ja!' he said. 'Me too.'

Suddenly I was nudged hard in the ribs from behind. 'Hey? Hey?' Garth leaned back against the wall and folded his arms across his chest to spread out his biceps. He looked different in the daylight. Younger. Sillier.

'Hello, Garth,' I said.

' "Hel-lo, Gaahth"!' he imitated. 'How d'you know Clive?' He wanted to know everything about my connections, nothing about me.

'I don't. I know Lucy.'

Garth stared at Lucy's breasts.

'I live next door,' she said.

'Junk, man!' he laughed. 'Come off it!'

'Oh, yes I do! Ask Ruth.'

I nodded. 'She does.'

'Ask her anything about me,' Lucy insisted. Her face purpled, even through her make-up.

'Do you still have all those wishbones?' I asked.

'Ja! Millions, hey Clivey? All around the lounge.'

'You go to Rangston too?' Garth asked, with more respect.

'Na, man! Morningside High.'

'Forlorningside!' He jumped backwards on to the wall and caught me between his feet. 'Gotcha!' he said.

I stood there, caught, wishing I could trust myself to squeal and struggle. I even tried to feel as I'd felt when Bernard had come that first time in his sandals and ordered me to turn and turn. But Garth had no power to enrage me. I wasn't even ashamed of last night anymore. He seemed like a baby, not a real man.

'Ice cream!' An Indian vendor, with his eye and ear for flirting, stopped behind Garth. 'Candy floss! Toffee apples!'

'Want something?' Garth asked.

I shook my head, but he jumped off the wall anyway and

burrowed into his swimming costume for some coins.

Lucy nestled the top of her head into Clive's neck. 'Clivey,' she whined, 'buy me an ice cream!'

'Ag no, man! You already had one. It's nearly lunch.' He seemed pleased to be able to scold her. He pulled her round and kissed her on the lips.

'Here –' Garth handed me an eskimo pie.

I blushed at last. 'Thanks,' I said. 'Want a bite, Luce?'

She giggled up at Clive. 'Clivey? Can I?' She was good at this, better than I could ever be. He shook his head.

'Want to put your things with mine?' Garth asked. The eskimo pie had given him a claim on me, and me to a place on the wall.

'Why don't we stay here?' I asked.

'Ja, go on, stay!' Lucy sing-songed.

Garth walked off. 'Come on!' he said.

I followed him along the tiny ledge of pavement, struggling between the crowds of people and the bumpers of parked cars. As we moved further and further down the beach, my pulse began to leap in alarm. Even though I had woken that morning to Jocelyn's words, not Valerie's – full of daring, mad to start the journey out. But now, just as far as the beach, every squeal and yelp of the people we passed startled me. I seemed to hear my name in every shout.

'Here!' He pointed over the wall to a group of strangers sitting on the sand. 'Hey, your ice cream's melting, man.'

I held it out to him and he leaned forward, gulping at it as if he were a child and I his nanny. How had Catherine done it, I wondered? How had she replaced them with Jeffrey? I wasn't ready. I wanted to drop the ice cream and run.

He held my wrist and sucked the chocolate off my fingers. 'Mmm!' he murmured.

'I have to go.'

'Ag no, man! It's only half-past eleven!'

I wiped my hand on my shorts, front and back and between the fingers. I wanted to be sick.

'Come ooonn!' He took my shoulders in his hands and pulled me towards him.

People around us turned to look. His eyes flicked left and right and over my shoulders.

'No!' I tore my shoulders away and fell backwards on to a parked car, scraping my leg.

Some of the audience laughed. 'Hey! Let her go, man! You don't want to be had up! Ha! Ha!'

'Why're you making a fool of me?' he hissed.

I scrambled around the car, clutching at my calf.

'You're a bloody baby! Jeezuss Christ!'

A car stopped to let me cross the road.

'Needs a bloody nanny!' he shouted.

'Ha! Ha!' they laughed.

They were on the verandah when I got home, drinking pink gin and eating nuts.

'Hello, darling! How was the beach?'

Jocelyn stared at me over the rim of her glass. 'Is this beaching season?' she asked.

My mother scrunched one eye down in an exaggerated wink. 'I think there's a special interest there!'

'Rubbish!' I said. I blushed and flopped into a chair and crashed the nut dish off the table by mistake.

My mother raised an eyebrow at Jocelyn.

'Up for some tennis this afternoon, Chops?'

'Not really.' I stared out to sea. The afternoon wind had blown away the clouds. Yachts were out, and two ships waiting to come into the harbour. Everything seemed normal, but it wasn't.

Reuben brought out a bowl of cheese sticks.

'Try these, Jocelyn,' my mother said. 'They're the imported variety.'

I felt a fool now for running home. And I couldn't bear Jocelyn to go.

'Mmm. Yum!' she said. 'How I'd love to take some of this sunshine back with me.'

She'd been packed before breakfast. I had to bite my lips together not to cry again. It was like sickness or madness. I

201

was sick now at the loss of Garth. Even though I hadn't wanted him. Didn't want him still. A hole had dug itself out of my stomach.

'Sarah, you must promise to keep in touch. I want to hear all about the next production.'

'Ah!'

'What about *My Fair Lady*? Can't I just see Roger as Professor Higgins!'

'Ah! Pipe dreams! Where would we find the voices? Not to mention the rights.'

Not to mention the money, I wanted to say.

'I think you'd have a whopping success. Perhaps it's worth taking a chance.'

My mother just smiled. She swirled her gin around the glass and stared into the vortex.

'I say!' my father said. 'Wouldn't Sarah make a marvellous Mrs Higgins?'

My mother threw her head back and gave one of her sudden sarcastic barks. The dogs sat up.

'Only a suggestion.'

'First you have me playing Valerie's rival in love! Then you suggest I play your mother! Next, I suppose, you'll want to be casting Valerie as Eliza! Ha! Ha!'

'Cast me as who?' Valerie stood at the top of the verandah steps.

'As *whom*!' I said.

Jocelyn smiled down into her lap.

'Nothing! Just another brilliant idea of your father's.'

Valerie sauntered on to the verandah and kicked me as she passed. 'Good, because I'm resigning from the theatre school. What are these?' She picked up a cheese stick delicately and sniffed it, put it in the ashtray with a grimace of disgust. 'I've asked Janet McGuire to take me on as a junior teacher.' She smiled into my mother's startled face. 'Don't worry, I won't snatch any of your precious students. Although God knows –' The rest was lost. She'd lowered her voice on purpose as she reached the lounge.

202

'Well!' Jocelyn said. 'This time next week –'
'Ah!' My mother sighed and gulped the rest of her gin. 'What wouldn't I give to be coming with you!'

14

For weeks after Jocelyn left I suffered a terrible sort of loneliness. Without her to talk to, or simply the assurance of her
silent observations, I felt my future disappearing again into the
madness that surrounded me. But then, once school resumed,
and there were tests and exams and the debate to worry about,
the loneliness began to resolve itself into imaginary conversations between us. I found these as comforting in their own way
as I had found the thought of Bernard, before Valerie displaced
him.

As the debate approached, Miss Robinson kept making
announcements about it in prayers.

'We will welcome the Brighton team, their teachers and
supporters, with the same grace and good manners that we
display towards *other* schools!'

'After the debate, tea will be served as usual on the pre-
fect's lawn. All girls in forms two, three and four are expected
to attend.' She raised one eyebrow. 'And to mingle and con-
verse with our guests! Three prefects will volunteer to serve
tea.'

One day she fixed her eyes on us over the tops of her glasses
and spoke in a deadly staccato. 'If – the – need – arises – the –
Brighton – gels – will – use – our – senior – cloakroom – ! – To –
set – them – at – ease – about – this – two – gels – from – form –

three – will – be – appointed – to – show – our – guests – how – to
– get – down – there.

'Any senior gel who must be absent for the debate will bring
her excuse directly to me. Take warning that I will not accept
sudden bilious attacks or other such poppycock.'

Cheryl McCormack nudged the girl next to her. She had told
us that she planned to put the thermometer against the light
bulb the morning of the debate and to drink a cup of vinegar.
The boarders had to use extraordinary methods to convince the
matron that they were ill.

'One would think,' I said to Edwina as we waited at last for the
Brighton girls to arrive, 'that we were debating against lepers.'

We had comforted each other with such pronouncements
during the previous weeks. Miss Robinson's constant reminders
of the trial ahead amused most of the girls in our class. They
had nothing to dread. They could burlesque for each other in
Indian accents about the cloakrooms smelling of garlic and
samosas for tea without the awful grip that anticipation of the
day exerted on our bowels.

Edwina nodded but said nothing. Her terror was fiercer than
mine. She swung her body from foot to foot and wiped the
palms of her hands on her skirt.

'There they are!' she whispered.

A crocodile line of Indian girls in white dresses and black
blazers wound in a curve down the path towards us. They wore
their long black hair braided into elaborate knots or loops.
This, together with the colour of their skin, their dark eyes and
thin noses, gave them a sameness of look that seemed to parody
our attempts to belong. With eyes and skin and hair of different
colours, hair short, hair long, straight or curly – we pretended
to a conformity that no uniform could achieve. But there they
were, all of a piece like cousins, neat and smiling, with their
teacher walking behind them in a bright-yellow sari. As a
group they showed none of the embarrassment we had been led
to expect. In fact they held their heads high and looked about
them at the school. Some of them pointed, some laughed. The

teacher laughed too. Already they seemed to have about them an air of triumph.

'God! I wish it were all over!' Edwina whispered. She flapped her skirt around to dissipate a fart.

The school bell rang. Behind us five hundred girls rumbled and stamped and shouted with the end of the day.

'How do you do?' The Indian girl at the head of the line held out a hand to me. 'I'm Maya Chowdree,' she said. 'And this is Suvreti Maharaj.' There was only the slightest curl of an Indian accent around her consonants, the softest Indian in her vowels.

'I'm Ruth Frank. May I introduce Edwina Sloane?'

Maya smiled with pearly teeth, straight and even. She was completely beautiful, her skin smooth and caramel, her cheekbones high and defined, her mouth wide, her eyes deep and almond-shaped and turning from black to purple as they caught the light. Around the lids I noticed the fine line of Gentian violet that Indians painted there for some reason.

'Ah! The opposing team!' Miss Robinson swept out of the vestibule in her black academic robe. 'Mrs Naidoo? Ah! Welcome to Rangston! Do come in! Ruth and Edwina, direct your opponents to the colosseum! Ha! Ha!' She roared heartily into Mrs Naidoo's bemused face.

We led Maya and her entourage to the hall. Girls were lined up all along the corridors, waiting for the Indian girls to be seated. They stared in silence as we passed. But teachers had been posted to watch them. No one dared to hold her nose in fun or even to snicker.

When the hall was full and quiet Miss Robinson stood up. She straightened her shoulders, closed her eyes for absolute silence. And then took a deep breath. 'There comes a time,' she said, 'when pioneers are born in every age. People with a vision. People who dare to dream.' She paused, looking out over the sea of black and white faces. 'When one says to oneself, "There is a job to be done and I shall do it! I – shall – do – it!" '

Our team sat at a table on the right of the stage. The Brighton girls on the left. They seemed to be listening carefully.

'Please God – dear Lord,' I prayed, 'let Miss Robinson go on

talking until my jaw stops shaking and I can breathe properly.'
I didn't dare touch the new prayer I'd created for the debate. It
nestled deep in the pocket of my gym shirt.

'When Jesus speaks of the rich man and the eye of the needle,'
Miss Robinson said, 'He puts us in mind of Allah, that great
prophet of our Moslem brethren –' Here she beamed at Mrs
Naidoo and her team, all of whom were Hindus. I saw Maya
lower her eyes to the table.

'All the great religions of the world hold learning in the
highest esteem. Teachers are valued above politicians, above
doctors, above lawyers, above merchants; or –' She turned on
me and contorted her face into one of her frowning smiles to
indicate a joke. 'Or psychologists!'

Some of the Rangston girls tittered politely and the Brighton
girls tittered too. But I couldn't even smile. In my fright the
muscles of my cheeks refused to obey. My nose too suddenly
stopped functioning. It would not take in any more air. I
dropped my jaw slightly and gulped.

'And so it is with great pleasure that I welcome Mrs Naidoo,
her middle school debating team, and their supporters, to
Rangston. May the best team win!'

She clapped as she sat down, leading Mrs Naidoo and the
entire audience to clap along with her.

In the silence that followed I reached for my notes and stood
up. My mother had coached me on the value of pauses. I
counted to five, slowly, smiling now, and breathing lightly. I
searched the audience, as she had told me to, for a friendly face.

'The subject of this debate,' I began in a voice half an octave
higher than usual, 'is, "Is it better to be born brilliant or
beautiful?" '

A few girls laughed. I took courage.

'I'm going to assume that we can only be beautiful and
unbrilliant, or brilliant and unbeautiful.'

Again they laughed. My breathing began to settle down.
Edwina and I, with the help of Miss Harding, had marshalled a
list of brilliant women for our argument. But in the end our
strength lay only in the elusive satisfactions of the intellect and

in the definition of 'better'. Our position, we had discovered, was without the backing of history.

'When Adam and Eve chose the Tree of Knowledge over the Tree of Life they made a very important choice for us all. They chose that we should grow old and die. Die.' I stared out at the friendly face in the front row. But she looked alarmed and stared down into her hands. Miss Robinson too frowned down at the table in front of her. I plunged on quickly. 'Everyone knows,' I pronounced, 'that we are all going to die.'

Mrs Naidoo smiled at me. She nodded as if there had been a doubt in her mind on the subject.

'The question is, how would we choose to live if we had a choice? Beautiful for the brief duration of our youth, with men and riches at our feet? Or brilliant for our whole lives? Think of it! All the worlds, past and present, their histories and litera-ture and music within the compass of our comprehension.' 'Worlds past and present' had come from one of my imaginary conversations with Jocelyn. 'Within the compass of our com-prehension' was my father's phrase. I liked it, the way it rolled off my tongue. But I was glad he wasn't there to hear me use it.

'Let me remind you,' I said, 'beauty fades. But a brilliant mind lives on. Brilliant people are never bored. Think of that! The world is their footstool. I shall now offer a few examples –'

As I paused to look up, Maya smiled at me across the stage. She had nothing on the table before her, no notes, not even a pencil. Suvreti too seemed composed and happy, as if she wore the immunity of a member of the audience.

'Madame Curie,' I said, 'Queen Elizabeth the First, Joan of Arc, the Wife of Bath –'

But the Wife of Bath caused Miss Robinson to explode into a snort, slapping both palms on to the table before her. We had only read a modern translation of the 'Prologue' to the Canter-bury Tales. I had liked the idea of the Wife of Bath's ugliness combined with her mastery of men. I wondered whether I'd be called to the office the next day to account for my choice of her.

'Think of our women writers,' I stumbled on. 'George Eliot,

Jane Austen, the Brontë sisters. Did they spend their nights attending balls, and their days choosing ribbon for their bonnets? No! They wrote, they read – um – and, most important of all, they live with us still. They are immo–'

Ping! Miss Harding's bell rang out. 'Time!' she barked. 'Brighton now opposes.'

I sat down, flushed. What could touch me now? It was done. I dug into my pocket and fondled the prayer.

Maya stood up. 'Miss Robinson, Mrs Naidoo, girls, we contend that beauty provides women with more power than money, brilliance or rank do. I think we must agree here that we are speaking not just of prettiness, but of great beauty. The beauty of a Cleopatra, or of a Princess Grace.'

She smiled slowly at the audience, her beautiful teeth sparkling in two even rows. There seemed in the bow of her head, the softness of her voice, a sort of feminine deference. As if to excuse her for making a point against her hosts. Only her eyes made no excuses. They stared at us steadily, quite assured, quite defiant.

'What, I am wondering, is this brilliance that my worthy opponent talks of? And how does it make life better?' She looked directly into the audience. 'I ask you. Did a riddle ever make you happy?'

The girls roared, and Miss Robinson's barking laugh lasted longest of all.

I felt double-crossed.

'How do we measure the happiness of geometry?' she demanded.

More roars came from the floor. Even the Brighton girls broke into shrieks and giggles.

'But to be fair, let's look at some of my worthy opponent's examples. Consider, for instance, the Brontë sisters. They were certainly brilliant, we must agree. But I have read that they were miserable, poor, and even mad. One of them anyway.'

I relaxed a little. She was resorting to qualifiers. Miss Harding had warned us off all indefinite statements.

'And Jane Austen,' she went on. 'She died young. Also she

never married or had children. How much better off was she?'

I held my breath.

'Judging by her books, I would think she spent most of her time watching beautiful women flirting at balls or choosing ribbon for their bonnets.'

Again the audience laughed. But Maya had placed her watch before her on the table and cut them short. 'Remember, please,' she said, 'that we are arguing about how much *better* it is to be *born* beautiful.' She smiled deferentially at Miss Robinson. 'Whatever our religions teach us, none of us, I think, can judge happiness after death.' She paused. 'Now let us consider the lives of a few beautiful women past and present –'

So it was lost. And yet how could I have known that my arguments – so carefully worded, so neatly written out – could fade and dissipate before the eloquence of this beautiful Indian girl? Justice was done. I couldn't even feel ashamed.

'Congratulations,' I said to her on the prefects' lawn. 'You deserved to win.'

'Oh, no!' She smiled and shook her head. 'Your arguments were far better. I felt like a fool arguing for beauty.' She lowered her voice slightly. 'I have the advantage, you see, of my dark skin. How could we lose?' She laughed, her black eyes flashing.

I had nothing to say to this. Never had I had such a conversation. It was like strange wine. Or a sickness coming on.

'Your mother is Sarah Frank, is she?' she asked.

'Yes.'

'I think she knows my aunt Devi.'

'Oh!' I exclaimed too loudly. 'Is Devi Chowdree your aunt? How funny!'

'A biscuit or some cake?' one of the prefects asked.

Maya took a piece of cake. 'Oooh! I love this vanilla icing!'

'I brought that cake,' I said. 'I'm sick of it, we have it all the time.'

'I don't think I'd ever get sick of it.' She smiled as she spiked a piece with her fork.

We liked each other. My heart and my head raced, trying to

210

know how to make her my friend. 'Do you play tennis?' I asked.

'Oh, yes. Every Sunday.'

'So do I.' I gulped. Valerie and Nora suddenly occurred to me. And Pillay. And the dogs.

'Would you be able one day to play with me at my house?' she asked.

'I'd love to!' I laughed in the mad hope that laughing would hide my blush.

'Well, would you give me a ring?' She touched my arm. 'I would like that very much. The number's in the book. R. Chowdree. Eglantine Drive. We could come and fetch you, if you like.'

'Oh, my mother will bring me,' I said. 'I'll phone.'

'Just look at this!' my mother beamed, flapping the newspaper at my father. 'Half a page on our little one, and not a bad photograph either.'

'Hmmm,' he said, smiling from the newspaper to me. 'Looks as if our Chopsticks is making quite a name for herself.'

'It's only the "School News" page,' I protested. But I too was thrilled. Miss Robinson and Mrs Naidoo, Maya and I beamed out above three columns on the debate.

'Devi Chowdree's niece!' my mother exclaimed. 'Lovely-looking girl!'

'Can I go and play tennis at her house?' I gabbled. 'She invited me. *Please*?'

My parents looked at each other. 'I don't see why not?' my father asked my mother.

'Why not?' she asked back.

I jumped up to go and phone.

'But I wouldn't advertise the fact, if I were you,' my mother called after me. 'You know what people in this country are like.'

'Advertise what?' Valerie asked, coming down the stairs.

'Mind your own beeswax!'

'What?' she asked my parents.

But I raced back to the lounge door. 'Don't tell her!' I shouted. 'She spoils everything!'

'Ruth has been invited to tennis at the home of Devi Chowdree's niece.'

'Ha! Just where she belongs!'

'Now come along,' my father crooned. 'Have you seen this lovely article on your sister in tonight's *News*?'

'Yes, but she lost!' Valerie sneered. 'What's all the fuss about when she can't even win her first debate? And against curry-munchers at that!'

My father laid down his Scotch and closed his eyes for peace. 'Valerie! You must adjust your sights, my young woman. Apart from the fact that Ruth seems to have put up a jolly good show, the debate itself was something significant in this country's rather awkward political set-up.'

'Bla, bla, bla,' she said.

'Flop, flop, flop,' I sang back. 'Crystal's toenail!'

My father was still too pleased to be provoked. 'For your information, Madam, Valerie gave a very creditable performance.'

My mother sniffed and turned to look out of the window.

'Very creditable!' he repeated, fixing an eye on my mother.

'Tart!' Valerie shouted. 'Cheap trollop! Do you know what she lets boys do to her?!'

'Girls, girls, *girls*! I just wish that you two would behave more like sisters and less like a pair of vixens!' He reached for the paper and held it up under the lamp. 'Now let's have another look at this. "Ruth Frank, youngest daughter of local theatre stars Roger and Sarah Frank, argued valiantly that it is better for a woman to be born brilliant than beautiful." Ha!' He clapped the paper down on to his trousers. 'Who would have thought we'd produce a suffragette? A suffragette Bolshevik no less! Ha! Ha! What a lark!'

After dinner I carried the newspaper to the kitchen. 'Look,' I said to Nora. I could count on her to be bowled over.

She brought the newspaper up under my nose. 'Hhawu!'

'It's me. See? There.'

'Who that one?' She touched one finger lightly on to Maya's face.

'Maya Chowdree.'

'Coolie?'

'Nora! She's an Indian girl. She's nice.'

'Why your teacher let coolie rubbish in your school?'

I snatched the paper back. 'I'm not going to show you if you talk like that.'

She leaned over and pinched my breast hard. 'Big surprise!' she said.

'That hurt!'

She bustled to the back door. 'Come! Quickle!'

I dropped the paper and followed her out across the laundry lawn. The light of her room shone brightly through the curtains.

'Who's there?' I asked. Nora's surprises were always good.

The door was ajar. She pushed it wide and pointed to the bed. 'Look!' she said. 'Big surprise!'

Two babies lay asleep on a bright-yellow crocheted blanket. Despite the heat each wore a knitted yellow pram set – cap, jacket, leggings, and mittens. The small faces were distinctly round, perfectly the same, the eyes like small brown grapes, two tiny Kewpie mouths.

'Twin. See?'

I wanted to weep at the sight of them, at the sight of Constance sitting on the chair giggling as I looked at her babies, her hand clasped over her mouth in pride.

'Oh, Nora! Why didn't you tell me? When were they born ? They're beautiful! You're so lucky! Oh!'

Nora beamed. There was no hint of the back yard scene. It was as if she'd always wanted them. Almost as if she'd given birth to them herself.

'Girls or boys?' I asked.

'Girl. Same like me!'

I touched the one on the cheek, the other one. 'How long will they stay?'

She busied herself with her dressing table. Dusted off the

213

arrangement of florists' bows, emptied some hairpins out of an old cut-glass bowl, wiped it out, and then put them back. 'Constance she got a job in Westville, start next month,' she said.

'What kind of job?'

'Wash girl.' She couldn't look at me.

'What will happen to them then?' I looked at Constance's impassive face. How did she know how to be a mother after all those years in standard four?

'Maybe they stay with me,' Nora said.

'Here? Oh, goody!'

'Maybe the Madam she say no.'

The probability was high. I raced through the voices and tones I could use to talk her into acquiescing.

'Grandmother she too old. Too sick.'

I would mention this.

'When Constance she sure of her job, she take them there.'

This too.

'And then they go back. When they walking and talking.'

'Back where?'

'To the mission station. My aunties they look after them.'

My parents were listening to Lux Radio Theatre when I came back in.

'Have you seen Nora's grandchildren?' I whispered.

'Shhh!'

I waited until the first commercial. I knew I should wait another day. They liked to discuss the actors and the play during commercials. But I couldn't bear to think of the babies sent back to the mission. 'Have you seen Constance's twins?'

'Yes. Nora brought them into the kitchen this morning.'

'Aren't they beautiful?'

She nodded, examining the *dramatis personae* in the SABC bulletin.

'Can they stay for a bit after Constance leaves?'

She sighed. 'I might have known you'd start something about that!'

'But they're so small. They won't be trouble.'

'What do *you* know?'

'It's just till Constance is sure of her job.'

'Can you imagine anyone keeping on that moron, even as a wash girl?' she snorted. 'She's literally half-witted!'

'But what about the babies?'

'The babies are not my concern! Why didn't Constance think of the babies before she had her fling? Hey?'

There it was again – her nose and mouth turned down, the turning of my stomach. Men's things and cheap little things and the distaste in her voice for women who were womanish. I thought of Garth for the first time in ages.

'Well, they shouldn't suffer. They're only babies.'

'Oh, come on, Ruth! Have a heart! I have a household to run. How can Nora possibly do her work and look after not one but two babies at the same time? Apart from anything else, there's something wrong with her these days. She's been in one of her states ever since that contretemps with Reuben. And, might I say, he isn't the servant he was either!' She sighed. The music came up for the second act. 'Look, my girl, I've got more on my fork at the moment than I can handle. I don't even know how I'm going to keep the theatre running, let alone this household!'

My father leaned over and patted my knee. 'Lay off your mother, Chopsticks. She's not having an easy time, you know.'

I stared out into the night. It was very dark, no moon. The doors to the verandah had been opened wide. In the street a black man whistled loud and shrill through his fingers. I jumped. Anything these days, any normal sound, seemed to signal the knife at the throat. My parents' indifference only panicked me further. Their words too. Her words. There was a different drama in them now. They were formed into the clichés of a real people. Real life. What would Jocelyn have made of this? I couldn't imagine. I flew to the doors and pulled them closed. Locked them. The windows too.

'Hey! Chopsticks! We'll suffocate!'

'It's not safe,' I insisted.

'What rubbish! We always keep the house open at this time of year.'

The front door rattled. I stopped still in fright.

'Ah,' my father said. 'She's back already.'

My mother reached over and turned up the volume. 'Sounds as if she's bringing him in too.'

My father raised his hands to his temples.

'You may as well just get used to the idea!' she snapped.

Valerie giggled. She threw open the lounge door. Bernard stretched his arms between the door posts and lifted himself off the ground, waving his sandals in the air.

'Guess what?' she said. Her eyes flashed between our parents, black and glassy.

My father kept his hands on his temples and stared at her with liquid eyes. My mother always refused to guess what.

I yawned and set the rocking chair in motion. 'You're getting married,' I said. 'Ho hum. What a bore.'

15

My mother insisted on driving me to Maya's house although I could easily have ridden there on my bicycle.

'I'm not happy about your riding around on your own in that sort of neighbourhood,' she said.

There was no point in arguing with her. She would only have forbidden me to go at all. Which would have been far more embarrassing than the flock of misgivings that already had me sitting silent in the car as we drove up to number 123 Eglantine Drive.

A high stone wall topped by chips of brightly coloured glass obscured the house from the street. At our approach an Indian gardener pulled open two heavy wrought-iron gates painted livid pink and green.

'Just look at those colours!' my mother said. 'I *am* surprised at the Chowdrees!'

My stomach turned. We crunched over the gravel driveway and pulled up beside two white Jaguars.

'Thanks, Ma.' I jumped out quickly. But as I turned to climb the front steps, Maya came out of the house with an elegant Indian woman at her side.

'Sarah!' the woman exclaimed. She came around to my mother's window.

'Devi!'

'I thought it might be you! Isn't this a lovely coincidence with our two clever girls?' She gestured lavishly towards Maya and me.

'Indeed it is! Do you live here too, Devi?'

Devi laughed so that her earrings tinkled like bells. She had Maya's teeth and eyes and smooth, smooth skin. 'Oh, no!' she said. 'I'm just here for lunch. But you know us! We Indians are like little rabbits. We like to live in one big happy family.'

My mother sighed knowingly. 'We too, you know. We've had Roger's father with us for umpteen years!'

'Can I persuade you to come in for some tea?' Devi asked. 'I'd love to introduce you to the rest of the family.'

Terror almost made me shout out 'No!' My mother exercising her charm amongst Indians would have been unbearable.

But she shook her head. 'Thank you very much, Devi! I simply wish I didn't have to fly down to the theatre – one of the junior rehearsals, you know. Sometimes I wonder what we're doing in the wretched business, don't you?'

I was safe. She had released the brake of our old Desoto and ground it into gear. 'Goodbye, Devi!' she called out. 'Bye, darling! Have a lovely day!' Then she stared rigidly over her knuckles on the steering wheel and chugged and braked around the driveway and out of the gate again.

'Come,' said Maya. 'Let me take you in.'

I followed her through an enormous front door and into a dark, wood-panelled hall, two storeys high. Beams of coloured light, bent and angled by the jewelled windows, glanced off brass bowls, copper plates, gilded frames, the curve of a smooth teak banister. I stopped in the middle and looked around me. Massive portraits in oils of Indian men in Eastern and Western dress hung high and low on the walls. Indian rugs in purples, oranges and golds covered the floor. A runner in a luminous paisley of green and scarlet wound up the circular stairway and out of sight.

'Come,' Maya said. 'Let me introduce you to the flesh and blood.'

She opened a door into a morning-room, bright with sunshine and white walls.

'This is my grandmother, Mrs Chowdree, here – and my other grandmother, Mrs Singh – my grandfather, Mr Singh. My father, my mother. Yuvassi, my little sister. And this is Aunt Vanitha. You've met Aunt Devi already.'

'Welcome! Welcome! Welcome!' Mr Chowdree chanted. He sounded just like Valerie's imitation of Indians saying things in threes.

'And how lovely it is to have you in our home!' Maya's mother added.

They watched me, smiling, smiling. 'Sit down?' they asked. 'How about a drink?'

I stood as if on stage for the first time. They smiled and nodded. One of the old women patted the seat of a chair next to her. But I could feel it coming on again – I knew the signs by now – the panic that had visited me at the beach. Their sing-song voices, their strange smiling, the smells everywhere of curry and pungent hair oil, the bright colours and the dark hall brought on the sickness. Homesickness. Nostalgia after five minutes for Nora, for my mother, for the dogs, the smell of our Sunday duck and of my father's sweat after a morning of golf.

'Maya has been talking of nothing but you since she was at your school,' Mrs Chowdree was saying.

'Jabber, jabber, jabber,' Mr Chowdree chortled.

'Oh, Daddy!' Maya reached for my hand and held it in hers. 'Does anyone mind if we have a few games before lunch?'

'You girls must do whatever you like. Want us to send out some juice?'

'Yes, please, Mummy.' She led me out on to a verandah and down into the garden.

I had seen Indian girls our age and even older holding hands, or walking arm in arm. It seemed silly. I felt silly, more silly than panicked now that we were out of the house and away from her family. As soon as I could, I uncoupled myself to retie a lace. Then I plunged my hands into my pockets and followed her along a path, through a stand of mango trees, and down a long sloping hill behind the house.

The garden was unkempt and overgrown, rank with weeds and rotting fruit. A granadilla hedge wound along the boundary.

'I've heard that snakes live in granadilla hedges,' I said nonchalantly.

'Oh, they do!' she cried. 'We have lots! The gardeners catch them all the time! Even mambas. Yuvassi won't set foot off the path.'

'My sister's terrified of flying ants!' I laughed, keeping my eye on the hedge for signs of life.

'Shame,' she said, 'poor thing. It must be awful for her when it rains.'

Had she scoffed at Valerie's terrors, or included me in some joke against her own sister, I would have felt less strange. It would have cheered me up perhaps. But she sprang beside me now, chatting about the newspaper article, telling me that her mother had framed it in a golden frame and placed it on their piano.

'Do you play?' I asked.

'Oh, yes.'

'Which exams? Royal College or Trinity?'

'Royal College,' she said. 'I'm taking Advanced I this year. And you?'

Nothing was right. 'Same,' I said. 'But I'm still on Intermediate.'

'Yuvassi too!' she cried. 'Have you got those three-part inventions?' She hummed a few bars from each.

I nodded.

'You lucky fish! I'm stuck with the Prokofiev variations.'

I'd never heard of the Prokofiev variations. And she loved Bach. Her ponytail sprang around her head thick and lush. There were two Jaguars in her driveway. And she had a family that she loved without embarrassment.

'Shame, poor you,' I said.

After tennis we drank granadilla juice on the thatched

220

verandah of the change-room cottage.

'Do you really want to do psychology when you leave school?' she asked.

'No! Why?'

'Miss Robinson made that joke before the debate.'

'Oh, that!' I giggled. 'She's quite bats, you know.'

Maya giggled too. 'I know! Mrs Naidoo warned us before we came.'

'Did she?' I loved the idea that Rangston wasn't sacred to the Indians. Things were getting better. Alone down there we could become friends.

'She said she's a bit of a battle-axe.'

'She's more than that,' I said. 'She's mad. She punishes us if we cough or scratch in prayers. And now we have to go to the cloakroom if we want to blow our noses!'

'Mrs Naidoo warned us about the coughing and scratching too. We were terrified, I can tell you!'

I laughed, wondering whether I could go any further. 'This juice is delicious,' I said.

'They're our own granadillas. We can pick some after lunch, if you like.'

'She's also a lesbian,' I said quickly.

'Who?' She stared at my smile as if she hadn't caught the joke.

'Miss Robinson!'

'Oh!' She laughed at last. 'Golly! She's even more of a cliché than I'd thought! Wait till I tell my father!'

Their Sunday lunch took place in a room even larger and gloomier than the hall. But here all the wood had been elaborately carved. Gargoyles, Vikings, lions' heads, eagles and even snakes glowered at each other across the table from the high-back uncomfortable chairs in which we sat. Mauve damask, streaked and stained, covered the walls. And the windows were draped in deep-purple silk, with pelmets, cords and tassles to match. Months or years of dust had settled into the crevices of the carvings, over the pelmets and drapes, and on all the vases and jugs, the picture frames, the pictures themselves. I stared at the table and the food on it for signs of dirt.

It was spotless. Bright silver salvers of curries and sauces, platters of samosas, nan, fruits of different colours, peeled and sliced into cut-glass bowls, had been placed down the centre of the table on a runner of pure-white lace. The table itself had been polished to a gleam. Three servants holding silver jugs stood against the walls waiting to fill our glasses. And over everything hung the heavy aroma of curry, cardamom, bananas, mangoes, and the soured milk and cinnamon of Indian sweetmeats.

'Well, girls, how was tennis?' Mr Chowdree asked. 'Are you two a match for each other?' He sat in tennis whites himself at the head of their long table. Just like my own father, he seemed amused and pleased by the presence of all his dependants around him.

'We're very equally matched,' Maya said.

'*Very* equally?' he asked, laughing. 'How can you be *very* equally matched. You are either equally matched or you are not. Not so?'

In our house such a speech would have brought out groans. But Maya laughed. 'Oh, Daddy! You're so pedantic! You know exactly what I meant!'

'The function of language,' he said, 'is not simply to communicate, but also to express. Excessive expression pollutes.'

Maya laid her hand on my arm. 'You must excuse him,' she said. 'He loves quibbling about these things.'

I laughed. 'My parents do too,' I said. But I couldn't yet love them for it as she loved her father. I decided to watch her more carefully.

'Of course they do!' Devi Chowdree said. 'Your parents are our shining examples of how the King's English should be spoken.'

'Well —' I hesitated. My speech caused consternation at home. From the start I had found excuses to miss my elocution lessons. And my parents, intent on their romance with Catherine and Valerie, hadn't noticed until it was too late. Even so, I accepted their assessment of my shortcomings. And I didn't want Devi to think they considered me one of the King's shining examples. 'Not me,' I said. 'They don't approve of my speech at all.

'We are all wondering what the next production will be,' Maya's mother exclaimed in her heavily Indian English. 'I'm sure it will be a very great success.'

I blushed. Indians couldn't come to white theatres. Even my parents were outraged to have their audiences so constrained. And I didn't know if there was going to be a next production. I didn't know what to say.

'We're putting on *Pygmalion* at our own little theatre in December,' Devi said. 'I'm already worrying about the casting.'

I sent a prayer of thanks to my God under the ceiling that Valerie wasn't there. She would have loved the idea of Eliza with an Indian accent. I could hear her voice torturing the words. Even see myself laughing at the funniness of it. Despite the fact that I was beginning to enjoy myself among them. Despite everything.

'My parents are thinking of *My Fair Lady*,' I said.

'Oh! What a coincidence!' Maya's mother cried. '*My Fair Lady* and *Pygmalion*! Isn't it a coincidence, everyone? Would you like some juice now, Ruth?'

Two servants leaped forward with their jugs.

'Coconut or granadilla?' she asked. 'Or both?'

They all laughed merrily at the thought of both juices together.

'Both!' I said to please them. They laughed. The old people rocked back and forth in their chairs.

Their humour seemed as silly to me as girls holding hands. But even so, the kind of laughing that this family practised had eased away the last of my discomfort. It allowed me to taste the food I ate with pleasure. No one commented on my appetite or nagged me to eat more, as Lucy's family used to do. The food itself seemed to be only food. A source of pleasure.

But they teased the old people a lot. 'Grandma, want the whole dish today? Shall we order another from the kitchen?'

The old lady clasped a plump hand over her mouth and

giggled. Her jewelled nostril kept catching the light and flashing mercurial red beams all over the room. 'No, no, no!' she shrieked.

'Hee! Hee! Hee!' The grandfather, a smooth round bald old man, giggled between the two old women.

Mr Chowdree turned to me, still smiling at his mother's embarrassment. 'Your father, I believe, preceded me at Balliol,' he said.

'Oh, yes,' I said. 'Yes.'

'I remember hearing him spoken of so many times. He was a fine scholar. And a rower too, I think.'

'He plays golf now,' I said.

He smiled. 'What about you? Maya tells me that you want to study psychology when you leave school.'

'Oh, no, Daddy!' Maya explained. 'I said the headmistress said so.'

'Is that your wish?' he asked again, inclining his head gently.

Having no idea how to answer him, I risked the truth. 'I was just being perverse,' I said. 'Miss Robinson only wants us to be teachers or nurses. She despises psychology. So I just said it. I don't really even know what it is.' I flushed as I looked at them, hoping they didn't think me flippant about my future.

But Maya's parents laughed, as if I'd told an hilarious story. Even Yuvassi began to laugh. And then Vanitha and Devi and Maya too.

Tears rolled down Mrs Chowdree's cheeks. 'You two girls!' she cried. 'Two peas in a pod!'

It wasn't that funny. But I laughed anyway, glad of my success.

Maya laid her hand on my arm again. 'My parents love to hear stories like that. They think of people like Miss Robinson as the worst relics of the Raj.'

I smiled. But my mind raced around trying to track down the meaning of 'Raj'.

'She's a lesbian too, Daddy!' Maya said. 'Isn't that just perfect?'

'Ha! Ha!' he laughed.

Mrs Chowdree stood and smiled around the table. 'Let's have tea on the verandah,' she said.

We drank our tea in wicker chairs facing the hills, looking over the tops of their mango trees, down into the valley. A flock of hadedahs whooped across the sky. The three old people sat indoors, talking to each other loudly in high-pitched Hindi.

It was Sunday. But in that house the peace of the afternoon carried no menace. Even the thought of school the next day and of my English essay still to do could not depress me. Perhaps it had been the mention of my father, a common past, or maybe the people themselves, their laughing, the place itself, and me there with them, that had threaded together to banish my discomfort and make me happy.

'Tell me, Ruth,' Mr Chowdree said, 'how do you like to spend your time best of all?'

I blushed. I had no idea how to play this game. It was nothing like our fun with Lucy.

'It depends on the circumstances,' I offered.

He rubbed his hands together. 'Good, good, good!' he said.

'I like the idea of being free,' I suggested, encouraged.

'Ah!' He sat forward. 'Free of or free to?'

I envied them their dark skins. By now I knew my cheeks and ears were on fire. 'Well, free of − free of −' I shrugged and laughed. 'I don't know. I'd like to travel, I think. I'm not very patient.'

He clapped his hands in delight. 'Patience, patience, patience!' he chanted. 'The best people have trouble with patience.'

'Two peas in a pod,' Mrs Chowdree chortled.

'I too want to travel,' Maya explained. 'But I have to wait until I've finished school.' She pretended to scowl.

I thought of the two Jaguars in the driveway, all the branches of Chowdree and Sons in Indiantown. It was easy for her. All she had to do was to wait.

'With a bit of luck Maya will go to Oxford too when she's finished school,' he said.

'Luck and hard work,' Devi added.

Maya jumped up. 'I promised to pick some granadillas for Ruth. Come, let's go.'

'Oh, no,' I cried, remembering the snakes, 'it doesn't matter. Really.'

'Let's send a servant!' her mother suggested. 'Think of all those snakes, Maya!'

'We're having such a good time!' her father wailed.

Maya laughed. 'Well, you'll just have to suffer! Go and play tennis or something. She's *my* friend!' She took my hand and led me back into the garden.

I waved and smiled. It was lovely to be wanted by these people. And yet nothing I had said was brilliant. For most of the lunch I'd been silent. Now that it was almost time to go, I wished we could start again. So that I could try from the beginning just to be myself. Now that I understood their rules. Now that I knew the value that they placed upon candour.

'Nothing wrong with cordial relations between the races,' Abba said, tapping his hands together lightly at the fingertips.

He had been waiting for me at the door of the boudoir when I returned. 'See here,' he had said, almost in a whisper, 'I have cashew nuts.'

'Oh, Abba –'

'Just a minute –'

And so I went in and sat on the chaise longue in the fading light.

'There are dangers,' he said, 'in overstepping the mark. I knew old Ravi Chowdree, the grandfather, and his two brothers. I knew the whole family. Not a scoundrel amongst them.'

He held out a bowl of cashews to me but I shook my head.

'I'm not saying one shouldn't respect one another,' he went on. 'But respect and social intercourse are two different things. I, for instance, have always respected the Indian above the other dark races. He is ambitious. He cares about the education of his young. He takes care of his sick and his aged. Mind you, that doesn't mean we are not to respect the Bantu as well. Most particularly the Zulu. His is a proud race, a loyal race.'

I had heard all this from Abba many times before. What I didn't want was any more about Maya's family. I began to feel sick again. And I longed for Jocelyn.

'Our own Jewish heritage, as you know, is the oldest and finest of all. We have been persecuted, discriminated against, excluded, exiled. But we have survived. It is our traditions that have held us together.'

He leaned forward in his chair, looked at me through the gloom. 'It would please me very much indeed to see you mix more with other young Jewish boys and girls, my dear. That fine boy, for instance, who invited you to Habonim. One day you could think of a visit to Israel. As I visited Palestine that was. You could —'

'Abba! I'll *never* join Habonim! To tell you the truth, I hated it! I don't want to mix with Jews only!'

He hung his large head and shook it heavily from side to side. 'Ruth, what has happened to you? Do you know what you are saying?'

I could barely breathe. All my belonging right then seemed to be slipping away. What I had had, the bits and pieces. Even Abba. And yet it was the bits and pieces in me that the Chowdrees had welcomed. Roger and Sarah's daughter. Oxford. Rowing. The things to which I had thought I belonged.

'I want to go to Oxford,' I said.

'That's a fine ideal. But you would go as a Jew, my dear,' he insisted. 'As a Jew first.'

'As me, just me.'

'A Jew and a South African,' he insisted. 'That's how you will be thought of, you know. That's what you are, my dear. What you should be proud of.'

'I'm not proud!' I shouted. 'Why should I be proud?'

He shook his head again. 'I think your dear parents were most remiss in allowing you to stop your Hebrew lessons.'

'They weren't! I hated Hebrew.'

'And do you not think that the young Chowdree girl receives instruction in her own language and religious teachings?'

I don't care!' I shouted. 'That's her business!'

But I wondered suddenly about Maya. She seemed so comfortable being different. And yet different from what? In her world, with her family, with the other Brighton girls, she belonged, she was comfortable. Perhaps it was her sort of belonging that allowed her to be comfortable everywhere, even at Rangston. It was I who was different, not she. And I knew it had nothing at all to do with Hebrew or Hindi. It had to do with me and us.

'It puts me in a damned awkward position,' my mother was saying as I came into the lounge. 'What do I *say*?'

My father cleared his throat. 'Well, is it out of the question? It's not really against the law, you know.'

'It's not just the law!'

'Well, how exactly did she put it?' he asked.

'She said that she wants the girl properly trained. Eventually, she says, the parents intend her for Oxford. And we're the best people to do the job.'

'We know that. They're no fools, these Indians.'

'Where would we put her? I can't just throw her in with the intermediates –'

'Who? What?' I asked. 'What "intermediates"?'

'Oh! You!' My mother stabbed at me through the air with one scarlet fingernail. 'You're the cause of all this.'

'What?' I knew already what. My pulse beat for joy in the nape of my neck.

'Devi Chowdree has asked me to take on that Maya at the school.'

'So?' I asked.

'So? So? So, it puts me in a damned awkward position! Gugh! As if I haven't got enough on my fork! And all because of you!'

I was quite used to her need to lay blame. There was no point in setting up a defence. 'If you take her, you could put me and her in a class together.'

'Her and me,' my father said.

'What?'

228

'What?' he echoed.

'I'll go with her,' I said.

My mother stared at my father. 'Now that's a thought!' she said.

'Two birds with one stone,' he replied.

'We could give them both to Alethea. Devi said she only wants voice. I think she understands the position she'd be putting us in with acting.'

'How can she fail to?'

'How indeed?'

My mother beamed at me. 'Well, darling, you've certainly got us out of a tight spot!'

'Ha! Perhaps our Chops will learn to open her mouth and speak properly into the bargain!' he said.

16

A few months later, the newspapers were carrying photographs of black bodies lying in the dust at Sharpeville. Bare arms and legs and feet, the heads face up, face down, children sprawled out dead. The government declared a state of emergency. Blacks marched and refused to go to work. People fasted all over the country. They joined together to pray to God for a solution. White liberals began to pack up and leave for England. 'It's just a matter of time,' they said. 'The winds of change, you know.'

'I hear the Goldbergs are leaving,' my mother said. 'Their house is up for sale.'

Abba shook his head. 'No point in running away.'

'It's all very well for them,' she snorted. 'They've got the money! They can afford to sell their house for next to nothing.'

Money had become a member of the household at last. It had taken the place of romance.

'But it's the principle of the matter, my dear,' Abba insisted. 'Running away is cowardly.'

I too wanted to run away. My dreams were filled with flight – over streets, over mountains, over continents. And then I would wake up just where I was, the sun beating hot through four thicknesses of curtain, the hadedahs wailing overhead, the snick-snack of Pillay's clippers in the garden.

At least Valerie was gone. Without her the house had lost its menace. I could climb the stairs or enter a room or sing or laugh, unstretched by caution. Rooms had become just rooms. The sewing-room. The music-room. Even her bedroom, just another spare room. It had been opened up, its perfumes and pictures gone, the walls scrubbed. I would walk in there simply to feel the current of freedom that her absence charged through me. I could sit on her chair or her bed, open her empty drawers. No longer hers. Anyone's. Ours.

But still there was the knife at the throat to worry about. And a strange sort of Sunday afternoon silence that had settled over us all the time. Since Jocelyn and Gwen and *The Women* my mother had taken on a new sort of silence herself. She mulled and mulled into her glass of Scotch, and then poured herself another, and closed her eyes, and threw her head back over the couch. Some days she didn't seem to see me at all. Nor did she complain that my father was often late for supper. Or that Nora's cooking hadn't improved. Most nights now there were only the three of us anyway. Often Abba didn't come down at all. He ordered a soft-boiled egg and toast for his room. He was going a little potty, my mother said. Up there all day with his photo albums and paraphernalia. It was as if he knew how useless his life had become to us. He'd already divided up his money. There was no more to be had. No one listened to what he had to say, not even me. For everyone but him he might as well have been dead.

Nora too was different. One day she appeared in the kitchen without any teeth. They had been paining her, she explained. Without them her voice flew up into her nose, her cheeks were sucked in, she lisped and spat as she spoke. My mother shook her head. 'They think it gives them a winsome smile,' she said. 'Perhaps she wants that Reuben back again.'

But I knew it wasn't Reuben. Nora seemed to have shrunk into herself. And her body had shrunk too. So had her breasts. She moved more slowly now. She had to keep hitching her uniform up over her belt. She complained a lot about her womb. And she talked constantly of her grandchildren. She crossed off the days on the kitchen calendar till she could see them again. She told me of a special savings account she kept at the building society for their future. They were clever, she said. Like me. One day they would be teachers perhaps.

Every week Maya and I met for voice class. And often on the weekends at each other's houses. I loved to go to her house and the Chowdrees loved to have me. They seemed to have formed an idea of the person I was and I liked to step into that idea, to be that person for them and for myself. It was different from Jocelyn's way of seeing into my future. It was more of a game. But not the sort of sport that we had played in our house with Lucy. There was no bloodshed in it.

'What will you do after Oxford?' I asked Maya. We sat on her verandah listening to the plock-plock of tennis balls.

'I'll come back here,' she said.

'You're mad.'

'No, I'm not. You tell me where I'd be better off!' She smiled her checkmate smile.

'England?'

'Without my family? A curry-muncher? Ha! Ha!'

'Better than being a second-class citizen here,' I said.

'Look at it my way. I don't need to take buses. We never go to restaurants. And we have our own theatre. It would be much worse in England.' She loved these arguments of ours, the ironies in them.

But I didn't. I could never admit to the real differences between us – money, beauty, happiness. Or accept as she did our common indifference to the black man's plight.

'Well, anyway,' I said, 'there's going to be a revolution.'

'No, there won't!' she laughed. 'My father says things will settle down in a year and everyone will come running back.' Maya knew more about the political situation than I did. Her family discussed it every night. They read the London *Times* and listened to the BBC on a special radio.

'But look at the numbers!' I cried.

'Look at the history! Look at our strategic importance.'

Our. It sounded funny from Maya. I never used it myself. Jews and Indians seemed to have no stake in the future of the country.

'Do you ever worry about anything?' I asked her. We had never discussed our separate futures as women. I didn't even know whether her family would arrange a marriage for her, as other Indians did. My own worries jangled and chimed in discord. Getting out. Money. A man of my own.

'I worry a lot about my A-levels,' she admitted. She leaned forward on to her elbows. 'I worry about it all the time. Don't you?'

I shook ny head. 'I don't think I'm doing A-levels,' I said.

'Why not?' Her eyes fixed their dark centres on mine.

I shrugged. 'I'll probably just stay here for my BA.'

'But why?'

She wouldn't, I knew, take any satisfaction from my shame. We were that different.

'I don't think we can afford it at the moment,' I said. 'My sister got married – there was the whole wedding, you know. And – you know people are leaving. My parents have lost a lot of students.'

I saw the slight nod of her head, felt the images passing between us in silence. House, theatre, family. We usually discussed history and music and teachers and politics. We amused each other with our clevernesses. How much had she actually seen of my family when she was in it? Of Valerie's viciousness? Or my mother's despair? What did she actually think of us, this friend of mine from the other side? I had no idea.

'What about scholarships?' she asked.

I shook my head. 'Who would give me a scholarship? Everyone thinks we're rich.'

She nodded.

'But I don't care.' I laughed loudly into her serious clever face. 'I'll go even if I have to stow away on a ship!'

She turned away from my laugh. Her father and Yuvassi were walking back from the courts through the high grass. They waved. We waved back. 'There must be a solution,' she said. 'Let's think about it sensibly.'

When I arrived home that evening Valerie and Bernard were there. They often dropped in at the last minute for supper. To save money, my mother said, because he kept Valerie on such a short stick. But I could see that Valerie liked to be back. She liked to sit, pregnant, beyond my father's reach. She liked to criticize the food. And to have Bernard run his hand over her stomach to our audience. She didn't seem to notice that the rules had changed. The stage was all torn up now. No one wanted a show anymore.

'What are those?' I asked.

Six or seven canvases had been propped around the window seat. I dropped my tennis racquet on to a chair and stood in front of them. They were awful. Naked bodies of women in lightning blues and dark purples, dead-looking women with arms and legs spread to the edges of each canvas.

Bernard had sprung silently behind me. He cupped one of my buttocks in his hand and ruffled around in the frills of my tennis pants. 'Like them?' he crooned.

I looked at my mother.

'Bernard!' she sighed. 'You know they're perfectly ghastly! If you have to sell them why not try someone with money! Try that Jeffrey. Why us, for God's sake?'

'We tried Jeffrey,' Valerie said. 'His taste is up his arse.'

'Valerie, my girl,' my father said softly, 'you're still in our house. Please don't be vulgar.'

'*Up his arse!*' she sneered. 'There's lots of room.'

My father lifted the paper again and shook his head behind it.

'Only an arseface like him would get us all into a mess like that!' She waved her hand at the paper.

'What mess?' I asked.

'Jeffrey's workers went on strike,' my father said. 'And he's refused to rehire them. There's some sort of hue-and-cry.'

'Fascist!' I said. It was a new word for me. Generally it amused them.

'You had better stop throwing those terms about so lightly, young woman,' my father said. 'Catherine has apparently received some threatening phone calls.'

'Maybe she'll get us all into the paper,' Valerie sneered. It was what she wanted for herself. Threatening phone calls. A husband in control of hundreds of lives.

Bernard opened the piano and began to pick out 'Some of These Days'.

'Valerie!' My father appealed to her with liquid eyes. Bernard's antics either gave him one of his headaches or brought him to tears these days. 'Please!' he said.

Valerie hauled herself out of the rocking chair and went to sit on the arm of the couch, next to my father. She laid her cheek on the top of his head and hugged him. He leaned against her with the convulsive relief of a lost child now found, and closed his eyes. She rocked him gently.

My mother crashed her glass on to the table and stood up. 'I'm going to ring for supper,' she said.

Bernard leapt across from the piano and took hold of Valerie's free arm. He gnawed and growled along it, up towards her armpit. 'I feel like crayfish,' he said. 'Let's go down to the Oyster Pit, Cheeky. C'mon!'

'No,' she said. Her black eyes flashed. 'I'm staying.'

He cocked his head at her and then turned suddenly, pounced over to me and laid his hands on my shoulders. 'Little one, want to come and have some crayfish with me?'

I shook my head. I was used by now to the effect of his eyes and his touch. 'It's a school night,' I said.

'Oh, c'mon!'

'Bernard!' my mother snapped. 'Don't be absurd. And leave that child alone. Haven't you caused enough trouble already?'

Valerie sat still, with her arm around my father. She even smiled. I didn't understand.

'Child?' Bernard crooned. 'This? A child?' His eyes ran over every contour of my body, my tennis shoes, around each toe inside.

I shivered. 'I don't want to go,' I said. 'Go by yourself.'

Valerie bent over to kiss my father's shining forehead. 'Will you take me home?' she asked.

'Supper it's ready, Madam,' Reuben announced from the door.

Bernard waved at us. 'Cheers!' he said. 'Enjoy yourselves.'

'Take away one place, please, Reuben,' my mother said. 'We'll only be five.'

'Manga-mang-ahhhh!'

'Manga-mang-ahhhh!'

'No! Resonate the "ng" right up here –' Alethea Davis circled her hand in front of her forehead. 'And then place it out there –' She pointed to a spot on the floor.

This was impossible for me. The sound came out of my mouth. I couldn't imagine how I was supposed to place it three feet away. And even if I could have, I didn't want to.

'Half a tone up now. Mingee-mingeeeee!'

'Mingee-mingeeeee!'

'Behind the nose this time! Wait! Let me feel that diaphragm as you take a breath.' She prodded me in the ribs. 'Shoulders down. Expand! Expand those ribs!'

Alethea was determined to take credit from my parents for transforming my speech. And I was equally determined not ever to talk as she did. All those carefully contrived vowels, the voice too deep for her small, pinched face.

'All right. Now Maya.'

For Maya this was different. She knew what she wanted – no trace at all of her Indian vowels and consonants. Her too-soft t's and too-voiced d's transformed for her arrival in England. She tried much harder than I did.

'T-t-t-t-t-tit.'

'T-t-t-t-t-tit.'

'Still too soft. The very tip of the tongue – see? – the very *tip* against the hard palate, just behind the teeth. Look –' Alethea opened her thin-lipped bird's mouth. 'Ti-t. Ti-t. Again.'

'T-t-t-t-tit.'

'Better! D-d-d-d-dad.'

236

We could hear my mother's voice on stage, booming and blasting at her advanced acting class. My father had his fencing class lunging at the back of the hall. Garth was one of the fencers. He turned away when he saw me now. It was as if we had never been out there in the garden, with his tongue in my mouth.

'All right. Each of you in turn. Let's take the Tennyson. Maya, do you want to begin?'

' "On either side the river lie –" '

I watched Maya trying not to sound herself, her whole body rigid with the effort.

' "Long fields of barley and of rye. That clothe the wold and meet the sky –" '

'Stop! Let's go back to the beginning. Now this time relax. If you think of each vowel and consonant as you're saying it, you'll miss the poetry of the piece. You've got to make the technique second nature.'

But Maya couldn't let go of each vowel and consonant. They were there in the anatomy of every thought. She had to learn to think a different way, so that when she opened her mouth to speak her voice and utterance contradicted the dark of her skin, her oiled hair, the way she took my hand in hers as we walked out to the street to meet her father.

'Hello, Daddy.'

'Hello, my dearest darling. Hello, Ruth! Climb in, girls.'

Mr Chowdree drove us home every Thursday. Maya was never allowed to take a bus and I was delighted not to have to wait for my parents at the school. The old chaos of the place was gone, the way the students hung about after their classes on the steps, or flocked around my father telling jokes. Parents came to fetch their children now that the winds of change were blowing. And the paint was peeling off the walls. White ants still ate away at the foundations. Jim had gone. My mother brought Johnson, our gardenboy, three times a week, to clean and tidy the place.

'How are you two coming along then?' Mr Chowdree laughed cheerfully.

People always stared at us as we drove down Market Street. The white Jaguar. The Indian in the Jaguar. The Indian school-girl next to him. And then at me in the back where the servants sat, in my Rangston hat and blazer.

'I'll never get it,' Maya said.

'Yes you will!' I said. 'I mean you have! You do!'

'Will. Have. Do.' Mr Chowdree chuckled. 'Future. Perfect. Present.'

'Daddy!'

'Do you think we have a future in this perfect present country, Ruth?'

'Daddy!'

We? What we? We rich? We Indians? We Jews? 'I don't know,' I said.

'But Maya tells me you predict revolution.' He laughed heartily.

Did Maya tell them everything? About the money too? And Oxford? I blushed. 'I think there will be,' I said. 'It's inevitable.'

'Ah! In-ev-i-table!' He plunked the syllables down the scale. 'Would you like to know what I think?'

'Yes.'

'I think there will be no revolution in South Africa. If there is, it won't happen until you and Maya have great-great-grandchildren.'

'But what about the ANC?' I asked. ANC was all I knew.

'Oh, the government will get rid of those trouble-makers. Look at what they're doing already.'

We were flying through the race course now, on our way up to the ridge. I knew that the government was 'clamping down'. But the clamping didn't seem enough to discourage the knife at the throat.

'Daddy, you won't convince her, you know.'

'No, no,' I said. 'He can.'

'You mean I *can* convince you?' He laughed. 'Or I can try?' He seemed very amused by the politeness that his presence en-forced on me.

I laughed too. We were almost home.

238

'Look,' he said. 'I happen to think we arc going to need our bright young people here to balance things a bit. If people like you and Maya, your family, our family, just leave, who will be left to work for peaceful solutions?'

'I don't know,' I said. I wondered what peaceful solution there could possibly be to all the hopeless numbers they kept printing in the paper. That kept turning in my head.

'Thank you very much for the lift, Mr Chowdree.'

'You're very much welcome, Miss Frank!' he laughed. He leaned over the back seat and looked into my face. 'Will you do me a favour, Ruth?'

I nodded. 'Oh, yes, of course.'

'Well, you don't know what it is. Be cautious with your agreements.'

'Daddy!'

'Before you make your big life decisions,' he said, 'come and talk to me. I have some suggestions you might like to consider.'

It was the money. She had told him. I thanked the God that watched over my life that I'd never talked to her about boys.

'You're almost a member of our family, you know,' he said.

The dogs barked and snarled and snapped behind the gate.

'I know,' I said. 'Maya too, with us.'

My parents arrived home silent from the theatre that night. They called for the drinks tray and sat at either end of the couch, staring ahead.

'Now what?' she demanded.

'We carry on.'

'You and your carrying on! Gugh!'

'There are plenty of other shows. You weren't even so sure if we could do it.'

'But to be pipped at the post.'

'We weren't pipped. They must have applied for the rights a good six months before we did.'

'Rights for what?' I asked.

She didn't see me or hear me. 'Let's face it,' she said, 'we're no longer the only crew in town. The public loves that rubbish they put on.'

'The public loves our stuff too. And it's not rubbish.'

She sighed and flexed the sinews in her neck.

'If I could borrow the money to go to Oxford –' I said into the silence.

'You could what?' my father asked.

She tossed her head. '*I* thought *Fair Lady* was a risk from the start. We haven't got the voices. Not to mention the where-withal!'

'Chopsticks?' he asked. 'What was that you said?'

She frowned up at me.

'I mean if someone offered to lend us the money, could I go to Oxford, do you think? I mean if I could get in. I was just thinking.'

'To *Oxford*! Ha! That's a joke! From where? From whom? If you're thinking of Uncle Leon you can think again. I'd rather starve!'

'No one's going to starve,' my father said.

'I wasn't thinking of Uncle Leon,' I said. 'I hate Uncle Leon.'

'Who then? The man in the moon?'

I shook my head. I couldn't bring myself to tell them. I wasn't even sure. But my heart galloped in hope. 'I mean just *if* someone could, would you?'

My mother looked up at me through bloodshot eyes. ' "Would you? Could you?" ' she mimicked. She screwed up her mouth and nose in a parody of mine. 'I think you use that dreadful squeak just to annoy us! Alethea has told me you have a voice! Just why you won't use it I can't tell her!' She slammed her glass down and poured herself another Scotch.

But her mimicking of me, her distorted face, her use of the weapon I'd so often used on others – on me, the one she'd always spared – killed suddenly the diffidence I'd felt in asking them for something for myself. I leapt up out of my chair and stood before her.

'You don't give a damn what happens to me, do you? All you care about is yourself! Even more than your stupid theatre!' I turned my mouth down at the corners like hers. 'The famous Sarah Frank!' I spat out. 'Famous! Ha! Ha! What a laugh! You're a fake! You can't even act! That's why you came back from England, isn't it? I'm sick and tired of all the lies you expect us to swallow!'

I faced her panting, my throat aching. And they stared back at me motionless, frightened, as if I'd run in out of the night, a stranger with a deadly weapon. It gave me hope.

'You're always pretending we're so special!' I shouted. 'What's so damned special about us, that's what I want to know? Valerie's sick in the head! Catherine hates you! And I – And I –' Tears stormed down my face now. I didn't know how to tell her that I loved her even so. 'I can't wait to leave! I'm warning you! I'd do anything to get away from here!'

'Hey, hey,' my father said. 'Steady on, Chops –'

I turned on him. 'I won't steady on! It's her fault! She drags everything down with her! How dare she drag me down too? She's like a disease! I hate her! I really hate her!'

It was said. She had heard me. I saw her cover her eyes at last and grope into her bag for a hankie. And, seeing her, I had to turn away to stop myself throwing my arms around her. I wanted to hold on to the truth a little bit longer.

My father waited for her to finish blowing her nose. 'If you've had your say, young woman,' he said carefully, 'perhaps you should now consider apologizing to your mother.'

'Awu!' Nora came to examine my bloodshot eyes. 'You too cheeky. I hear you scream bad words.'

It was Beauty's day off. She had come up to turn down the beds.

'Why you scream bad words at the Madam?' she whistled through her flaccid lips.

I shrugged. Nora's questions didn't interest me anymore. Nor did her opinions. I'd outgrown them. And she was changing her tone with me. She was more polite. Diffident even. If my mother was out she asked my permission for things. I had almost become a Madam myself.

241

'The Lord he say we must honour our mother and our father.'
She folded back my sheet and tucked it in. 'Every mother she
have trouble,' she said.

'Let's sing, Nors,' I suggested, to change the subject.

She smiled, baring pink and grey gums. ' "Lord Is My
Shepherd?" ' she lisped.

'The Lord's my shepherd,' I began.

She clasped her hands before her and gazed up at the ceiling.
Her voice wavered into the harmony. Her eyes moistened. By
the time we reached the 'amen' a few tears had run into the
hollows of her cheeks.

'Awu!' She wiped her eyes on her apron. 'Nkosiyami!' She
shuffled off to the wardrobe for my nightie, laid it carefully
across the bed. 'Old Nora going to die one of these days,' she
whispered.

'You won't die, Nors, don't worry.'

'Who they going to look after my twin?' she asked.

'Constance?'

She shook her head. 'I got *Napoleon Book of Fate*,' she said.

'You can't believe that rubbish!' I said. 'What is it?'

'Everything it's there. Everything. Even you.'

'Me?'

'When you born and when you die. Everything!' She straightened the hairbrushes on the dressing table. 'God move in a
mysterious way,' she warbled. 'His wonder to per-form. He
plant his footstep in the sea. And ride up-on the storm.'

17

In my eighteenth year Bernard became my first lover. I had been sent by my parents to comfort Valerie after her third miscarriage and was to stay with her for the entire Christmas holidays. She and Bernard had bought a small holiday farm inland the year before, with money borrowed from Jeffrey.

They were both at the station to meet me.

'My God, you've lost weight!' she said. She still looked pregnant. Her stomach stuck out and her arms were fat. Her face had lost its angles. Her eyes seemed smaller and lashless. She grasped the back of my sundress and turned it inside out. 'Hmm,' she said. 'Jonathan Logan. Who got you this?'

'Ma. They were on sale at Cottams.'

'This your case?' Bernard shouted out of the train window.

'I don't know what you're going to do here for three months,' she said, striding off down the platform. 'The place is full of old farts and young couples. You'd better learn to play bridge and bowls.'

Valerie's letters had been full of the triumphs of her new life. Dining-room menus. Speech-training classes for farm children. Bottled jams. A sewing circle. Could we please send her the sewing machine until she had time to look for one for herself? She needed to make curtains for all the guest-rooms and crib sheets and things for the baby. The farm labourers were lazy and drunk. Where she would find a nanny, she couldn't imagine. What about lending her Nora?

'Welcome to Chaka's Rest Farm Hotel,' a sign said. 'Licensed to sell wine, malt and spirituous liquors.'

'See, little one?' Bernard waved his sunburned arm out over a mess of long low buildings with corrugated iron roofs. Jacarandas and Old Cape chestnuts towered here and there, blooming in clouds of mauve and pink. Smoky steam rose from the hotel laundry. A few farm dogs ran along barking next to the car.

'It's lovely!' I said. 'It's really like being in the country.'

We were driving up a dirt road, past a patch of bare ground, with an old slide and a see-saw and some rusty swings on it. Two nannies pushed children on the swings. Others sat on the ground in the shade, knitting. Nearby there was splashing and the shrieks of children playing in water.

'Do you have a swimming bath?' I asked.

Valerie tossed her head away from Bernard and looked out of the window. 'If you can call it that,' she said.

A waiter marched up and down the verandah banging out a simple scale on a xylophone.

Valerie and I sat in old wicker chairs, looking out over the hills and drinking lemonade. It felt odd to be in such a place with the loud-voiced people sitting all around us. Chaka's Rest was the sort of resort Lucy's family saved up for. For one week's holiday every two years.

'Yoks,' Valerie said, seeing me looking. 'Let's go in for lunch.'

I followed her through glass doors covered in nylon netting, and into a dark, musty lounge smelling of old smoke and beer. It was furnished with walnut chairs upholstered in burnt-orange coarseweave, turquoise formica tables, and an old dirty flowered carpet. The chairs wore greasy antimacassars and special wooden depressions for glasses at the end of each arm. An Indian waiter in a red fez bowed to Valerie as we passed. Behind him, from a room off the lounge, came the noise of men in a bar. Bernard's voice roared and hooted above the others.

'He has to,' Valerie explained. 'We make most of our money from the bar.'

The dining-room was dark, the chairs stained black. On the floor an old, cracked, patterned linoleum had been worn through in black thready patches here and there. The curtains, crude and unlined, were of the sort of nylon floral that my mother bought in Indiantown for the servants' rooms. They looked as if they had never been washed. The tablecloths were stained and fraying at the edges. Bottles of Chef's and Worcestershire sauce stood on each table. And cheap cut-glass salts and peppers. The waiters smelled of body odour and wore dirty uniforms. One of them thrust the menu under my nose.

'I'd suggest the liver,' Valerie said. 'Don't have the rarebit, if that's what you were thinking.'

I looked up. She was staring at me, my bare tanned shoulders, my new haircut, the way I sat up straight. And there was something missing in her voice now, the old serrated edge.

'Liver, please,' I said.

'Same,' she said. 'And make sure it's right this time.'

People stared at us from other tables and then lowered their voices to gossip.

'Ma sent you the material you wanted,' I said. 'And a whole lot of other things.'

She nodded. Her jaw seemed to be working as if she were trying to stop herself crying.

'I'm so sorry about the baby,' I blurted. 'I know how much –'

'You know nothing! What do you know?' Her eyes flashed at me in the old way. 'I don't know what she thought she was doing sending you here in the first place.'

My heart lifted. Perhaps she'd send me back. Maya would be waiting. And Edwina too. I was thin now. Men turned to watch me on the street. I could even think of trying the beach again.

'Did you hear what happened to Luc–' I coughed. I blushed. Everything I could think of saying seemed to poach on the forbidden subject.

'Yes, I heard!' Valerie sneered. 'Cheap bit of fluff!'

245

'Shame,' I said.

She looked at me with scorn. 'You would say shame!'

But I did feel sorry for Lucy in her yellow bunnywool bolero, carrying her own suitcase to the bus. And then to the train. And then to some cousin in Colenso until her baby could be born and given away. We had all heard her shrieks and screams during dinner as Mr Knowles strapped her with his belt. And then the next night her pleas as her mother snapped every silvered wishbone into pieces – 'See that?' Mrs Knowles screamed. 'That'll teach you! See that?'

'That Clive Spilkin's got his taste up his arse,' Valerie said.

Two waiters leapt to attention as Bernard stalked in. He wore khaki shorts and his rubber sandals. He was tanned. He stopped here and there to talk to his guests. 'Daisy! Hoe gaan did? Piet? Watch out tonight, hey? I'll get you six nil.'

'That'll be the frosty Friday!'

Bernard pounced down next to Valerie and waved to the bar steward. 'Hey! Three shandies! One-two-three!'

A chipped plate of oily liver and onions landed in front of me.

'Wait!' Valerie said. She cut hers open in the middle. 'See?' she said to the waiter. 'Overdone. Take them back. And just tell that munt in there that if this happens again I'll get another chef.'

The waiter stared at Bernard as he took away our plates.

'I've told him and told him,' Valerie explained.

But Bernard had turned to me. He handed me my tankard of shandy. 'To the littlest Frank!' he said. 'Welcome to Chaka's Rest.'

The mock in his voice was gone now. And his eyes seemed bluer in his tanned face, his beard lighter. He smelled of fresh sweat. I blushed and sipped the bittersweet gold liquid.

'Now what?' he asked. 'Rag princess, hey?'

I shrugged. 'I'm waiting to hear about a scholarship. Hope-hope!' I blushed.

'For where?' Valerie demanded. Her jaw was working again. She unscrewed the lid of the salt cellar and loosened the salt with the end of her fork.

'Oh, I don't know. It depends.'

'Well, if you're still thinking of overseas you'd better think again. No scholarship's going to cover that.'

I nodded. She could still kill my hope. It came and went all the time anyway, the way distances expanded and contracted in dreams. The nine thousand miles north. The five hours back home in the train.

'This one will do it, you mark my words,' Bernard said. He looked at me, smiling, the way he had done so long ago. He reached over and touched my arm. 'This one's got it, you can see that a mile away.'

Everyone dressed up on a Saturday night. Women wore diamanté necklaces and earrings and peep-toed shoes. My mother had insisted I take Catherine's old black velvet evening dress with glass buttons. Valerie wore one of her trousseau dresses, too tight, and shiny at the seams. I understood now why her eyes looked lashless. She wore no make-up anymore. No polish on her nails either. Her hands were rough and cracked, and a blue vein stood out behind her left knee.

After dinner we sat in the lounge drinking coffee out of thick cups while the waiters cleared a space in the dining-room for dancing. The music crackled on through a loudspeaker over the glass doors. 'You must have been a beautiful baby,' Ray Conniff's singers crooned. It was one of our records, taken by Valerie when she left.

'Madame Defarge?' Bernard bowed in front of me. Unlike the other men, he wore an open shirt, short sleeves, and the sandals.

I glanced at Valerie. She pulled on a cigarette and stared ahead of her.

People watched us as we left the room. We were the first to dance. He grasped me strong and tight, swooped me here and there, his sandals catching on the linoleum. Others came too. They smiled at him, and he looked down at me, like the peasant dancing in the Renoir print my parents had in their bedroom.

He held me tight, waiting for the next dance. The velvet

247

dress and his body flat against mine made my skin run with sweat. My feet squelched in my sandals. 'I think maybe we should keep Valerie company,' I suggested.

'All the Things You Are' started up.

Bernard barely moved me now. We swayed together, his beard at my forehead. 'Tomorrow,' he said, 'want to come around the farm with me?'

I nodded. I decided not to ask about Valerie anymore. I told myself she didn't care.

'I'll show you the things I love,' he said.

My room was small, without a bathroom of its own, at the end of a long barracks of similar rooms. Each had a bed or two, a table covered with a crocheted doily, a jug for water and a basin. It smelled of Cobra polish and smoky sheets. Rough, heavy blankets covered the bed. The floor was bare except for a small square of worn carpet next to the bed. And the night was very dark, and much cooler than the coast. Things hooted and whooshed in the country silence. I stumbled to the door several times to check that I'd turned the key. By the time the sun rose I had just fallen into a real sleep.

When I woke up the room was hot. Someone seemed to be banging somewhere.

'Ruth! It's lunchtime! Ruth?'

I ran for the door and turned the key.

'Why do you lock the bloody thing?' Valerie demanded. 'We're not in the bloody bundu, you know.'

The sun streamed in over the green polished floor. I blinked at her. 'Sorry,' I said.

She was at the cupboard, leafing through my dresses. 'There's the lunch gong,' she said. 'Hurry up.'

Bernard didn't come to lunch. And afterwards Valerie took me to their bungalow. It was apart from the hotel, an old building with an old-fashioned verandah all around it. She led me through each room, lecturing me on the improvements she had made. I followed her, nodding and praising, wondering just how I was meant to give her comfort. But every now and then,

248

as she would stop at a chair, or some shelves just built, as she'd lose the rest of her sentence and stare at the chair or the shelves or at me, I wanted to embrace her as I'd wanted to embrace my mother. They both seemed to have fallen so far from their power.

'Would you show me the baby things?' I asked.

We stood in her pantry. She had been showing me bottles of jams and preserves, labelled in her neat hand, and gem squash and paw-paws and lemons from the farm. She shrugged. 'This way,' she said.

I followed her along the corridor and into a small room painted white. In the middle stood a crib, lined and skirted all around in cascades of dotted Swiss. Inside were baby blankets and a satin eiderdown in white. She pulled open a cupboard. Tiny jerseys and booties, knitted by Catherine and my mother, were folded into piles. Nappies, harringtons, embroidered vyella nighties filled the drawers. A voile-and-lace dress hung on a miniature hanger. I reached for it.

'Oh, Valerie! Did you make this?'

She nodded. She bit her lip.

I thought of Nora and her *Book of Fate*. I grabbed her hand and turned it up, pointed at one of the meaningless creases on her palm. 'Look there,' I said. 'Two or three children. At least!'

She pulled her hand away and fell back into a white wicker rocking chair. She turned from me to hide her face. I'd never seen Valerie cry like this before. There was hardly any sound, and no joy in it. I walked over to the window and looked out. Bernard, wearing a straw sunhat and red gingham shirt, rode a tractor in the distance. Last night seemed never to have happened.

'I'm going to give it all to that bloody church bazaar,' she mumbled.

'Oh, don't!' I said.

She smiled at that, her old menacing smile. 'Why not? Why shouldn't I pass on the bad luck?'

I thought of my mother knitting as she listened to Lux Radio Theatre, the pride she took in each new garment, the way she had searched all over town for blue tissue paper to wrap the things in. 'Please, don't,' I said.

'Oh, don't be stupider than you can help!' She pushed herself out of the chair, leaving it rocking gently.

'Would you like me to clear it out then?' I suggested. 'I can put it all into boxes and things, you know. That'll save you –'

She turned on me quickly. 'You leave them alone! Don't you dare touch one of those things with those filthy hands of yours!'

I looked down at my hands. 'Don't provoke her, darling,' my mother had said. 'You can't know what it's like unless it's happened to you.' My fingers were dusty from the undusted sill. I understood then that provoke wasn't the word for it. And that the duty I'd been sent to perform was not to comfort Valerie. I'd been sent to give her someone to blame. Since I'd shouted the truth at my mother she seemed to consider me strong enough for any task.

The next day Bernard took me to see the farm. The sun was just up and the air chilly. Workers straggled up the hill from their barracks, some barefoot, some in gum boots. He shouted at them in Zulu and pointed here and there. They broke away and ran at his command. 'Come!' he said to me, stalking off.

I had to run to keep up. He climbed into a jeep parked behind the kitchen. I climbed in after him. 'Here –' He dropped a greaseproof paper package into my lap. 'Breakfast,' he said.

Inside were scones, buttered and jammed, yesterday's tea. 'Want one?' I asked.

He shook his head. 'Later,' he said.

I bit into a scone and he turned to watch me, smiled the smile of a man providing food. I smiled back, his woman for the moment. 'It's delicious,' I said.

'Wait till you see the calves. There's a lamb too.'

There was nothing ridiculous about him here, not even the straw hat. Workers stopped to stare at us as we passed. He shouted things at the top of his voice, stopping the jeep every now and then to complete the command. I saw them bow and run. He was master here. I wondered whether Valerie had ever been out with him like this. She never seemed to leave the hotel.

'Here. Out.' We were at the dairy, a set of low whitewashed buildings behind a cattle dip. He jumped out leaving me to follow. Inside, cows lowed and shuffled in their stalls. The place smelled of dung and disinfectant. I hung back against the doorway while he spoke to the cow herd in Zulu. He unlocked a cupboard and pulled out a few medicine bottles, took out a syringe and filled it, squirted it in the air like a doctor.

'What are you doing?' I asked.

'Sick calf,' he said.

I followed him, watched him squat next to the small ungainly creature. He whispered something into its ear and then grasped it tightly and plunged the needle in. The cowherd pointed to another calf. And then another. I loved watching him hold the animal like that, not scared to touch things that might be dirty, the way my father was. And his jeans pulled tight at the fly, the muscle in his arm flexed hard as he pushed in the syringe.

'I'll have one of those scones now,' he said when we were back in the jeep. We were bumping down a hill towards a bridge. 'There's a place I want to show you over there,' he said, pointing to some wattles. 'You can see the whole farm from there.'

I had to hold the scone up to his mouth as he drove, like Jeffrey had Catherine do for him. Crumbs scattered around the seat and floor. I tried to wipe them away, but he laid his hand on mine without a word. The sun was full up now and shining through the wattles, pink and gold.

'It's so beautiful here,' I said.

'Wait. Wait till you see.'

We drove in silence over the old stone bridge and up the meadow on the other side. He stopped under some trees. 'Here,' he said. 'Get out.'

We were on a ridge, higher than the hill on which the hotel buildings sat. The sun had just caught the window glass there, and the roof in places. It lit the whitewash of the walls into a soft grey. African women sang somewhere down at the river. Turtle doves had started in the trees. Bernard took my hand and led me higher, into the trees.

'Here,' he said. 'Listen. Isn't it wonderful?'

I listened. But with my hand in his I could hear nothing anymore except the blood beating in my ears. 'I love this place,' I managed to say. 'I think you're very lucky.'

He dropped my hand and sank down on to the grass, brooding forward over his knees. I sat down too.

'You understand,' he said.

I wasn't sure what I understood or whether he just liked the idea of being understood by someone. But I was glad he thought I did. Especially because I knew he meant Valerie didn't understand.

'I want to paint you, little one, just the way you are now. Before you change. Will you do that for me?'

I thought of the naked women, all sinews and muscle in electric blues and purples. I wondered whether he'd do that to me. 'OK,' I said.

He leapt up. 'Come. The light's perfect. We can go to my studio right now.'

His studio was an old farm shack, hidden behind the hill we were on. He had whitewashed it inside and out and put in enormous windows, and a skylight in the corrugated iron roof. Inside there was barely room for a divan, a table, two chairs, and an easel. His paintings hung all around the walls – the ones we'd seen and more like them. Suddenly I felt shy.

But he was setting a canvas on the easel. He waved towards the divan. 'There,' he said. 'Let's try you there.'

I sat carefully on the edge of the grubby hotel blanket that covered the divan. What would he make me do? Take off my clothes?

He stood up and squinted at me, cocked his head. 'Kneel,' he said.

'Where?'

'In the middle of the bed. Just kneel so I can see how it looks.

Here –' He upturned the box in which he kept his paints and placed it next to me. 'Look into that. Ah! Aha! Pandora! That's what I'll do!'

Pandora? The only picture of Pandora I'd seen was an Arthur Rackham one, with bats and vampires and her with nothing on, not even breasts.

He came to the edge of the divan and looked down at me kneeling there in my shorts and sandals. He planted his hands on his hips. 'Little one,' he said softly. 'How would you feel about taking off the clothes? Just for the picture. I won't eat you up, I promise.'

I blushed. Anything seemed normal with Bernard. Clothes on, clothes off, inside, outside. I couldn't think of a reasonable objection. 'OK,' I said.

He returned to the table and busied himself with tubes of paint while I pulled off my jersey and then unbuttoned my blouse. I couldn't think of what to do with the bra, so I stood up and wriggled out of my shorts, stamped them on to the ground. He looked up. 'My God!' he said. His eyes moved up and down, up and down. 'Little one, could you take off the bra and pants? Just for me?'

This time he watched as I unhooked my bra and wrapped it into a ball, pulled down my pants. I jumped back on to the divan and tried to hide my breasts with my arm and my pubic hair between my thighs. Everything was on fire. And all my old daring seemed to have vanished. This was nothing like that time, so long ago, on the window sill with Lucy.

He walked over to me slowly and touched my shoulder. 'I just want to look at you,' he said in the same soft voice. 'Please stand up.'

I scrambled to my feet on the bed. He backed away, banging into the table. I had never seen his face like this, the way it had been in my dreams. Adoring, amazed, wanting only me.

'Little one,' he murmured. 'My God!'

I felt beautiful under his gaze.

'You are beautiful,' he said. 'How can I paint such a thing?'

Even his words were the words of my dreams. The same tone.

The awe. I had incapacitated him the way Catherine had swept off Jeffrey or my mother had stunned my father.

'May I touch you?' he asked. It was a real question. If I said no he would stay away.

I nodded.

He stepped up to the divan and laid his hand on my thigh. He stroked my leg, down towards the ankle. Then he placed both hands gently on my hips and held them there.

'Soft, soft,' he murmured.

My knees weakened. I wanted his hands all over me. I didn't care. I'd forgotten all about men planting their seed.

He pulled me towards him and laid his cheek against my stomach. My blood rushed to the spot and left me faint. He pulled me down, he laid me out on the divan, lay down beside me, kissed me and kissed me and stroked and murmured. All the time he praised me, my breasts, my skin, my thighs. He loved me, he said as he wrenched off his own jeans and shirt. He adored me, his little one, oh God! Did that hurt? No? Oh, little one, little one, little one! OH!

The sun had heated the room to a hundred degrees. In the distance machines whined and farmhands whistled and yelled. Bernard was asleep and I was stuck between him and the wall. I edged myself up a bit and looked down at him. The madness was gone. He lay on his back snoring. His penis flopped to one side, small and pointy. I still didn't understand. Looking down at him then I couldn't even remember my dreams anymore. Suddenly I remembered Miss Robinson's unmarried mothers' home. And Lucy. I sat up and banged my head against the wall. 'Ouch!' I said.

'What?' Bernard groped towards me. 'Little one?'

But I didn't want his hands on me anymore. They seemed like a trick. 'I'm worried about falling pregnant,' I said.

'Pulled out.'

'What?'

'I pulled out, you silly little clown. *Pulled out.*' He turned away from me and went back to sleep.

I went to the studio with him every day after that. Every day it was the same. The madness, the words of praise, the snoring afterwards. Valerie didn't seem to suspect. She slept until noon and then sat with me silently at lunch. In the afternoons, while she taught her few students, I swam or slept myself. At night, in front of her, Bernard was just the same. He fingered my neck or caught me by one buttock. He clowned around me to squint down my dress. But in his studio he was always my real lover. At worship. The finest audience I'd every had.

After two months I'd had enough. He whispered that he would find a way to come to town alone. He'd take a flat, he said. And when could I come again?'

I shrugged. I knew I'd never come back the same way. I was already beyond his reach. Almost free.

'Little one,' he asked me on the last morning. 'I want to ask you a question.' He was tucking himself into his jeans, watching me dress. 'That first morning – why did you let me touch you like that?'

'What?'

He smiled, embarrassed. 'Why did you let me?'

'Let you what?' I asked. I stared at him. I knew what he wanted to know, but I couldn't believe that he was asking the question or that he couldn't use the right words to ask it.

He blinked at me. I'd never seen him at a loss before.

'I didn't "let you" make love to me,' I said. 'I wanted you to. I could have said no.'

It was not what he wanted to hear. And I knew I couldn't tell him the whole truth either. It hadn't really been him at all.

My parents were both at the station as I'd hoped. They waved wildly as the train pulled in.

'*Darling!*' my mother boomed. 'How simply marvellous to have you back!'

'How's Valerie?' my father asked.

'Fine. They're both fine.'

'Well, I only hope she appreciates your visit,' she said. 'You never know what response you're going to get out of that one.'

255

'Hey, don't carry those, we'll get a porter. Porter! Here!'

Two black men leapt for my luggage.

'Come on,' my mother said. 'Tea's waiting at home. 'I'm afraid Dad and I have to go to the theatre tonight. Oh, and there's a letter for you from Jocelyn.'

I threw my arm around her shoulders and squeezed her tight. A letter from Jocelyn. And my period just come on the train. Everything was right.

'Just one of you, please!' my father barked at the porters. 'Follow me.'

It was hot. And there was the sweet, sweet smell of the sugar refineries again. The sour fetor of dead whales. Sutherland Road. Steiner Street. A Zulu woman walking with a sewing machine on her head. I felt as if I'd been gone for a year.

We pulled into the garage and my father hooted for someone to fetch my luggage.

'Darling,' my mother said, as he got out and walked around to the boot. 'I think I should warn you that we've put the house on the market.'

'What?'

'It's of necessity, darling. Everything happened at once. We had no choice. She lowered her voice. 'You might refrain, by the way, from mentioning the subject to Dad. You can't imagine what's been going on every time the estate agent comes round. Migraines. The lot!'

Her tone was different, the words she chose, everything.

'Abba's no help, of course. His mind seems to be going, poor old thing. If it weren't for Jeffrey, you know, we'd have had to put the theatre up for sale too.'

'Jeffrey?'

'He bailed us out a bit,' she whispered.

Johnson, the gardenboy, arrived to fetch the luggage. The dogs snarled and snapped behind him.

'Let's go in for tea,' my mother said, wagging a finger surreptitiously at the 'For Sale' sign tied to the fence.

Beauty brought in the tea tray.

'Where's Nora?' I asked.

They glanced at each other.

'Where is she?'

'In her room, darling,' she said. 'I'm afraid she's not been at all well.' She blinked and sighed and shook her head, dangerously close to her old role of bereavement. 'She's not what she used to be, darling. We had to force her to see Slatkin last week.'

'What's wrong?' I whispered.

She breathed in deeply. 'It seems that Nora's got cancer, darling. Apparently she's quite far go–'

I ran from the room and out through the kitchen, across the laundry lawn to the compound. I knocked softly at Nora's door. Listened. Pushed it open into the gloom. The curtains were drawn, six mattresses piled high on the iron bed, and in their centre – in the hollow made by what she once had been – Nora. There was no flesh now on her face, her lips and cheeks were sucked in to reveal her skeleton. Grey fuzz stood up around her head. Her arms, legs, chest were all bones and soft black skin. And pushing up against her nightdress was her stomach, huge and shaped like a melon.

'Nors! Oh, Nors!' I stood panting beside her bed.

'Awu! You back!' she whispered.

'I brought you some perfume,' I shouted, as if her illness had made her deaf. 'And some XXX mints!'

The room smelled of old urine, old sweat, the sweet-sour stench of death.

'Awu! You not cry!' she whispered. 'How is Val?'

I sat on the chair next to the bed. 'Please don't die,' I said.

'Ruth! Ruth!' My mother shouted out of the kitchen window.

'You go!' Nora rasped. 'Please. You go now.'

'No one is taking Nora to the King George,' my mother boomed. 'Have you gone quite mad? There's a cholera epidemic on! These poor devils are dying like flies! And you're suggesting you take her to the King George! I forbid it!'

'But she won't go in an ambulance!'

'She'll go as she's told to go!'

'I don't know why she can't simply be allowed to die peacefully in her room,' my father suggested. 'It is her expressed wish, you know.'

'Because there's no one looking after her!' I shouted. 'She's lying there in her own filth! And she's in agony!'

'Just keep your hair on, please!' my mother said. 'Calm down! Beauty is supposed to be ministering to her. She's been doing it for two weeks. Since this whole thing came on.'

'Nora hates Beauty and Beauty hates Nora! You know that! They've always hated each other!'

'Well, what about that Constance of hers? She's the daughter! She should be here looking after her mother!'

'Constance has got a job! She can't just leave a job!'

'They leave when it suits them to leave. Don't you believe it.'

As soon as my parents left for the theatre that evening I went to Nora's room.

'We're going to the King George, my darling,' I said.

'Awu, no!' A tear rolled out of one eye and down into the crevice of her cheek.

'Nors, it'll be better. They'll wash you and watch you and give you medicine for the pain.'

'Awu, no, please, Ruth.'

I knelt down next to her bed. 'Nors, you know Lord Jesus?' She blinked.

I pointed to a picture of Christ on the cross above her dressing table mirror. 'There he is, see? He's waiting for you. But he wants you to be clean. He wants you without pain. Please, Nors, we don't have much time.'

Again she blinked.

'Tell me what you want to take with you. Where is your suitcase.'

She pointed to an old cardboard suitcase on top of the wardrobe, to her top drawer, her bag, her keys, the photograph of her and Constance against the mountains and waterfalls.

'I'll get a clean nightie,' I said. I pulled open a drawer and grabbed a pink brushed-nylon nightdress, still in its cellophane bag, given her at Christmas by my mother.

'Nors, I'll change you. I'll put it on. Don't move.'

258

As I lifted each arm, pulled her fetid nightie up and over her head, tears rolled freely over her cheekbones and down towards her ears. I opened her bottle of 4711 cologne – another year's Christmas present – and poured some on to a tissue, dabbed at her arms, under an arm, into the sunken, curly pit.

'Awu, no!' she whispered, ashamed.

'OK. I won't.'

I rolled up the new nightie and pulled it over her head, each arm into a sleeve, the tent of it pulled down around her two flaps of breast, her distorted hump of a stomach.

'*Book of Fate*,' she rasped.

'Where?'

She pointed over her shoulder, next to the bed.

I grabbed it. 'We've got to hurry,' I said. I ran to the back yard and banged on Johannes's door. 'Take us to King George's, please,' I said.

He hastily buttoned his uniform. 'What about my Master?' he asked.

'He says it's OK. Hurry.'

I ran back to Nora's room and picked her up, carried her out to Abba's old Vauxhall. She hung across my arms like a child, her head against my chest. Reuben followed with the cardboard case.

'Awu!' he said. 'Hamba kahle!'

'I'll sing something for you, if you like, Nors,' I suggested. 'What would you like me to sing?'

' "Oh God Our Help",' she whispered.

'Oh God our help in ages past,' I sang.

'Our hope –' She tried but couldn't sing.

'Our hope for years to come. Our shelter from the stormy blast. And our eternal home.'

18

'You can speak to him tonight,' my mother said. 'Dad has already mentioned it, you know. He seems quite open to the idea.'

'I won't! I can't stand the thought of asking him!'

'My dear, don't be absurd. You want to go. How else do you think we're going to manage it?'

'Mr Chowdree?'

'Look –' She pointed her nose right into my diffident question. 'I told him, I've told you, and I'm telling you now finally! We are not accepting charity from that Chowdree man.' She waved her hand against any objections. 'I know what you're going to say. I've heard it all before. But will you please try to think of someone other than yourself for a change? How on earth do you think Dad and I could face such a thing?'

'Accepting money from an Indian?' I said.

She stared at me. The skin around her eyes was stretched now from all the rubbing, draped into folds and folds of wrinkles. 'You have a very bald way of putting things these days, don't you?' she said. She glanced at the tea crates piled around us, the bare floors. 'Hard,' she said, her voice echoing against all the hard surfaces. 'You've become hard. It's very unattractive.'

'Ma –' I reached for her hand and stroked it. 'When you wanted to go you went in your own way, didn't you?' Playing

260

mother to her now played down my own desolation. Nora dead. Abba sent off to Our Jewish Home. The house sold. No hope for me but charity from Jeffrey.

Her mouth began to pucker. Tears spilled down her cheeks. She wrenched her hand away in anger. 'Jeffrey is family!' she sobbed. 'At least he's family!'

'Shall I tell Beauty to bring us some tea?'

She shook her head as she blew her nose. 'Catherine's coming. I asked her to come and help me with the auctioneer.'

We had tea in the dining-room, where the table still stood. There were fairy cakes, baked by Beauty now, with the same light touch as Nora's. 'She's got a lot to learn,' my mother told Catherine, 'but she's very willing.'

Catherine looked at her watch. She always looked at her watch when she came to the house. Even now. It seemed to reassure her that she had the right to leave again. 'When's this auctioneer specimen arriving?' she asked. She rolled her eyes at me and I smiled back. My heart still leapt when she made me her friend, even with my mother as victim, with anyone. Lately she had been including me in little gestures against our parents. Sometimes she even asked me to tea. When we were alone she would question me about university. What subjects did I think I would do? How much would a scholarship pay? It was as if my future mattered to her now in some secret way, as if it had become part of her own revenge.

The doorbell rang.

'Ah!' my mother said. 'Perfect timing!'

My father spent most of his time at the theatre now, supervising the repairs. He couldn't bear the thought of himself watching his house sold to strangers. Or to hear them pacing out each room for the improvements they planned to make. He couldn't bear the thought of selling anything at all, even the excess furniture that the auctioneer was coming to appraise.

I slipped out into the passage and past the pantries, piled high with crates. My mother's heels echoed into the breakfast-room. 'Let's start here,' she said. 'This whole suite must go. Except that lovely little corner cabinet, of course.'

261

I wandered through the kitchen and out on to the laundry lawn. Only Beauty and Reuben were to come with us to the new flat. Johannes had gone with Abba. And Pillay and Johnson were to be let go. Pillay looked up from the dahlia bed and grinned at me, baring his toothless red gums. 'Please, Miss – Miss?'

'Yes?'

He hawked and spat into the turned earth to clear his mouth for a request. 'Miss, please, Miss, ask Madam to find another place for me, Miss. I'm not too old, Miss.'

I nodded. It was all the same to me now. Please, Miss. Other people's needs so much greater than my own. The walls were down. They could all come in asking. And what was there to give?

I wandered up to the tennis courts. The surface was beginning to crack and sprout weeds. Up to the fence. Tickey-draai music came from the servants' shack on Lucy's side. Nothing from her flat. We never even heard Mr and Mrs Knowles anymore. It was as if Lucy had died, and together with her all the incidental noises of her life.

The dogs frisked beside me, up and down the rockeries. There were only two left, Temba and Chaka. But they too had to go. The flat had a rule against pets. Catherine couldn't take them, they would fight with hers. Perhaps Valerie and Bernard might, although Valerie wasn't one for dogs, my mother said. But the dogs, she assured us, were the last thing she was going to worry about.

I climbed down through the rockery. The zinnias had dried into stalks. No one had time to supervise Johnson's watering anymore. Now that the zinnias and everything else belonged to 'that bloody Englishman'. They were coming in in droves, my parents said, those bloody Englishmen. Buying up houses like ours for next to nothing. At least *someone* seemed to have confidence in the country's future. Ha! Perhaps they knew something we didn't.

Rotten mangoes lay under the trees. Avocados too. The servants had picked all the best ones and sold them or eaten them. No one was there to stop them. Nora was dead, and Beauty hadn't yet learned to guard the pantry like a cook.

I pushed open the compound gate. Chaka and Temba sat down in the shade to wait. Nora's door stood open to air the room. Johnson had been told to scrub it clean. It reeked of Dettol. And it looked bigger. The mattresses were gone, the carpet, the vase of bows, the puppies and kittens on the walls.

I sat down on the globe chair and hid my face in my hands. There were still things I wanted to tell Nora. And things she would have known anyway. One look and she would have known about Bernard. She would have understood about Jeffrey too. She would have given me hope. She would have shouted at me and made me feel more special than the rest. 'You! You the one!' she would have shouted. 'You! You the best of the lot!'

My mother's voice approached the compound. Catherine's children shrieked up the hill in a troop from the swing. 'Parselina!' Catherine called. 'Please keep the children away from the compound.'

'And then, of course,' my mother was saying, 'there are the bits and pieces in the servants' quarters. Our new place, you know, is equipped with all the modern conveniences for them.'

The gate squeaked open and they clopped down the path towards me.

'It's hard to believe, isn't it, that things are changing as rapidly as they are?' She laughed. 'I hear the new people are going to tear all this up and replace it with a proper toilet.'

The man laughed too. 'That'll cost a packet,' he said.

'Now this is our old cook and housekeeper's –'

The trio stopped in the doorway and stared down at me.

'Ruth! What on earth are you doing in here?'

I shrugged. 'Just looking,' I said.

'Mr van der Walt wants to examine the furniture in here, darling. Mr van der Walt, this is our youngest daughter, Ruth. She's the one I was telling you about, the one who wants to go to England.'

'England, hey?' he laughed. 'Our local chaps not good enough, hey?'

Jeffrey rested his chin on his knuckles and frowned at me. I understood the game he was playing with silence and tossed my head and pretended to examine the room. Everything was wrong with it. It had been built as a library, not an office. Beautiful yellow wood bookshelves covered two walls. But now, except for a set of *Encyclopaedia Britannica* and some old school books of Catherine's, they were empty. A photograph of Sol Goldman shaking Ben-Gurion's hand hung on the wall behind Jeffrey's head. On the other hung an Israeli relief of a boy with a horn, in greening copper.

'So,' he said, grinning. 'Tell me something.'

'What?' I asked.

He bounced back into his chair and pushed it into a recline. 'I hear from your Pop that you're dead set on Oxford.'

I nodded.

'Why?' he asked.

Blood rose immediately to my cheeks and ears. All afternoon I had been dreading that question from him, and resenting the right he had to ask it. I had no words for an answer. 'I've applied for a whole lot of scholarships,' I mumbled.

'Can you bring me a list?'

'A list? Why?'

'If I'm going to make an investment I have to know who my co-investors are, don't I?' He lilted through the question as if he'd been saving it up for days. Black hair curled up over his tie.

I tried to remember how Alethea had taught us to keep our voices down at their normal level. 'There's no point in that until I know whether I'll get one,' I croaked.

'That's for me to decide, isn't it?' He reached over for a magazine and began flapping through it. 'What's wrong with staying here?' he asked into its pages.

'Nothing's wrong.' The drama was gone, the silence was everywhere. There was nothing anymore to stand between us and people like Jeffrey.

'Then why do you want to go? What have they got there that's so special?'

'History,' I said, breathing lightly. The word arrived in my mouth from nowhere.

'You can't do history here?'

'*A* history. They have *a* history,' I explained in a careful teacher's voice. Even though I knew he would hate me for it. Even so.

The chair sprang forward, the magazine dropped. 'Oh? *A* history!' he mocked. 'Don't you think *we've* got *a* history?'

I shrugged.

He gripped the edge of the desk. 'All I want is the facts. Forget about all this blooming intellectual rubbish. You and your lot cause nothing but trouble.'

'My lot?' I asked. Burning my boats had brought my voice under control again. 'What lot?'

'Trouble-makers!' he said. 'With their heads in the clouds! Why don't you take a leaf out of your sister's book?'

'Which sister?'

'Are you trying to be funny?' He stared into my face for a hint of mockery. He blinked and twitched and flushed.

I understood then that he stung still from our sport with him. And that nothing I could say would make him feel safe with me. He couldn't like me. He was scared of me, of my mother in me. He was even scared of my jokes. I shook my head. 'No,' I said, 'I'm not trying to be funny.' I was trying now to like him. I wanted him to know that.

'Because if you are –'

I pushed my chair back and stood up. 'Jeffrey – please – I just don't know how to answer your questions. Whatever I would say to you would sound wrong. Let's just forget the whole thing. It wasn't my idea anyway. I'm sorry.' I opened the door and walked out into the hall.

'Look,' he called out, 'you can't expect me –'

They were all on the verandah having tea. My mother stretched her hand out for mine and squeezed it confidentially. 'Want some tea, darling?'

I shook my head and stared out into the dark. A strange orange haze brightened the dark sky as if the sun were rising.

Catherine yawned.

My father clapped his hands together on cue. 'It's late,' he said, standing up. 'Come, women, let's go.'

'What's that light?' I asked.

'What light?' He shaded his eyes against the light of the verandah. 'By Jove! It must be a fire!'

'Fire? Where?' my mother asked.

He pushed one of the footstools next to the pillar and stood on it.

'Where?' she demanded.

The phone rang.

Catherine clicked her tongue. 'Who's phoning at this hour?'

'That's some blaze!' my father said. 'I wouldn't be surprised if it's three or four buildings.'

Jeffrey flew out on to the verandah. 'Pop!' he shouted.

'We've seen the fire,' I said.

'Phone, Pop! Quick!'

Abba died the night the synagogue burned down. They said at Our Jewish Home that his heart just exploded when he heard the news of it.

'I'm glad he didn't live to see all this,' my mother said, gesturing around at all our old things out of place in the new flat. 'It would have broken his heart.'

She spoke this way about the dogs too, and about Pillay, and even Nora. 'Willing that Beauty might be,' she said, 'but she doesn't listen! How many times have I told her not to overcook those rissoles?'

My father and I never answered these questions. And I never pointed out to her that there was no one now to teach Beauty what overcooked meant and how not to do it. My father simply stood up quietly and left the room. But there was nowhere really for him to go now. She only had to follow him to the study or the bedroom to shout her complaints. The lounge and dining-room were all one room. The study and three bedrooms

266

led off one long corridor. And the lift and stairs caught the smells of other people's cooking. The garden was three floors down and belonged to everyone in the building. From noon on anyway it was cast into shadow.

We lived in the luxury flat like refugees. At night the three of us squeezed ourselves around the old dining-room table, far too massive for the enclave that served as a dining-room. There were no doors to close the servants out of our conversation. There was no conversation anyway. Just money, and Valerie having to stay in bed for the duration of her new pregnancy, and how not to renew Alethea's contract.

There wasn't even enough work at the theatre now for both my parents. There weren't enough students. And there was no money for anything but student productions. At my mother's request, Jeffrey offered my father a part-time position doing PR at the factory. My father thanked Jeffrey, but said he needed time to think. For three days he lay in his darkened room, accepting only clear soup. Dr Slatkin whispered to my mother that perhaps it was psychological. She nodded. She told Jeffrey no, and asked him please not to bring up the subject again. When my father recovered he busied himself installing an electric bell from the dining-room to the kitchen. I laughed. 'Let him!' my mother whispered urgently. 'What's the difference if it makes him feel more at home!'

She, however, had agreed to run the Zionist women's annual fête. Mrs Goldman had asked Jeffrey to ask Catherine to ask her. Sarah Frank would be a draw, she had explained. The Zionists were suffering like everyone else.

'Ha!' my mother said. 'Why not? Perhaps for once they'll see how things should be done!'

She attacked the task like a new production. Every evening now she sat in the study with lists. She phoned Zionist women to find out how many tea cosies she could expect for the handiwork stall. Or who could take the two-to-four shift at the tombola.

I concentrated on my future. Three times a week Maya and I met with her tutor for A-levels. 'I don't see any harm in it if they're paying,' my mother said. 'Although God knows you threw away a good thing with Jeffrey.' She'd dropped the 'that' for Jeffrey now. And she considered me a fool. Loved me for it in a strange new way, with tears in her eyes for my obstinacy. When my father wasn't home she handed me scripts to read and asked for my opinion. She bought no clothes for herself now, but brought things home for me on appro. 'Just something I found at Morgan's on my way back from the theatre.'

She loved to sit in my bedroom chair and watch me try things on. 'Oh, darling! We must take that! Just look what it does for that gorgeous neck of yours!'

'But, Ma!'

'Don't you "but, Ma" me! That one definitely. Now try the twinset.'

Sometimes I had to turn away in tears too now. It was her loss, my gain, the way she turned up a collar – 'There! Like that! Now don't you go mentioning this to Valerie, please.'

Bernard had come to town several times to buy things for the farm. He pulled me out on to the porch and pushed me up against the wall. 'When?' he demanded, breathing all down my neck. 'I came all the way to see you.'

I shook my head.

'What's happened to you?' he whispered, his whole body tight and quivering.

'Nothing,' I said. I still wanted him sometimes. When I saw myself in my new clothes. Or men turned in the street to whistle. But the thrill was gone. I never wanted him when he was there to be had.

'I'd watch out for that Bernard, if I were you,' my mother said. 'I wouldn't put it past him to make one of his passes now that you've blossomed into a beauty.'

'He made passes at me even when I was fat and pimply,' I said.

She nodded and sighed. 'Ah!' she said. 'What's happened to us all, hey?'

It was always there now, what had happened, what could happen. Jocelyn's curtain gone. And my parents scared. They lacked the normal skills and judgement for the world they found themselves in. They couldn't even judge the stares they got from other people living in our building. Or the gloomy headlines in the newspaper. The slump. The dangers. People putting in burglar alarms. Jeffrey's oration at Abba's memorial service.

'It wasn't that bad,' my mother said, sipping tea. 'If only he'd learn to modulate that voice a little, and not to thrust his hands into his pockets.' She peered into her teacup. 'Will that girl never learn to wait until the water boils?'

'I didn't mean the delivery,' I said, 'I meant the content. What a lot of crap.'

'Chopsticks, I'll thank you not to use that kind of language in this circumstance,' my father said. He sat like an old man himself now, his knees together, a hand spread out on each knee. His eyes had begun to stare out from the middle of deep, grey circles the way Abba's had done. The debonair twist of a smile was gone, the way he angled his chin to give you the best view of his profile.

I had begun to feel responsible for them. When I came home from school now they both looked up with hope. My mother would jump up and offer me tea, as if to make me stay a little longer. Jocelyn had said I'd always have my world to come back to. But she couldn't have known that this would happen. And I couldn't imagine how I could ever leave them. Or what there would be to come back to if I did. I avoided passing the old house now. The new people had pulled down the palm trees along the front fence, and also the summerhouse. They'd put in a swimming bath on the lower lawn.

'We've decided to rent the theatre to Janet McGuire three days a week,' my mother announced one day. 'Jeffrey's the one who suggested it, you know. I must say he's got a head on his shoulders that one.'

Janet McGuire now, and not a hint of scorn. I stared down into the courtyard where two men walked out of their garages, home from work in suits and ties. I felt much older than my parents. Agéd sometimes. Close to death.

'By the way, Jeffrey's asked us to come round after dinner. Some urgent business matter.'

'Fine,' I said.

My mother pointed her nose at me in the old way. 'You too,' she said. 'Jeffrey asked particularly that you be there.'

'I've got work to do. I'm particularly sorry.'

She leaned over to me, hiding her face from my father. She clamped her hand tight over my wrist like a claw. 'Don't be such a little fool!' she whispered. 'He might have decided to give you another chance!'

Jeffrey was waiting for us when we came. His face was flushed. So was Catherine's. She even looked up and smiled as I came in, a real smile. She offered me a sweet.

In his hands he held a sheaf of papers. He flapped them nervously against his calf as he waited for us to settle into the study chairs.

'We've sorted things out now,' he said in his sing-song voice. 'No point in beating about the bush.'

I bent down to ruffle one of the dog's ears. I would not sit in reverential silence like the rest, waiting for Jeffrey to make one of his pronouncements.

'Ruth!' Catherine said. 'Leave Jason alone and listen!'

Jeffrey frowned over at me. Red splotches had spread across his forehead and cheeks. His lips were white and dry. ' "To Ruth Leah Frank," ' he read, ' "youngest daughter of my only son, Roger Albert Frank, I leave the sum of –, to be held in trust until she reaches the age of twenty-one years. The funds are to be used for the purposes of acquiring a university education; for travel to and from said university; for board and lodging; for books and clothes, and for such other necessities as beneficiary and trustee both see fit. I appoint as trustee Jeffrey Mervyn Goldman, husband of my oldest granddaughter, Catherine Jane Goldman, *née* Frank. Signed, Abraham Mordechai Frank." '

19

Maya stood garlanded with marigolds on her side of the fence. Thirty or forty people had come to see her off. She waved at me. We all waved back. Valerie waved her baby's arm like a paw.

'I'm glad you girls are going to have each other,' my mother said for the tenth time. She reached up to straighten the collar of my suit. 'Darling,' she said, 'please write regularly. I implore you!'

'I will, Ma.'

'Chops –' My father stood to attention. 'Only five minutes now.'

'Roger! Stop chiming in like a damned clock!' my mother snapped.

He jumped at Valerie's baby and beat out a rhythm on its nappy. The baby laughed. Catherine looked at her watch.

'South African Airways announces the departure of its flight –'

I dropped my bag and threw my arms around my mother. 'Oh, Ma!'

She shook her head. 'I don't want to cry,' she sobbed.

I shook my head too, sobbing too.

'Come on, Chops,' my father said. 'They're boarding.'

She held me away by my arms. 'Darling – Darling –' But there were no more clichés behind which to hide her loneliness.

My father stepped up and took me by the shoulders. He too had tears in his eyes, tears of nostalgia, for himself left behind, for himself having left so many years before.

'Would all passengers please proceed to the fence –'

'Here –' My mother handed me my bag as if I'd left it lying around in the lounge again.

'Don't forget to grab four seats across after Jo'burg,' Catherine said. She had been advising me on aeroplane travel for weeks – blankets and pillows and seats over the wing. My going away seemed to have confirmed our friendship.

The Chowdree party moved in a swarm to the fence. Maya was on the tarmac already, waving back at them.

'Darling, go now,' my mother whispered. She hugged me to her again. 'God bless, my darling.'

Some of her Black Narcissus had rubbed off on me somewhere. I smelled it as I climbed the steps with Maya.

'Welcome on board South African Airways,' the stewardess sing-songed. She threw a look at the steward when she saw Maya. 'Down there, please. Follow him.'

I turned to wave. Turning to wave from the top of the steps had been rehearsed in my dreams for years. But this was nothing at all like my dreams. There was no drama in seeing my mother clinging to the fence with both hands, like a prisoner in Auschwitz. Or my own throat tight with tears, the panic I felt, the mad way I wished now that I could turn back.

'Excuse me, Madam, would you please be seated?'

I plunged into the plane and they shut the door behind me. Maya waved at me from the back and I began to make my way towards her.

'Here, please, Madam,' the steward said. 'This is your seat.' He smirked at me. 'You can join your friend after Johannesburg.'

I pressed my face against the glass of the window. They were still at the fence, their heads moving this way, that way, along the plane, looking for me. I waved and banged. But the propellers had started up already. They covered their ears and backed towards the airport building.

The plane moved forward and turned in a circle. There was the bluff now, and the oil refineries. We turned again, poised in place, while the propellers whined louder and louder. Then suddenly we lurched forward, roared past the airport and rose into the sky. We banked over factories and sugar refineries, sugar-cane fields, and the hills starting their corrugations. Home, I thought, trying to turn the lump in my throat into tears. I stared down at the smoke hanging low over a kraal. Home, I thought. Home, home, home. But my father's nostalgia wouldn't work on me. My heart lifted instead. I remembered that I could come back. Jocelyn had been right. I could leave and I could return. Like Maya. I was free.

FOR THE BEST IN PAPERBACKS, LOOK FOR THE 🐧

In every corner of the world, on every subject under the sun, Penguin represents quality and variety – the very best in publishing today.

For complete information about books available from Penguin – including Pelicans, Puffins, Peregrines and Penguin Classics – and how to order them, write to us at the appropriate address below. Please note that for copyright reasons the selection of books varies from country to country.

In the United Kingdom: For a complete list of books available from Penguin in the U.K., please write to *Dept E.P., Penguin Books Ltd, Harmondsworth, Middlesex, UB7 0DA*

In the United States: For a complete list of books available from Penguin in the U.S., please write to *Dept BA, Penguin, 299 Murray Hill Parkway, East Rutherford, New Jersey 07073*

In Canada: For a complete list of books available from Penguin in Canada, please write to *Penguin Books Canada Ltd, 2801 John Street, Markham, Ontario L3R 1B4*

In Australia: For a complete list of books available from Penguin in Australia, please write to the *Marketing Department, Penguin Books Australia Ltd, P.O. Box 257, Ringwood, Victoria 3134*

In New Zealand: For a complete list of books available from Penguin in New Zealand, please write to the *Marketing Department, Penguin Books (NZ) Ltd, Private Bag, Takapuna, Auckland 9*

In India: For a complete list of books available from Penguin, please write to *Penguin Overseas Ltd, 706 Eros Apartments, 56 Nehru Place, New Delhi, 110019*

In Holland: For a complete list of books available from Penguin in Holland, please write to *Penguin Books Nederland B.V., Postbus 195, NL–1380AD Weesp, Netherlands*

In Germany: For a complete list of books available from Penguin, please write to *Penguin Books Ltd, Friedrichstrasse 10 – 12, D–6000 Frankfurt Main 1, Federal Republic of Germany*

In Spain: For a complete list of books available from Penguin in Spain, please write to *Longman Penguin España, Calle San Nicolas 15, E–28013 Madrid, Spain*

CRIME AND MYSTERY IN PENGUINS

Deep Water   Patricia Highsmith

Portrait of a psychopath, from the first faint outline to the full horrors of schizophrenia. 'If you read crime stories at all, or perhaps especially if you don't, you should read *Deep Water*' – Julian Symons in the *Sunday Times*

Farewell My Lovely   Raymond Chandler

Moose Malloy was a big man but not more than six feet five inches tall and not wider than a beer truck. He looked about as inconspicuous as a tarantula on a slice of angel food. Marlowe's greatest case. Chandler's greatest book.

God Save the Child   Robert B. Parker

When young Kevin Bartlett disappears, everyone assumes he's run away . . . until the comic strip ransom note arrives . . . 'In classic wisecracking and handfighting tradition, Spenser sorts out the case and wins the love of a fine-boned Jewish Lady . . . who even shares his taste for iced red wine' – Francis Goff in the *Sunday Telegraph*

The Daughter of Time   Josephine Tey

Josephine Tey again delves into history to reconstruct a crime. This time it is a crime committed in the tumultuous fifteenth century. 'Most people will find *The Daughter of Time* as interesting and enjoyable a book as they will meet in a month of Sundays' – Marghanita Laski in the *Observer*

The Michael Innes Omnibus

Three tensely exhilarating novels. 'A master – he constructs a plot that twists and turns like an electric eel: it gives you shock upon shock and you cannot let go' – *The Times Literary Supplement*

Killer's Choice   Ed McBain

Who killed Annie Boone? Employer, lover, ex-husband, girlfriend? This is a tense, terrifying and tautly written novel from the author of *The Mugger*, *The Pusher*, *Lady Killer* and a dozen other first class thrillers.

CRIME AND MYSTERY IN PENGUINS

Call for the Dead   John Le Carré

The classic work of espionage which introduced the world to George Smiley. 'Brilliant . . . highly intelligent, realistic. Constant suspense. Excellent writing' – *Observer*

Swag   Elmore Leonard

From the bestselling author of *Stick* and *LaBrava* comes this wallbanger of a book in which 100,000 dollars' worth of nicely spendable swag sets off a slick, fast-moving chain of events. 'Brilliant' – *The New York Times*

The Soft Talkers   Margaret Millar

The mysterious disappearance of a Toronto businessman is the start point for this spine-chilling, compulsive novel. 'This is not for the squeamish, and again the last chapter conceals a staggering surprise' – *Time and Tide*

The Julian Symons Omnibus

The Man Who Killed Himself, The Man Whose Dreams Came True, The Man Who Lost His Wife: three novels of cynical humour and cliff-hanging suspense from a master of his craft. 'Exciting and compulsively readable' – *Observer*

Love in Amsterdam   Nicolas Freeling

Inspector Van der Valk's first case involves him in an elaborate cat-and-mouse game with a very wily suspect. 'Has the sinister, spell-binding perfection of a cobra uncoiling. It is a masterpiece of the genre' – Stanley Ellis

Maigret's Pipe   Georges Simenon

Eighteen intriguing cases of mystery and murder to which the pipe-smoking Maigret applies his wit and intuition, his genius for detection and a certain *je ne sais quoi* . . .